A debutant novel about life, people and places,

fact and fiction.

A book about travel, but not a travel book

A catalogue record of this book is available
at the Royal Danish Library, Det Kongelige Bibliotek
in Copenhagen, Denmark.

ISBN 9788797058206

Revised edition II.I
Spring, 2020

Hallelujah Canyon

They experience everywhere,

they go nowhere

"The journey is the reward.' Old Taoist saying

Richard Lightbody

To Britt; to Sally, Simon, Jilly and Christian;
to Maureen, Rodger, Valerie, David, Dee and Rosie;
to Nathan, Ali and Thomas.
Without whom, life is just a word.

(that should guarantee at least a dozen sales)

but before you set out on this journey a word about three
inspirational people, Jack, Pete and Bill.

Jack and Me

Not Jack Daniels, but Murphy. If any single person is responsible for what follows, it is 'Black Jack', an English master at Bangor Grammar School who, after I'd failed my national exam for the second time with a second abysmal mark, suggested that if I failed again he'd demand an enquiry. He believed this mis-spelt youth should go into journalism. Third attempt, I passed, with ease. Jack Murphy, was young, but died way before his time. Fifty years on, I'm still here, and still doing what Jack suggested thanks to his inspiration.

To Jack I apologize for the non-use of standard English. This is an American tale and both deserves and demands that I fill the pages with z's, omit the u's and refine the ll's to l's. If you miss these to distraction, please contact me and I'll send you some. I've also stripped Mr. and Mrs. of their regulation full-points because I think it over-formalizes the flow. Stock up here...........

For me journalistic life began as news and then sports reporter for Northern Ireland's national newspaper. This was followed by a BBC career that also started in news but ended in London directing documentaries, for both the BBC and the independent channels. It is from the thirty years of global opportunities that work and life gave me, that many of the interweaved stories and flashes of trivia originate.

Why write a US-based book about Europe from Denmark? That's because, that's where happy circumstance has brought me to live.

Pete and Me

'For seven years I traveled the world making programs with a charming and hilarious Ulsterman with a strong County Down accent that made no concession to people who had learned standard English from Linguaphone or the BBC World Service. From Moscow to Vanuatu, from China to Marrakesh. I watched as he told anecdotes, explained camera shots and paid compliments to people who couldn't understand anything he was saying. Then, when he was finished, one of us would translate.'

Pete McCarthy – The Road to McCarthy, Pete's second book. He was working on his third when, tragically, illness in its most terminal form robbed us of his huge observational wit.

The Ulsterman has continued to vocally confuse; with no one left to translate, he has put his mind to writing a travel book like no other. This is it. Words can take the place of the road that lies ahead, especially when the road itself is the lie.

Bill and Me

Before we start this journey a word about a kinder word from Bill Bryson, one of those on the cover. 'Funniest.' Many, many years ago I drove from London for many hours to the Yorkshire Dales to meet a then young author who had stormed it with his second book and first novel, The Lost Continent. Beside his log burning stove in his farmhouse kitchen, we drank tea and then for many years, beers in a broad selection of London pubs. I had long given up hope of coaxing Bill in front of the camera. Jenny Duff, series producer of Travelog, an award-winning television program encouraged me to persist and indeed nurtured the early seeds of this book when I'd conceived it as a film. Thank you, Jenny, for both. It took a while but eventually I did convince Bill to make a travel video in Washington DC for Channel Four. Bill described it as 'the best fun I've ever had with adults, with my clothes on,' a line I borrow deeper into this fictional adventure, with honor.

After that we resumed our all too infrequent pub sessions. I was actually in a bar, that's Irish for a pub without sticky carpets and a dartboard, in Clones, Co Monaghan when Bill who was in London, tracked me down on the phone.

Eleven months earlier he'd signed a contract with Carlton Television giving them the rights to 'Notes from a Small Island.' The television company panicked when they realized that they had only weeks to start production, or lose the rights. Bill had been offered a number of directors, but felt they'd missed the point of his farewell eulogy to the UK and insisted on the guy with whom he'd had the best fun he'd ever had with adults, with his clothes on.

What followed was a successful series, but in all honesty the book was so much better, and much better still than the actual six-part television version would have been a film of making the film. It was weeks of unplanned, frustrating un-controlled madness, but fun, even upon distant reflection two decades on. As the central character Zimmerman will tell you, there are only two memorable types of travel experience, the wonderful and the dreadful.

So that's maybe where the 'funniest' person came from, or maybe strangest, or oddest . . . . whatever, maybe what follows is a combination of all three.

Prelude

The sun cut a crisp shaft of brightness along the lower quarter of the wall; thirty years of daily ritual had taken the color from the wood, drained it of vitality, of its life, a bit like the arid landscape outside. Glancing at the clock sheltering in the shadow that crept along the back of the courtroom, Judge Marcus C. Heffner already knew that his immediate pleasure plans were ruined. The four-ball would need to be a three-ball today, but surely not tomorrow, this couldn't go on. Owner of a trio of the most active hemorrhoids in Maricopa County, the irritation on this particular day was coming from elsewhere. He looked down on another potentially annoying threesome who had disrupted his moment of intended minor sporting glory.

'Again please, how do you plea?

Sitting motionless, but anxious, in front of him were a slight-built man in his late forties maybe early fifties on a bad day, a muscular 35-year old and an attractive blonde-haired lady of discussable age. In the public gallery of around 50 people, at least half of them were wearing sunglasses, despite being totally in the shade.

'We plead not guilty, your honor,' said the eldest of the trio. He had in his head a defense as sturdy as a cardboard box in the rain. To avoid fruitless expenditure in a situation of little or no-hope, he had assumed the role of counsel.

Heffner fumbled a now redundant plastic golf tee in his pocket and muttered to himself, 'this better be good.

1.
DESTINATION NOWHERE

Thirteen months earlier: Interstate 40 Arizona

They were heading to nowhere in particular; it just had to be somewhere, anywhere else.

Destination wherever, whenever. As a means of escape the bus had always been his preferred mode. He hated cars and even more hated those driven by taxi drivers. Not for their ability to turn 'hello' into a political argument or their fabulous geographical knowledge, he just got riled at the way their mouths were their most industrious organ. He preferred to observe life passing by in controlled silence. He loved the way on buses passengers try to find the space with the most space, and most importantly, furthest away from the person most socially disconnected from themselves, like a form of human backgammon.

Anyway, he enjoyed the relative freedom of choosing from 38 seats and there was another potentially more crucial bonus. Buses don't need gantry gates, platforms or docks to disembark. Once on a plane, or a train, or a boat, you are at the mercy of the telephone call, the radio message; look at what happened to Doctor Crippen he reminded himself. He almost worshiped the infamous doctor. Not for his deeds, but his daring. A battered brown leather Filofax, stuffed with additional papers and inspirational notes, sat open on his lap. He was tired and the miles passed faster than the pages.

The Greyhound had crossed seven state lines and kissed a few more. On one occasion it had even come close enough to Hawley Harvey Crippen's Michigan hometown to consider hopping off, a detour, a potential moment of homage, or a moment of potential homage. It was difficult to imagine what kind of recognition anywhere would give to a murderer. Perhaps in Coldwater, Michigan there was nothing, infamy usually resulted in the bulldozers being called in.

Heading to nowhere in particular there was no estimated time of arrival for the three travelers encamped in the bus's two back rows. The detour would have been nice, like landing on a home-base in history, but he didn't pitch the idea, he knew the other two players were not interested in batting.

It had been a long day, part of a long week and an even longer month. Failure is a drag. Escape from failure, a sort of mild relief. After a prolonged period of stress and anxiety, he noted that even the moment of capture can provide release. Reports at the time mentioned that when they collared the homicidal homeopath after his transatlantic run with his girlfriend, he looked calmly thankful.

Perhaps that was because he believed he was innocent. In 1910 Crippen was the 20th Century's Osama bin Laden. A name destined to go into the history books as evil and wicked, but would he have been so notorious had it not been for the dramatic manner of his capture?

It was not his crime that made him famous, it was his detention by telegraphic communication that made him infamous. After all domestic murders were two-a-penny in Edwardian England. The disappearance of his wife Bella had led to considerable speculation and rumor, but without Marconi, Crippen would have been a couple of paragraphs on page seven of most papers and then discarded as he melted back into the States with his young lover. Caught yes, but the open

2

book on this escapee's lap suggested it was also an open case. There was one thing that even a mediocre modern-day TV detective might have asked, let alone any third-year legal student. On the downside of his defense, if, as Doctor Crippen had claimed, his wife had died and been cremated in the US, where was the paperwork? So, guilty, but for one hiccup, modern techniques proved the incriminating body parts found at his home , to be those of a man. They should have arrested the pathologist for missing the extra bit. Indeed, the jury should still be out. There were many strange questions left unanswered by the professional expertise of the executioner in Pentonville Prison on a cold and wet November morning, and more than a century later, unlike Crippen, still left hanging.

They puzzled Ernest Zimmerman III.

Ernie was a simple man crippled by a complex mind. 'Don't bend to beauty, nor kneel to power' was one of his many mantras. The unassuming live a simple carefree existence, without conscience or pain; the complex however cannot sleep for the constant zig-zagging of tangled thoughts. Ernie never saw the night without imagining the dawn, he never saw sun without feeling the prospect of rain on his shoulders, yet here he was in the back of yet another bus, fleeing from yet another perfect plan turned to pulp. Another pretty paper decoration caught in the rain. Flashes of beauty and brilliance destroyed by the bitter chilled puff of circumstance. These thoughts all ran through the semi-poetical section of his mind. There was a certain irony in that his initials combined to create his not often used schoolboy nickname, EZ, Life had never been so.

Yet what they were fleeing from had seemed so easy. All it took was a justifiably caring sounding charity, a flat open space with a school or sporting event in close proximity, some tape, a load of poles, a couple of laser measuring devices, a book of tickets . . . . and a cow. Oh yes, and the magic ingredient for maximum profit, saline laxative.

The cow they usually borrowed or, as on a couple of desperate occasions, hired; the venue they usually hijacked having scanned through local papers for a suitable event. Only on one occasion had their presence ever been questioned. It was the beauty of events run by committees, everyone always believes 'this is somebody else's pigeon.' Faced with some honest and valid questions, Ernie had immediately responded by showing the organizers some paperwork which indicated that they had a clear agreement from the school . . . only it turned out to be a different school, similar name, different county. Ernie fanned innocence, but with the potential hosts expressing anxieties about the animal's health, error accepted, the Cow Plop Bingo, was instantly added to the list of gala events. It proved to be one of their biggest and best days.

It was an ingenuous fund-raiser much loved in rural New England where it is generally, and more elegantly, called Cow Pie Bingo – Ernie opted to set up his own association as a potential safeguard, just in case there should be any enquiring busybodies who felt a need to make observations. He would reply that the 'o' in plop was for organic. Running it under a different controlling body gave Ernie the power, as the association's head, the supreme right to change rules as he went along, a bit like being a president of somewhere like, Russia.

As a money generating concept it was the forerunner of people putting Ferraris in airport departure lounges with 'win me' on the windscreen and $100 tickets to have any chance of doing so, like one in a thousand. The mathematics was simple. A $75,000

4

car with $100,000 in the bucket. With the more basic version, the field was roped off, 50 yards by 50, tickets were sold for each square yard and the cow was let loose to roam until nature took its due course. It happily fed on the grass whilst EZ & Co were even happier to feed on mans' greed. At $10 a ticket and half the total going to the winner, the other half, less expenses, to 'charity', the locals waited in line dreaming of what to do with their potential $12,500. One chance in 1,250 of a sizable return.

'Say no to one Big Mac Meal with cheese pops and soda and you could have a new car,' Ernie would chant out. He'd noted over time that thinner people were more likely to participate.

The hosting venue received 10% of the net, just to keep them sweet. In some more socially challenged neighborhoods he reduced the ticket to five dollars and the winnings correspondingly. Blinded by greed no one ever questioned what the organizer's cut was. Perhaps it was consumed by the 'less expenses' clause.

All the cow had to do was make a small deposit. Ernie and his buddy would then carefully measure the precise square the majority of the pat had landed in and announce the winner. There was one cunning addition to the plan. Rule 26 of the Cow Plop Bingo Association required the 'pay out plop' to be the first one deposited and that it was well-formed and at least the size of a soup plate. The saline laxative normally resulted in a minor anal explosion, a splattering of shotgun shit and the calling of a 'no plop'.

In such a situation in came Rule 26, or should the event by canceled due to a threat of lightening Rule 32A, or number five, if the cow defeated the saline and retained its prize-winning package for the two-hour event. Under all these circumstances all tickets would go into a free draw and someone from the crowd, picked totally at random, was blindfolded and asked to pull the winner from a bag.

That someone chosen at random bore a remarkable likeness to the lady presently sleeping in the seat opposite Ernie. Strangely the winning ticket was, unless the crowd seemed potentially hostile, an 'out of towner', someone who was passing through and had just left the event, but had, as was required of everyone, written their name, address and telephone number on the back. Once informed they had 30 days to claim their prize.

Never had they sold the full amount of tickets. They never could, there was always one in the random lady's hand, low numbered ticket in the twenties or thirties, low enough for the owner to have headed home, where for Ernie 'charity' began, and ended. In the situation where the plop was deposited in a blank square the winner would always be another 'out of towner' who Ernie would immediately ring up in public, on speaker phone, and tell the good news. The winner's voice had a remarkable resemblance to the Georgian tones of the lady currently sitting opposite Ernie in the bus. At one point in the summer they were clearing in excess of twenty thousand dollars a month. To avoid Saturday fete junkies, and the risk of being recognized, they always put at least a hundred miles between venues.

It had all been working so well until they reached Chelsea, Vermont. The cow they'd borrowed had seen better days, weary and tattered, you'd have struggled to get a moccasin out of it, let alone a pair; the school they'd chosen, politically hyperactive, the saline solution over-strong. From the outset, with a frothing mouth as if she'd just completed a steeplechase, the cow looked out of sorts. It was further stressed and harassed as the students staged an immediate animal's rights protest.in her benefit. She was having problems with her fifteen minutes of fame. The salty solution normally worked in about an hour. The Golden Hour Ernie called it as they whipped up sales, but the tattered bovine could not wait that long – she gave a sigh, a moan and dropped somewhere around squares M12 and N13 and O28 and O29. The cow that was, not the crap. Stone-dead Bingo was not the name of the game and Ernie and his team swept into plan C&C, his family motto – confuse and conquer, or in this case, cash and carry.

They grabbed the funds and made their way off through the school shouting 'Is there a veterinarian in the house?' Two old timers on a bench thought it likely particularly after what they'd witnessed. 'It's the sort of sight that would make anyone a vegetarian,' one noted.

By some sad chance there was, a veterinarian that is, and by compounded misfortune she'd witnessed the trio's performance some weeks earlier in Hanover, New Hampshire. Putting two and two together she started to ask questions out loud. It was one minute past time to leave, to head south, because that is really the only way you can leave Chelsea and stay in the United States. The cow wasn't worth involving the Mounties. Out of Chelsea, after a couple of hours free of the confines of the Green Mountains, you can opt for east or west. The west won. It seemed the more expansive option.

The $3,700 they had pocketed was bovine blood money. He fondled it along with their other cash reserve and wondered would it quickly dwindle or grow. He was a little concerned;

he had no plans for the latter. Three adults constantly on the road was like funding a permanent vacation.

Still sleeping in the row opposite, but with the tingle of musical tinnitus easing through her cheap personal earphones and cutting through the sound of exhausting diesel, was Rooster. He'd known her for four years; never known where or why she got the name, but recognized why men liked her. Not him of course, he, at a decade and a half her senior, was in the next division up, or down, depending how you viewed it. She was without over-playing her cards, sexy. Ernie could see it, but something in the decades that separated them neutralized his thoughts. It was not something he sought – perhaps it was his age, but the closest he'd been to having sex in the previous six months was in a late-night comfort stop. At a 7-Eleven in upper New York state, with ten minutes to re-join the bus, he waited in line and eventually to much relief, sat on a warmed toilet seat.

Rooster was in every sense of the word feisty, maybe 27 or 29, 32 or 34, but never 30. It was a barrier she'd either to break or had broken with a degree of grace. Anyway, she chose to ignore it. Rooster was an attractive mystery. The most she'd ever spent in one place was in her early teens, the six years in Savannah with an aunt were the most stable, body forming and accent grooming of her life. The aunt died when she was 17 and she found herself without a mentor, and worse still, a roof. She took to the road, working and moving on as she felt.

Behind her, laid out on the back seat like a dead Roman emperor, was Ryder. Ernie had never been sure how to spell it, with an 'i' or a 'y'. Whatever, Ryder was Ernie's Chico to Ernie's Groucho – not dumb, but pliable, in his mid to late thirties and still naturally physically intact. He put in the hours

8

and donkeywork to help turn Ernie's whims and brain flashes into projects. They were projects, which promised wealth with ease, but inevitably resulted in situations like the one they currently found themselves in – urgently moving on.

Ryder stirred, opened one eye, and muttered 'I'm hungry.' 'Think of something else, something nice,' Ernie quietly advised.

The eye closed like a sleeping turtle and a smile forced its way up the side of his tanned face. 'Quarter-pounder with cheese and bacon,' he thought. Thinking out of the happy box was not one of his strengths.

Ernie put his earphones back in. Apart from his cell, his eight-year-old CD player was his only concession to the digital age. He pressed the right facing triangle and Leonard Cohen flowed into his ears. He needed cheering up, and Leonard was his man.

-0-

Time was moving on too. Another night had just about passed and the sun was teasing its way up at the end of the long straight road they'd bussed along and forever towards – it was like the dot at the bottom of an inverted exclamation mark. Ernie smiled, another day, then grimaced, not another dollar.

Where that next dollar would come from was the anxiety that had kept him awake most of the night. In the western desert, Cow Plop Bingo didn't seem quite right . . .maybe a camel. They were surviving on their wits; their wits were their only tenable resource. At times it seemed as if they were running low, the well worryingly dry. Back in 8th grade he'd been stung

9

by a teacher's remark in his annual report, 'wit is no substitute for wits'. True Ernie had always had a very quick tongue, one which conjured up such strange responses that often people would never get what he was on about – and from that he gained an even deeper satisfaction than if had he managed to generate a hearty laugh. His philosophy was like a debit sheet, as long as his tongue could get him out of the trouble it had just got him into, with a little profit, he'd survive.

The sun had broken free of the exclamation mark; it was a totally independent full-stop and as the road, now just a line, rose and fell with the geography, it pushed its light deeper into the dips revealing a dry arid landscape.

For two days the signposts had called out the names of small towns, many named by desperate people who were amongst the first to appreciate the power of marketing, advertising and perception, or mis-perception. Like Erik, the exiled Viking, who in the world's first real estate con, named a huge freezing block of ice, Greenland, in order to entice other Vikings to abandon the negatively named Iceland and follow him.

It always amazed him how the Scandinavians held a torch for the Vikings. In the States, a land not rated highly for sensitivity, referring to Red Indians had gone, the Confederate flag largely mothballed and yet here was a vicious dysfunctional crowd of murdering rapists, they idolized. Somewhere along the line the word Viking would become taboo, like naming your child Adolf or Harvey.

There were marketing gems like the town of Hope, where there clearly was none, Central when that was exactly what it was - in the middle of nowhere, Progresso, which never did, and then of course Truth or Consequences, a single town with the

most convoluted of signs. It was Ernie's favorite, not so much a
con, rather an indication of how pliable humans are.

 Until 1950 the sign to Truth or Consequences read, to Hot
Springs. It was logical because that's what you found there and
at several other towns so favored and so named. Then an NBC
national radio presenter said they'd host the coast-to-coast
program from whichever town would change its name to that
of the show, Truth or Consequences. And so it came to pass
that the little nowhere town somewhere in New Mexico,
population 4,700, became a national institution for one night
and then quietly forever. By the time Ernie's bus passed
through it had soared to 6,023. For Ernie it was another
tempting diversion, but if he could resist Crippen's pad, then
not this time.

Was T&C as the locals call it, a bad example of the power of
marketing? Or maybe not, as Hot Springs, in all likelihood, it
would have evaporated into the New Mexican desert, just like
400 other towns, including one called Montoya.

Born as a cattle-loading point for the Southern Pacific Railroad
in 1902, it seemed as if it was blessed when twenty years later
the old Route 66 pushed its tarmac through and a gas station
ensured that drivers would stop. The population grew slowly
until the Second World War when the decline started. In 1930,
there were 152 souls, by the time of the chance to change its
name to Truth or Consequences it was 92, by 1970 there was no
one and the word ghost prefixed its status.

-0-

Then it happened, somewhere west of Flagstaff. In a landscape
of pan-fried geology, lay a green oasis held intact by a long

stonewall. Penned inside, tree-lined avenues crisscrossed at regular intervals with the junctions marked by lush bushes which even now, nearing mid-day, were being revitalized by pop-up sprinklers. The wall hid the secrets from the low-lying passing cars, but not to the elevated Greyhound passengers, or at least the few who bothered to take time from their Kindles, magazines or interrupted snoozing the miles away, to look up and out the windows.

Even in the heat of the day, the pathways had human traffic, making their ways shuffling independently, sometimes with assistance, past the sprinkled hazes. Ernie smiled; it was like a slippered Amtrak. Not unlike EZ, Ryder and Rooster, these inmates were heading to nowhere, but at least they knew where they were. Or did they? Their movements were stuttered and there seemed to be a curious lack of urgency to escape the heat. In the bus the air-conditioning disguised the already 32 degrees outside, yet still, rather than sit inside the impressive large building that poked out occasionally from behind the landscaped trees, they opted to drag themselves between shaded benches, some using walking frames, some just sticks.

Some of the walkways had shaded covers stretching along their entire length. In arid Arizona somebody cared for these people, either that or they just wanted them out of the house. Truthfully named Arizona was not the product of a Viking estate agent.

The wall curved round and a large sign ended Ernie's guessing game. In italics it simply read, St Anthony's Home for the Blind, Kingman. Another five minutes passed and they were about two and a half hours from what was his silently potential somewhere, Las Vegas. Ernie nudged his dozy and disinterested companions, 'we're getting off!'

Rooster was the first to resist. Looking around she asked, 'Why here Ernie?' Her voice had the tapered tag of a question that had often been raised before. She knew it was futile to oppose, it was just that she wanted to set down a marker that later could be a reference point when they came to reflect on the inevitable disaster. 'Ernie, I asked you at the time,' she'd state knowing that the only novelty would be in the reply.

Battle-weary, occasionally driven deep into frustration, she still liked EZ, enjoyed being part of a small tight team and wouldn't have tolerated the history of mishaps she'd endured with anyone else. Certain aspects of life with Ernie, the process of despair followed by inspiration, hope and hard work then being terminated by some predictably unforeseeable event and a quick exit, meant there was rarely a dull moment. Ernie, often unconsciously, made her laugh, a smile that took away all the misery and lit up any room. Like some loser buying lotto tickets and then delaying checking them to extend the fantasy of potential wealth, she held onto the dream that one day, Ernie would hit the jackpot for her.

The bus pulled up outside a railroad station of rare design and beauty. It looked like it should have been on the set of the Alamo, the scene before Santa Anna blew great holes in it, and in Davy Crockett.

They stepped out onto Andy Devine Avenue as a tiny man with a high-pitched voice, dressed in purposefully baggy cowboy gear, broke the silence of an exhausted group of seniors, also debussing, also looking like they'd been through a rough ten-hour bus trip. 'Step this way ladies and gents for a tour of Kingman the city, by Kingman's most famous son . . .' He wandered off, totally unfollowed and unaware, pausing only at the corner to point out, 'it was just over here that Andy

13

used to . . .' His voice drowned by the horn of a massive freight train.

'Why?' said Rooster fighting the tail end of the train's rumble.

'Why?' Ernie paused. 'I know that we've had our disappointments, but today, believe me, we've landed in the land of milk and money.'

Rooster looked at Ryder, Ryder looked at Rooster, in sync they turned to look at Ernie and then each did a 180-degree scan of downtown Kingman. There was not a cow in sight.

'I can see a soda bar and a bank, I hope it gets better than that,' said Rooster picking up her bag.

They made towards a motel boasting 'clean rooms and air for just $29' as the high-pitched voice made a brief comeback from an alley behind a liquor store, 'Sixty-two was a great year for him, The Man Who Shot Liberty Valance was followed by How the West Was Won . . . '

Ernie looked back at the motel, 'how much without the air option' he thought. He took in the broader view and smiled - for the first time in a long time he felt he was going to win in the west.

2.
FIRST GLINT OF A GEM

Kingman, Arizona

Rooster woke up to look around her room. It repulsed her. Cleanish if you didn't mind the mild stickiness of the carpets; cleanish if you looked to the calcium-encrusted showerhead rather than the hair filled plug; cleanish if you erased from your mind just how often the top cover of the bed had been exposed to instant human post check-in passion and then how often it hadn't been to the dry cleaners. Cleanish apart, it was all pretty grubby.

She'd had a fitful night's sleep. Exhausted from days of bus-napping and a bit disorientated she'd left the light on, a beacon in case she needed to find her way to the bathroom without touching anything. From east to west motel rooms smell and look the same, and she still hadn't forgotten the time in northern Maine when she got up, took the wrong door option and found herself locked out, standing facing a car park with only her briefest of briefs and loosest of vests keeping what was left of her privacy from a gathering bunch of early morning hunters. No matter what other three B's, bison, bear or beaver they would encounter that day, they'd remember the 3B's, the blonde babe on the balcony.

When she woke she noticed that the beacon was off and then realized that she hadn't been dreaming when the door had been opened sometime after midnight. A hand had slipped in and turned off the light, she'd screamed and a retreating apology of sorts came from along the gangway. She turned the light back on, put a chair up against the door and then eventually returned to an uncomfortable and fitful sleep. Upon the dawn, plus an hour or so, the light was off, but chair was still there, proof. She flicked the switch up and down; the bulb had blown.

Down at reception, waiting for the others before walking across the road to a diner for breakfast, a pair of eyes appeared from out of the darkness of an inner office. She could make out a kettle, a chaise lounge and an old TV, on, but muted, its intermittent glow lowlighting the highlights of a dismal workplace; emerging from it eventually the eyes became a face and a face became a body and a sleepy lump of humanity became the night manager, who in the next few minutes, through necessity rather than ability, would become the day manager. Before she could launch her grievance and request a new bulb, an Indian accent, more Chennai than Cherokee, broke the silence.

'I'm very sorry for to disturb you. I saw the light and thought the room empty – most of our guests don't stay the night,' he said.

Rooster tried to remember, had she washed her hands after removing the bedcover? The images were still burning in her head as Ryder and then Ernie emerged from their rooms opposite.

Breakfast was a fine up-lifter. Bacon, eggs, coffee, toast, Ernie setting aside any religious intolerances to take all four, twice, not that toast was an issue. He never ate bacon without thinking how expensive it would be if the Jews and Muslims wanted it too. 'Dearer than oil,' he reflected. 'Oil or bacon, no choice.' He turned to his companions.

'If Jesus was God's son, and Jesus was a Jew, then heaven must be baconless. The devil ain't just got the good tunes, he's got the smoky Canadian,' sparked Ryder in a rare moment of philosophizing and considering his fate.

'We were too tired last night to take it on board, so I left telling you until now,' he started. 'Did you notice, the big building on the way into town?' Ernie started again
.

'A prison,' Ryder muttered with more than a degree of experienced angst.

'No,' he paused, 'but of sorts,' said Ernie.

It wasn't just a case of fatigue that caused Ernie to hold fire on his idea. He had had the flash, but not until he sat quietly with the half bottle of bourbon he'd picked up from the liquor store, did the flash became a sustainable flame.

He gently led them through what he modestly said was pure genius. What he'd seen in the St Anthony's Home for the Blind was not a collection of unfortunate people being cared for. It was, in his mind, a holding center where relatives offloaded their weak-willed responsibilities and even weaker consciences. Here they planted time-consuming uncles and aunts, moms and dads into the best possible care that money could buy, providing it wasn't their money. Sadly, St Anthony's, chosen for its dry climate and clear air, was not readily accessible, so visiting destabilized from weekly to monthly, to seasonally, to almost never. But regardless, they were in the best possible care, as they would re-assure themselves and anyone else who asked, including their lonely aunts and uncles, moms and dads. It was sort of a safety deposit box for discarded relatives, a box that was only opened to reveal a last will and testimony.

Ernie assumed there were three common factors that turned this flash into a sustainable business. He always preferred to see ventures as business opportunities when others might have seen them as scams. This business was founded on the rock-hard pillar of guilt. Guilt was the final of the three common factors, blindness and money being the other two. Here close to the Mojave Desert, isolated and abandoned, lay perhaps a hundred souls, if not in need of salvation, in need of stimulation.

Ernie looked at Rooster and Ryder. 'We are going to stimulate them as never before. Welcome to the *European Experience*.'

'Lectures?' said Rooster thinking of her mind.

'Cooking?' said Ryder thinking of his stomach.

'No, no. Yes, yes in a way. We are going to take parties of about 15 and let them experience Europe.'

'Ernie that ain't easy,' shrugged Rooster. 'Travel is a long hard road to make a fast buck on. Everyone says so. We're not trained in caring, in organizing trains, planes and automobiles, let alone hotels, restaurants and attractions. A group of blind people relying on us for how long, two, three weeks? It's probably the maddest idea you've ever come up with.'

'Europe's a long way,' pumped in Ryder, ever happy to share his grasp of geography.

London, Paris, Rome, they won't touch an inch of them, but they will experience them, totally. We are going to create our own Disneyland, a world where everything smells right, feels right, sounds right, but it just won't look right, but then it doesn't have to,' smiled Ernie. 'Think of it we take 15 people out of their monotonous daily lives, they come back refreshed and breathe so much new life into St Anthony's, they'll all want it. After that there's the Asian Experience, the African Experience and then back to, by popular demand, European Experience II. This is the ultimate package holiday.'

Rooster went into a bubble. She often did it when she needed to reboot her mind. Mad, yes, easy, no, but potentially brilliant, could this be the lotto moment? It was certainly a little more complex than deciding on what square some cow shit had landed.

-0-

Ernie's shopping list was long and split into three. Kingman the town had many virtues, although it was a bit limiting to someone wishing to create a new Europe. Ernie liked its remoteness; it was out of the way enough to host the near-secret Hollywood marriage of Clark Gable and Carole Lombard. Its most famous son, Andy Devine, he of the boulevard, the short-arsed cowboy sidekick with a high voice, was its biggest draw today, alongside a certain road. Being at the heart of Route 66 it's mentioned in the song, twice, as a cautionary note,

You see Amarillo and Gallup, New Mexico
Flagstaff, Arizona don't forget Winona
Kingman, Barstaw, San Bernadino'

Although Ernie loved the song enough to know it by heart he had forgotten Amarillo and Gallup, not the words, the towns - perhaps he'd slept through them.

Ernie wasn't going to sleep through Kingman. St Anthony's for The Blind had opened his eyes and he was already warming to it. The city had, he now discovered, a dark underbelly. One time home to the Oklahoma City bomber, Timothy McVeigh, it had also been a home from home for La Cosa Nostra members who took advantage of Arizona's neutral status and that fact that Las Vegas was just up the road. 'God damn it even an episode of the Sopranos kicked off here,' he noted. The last of these three facts Ernie found in a booklet at the tourist office, the first two strangely omitted, or maybe not. But the booklet did mention another minor brush with the law. Kingman had attracted Pamela Anderson to do a Playboy photo shoot. It was all going swimming-costumely well until she got down to business on a street corner, started to disrobe in order to boost potential readership and was promptly arrested for indecent exposure.

He walked around, down Beale, up Third, along East Oak, down Fourth, along Andy Devine, its longest street named after its shortest resident – within three blocks of the center the desert reminded him of who was the real boss around here. There were more houses than trees, kinda what he'd expect a moon settlement to look like. He imagined it a cross between Tombstone and Salt Lake City. He had to imagine since he hadn't been to either.

Looking like one of the hundreds of drop-in Route 66ers he'd popped into the tourist office searching for a list of local businesses and services. Although it was no stranger to film and TV crews, no movie mogul had ever put dollars into the city to build a studio. Which was exactly what Ernie wanted right now and in a strange way he was quite relieved that there was no local option, no temptation. When 'The Experience' started he wanted to be a healthy distance away from St Anthony's, about eight hours by train, five by road, would be perfect - precisely the distance of Los Angeles.

Within hours he was back on yet another Greyhound, this time not for personal security or escape, but to see what was out there, what could be used in The Experience. The whole project hung on getting every part of the jigsaw onto the table. If just one piece were to be missing the whole thing would crumble. He called Clinton the 'IKEA president,' one loose screw and the administration fell apart.

He toyed with approaching St Anthony's immediately. He felt if his pitch failed was always another St Anthony's out there, but first he needed to see if he could get the other pieces into the picture. If you don't have a freezer, never promise a fat boy with a gun, an ice cream, was another of his mantras.

Top of his list was a derelict backlot, a mothballed studio waiting for the industry to go retro and give the graphic artists some time off. The timing was perfect, even Paramount had a vacant lot, but Ernie was hesitant. He wanted a small fish, one that could be enticed into a complicated web of promises. One for whom the prize of maintaining a secret was a possible lifeline. One that was desperate.

He had three on his list. He curled up in the seat and glanced out of the window. A green and white signpost whipped by, one which sent a shiver down his spine, 'Arizona State Prison – Kingman.' About two miles to his right beyond some moonlike rocks he immediately imagined he could see, occasionally

21

poking out through the parched terrain, a harsh reminder of the consequence of failure. In his time he'd done some time. Not big time, but enough time to appreciate the fine line between incarceration and freedom. So here he was, attracted to a small city because of an institution on its eastern approach and fearful because of an institution on its western flank.

-0-

Ryder's initial list was a bit more practical, the complex would follow once Ernie had secured a studio lot, but hopefully many of the items would be to hand, having been discarded by movie makers; a plane interior, office space or dressing rooms to convert to bedrooms, cafes and maybe even a boat. For the time being one, a bus, stood at the top of his wish list.

He'd a good idea where to find one. On the outskirts of Kingman lay a world-famous retirement home, not for people, for planes. It might be the sort of place that a bus, maybe one once used by an airport or airline, had be tucked away and forgotten. There was only one way to find out.

One of Kingman's virtues was, in being a college town, it meant plenty of bookstores. Getting together a mini library would be the core of planning and Rooster's first duty. Not a difficult one by her standards since she'd clocked The Book Nook directly over from the station as they got off the Greyhound. She was also naturally talented in the world of computers and websites. A marriage of the two would be necessary to give credence to any blossoming firm and she quite looked forward to it, even if it meant hours researching, stuck in a tacky motel room. She could reward herself with breaks by the pool. She wouldn't swim, just relax, for she suspected the water was changed less frequently than the bed covers. The image of a passing salesman, who had hooked up at the local bar, introducing his new love to a life of sublime luxury with a luke-warm bottle of Cook's Californian, followed by a late-might skinny dip and some unimaginable, unattractive and unprotected communication, made the pool as attractive as an Afghan minefield. Still the minefield was marginally more appealing than her room.

Beyond the bus, Ryder's role was for the moment a little less clearly defined. The only thing that was assured was that it would be physical and mechanical and riddled with disastrous potential. He was neither a planner or a dreamer, regardless of destination, if the bus was on the right side of the road, he'd hop on. What else would he do? Ernie was a mate and a provider, the only two he had.

3.
GONE WITH THE WIND

Burbank, Los Angeles

Typhoon Films had seen better days, not many, but certainly
better. Elsewhere in LA the studios had grown and around
them a comforting degree of support; restaurants, bars, motels,
service stations. Typhoon looked like an orphan cast into the
wind and left to sort itself out. In a moment of self-flagellating
promotion, it had declared itself 'Home of the B Movie', but on
a sun-kissed morning as a taxi slowly pulled up, even that
seemed overstated.

Ernest Zimmerman III stepped out of the cab and looked at the
faded sign, the dust-blown security hut, the unpainted main
block and thought, 'perfect, God damn perfect.'

Charles Crawford sat in his office looking out over the silent
lots. Nothing had happened there since an advertising agency
had spent three days and not a lot of money two weeks ago.
The agency had wanted to make a spoof about a fading starlet
in a faded studio, it was 'perfect, God damn perfect', the same
GDP that the faded character walking in had grasped moments
before as he passed a dozing security guard doing his third job
of the day as thoroughly as he had slept through the other two.

As the Chief Executive and Producer Charles had many
anxieties, but he eased them by coming in early each day, at
about 8.15, looking for the mail, and then if nothing had
cropped up by eleven he and his secretary slipped off for a

24

light lunch and back for heavy sex. His secretary Roger was a former NBA starlet broken by pressure, but sustained by pleasure. Charles's wife didn't have the energy to suspect, she was too busy living off his past to see the present, let alone care about the future. Anyway, as soon as Charles came home she'd be off to the tennis club. She was being coached by someone called Beverley, but in reality Bev was Roger, a former NBA starlet broken by pressure but sustained by pleasure. Roger played for both teams. Hollywood, where odd is so commonplace it's normal, and yet even in its dimmest corners, it can still manage to flash a light on the improbable and the intriguing lifting the peculiar to down-right bizarre.

Strangely these where the virtues Charles most craved for in a script. 'Perhaps someday someone would walk in through my door . . ' he thought. The improbable and the intriguing were at that very moment walking along the creaking wooden veranda towards his office.

'You were expecting me, I believe,' Ernie said as he moved towards Roger.

'I expect nothing and nothing is expected of me,' said Roger in the kind of throwaway line he imagined Oscar Wilde would deliver and scriptwriters would die for, quite wrongly.

'The perfect KPI's' Ernie remarked, as Charles breezed by.

'Do follow' he nodded to Ernie and like a paper bag caught in the draught of a passing car he was sucked into and office littered with minor moments of nostalgia, but not achievement. Moments not monuments. Photos, old marked-up clapperboards, Variety covers, but no Oscars; the closest thing to an award was a grand-looking model of an Arri cine-camera that on closer inspection turned out to be a cigarette lighter.

'I'm a busy man' Charles started without a hint of guilt or realization that his dire situation was blatantly obvious. 'I can give you ten minutes.'

'I can give you a twenty-million-dollar movie,' replied Ernie going straight to Charles' Achilles and one hour later he was still causing Charles to swoon in his own good fortune.

The basic plan that lay ahead for Typhoon Pictures was that the Government was looking for somewhere discreet to conduct some secret social psychology tests for groups of people – the outcome of which would totally change not just America, but humanity. If Typhoon signed the Secrets Act, 'hosted' the experiment without interruption or intervention on a back lot, then they, Typhoon, would get the exclusive rights to the movie, once the findings were published. Even if Typhoon folded Charles would have the rights, his pension fund. It would cost them nothing, an old disused back lot and their temporary silence wrapped up in patience.

For any studio down on its knees, it was a long shot, but for Typhoon it was the first time someone had loaded the gun in absolutely ages. And joy of joys, it was the US Government, albeit in the shape of a very non-Washington Ernest Zimmerman. Charles looked across the table at Ernie, could he see this man in the Oval Office? No, but then he was a psychologist so he'd probably been there a few times, especially recently.

'What's the timescale, at what point do you finish and we can start?' Charles delivered knowing that this was vital whilst not wanting to seem like he was desperate.

'If all goes well 24 months, if it requires more study, maybe four years,' Ernie replied basing his judgement on whether he could hope to get one or ten Experiences through Typhoon before the balloon burst.

Charles didn't know if they could even last the 24 months. He stood up from the desk and said he'd think about it, by the time he'd got to the door he'd thought. 'I'm a movie-maker, but above all I am an American, I love this country, if I can serve it with this and then make a movie, then we are on.'

Ernie looked at him. A humble thank you was followed by his relief in the cooperation 'because I'd have hated to have to had to requisition the place. It's so perfect, so God damn perfect, but only if you make our lot a total "no go zone", and I mean total, I want the wind to ask permission to blow through.'

4.
CALL THE DOCTOR

Kingman, Arizona

Dr Ronald Dent was a man of considerable stature, and he considered his stature continuously in his own eyes. It was those very same eyes that caused others to shun away from automatic trust, openness, or friendship. Steel-blue, narrow and piercing they destroyed his other manly attributes of a fine muscular-build disguising his fifty-two years and hair so light in color that from a distance you were unsure if he were blonde, grey or white. Close-up you were never in a position to decide, so dominating and distracting were those blue eyes that you would forget to look. With a smile he could be the irresistible movie lover, without one, a cold-blooded assassin.

You could imagine him as the strict authoritarian running the federal prison on the western side of Kingman with an inflexible approach to anything mildly humanitarian. The irony was that Dr Dent held a post to the east of Kingman as Director of St Anthony's Home for the Blind, which he ran with an inflexible approach to anything mildly humanitarian.

Dr Dent was at his desk muddling through accounts. Ernest Zimmerman meanwhile was heading eastwards back to Kingman, glowing in the success of his LA expedition, unaware of the blue-eyed difficulty that lay ahead. He did know however that this one person was now the most vital link in his whole plan. Dr Dent could be a comma in a glorious sentence, or a full stop.

Courtesy of East Andy Devine Boulevard and a local bus, Ryder was about ten miles north east of the city. He'd caught an airport bus in the hope of finding a coach at the airport, having received the rather confusing instruction from an elated Ernie the previous evening. Ernie felt good about the prospects, but not yet good enough to move up to car rental. For the time being it was buses, anyway if Ryder did stumble upon a bus he'd need to drive it back.

Kingman has one of several airfields in the States that has more planes than most hubs see in a day. It is a plane spotter's Valhalla for, as with several other locations in the driest zone of Arizona, here was a rest home for those magnificent flying machines that had out-lived their usefulness, where maintenance didn't need paying because climatic conditions put the planes into a time warp. A bit like the 'guests' at St Anthony's, the planes were temporarily discarded by those who didn't want them anymore, in this case Delta, United and American Airlines, DHL and several others including a smatter of ex-military.

Mothballed in the dry air with some cannibalized at will to keep the rest of the fleets flying, they await an uncertain future. Slow decaying death by mechanic or worse, a new life in Africa flying unmaintained, in and out of airports that made the two tarmacked runways at Kingman seem like O'Hare. Flying, until they hit the ground and headlines.

At one stage you could have bought a twin engine light bomber from the lot at Kingman, like a Douglas A26, for the price of rundown second hand car or an hour at the tables and very fancy lady in Las Vegas, about $2,000. So said the guy in the bar that Ryder had talked to. 'Do they also sell coaches?' Ryder had enquired and the guy, not flinching at the off-beam

29

request, simply muttered, 'may do.' In truth Ryder wasn't listening, his mind immediately triggering to the fact that if you had 2,000 bucks you would have to decide between a car, or a plane or a hooker. The car he decided was the most desirable of the trio, even though he hadn't been in either of the other options for quite some time.

The request from Ernie and the information from the guy in the bar had merely resulted in a morning out, a very dry run. Rows and rows of commercial and a scattering of military planes doing what actors do between jobs, resting, but no cheap unwanted buses.

Rooster, having used up her allocation of free bytes on the motel Internet was in the local tourist office picking up brochures and asking for the code for the free Wi-Fi so she could 'book' something. Happy, later she'd sit on the bench outside trying to avoid sunlight on the screen and surfing with a sandwich.

-0-

Ernie was not just the CEO of the trio, he was also Chief Financial Officer, and he'd devised a method of fiscal control, inspired by the Olympics. All concepts were competitors, an idea had to show considerable promise to be bronze and to be silver it needed to be a near certainty, whilst gold required it to be purely exceptional. He distributed their investment funds in this way. He was so excited by the Kingman project he'd told the others immediately that it was certain bronze. In all the years they'd been together they'd never stood at the top of the podium.

Still on the Greyhound heading back eastwards EZ was nudging towards silver; well it would be after he'd cracked the next nut in the bowl, the man behind the wall nut. Somewhere in the Mohave about three hours out of LA, the highway had decided to part company with the escorting rail track and in the middle of nowhere Ernie noticed a full set of bars on his cell-phone. Not a full set of bars on his cell, which was something that never ever fully left his mind and was certainly nothing to phone home about. He punched in the number for St Antony's and was glad of the relative peace in the rear of the coach.

A warm voice welcomed him and she said she'd enquire if Dr Dent were available. In what seemed an age as the moonscape of the Mohave passed by, Ernie waited and practiced his opening lines.

'Good morning, Dr Ronald Dent, how can I help,' the voice was brisk, no nonsense, not cold, but still not anything half a degree warmer than business formal. After all it might be a relative of a potential inmate, potential revenue.

'Good morning doctor, my name is Ernest Zimmerman, I would like to request half an hour of your time to put something to you that will lift morale amongst your guests and reduce your workload.' There was a silence that matched a desert night and Ernie scrambled to fill it with 'and represent a potential cost-saving for your institution.' More desert night and Ernie chipped in, 'a considerable saving.'

The speaker-phone rumbled to the muffled sound of a diesel engine, and Dent looked the considerable length of his office, his head moving up down, up down. His shoulders eventually followed the movement and a light ping sent a ball on its way,

31

past the desk, through the chair legs and on to the electric hole. Had he been successful the golf ball would have shot right back, it didn't and clipping of the front lip in disappeared behind a bookcase. Dent shuddered with a mild rage, it was as if he'd lost the Masters and would never wear the green jacket.

Rooster had taken the time to look up the details of St Anthony's and Dent's profile on the web and had sent Ernie a summary and a pocket portrait of the doctor. Neither helped him as much as the un-grabbed and thrown pitched lines about financial significance. Cold and calculated was the man at the other end of the phone, he'd been in full-flow, ready to send this Mr Zimmerman, like the golf ball, on his way. He was multi-tasking, putting badly and ignoring this Zimmerman fellow simultaneously. Sod the golf, running the institution for an ugly profit was the real number one for Dr Ronald Dent. He needed it for his double life style. Maybe he should listen.

'Let me see,' went Dent, feigning to consult a diary. Ernie could hear pages turning, one, two, three. 'Was it a daily, weekly or monthly diary?' Ernie thought anxiously. It was already Wednesday, if the pages had flicked on to Friday and the doctor didn't do weekends, he'd be into next week with a considerable, perhaps even fatal, knock-on in costs. Every day lost, every cent spent, put the embryonic project in deeper jeopardy.

Ernie decided to flush the fox out. It was a gamble, but it just had to be, time wasn't on his side. Better to blow up in his face now than after a month of waiting and delays. He'd noted that St Anthony's had a board, but suspected that Dent was the kind of man who saw the board as his, rather than he, their obedient servant. He was so hard and arrogant that behind his back the nursing staff had nicknamed him 'The Count' – the non-nursing staff, who were treated even more subserviently, used the same title, only the 'o' was silent.

'I'm actually in Phoenix at the moment due in Vegas on Saturday, instead of flying I could keep the rental and drop by Kingman, you are near there, aren't you?'

The inclusion of a question, especially one requiring local knowledge, was always a good way Ernie thought of increasing the chances of communication and through that the chances of a positive response.

'It's a bit of a drive, not so much in miles, but more in monotony – I could do lunchtime tomorrow, or just after it would be better,' the doctor offered thinking so as not to disturb one of his non-sporting or sexual pleasures. 'But before we go any further, what is it you are offering?' Before he got more than the first few words of a reply, the bars on Ernie's phone evaporated in the desert heat. Mildly intrigued Dent sent another ball towards the cup. Smack center, perhaps an omen, he thought.

5.
THE PITCH

St Anthony's, Kingman, Arizona

St Anthony's lay about six miles out of Kingman. It had been built in the Thirties as a private home for a Californian industrialist who made his fortune in plastics and wanted somewhere free of the pollution he'd created and freer of people he employed. He got both in an expansive neo-Georgian house set far back from the Interstate they were busy constructing. It was modelled on a property in Connecticut the industrialist had long lusted after, but couldn't face the prospect of New England winters. What he got instead was twelve bedrooms, four reception rooms and a library in the middle of one of the driest and hottest of states.

He never got to properly enjoy it; after four decades of 12-hour days crammed with stress to create a fortune, his body couldn't cope with downtime. One month after moving in and whilst trying out the newly laid pathways, he stopped in the shade of a gazebo, turned to look at where he intended to spend the rest of his life, and spent it. An aneurism, he was dead before he hit the gravel he'd just paid for.

A bachelor who was married only to his fortune, his cousins were not so eager to enjoy peace and quiet in 80 degrees and sold the building on to a school. They added a dormitory block, a swimming pool, and a west-facing wing full of classrooms. The board of governors had intended to put in an assembly hall in a second-stage development, but the school too, at a time when the world was busy fighting itself, found it impossible to survive and it became a silent casualty of WWII.

And so the expanded house, like the mothballed planes at the airport, just sat there awaiting its fate. It was no short wait. The first sign of life was as a health spa in the late Fifties and then the demand for rehab created by the Swinging Sixties and Seventies, saw the establishment freed from any financial life-support system for the first time and it was able to breathe on its own. The very isolation made it work as a rehab center for people who saw their best years at best obliquely, through a drug-induced haze. The same isolation made it sound choice for families wanting to visit infrequently and for those who, even though out of their heads, realized that at Kingman there was no conceivable outlet for temptation and their half hoped for the chance of falling off the wagon.

The owners tired of dealing with other people's problems sold it, the new owners failed to grasp the concept and it closed. In the Eighties, a religious order moved in to use it as a retreat. The building, anonymous for so long, finally got a name, St Anthony's, which stuck even after the modern-day monks moved out because there was never enough of them to form a choir. Armed with a mock-up brochure and a pocketful of business cards, Ernest Zimmerman III had arrived by taxi and was about to make the biggest pitch of his life. He would explain the lack of hire car by way of puncture picked up downtown.

--0—

Nurse Patricia Swallow was from South Chicago; she could have been Miss America, not for her looks, although she was a fine lady in her mid-thirties, but for her genetic pool. She had

35

Lithuanian, German, Italian, Afro American and WASP blood in her, with a dash of Irish revealed as the sun hit her auburn to blonde hair. Ernest followed her closely down the corridor; he felt he had to. It was the only way he could avoid looking at the broken zip on the back of her pencil thin skirt. Today all concentration was on getting initial approval for the project, not on the moving black T, the fragile piece of undergarment revealed to the light of day by the malfunctioning zipper. Lingerie thought Ernie, what a great con, the more you pay, the less you get.

Unaware of her distraction she moved with silk-like ease bidding warm comments to those she passed. She knew them all, 'Mr Easterbrook, Miss Little, Mr Sharman, Mrs Clarke, Ms Jankowski as she passed or they passed her she would identify them chipping in a personal detail to show she cared. She didn't care quite enough to use first names, an insight Ernie thought that said 'these are not patients or guests, they are commodities. Souls deposited for disposal.'

One elderly man moved closer, sniffing the air as if drawn towards an apple pie cooling on the window ledge.

'Miss Dior?' he said within range of breath.

'Miss Swallow to you, Mr Wilcox,' she said backing off a pace, 'or I'd prefer, nurse Swallow.'

'No, the perfume, I know it is not, but it reminds me of Miss Dior, I never forget a smell,' he said as Swallow and Ernie broke free into open space, her inviting body glow creating a new trail.

She turned to the visitor. 'You've got to watch him. He's 72, he can smell like a bloodhound, it is akin to Miss Dior, but I wouldn't give him the satisfaction because the only thing that is more active than his nose are his hands. Encourage one and you unleash the other.'

Ernie smiled back in a consent that was deeper than the nurse could understand, for it included the thought of what Mr Wilcox would, if he only could, have made of her flashing G-String. A second thought struck him, why is it called a G-string? Girlie, groin, genitals, he'd get Rooster to look it up.

By now a fine double butterfly-carpentered door was all that was left between Ernie and his objective, he thought of the word quarry, but that made it too much of an unbalanced hunt. Dr Dent was not an animal under pursuit; he was a mission that had to be accomplished for the embryonic idea to even survive in the womb. He was a lion that needed taming. As nurse Swallow opened the door, the doctor was revealed looking out of the window. An unnatural action given the noise the door made upon opening, it was the doctor playing his first card. It said, 'this is my territory, my rules, you wait on me.'

Ernie recognized this and remembered the old intelligence service destabilizing trick at the first job interview where the interviewer doesn't glance at the interviewee, but beckons him to take a seat – except there is no seat in the room beyond the one the principal was sitting in. It was all about seeing how you react to non-conformity.

As the, seemingly preoccupied, doctor slowly turned, Ernie played his first card in this game of calculated chance. 'Doctor thank you for seeing me at such short notice. Ernest Zimmerman.'

'Ah Mr Zimmerman,' the doctor said in such a way it indicated that Ernie was not the highlight of his working day. The director then dismissed nurse Swallow with a nod and Ernie instinctively thought to himself that there was something between the two of them, even if her boss had failed to miss the broken zip on her exit. This was either going to be a very short or a very long day.

'So, this project,' the doctor kicked off, 'on the phone you briefly mentioned before the line went dead, that you want to take some of our, you used the word "patients", they are disadvantaged, blind not ill. I prefer the word "guests", you want to take them away from here, for a holiday – I think you called it The European Experience. I'm happy to hear about it, but I have grave doubts that it will work. As I said these are not sick people, but they do need professional care or they would become "patients", if anything should happen to any of them we would be sued out of existence, and so would you.'

Ernie gave the calm nod of a poker player facing a potential flush with two pair in his hand. This was a big question, perhaps the biggest, and it was his first. Throw the cards down now and he'd be back in the car before the blue light coming from the mosaic window had moved off the golf ball hiding in the corner. "Confuse and Conqueror," his self-generated family motto rang through his ears. Sitting room-side of the large leather inlaid desk, the world of professional healthcare was as remote a subject matter to him as if he'd pulled 'Italian tenors of the 19th century' out of the hat in a TV quiz show. The man sitting opposite, window-side of the desk, was pitching on home ground and all Ernie could hope for even at this early point was a dark cloud and a rain check.

'Of course, that is the number one fundamental issue – care is core and paramount and if I may I'll come to that in a moment or two,' said Ernie hoping for a moment or ten. 'There will be many care questions you will want to ask, and I want to answer, but some might answer themselves if I give to a from-the-ground-up brief on what the European Experience is all about.'

The doctor threatened to smile, didn't, he was mulling over the phrase 'care is core' and how it could look on the wall outside. Without speaking his eyebrows consented to Ernie carrying on down the road he'd selected.

As a sales pitch, Ernie was more than aware that his presentation was a little shy of glossy experience-filled brochures. Ryder had argued, what was the point since the intended targets couldn't see them. He had hit on something Ernie would, of course, turn to the advantage.

'I'm a bit shy on promotional ware here, for obvious reasons. Every time I'm in London I can't get over the pubs with signs outside saying, "Good food served here" what else are they going to say? "Our food is lousy microwaved garbage, so come inside.' He went on to deride online public-driven travel guides, 'the longer we can keep out of that snake pit of uncontrolled opinion the better.'

What Ernie did have was two pages of minimalist content and design, created by Rooster from her library visits and hours on the laptop. If less is more, then here he had a lot. What little he had actually looked quite classy with a logo EE to signify the whole core of the project, the European Experience.

Slowly Ernie took Dent on a verbal tour of Europe, Ireland, England, Denmark, Germany, Poland, Italy, Spain, France and back to Arizona; in all 23 days.

Ernie was desperate to break the naughty schoolboy in the headmaster's office atmosphere that prevailed. Unless he did something to lift his status he was in for a short spanking for not doing his homework. Anyway, a moving target is harder to hit. He rose from his seat walked round the desk and towards the windows. Looking out he added, 'For 15 of your guests this could be the most enlightening time of their lives. Forgive me but as I look out these people, unfortunate in circumstance, comforted by your obviously superb care, they lack the flash of stimulation that the European Experience can give them. And not just those who do the trip, the whole institution will have a new glow, refreshed dimensions.'

He moved back and daring to eat further into Dent's space, picked up the putter, prodded a rough ball out from beside a waste bin and sent it on its way towards the hole. To his surprise and Dent's nudging and begrudging admiration, it went in. 'You play? The doctor asked. 'No, beginner's luck,' Ernie said and smiled.

'I understand the proper concerns of care. This project benefits everyone. How many patients, sorry I keep saying it because I don't see them as people I yet know. Maybe participants would be a better collective name when they travel. Looking at them they are people who it seems as if they can survive on their own. Is it just so? Do they live in their own dark world or do they interact with each other and how many do you have

40

here?'

Ernie thought that a barrage of questions would reduce the
time he had to perform if Dent decided to answer any of them.

'Our optimum is 130, currently we are running at about one
hundred, 104, I think,' Dent offered. He looked out the window
as an anonymous white van pulled up. '103.'

'For you staff it would be about a 15% reduction in their
workload. For the Institution, a 15% saving in all costs like
food, A/C, hot water and, and lighting and . . . ' Ernie's mind
went a little blank as he thought of the insignificance of lighting
. . . 'and, and there would be a five percent booking charge
earned by the Institution.' He paused wondering if he'd over
done it in terms of seeming keen so he added 'to offset any
administration costs.'

Ernie wasn't sure where that had come from, did it sound
desperate? His immediate secondary thought was deep down
in his pocket, but it might just have proved to be the deal
maker, for Dent, like a low watt light bulb flickered up a notch
or two to full glow. Well as full a glow as Ernie thought
possible. Dent's cool personality was no room filler, but the
thought of funds that didn't really have to go through the
books and might find their tax-free way into his personal
financial zone, was so pleasing, the whole atmosphere warmed
up.

Ernie, back to the Zimmerman of old, the cow plop bingo fiasco
a trivial memory, was on a wave and reaching into the EE
monogramed leather folder he pulled out two sets of papers.
One in plain English was marked "Preliminary Booking" and
Ernie explained its purpose and saying it was too early in the

process slipped it back into the folder. By too early Ernie meant that he'd like time to re-adjust the figures to include the five percent he'd just given away. He covered this by saying that the five per cent was not necessarily on the books. He could see that Dent understood. It wasn't a backhander, just a sum for him to dispense as he saw fit. He moved away from finances to practicalities and said that naturally he would have to come and talk to the guests and fully brief them before they signed up.

The other set of papers was almost devoid of anything; near blank sheets with some small type at the base. The rest of the pages were a mass of embossed dots, braille. It was Rooster's idea and she'd found an online company that returned printed documents impressively quickly, converted into braille. It was a simple touch of genius and if he ever paid her he'd give her a rise, he thought. Just thought.

In a brief silent vacuum, Ernie looked around the office, apart from a couple of photos it was cold and business-like. There was a top line wall-mounted CD player and on a rack a dozen or so discs. Ray Charles, Jose Feliciano, Andrea Bocelli, Steve Wonder . . . . Ernie was just about to comment on the diversity of music when Dent spoke with some warming degree of understanding.

'Only a handful I'm afraid can read braille'

6.
LAST CHANCE MOTEL

Star of 66 Motel, Kingman, Arizona

Rooster was sitting at the mirror, looking into the future, reflecting on the past. She liked Ernie, even Ryder on most days, but all she saw this particular day was a girl sitting in the Last Chance Motel. Perhaps after this episode they'd end up in California, split up and go their own ways; she'd meet a nice sensible guy with a sensible career and a sensible bank balance and they could settle down to a stable comfortable sensible existence. The only word she could identify from her thoughts was existence, for that was all she had done for the past fourteen or fifteen years.

She'd existed as a trainee nurse before she couldn't face other people's blood and pain, she'd existed as a checkout clerk in a supermarket, she'd existed as a bartender and then as a croupier when this fast-talking funny guy walked in and she walked out to begin a career on the road. She smiled, then noticed the wrinkles and returned to thinking of the good, the bad and the darn right ugly events that had followed. Perhaps they were largely positive for she wouldn't have hacked it if they had all been nightmares of the same intensity as the dead cow in Chelsea. She closed and opened her eyes, this was the moment, after the European Experience failed, she was out.

The phone rang, breaking her deep reflection. For a moment she hesitated. The phone, like the room was grubby and out of date, the person at the other end of the line would not be the

43

sensible Mr Right, it would be Ryder with a problem or Ernie with good or bad news. It rang six maybe seven times, she didn't count, she just ended it by lifting the receiver to her ear. It was Ernie.

'Rooster my dear,' she knew that was either good or a plea for help, 'I think we are on the stagecoach out of here,' she couldn't work out if he meant that the project was on or off, 'the doctor has swallowed our pill and now we just need to get some bums on seats.'

It was semi good news demanding action. Rooster summoned up as much enthusiasm as previous experiences would allow her and added to Ernie's glee. She thought the little man at the other end of the line had never seemed so up and then thought there is no such thing as at the end of the line anymore. The wire stopped somewhere outside of her dingy motel room and translated into something invisible to everything except the number at the other end. That number was close to Ernie's ear in the back of a taxi. Driving was one of the skills Ernie hadn't acquired and he had had a storyline ready, if needed, to tell Dent why when driving from Phoenix, he'd arrived by cab.

Ernie rattled off a wish list like a seven-year old at Christmas, 'have you got all that?' he asked. Rooster replied no, for she hadn't and she knew that his recall was pretty-well total. One forgotten item wouldn't haunt her, but it would bug both of them. 'Never mind, I'll be back in fifteen, we can go through it together, and where's Ryder?'

She didn't know, but he wouldn't be far. They hadn't the funds to squander on the highlife of downtown Kingman, if there were any.

--0—

44

Re-united the trio set off on foot to find a neutral conference area, free from the rigor mortis induced by every waking second in the motel. They got as far as the car park and a sign that said "Parking - Residents Only" and realized that the only other reason for leaving your car here would be a breakdown. They thought that the rental car Rooster had picked up as the first item on Ernie's list, also deserved a chance of freedom and unselfishly returned to take it out of its dismal environment.

It was hot and dusty, the motel sign gently swinging; the only thing missing from this desolate glimpse of classic Americana was the stray tumbleweed. That and perhaps a sign indicating why the motel existed in the first place, although Star of 66 was a clue, though some visitors thought that was maybe the last year it was cleaned. The wide stretch of tarmac that eastwards took you north to eventually Chicago and westwards to LA was a two-lane carriageway, known locally as East Andy Devine Boulevard, but to the world as the most famous of all roads, Route 66.

Route 66 isn't a road, it is a culture, a bookmark in the history of America. A strip of tarmac, it is their Westminster Abbey, their Taj Mahal stretched out over eight states. It was in the American highways system for just 58 years, but still it's eternally embedded in the American psyche. Every inch of its 2,448 miles resounds to Buddy Holly, the Everly Brothers and of course Chuck Berry. It is not a road, it is a track, an American soundtrack. It is the page that says Harley Davidson, leathers, open Corvettes and Mustangs, even open space, soda jerks, drive-throughs with girls in fairy-like dresses stepping out of open-topped Cadillac's and dreamers fulfilling their dream.

Today the red rental wouldn't live or drive much of the dream.

It turned right and briefly onto the historic highway and then left into a Walmart. Ernie knew they really didn't need a confidential area, what they were discussing was so far off the wall that no one outside of little group could or would understand what on earth they were going on about. Even Ryder, with all the story slowly revealing itself, at times struggled to keep up. A corner of the coffee shop would do for this outline meeting. Later he would then take them downtown and do something totally out of character, put his wallet on the bar and let his team eat and drink themselves into happiness. They were moving from silver to gold.

Like the car they had just parked, they had clearly defined roles. Ernest was in charge of the steering wheel and gear stick, basically in control although he'd no license; Rooster was seats, safety and in-car entertainment and Ryder was the engine, called upon to pull-push carry. Like most engines, it was only on the occasions of failure that he received any attention and then it was, by instinct, fairly negative.

-0-

Like all good ideas, the basic concept was simple. They would assemble a party of blind people, now called participants, take them out of their current environment by putting them on a trip where they fully experienced Europe. Well not quite fully, because they would never leave the United States, but as fully as you could get in the circumstances. They would taste Guinness in Dublin, enjoy an open-air Shakespearian play in the bard's home of Stratford-upon-Avon, do French vineyard tours and attend a Papal Mass in Italy, gambling in Monte Carlo and enjoy Paris nightlife.

All that the EE team needed was two half-witted sound engineers, a fairly comfortable bus, the conversion of the accommodation block at the studio into fifteen very different feeling bedrooms and an old plane fuselage. The last item Ernie had already joyously spied when at Typhoon. Along one side of the studio was a cut open model of a commercial aircraft, fifteen rows of seats, a toilet, a crew area and a cockpit. The whole platform was on hydraulics. It was perfect. The hydraulics might make the frame creak a bit, so Ernie was into keeping a fairly noisy in-flight atmosphere track booming throughout the two long haul and several short haul 'flights'. There were other things more basic, some of which could even be sourced from the shop they were now in.

Ever the realist Rooster brought up the subject of funding. Ernie rarely went into this zone unprompted or positively forced – unknown to the others, he did have a nest egg, 'the bundle' he called it. It was the only sensible thing he'd ever religiously held on to. Many times in the past the temptation to fall back on it was immense, but he'd resisted. The $15,000 he had stashed away from a very successful sting in upstate New York was his combined Get Out Of Jail ticket and, as of today, the priming money for an idea about to move a project to gold. He still couldn't bring himself to admit to the others that they had ever had resources. Such a revelation could only stir up resentment for the nights they had spent in bus terminals rather than hotels. The café menu instead of a restaurant. What they didn't know, didn't hurt.

They still wouldn't know even now. In the eyes of R&R, the rainy day bundle would simply be added anonymously to the money raised by the deposits and then be extracted from the full revenue, when earned, and returned to its 'bunker' hopefully increased. It was a staggeringly simple piece of bookkeeping. It just required constant resolve. It was like a financial iCloud, it was there, it works, but no one can really understand how.

'I've upped the cost of the trip to $8,500 – it is all in because we can't afford for people to make decisions about excursions, what one does they all do,' explained Ernie.

'That's $127,500,' said Rooster.

'Yes, but not quite, about six grand goes to St Anthony's, or I should say, Dr Dent. I had to give him a sweetener. It's really a bit more than that, but I've explained to him that there are some administration costs.'

'Corrupt bastard,' Ryder murmured in mild disgust, totally ignoring what fiscal misery they had amassed during their relatively brief time together.

'The profit on this one is not huge, about 25 to 30 per cent for us, but any subsequent tours, and they will happen because of peer pressure and the ravings of group one, will up our profit to 70 or 75,' said Ernie. 'These people are not short of cash, many are independently wealthy, they have been put in St Anthony's by relatives who don't want anything to threaten the natural filtering of their inheritance. I see four groups here, at least, especially if the caring doctor is locked in at six grand a trip.'

At Ernie's request, Rooster had researched beyond the walls of St Anthony's. There were 20 million Americans with sight loss, not always total so it was a figure that contributed nothing to future planning. However, she had listed 14 separate institutes on the western side of the country, all within two days drive to LA.

Ernie went on to expand how he roped in Typhoon Studios and that two extra hands would be joining them. Earlier he'd been on the phone to Charles Crawford, firstly to confirm that the 'project, I don't want to say more' was on and secondly to see if the studio could provide, at a shared cost, two technicians who could be sworn to secrecy about the mission.

The movie executive knew of five guys, currently looking for work who could fit the bill, three sound engineers and two from the special effects department. He then remembered two others who might be able to cope. They had the extra qualification of being a free asset to Typhoon. They were on site and, as Charles put it, 'currently living under special circumstances.'

Bolstered by Dr Dent's inclusion, Ernie listened to their CV's and immediately opted for the two guys with the special circumstances. 'But hold the others for later,' he told Charles, 'since the Government was keen not to rely on just one set of tests.' Ernie had already calculated that dumb as Charles was, there would be a day of realization if he pushed it too far. If they could get three trips out of Typhoon, that might be it. From then on with capital flowing, hiring another down-at-heel lot would be the more attractive option, or he could simply remain at Typhoon as a paying long-term client. The plane fuselage alone made this an attractive option.

Charles, sworn to the Secrets Act, could do little but sit back and wait. It was something he was good at. Presently he was sitting back and waiting for Roger to return and 'to finish what they had started' sometime earlier. Meanwhile Mrs Crawford

49

was several miles away, being finished by Roger in a shower room of the Belvoir Valley LTC. The Belvoir Valley Ladies Tennis Club was famous amongst the local in-crowd for one notable fact, it didn't have a court. Private changing rooms with massage tables and showers, yes, but nothing needing an umpire or even a net. It was very popular with the hungry wives of exhausted executives, most of who invested in the best in fashion sports clothing and most expensive of racquets – the latter never making it out of the trunk. Many a Smartphone diary contained the initials BV, once or twice a week. There were rumors of a Belvoir Valley Golf Club starting up for those who wanted just a little bit more, like a whole day's sport, with the clubs tucked safety in the trunk.

7.
SHOWTIME

St Anthony's, Kingman, Arizona

Ernie thought the turnout for the introduction to the European Experience impressively high. But then anything out of the normal was an event at St Anthony's. Any attendance less than 100% caused the staff to panic and do a quick room search, expecting the worst. Ernie had asked nurse Swallow for what she thought might be the optimum time-slot. The guests at St Anthony's relied on radio and music for a large part of their entertainment; eating, walking and sleeping filling most of the rest of their considerable free time. Unlike conferences where the dead zone for speakers was the session after lunch, at St Anthony's it was the point when spirits were highest with most people confined to indoors because of the striking heat. Nurse Swallow said that because they were together, once they'd finished eating they generally chatted for about an hour before wilting and taking a snooze in the many winged armchairs. At Ernie's suggestion, the cook had given the lunch a twist of Europe feel with French pates, Spanish olives, Danish fish, English cheese and Italian hams. He didn't request German or Polish delicacies because he couldn't think of any.

Ryder, standing at the back of the 130-seat auditorium, had been looking forward to this day since he'd heard about nurse Swallow and the broken zip. His spirits tumbled when she entered. Striking yes, but the white medical coat, buttoned and stopping at the knees, dispelled any chance of the mildest titivation. Best get on with the work as detailed he thought.

In his left hand he held a small digital camera and he explained to nurse Swallow that he'd video some of Ernie's performance for their forthcoming website, if that was ok by her. She consented, but with the condition that the guests were informed and should they request it, they would be excluded from the video. In response to Swallow announcing the video just one hand raised, an Afro-American guy in his early thirties and he was subsequently escorted to a row near the back. Ryder noted that his name was Harley, for that was the sole purpose of the video. There was no website, there never would be, but footage of potential customers would be looked at later by the trio to identify suitable 'marks' and danger areas.

It was a trick that Ernie had picked up from a tour operator in Puerto Rico. The tour company always overbooked, they had to in order to satisfy their delicate profit margins. The plane would arrive and the tour operator knew that he had to cull up to six people from their hotel and holiday of their choice. Something they'd spent hours at home discussing and deciding would change in a flash. He would watch from the moment they stepped off the plane, but the most telling area was when they stood by the carousel awaiting their luggage. Then he would strike, hitting those looking nervous and unsure. It was Darwinian in principle, survival of the fittest, but he had to be quick. Noticing the baggage tag he'd move in, 'Mr and Mrs Wilkinson?' They would reel at the identification, nodding a very uncertain consent whilst thinking things at their very worst. 'Has there been an accident at home, are our visas invalid, should we be here at all?' He'd smile 'Good I caught you before you got on the wrong coach. I'm delighted to tell you that you have upgraded. We care about our visitors and we decided that the Pablo Casa wasn't what we'd like for Mr and Mrs Wilkinson.'

Bewildered he'd usher them aside into a corner, dismissing their anxiety that the new hotel was in a city when they'd booked a resort with sea views by stressing that they would have the best of both worlds, city shopping and nightlife and a complimentary bus to take them to the beach during the day. He would then return to the carousel to repeat the process until his overbooking was relieved. If he couldn't read the baggage label, he'd throw out a name, they'd usually correct him with their name and he'd say, 'Oh excellent Mr Jones, you are also on the VIP list.'

As a delightful twist to the scam, Ernie loved the way that the tour company headquarters back in Miami, had laid on the bus to the beach, which the rep used to its fullest extent by transporting anyone and everyone, mostly the locals, all day long. The resulting funds had already bought the rep two holiday villas on the island. The tour company back in Florida couldn't work out why the diesel bill was so excessive. To Ernie it was a money-making-money poetry and standing in front of perhaps 90 plus people he was seeing similar dollar signs.

'Thank you for taking time out of your lives to listen to me today,' he began, thinking at the same time what else would they be doing. 'I'm Ernest Zimmerman III, co-founder and President of the European Experience. I hope you enjoyed your lunch today and noticed the hints of Tuscany, the Dordogne, la Rioja. What we'd like to do is for a party of you to experience a fuller taste of Europe. Twenty-three days of,' he hesitated and a flash frame of John Cleese classically failing to avoid mentioning "the war" to a German guest, caused him to stumble away from sight-seeing, 'of what we can only call experiencing the joys of the cultures which are the foundation bricks of this great building we proudly call the USA.'

53

Ignoring a call, 'So we're going to Africa then,' he threw open the presentation to the floor asking hands to raise in order to take note of the rich diversity of ethnic origins. Where there any Poles, Russians, Lithuanians. Irish, Italians, Germans, Jews? Hands went up, from some repeatedly with them offering a percentage of what they were. 'Scots/Irish on my father's side, Swedish/German on my mother's.' Through it all Ryder videoed, capturing the cultural DNA of the group and something that could influence the trip's 'destinations'. After all it could be a fatal planning error if you had native French or German speakers wanting to interact with the local population, a population that was 4,000 miles decidedly un-local to the east.

The potential travelers identified themselves by asking questions as Ernie continued with his audio presentation. Already he was sensing that there was more to the success of this project than he'd simply outlined in the Walmart coffee shop. These were not the sad zombies shuffling round the pathways he'd seen just eight days ago. Several of the patients were not totally blind – they could clearly identify shapes, an unfocused ability that immediately put them on Ernie's permanent waiting list. The introduction session had been a two-way exercise and a slow respect and deep caution was growing inside Ernest Zimmerman III. Get this wrong and escape would not be on a bus, they were going federal and whatever his nickname, this was not going to be EZ.

One by one they stepped up, not signing but signaling that there existed a genuine desire to get out of St Anthony's, if only for 23 days. Mr Wilcox wanted to know if Provence and its perfume creators were part of the package, Bob Protz desired German weiss beer, Jack Megaghy whiskey, Arthur J. Hilton questioned which cathedrals they'd visit and Ben Nelson at 22 asked if and how they would cater for the younger age group.

'There's something for everyone, there will never be a dull moment,' Ernie reassured the assembled, not knowing just how accurate his prediction would be. A show of hands as to who was initially interested stunned the trio, twenty hands shot up instantly and the number slowly grew to almost double. He froze, never before had he stood in front of a quarter of a million dollars.

8.
SO SIMPLE, SO CLEVER

Los Angeles, California

Although all in LA, the trio had gone their own separate ways, temporally scattered. Rooster was out sourcing European-style food suppliers, Ryder organizing transport and Ernie supervising the conversion of offices into bedrooms. The trick he'd decided to employ was to make them all feel different. It had been relatively easy. Passing a final day closure of a furniture store he bought 10 beds for a fistful of dollars, a small fist. The secret stash would oil the first few purchases, but he needed the deposits from the travelers to move on.

The next day he had Ryder fetch the furniture, but in confusion he went to be the back of the now empty building, opened a garage door and loaded the hire truck. He returned bemused, 'why Ernie didn't you say you'd bought 22?'

'I didn't, because I didn't,' Ernie said in clarification.

'Well we've got 22 now.'

Ernie went outside to inspect the catch. A full set of beds was brilliant, but they needed to feel different, hard soft, high low, midsize singles, wood, metal. A process of rotation as they party moved from 'country to country' would mean the guests at breakfast would have something to chat about, constant change. It's just about the most frequent question on a road trip, 'did you sleep alright?' It was a question that particularly irritated Ernie for its sheer insincerity. When asked he always replied with the most facetious answer he could muster. Most times it would fly over the head of the uncaring questioner. It wasn't his most passionate human hate, that was reserved for the relatively new trend to welcome someone with a 'mugh mugh' kiss about three inches from either cheek. In his lifetime he'd seen this social greeting grow from a few society upstarts to stretch right through the middle classes. Thankfully the blue collars had yet to adopt it – it certainly hadn't reached Kingman where the buddy handshake remained solely demonstrative.

The variety of beds was a small, but vital, part of the overall plan. Ernie had a catchphrase which he often used, 'follow the family motto, confuse and conqueror.' To further the illusion process Ryder had built a number of plasterboard flats and put them on lockable roller wheels. These they called G boards, geography boards, their purpose being to give a different feel to the walk from bedroom to dining room to reception. Although they were experiencing eight countries, Ireland, England, Denmark, Germany, Poland, Italy, Monaco, Spain and then on to France, most nights meant a change of hotel. Only in Copenhagen and Berlin was the stay, for the time being, scheduled for two nights.

On the main wall of what was going to become the floating reception area come lobby, hung two huge maps, one of Europe and one of the western states. On the maps different colored ribbons, anchored by black and white pins, the black signifying a stopover, white a drive through. There were also red and green pins to mark airport departures and arrivals. The color of the ribbon on the European map corresponded to a similar ribbon on the western states. It had all the hallmarks of a military campaign. In fact, many a warring campaign would have been shorter with such precision planning. The ribbon color also matched the color of the paper of printed scripts or the color of the text on the script should it be impractical to read. One such case was with the purple ribbon which took them from east to west Berlin, from the old DDR parliament to Marlene Dietrich's grave and then on to the steps of the Rathaus Schöneberg for a bit of JFK. The instructions in purple ink on white paper were clear, but vital. Ryder had to source and hire a Trabant for a couple of hours, failing that an old Fiat 500 with a dodgy muffler, Rooster was to source a Dietrich track and JFK's famous speech, which they would mark by handing out the cream donuts that were also on her list. The purple type included the contact details for a German deli in Van Nuys where she'd have pre-ordered sausages and beers along with a box of steins. Most importantly two pinned national flags marked where they actually where and where they thought they might be.

For continuity, the last page in every instruction was a copy of the first page on the next in order to smooth transition without surprises. So simple, so clever, yet to look at it on the wall it was a complex web which would need an Enigma code-breaker to crack.

--0--

In a corner of the studio block two new faces where hard at it with several boxes of wires and some fairly massive speakers. Pang and Ngoc had been suggested by Charles and vetted by Ernie. Cambodian and Vietnamese respectively, they had been in the country for less than a year, illegally. Roger had introduced them to Charles as a potential exotic diversion, but they struggled with English and were not keen on the hinted boy-on-boy games and only as a favor to his secretary, who

58

had taken an uncompromising shine to them, had the studio boss given them odd jobs on the back lot.

Anyway, they signed up to the Secrets Act not having any real clue what it was all about other than keeping silent. They were as happy as sand boys to be working at all let alone for a secret government department which, if it were real, would have them on the next plane out of their new world. They also were enjoying the freedom Ernie gave them to experiment, within a strict budget, with sounds and special FX. The moments they spent relaxing in the old caravan that was their home were tortuously long and they were happy to spend anything around 14 hours a day just working. Naturals with anything electronic they'd already come up with one suggestion Ernie loved, three large portable speaker systems, bolted onto soft-wheeled trolleys. These were called Ambients A, B and C and would be constantly be moved into a triangular configuration around the action areas to lay a foundation of sound relevant to the situation. Using some pretty muscular SD cards they had already recorded a number of scenarios, including bustling central London and the peace and quiet of a Tuscan vineyard although the constant trickling water and occasional wind chimes might have suggested more Saigon than Sienna.

It was the subtler sounds that caused the most work, or rather excluding or disguising them. These were noises that are there, but shouldn't be. In this case, sounds unheard or generally ignored by the sighted, but picked up by those who have to compensate for the loss of one sense. The studio was set back from any freeways, but there was always a very low distant rumble of LA traffic in anywhere except the sound-proofed stages. To combat this Ernie had adopted Greenwich Meantime as the studio clock. It had the twin virtue of allowing most of their activities to be conducted when it was cooler and quieter.

59

The Ambient speakers were complimented by what they had decided to call mini-sound; small Bluetooth speakers carried around by the team. These would play single clean sounds like a passing bicycle or bus or kids chatting in the appropriate language.

Relating to language the expanded EE team had started to devise signage to employ when necessary. Holding hands high with index fingers crossing each other in an 'X' marked caution alarm, two fingers from each hand forming two 'XX' was the signal for Ngoc to deftly start a sprinkler system, for someone to shout 'rain' and for the party to be bustled back on board their coach. Clasping all fingers together meant 'terminate current operation and return to base'. It was all part of Ernie's policy of confuse and conquer, or in this case, retreat and repair.

Two large Marshall speakers that Pang and Ngoc had dug out from an old storeroom and dusted down were earmarked for near permanent installation on top of the bus that would transport the party around. They were due to be covered with light tarpaulins to stop the whole exercise becoming a spectacle.

The coach was a major issue and potential investment. Ryder had again been dispatched to search and source. He'd already been to four new and used bus dealers and was unimpressed. The seating in school buses was simply too hard for the purpose of long distance luxury coach transportation, the long-distance luxury coaches were simply way out of budget.

The bus would be the workhorse of the project. Although the base camp would be in Typhoon Studios, the plan was to take almost daily expeditions, some more trying and dangerous than others. A trip up the Napa Valley for some Rioja was easy when you compared it to recreating visiting the top of the Eiffel Tower, but Ernie knew that risks had to be taken. The greatest risk was boredom for it generated negativity and questioning thoughts. Unknown to Ernie questioning thoughts were being generated elsewhere.

--0—

Nurse Swallow moved the plastic slider on the door from green to red, from disturb if you really have to, to do not even think about entering. In a single movement she tapped the panel once and opened the door, slipped inside and gently closed it. Dent, putter in hand, had his back to her and didn't flinch. He was in his own world, singing along to Madonna on his headset and about to putt for the PGA title.

The ball rolled nine feet and into the hole, as it popped back it broke out into 'We started singing bye, bye, Miss American Pie Drove my Chevy to the levee but the levee was dry Them good ole boys were drinking whiskey 'n . . . . .' He looked up, not embarrassed because he and the nurse knew each other better than that.

'Nice goal Ronnie' she started and he realized that it was sex or favor time . . or both. 'Ronnie about this European Experience, don't you think, for our sakes we ought to have a St Anthony's staff member on the trip? Somebody with a nursing background . . . and long legs, like the ones you like wrapped around your neck.'

The thought of her naked fulfilled just about every fantasy he'd ever had. It was a fantastic fantasy they had acted out many times in the four years she'd been there. She was his Miss

American Pie, with the emphasis on the miss. Dent replaced the putter in the bag, picked up the ball and moved to the center of the room.

'I mentioned this on day one to Zimmerman and his stance was that the experience would work best if it was a total break from all routine here. Just our names he said would break the new spell,' Dent found himself speaking words that actually conflicted with his true thoughts. Would he trust Zimmerman enough to take a comfort break whilst he was in the office, no. Yet here he was defending him.

Swallow rested herself against the desk, raising her right foot and latching her heel onto a drawer handle; her white lab coat flapped open to reveal no broken zip, no skirt. Dent looked on in the admiration he'd long held for the legs that from where he stood formed the perfect 4.

'Ronnie, London, Ronnie, Paris, Ronnie, Rome . . .' she purred, 'and we don't necessarily have to do it in the same order as the tourists. We could maybe spend a day or two with them somewhere along the line.'

The savage instinct that was priming him to go over and sweep the desk free of paper and roll her back onto it was the same savage instinct that said he didn't want her to leave him for 24 hours let alone 23 days

Moving towards her he reached out his hand and brought it up the inside of her left thigh, 'So you would prefer 23 days with Mr Wilcox, rather than to be with me?'

'I said "we" didn't I Ronnie?'

Swallow smiled for the logic was priceless, both options offered the potential of persistent groping, one annoying, one enjoying, 'that's not fair, you know where I'd rather be,' she said moving her hand into a similar position on his golf trousers, 'but I've never been to Europe.'

Dent immediately thought of his cash windfall created by the Experience, the invisible five per cent. He'd already earmarked it for a Bermudian golfing trip with his buddies, but what if they took a week out together, free from work, one funded in part by the Institute.

'You would not enjoy it for the responsibilities would, I'm sure, be stacked straight onto you by Zimmerman. He's an organizer and user. That, strangely is why I feel semi-confident in not sending someone from here,' he paused and looked into a neutral corner of the room, like a golfer eyeing up the winning put, 'but what, what if we were to go for a week in the middle of the trip? As you said we could catch-up with them, say hi, but then be free to enjoy the sights. Ronnie and Patricia in Rome' his hand reached further up her stocking-less leg.

'But that sight you've already seen, many times' she said moving his hand away, adding 'dot, dot, dot, dash, dash, dash, dot, dot, dot.' He looked at her puzzlingly, 'What?'

'Three dots, three dashes, three dots, SOS, you were in the Slap Or Smile zone,' she again smiled, indicating that the slap was unlikely, maybe even a fuller smile later. She was already totally on board for a week with him in Europe, six nights with Ronnie or 23 avoiding Mr Wilcox's hand was no contest, but she didn't want to make the negotiation process too easy, she liked the sound of Mrs Ronald Dent on hotel forms, even if there currently was a Mrs R. Dent in the Kingman telephone book.

'Interesting idea,' she said as she tightened her buttocks to propel herself from the desk and head to the door. 'I'll go and check my diary.' Again, in one silk-like movement, she opened one side of the double door, slipped through and moved the plastic strip back off the 'do not disturb.'

Dent had been disturbed in his trousers and now in his mind, 'Diary? What was she on about? She damn well nearly runs the place.'

9.
THE FOURTH SENSE

Back lot, Typhoon Studios, LA

At the studio Rooster was busying herself. The clock was ticking. It was more than a month and a half since the Greyhound motored past the high walls of St Anthony's. The European Experience would kick off in just eight days. Ernie was not one to hang on and deliberate. Thankfully the positive flow from the Institute had enabled Ernie to opt for immediacy, gambling losing prep time against exposure to awkward questions and change of mind time. Encouragingly twenty-two of the guests at St Anthony's had signed up and put money on the table. That was seven too many for feasibility so Ernie would need to cull them. The target was to find those most eager to go and then put them onto trip two, for they were the most likely not to immediately request their deposits back. To encourage them, based on the greater profit margin of a repeat expedition, Ernie gave them a better price for the second trip and an upgrade, whatever that meant.

The studio back lot had not seen action since a series of cheap television ads some months back. Typhoon Studios was not totally dead in the water, the main lot was ticking over, the body was floating, but not moving at a rate virile enough to be classified as swimming along nicely. The projects tended to last no longer than a few days. Each one created an extra prop, which was inevitably left behind and would find its way onto the closed lot that was EE's new domain. Charles had promised that the dumping would stop and true to his word it had,

65

largely because of lack of business and the reliance on graphics, but Rooster and Ryder were faced with creating space whilst wondering if any of the B movie props could have a use in Belfast, Berlin or Barcelona.

And they had potential. Apart from the priceless plane fuselage, a bar used in a television sitcom from the nineties would become several anonymous hotel bars right across Europe including starring roles as a German beer hall and the tasting area for a tour of the Guinness brewery in Dublin. One hundred tons of sand from a Moroccan desert scene would become a Mediterranean beach when dumped beside the lagoon they'd used for a jungle scene, three shacks from a cowboy film could become the sad accommodation of a Nazi prison camp and a larger paved area that doubled as a car park would become some of the most famous squares of London, Paris and Rome. There were also a number of cars and trucks that could be used to create exterior 'G boards' blocking exits and movement.

The demands of sound and touch were slowly being met, climate was pretty well a wildcard, but as Mr Wilcox had proved on day one, smell was also a crucial issue, especially smells that were silent and ubiquitous. Atmosphere is a strange concoction of sound, smell, taste, touch and sight, with what you see mistakenly given dominance over the other four. Rooster had read in a book that the senses that transported you furthest back in time were taste and smell. Sight was a relatively short-lived part of the memory bank.

The trio had devoted long hours towards confronting this area knowing that when you lose one sense, others compensate. The second and fourth senses, sound and smell never rest. Go into a room at night and look around Ernie had advised, then turn off the light. Darkness has no memory, but smell resonates.

There were easy zones like the hotel rooms. They were to be sprayed with different aerosols. Ryder had been online and every day or so the front office at Typhoon would ring up the lot saying that something or other had arrived. His odor armory ranged from fresh baked bread to farts, a particular favorite of Ryder's. The problem remained about how to get the smell into the required zones. The hiss of the can was a dead giveaway. Almost as bad as a beleaguered husband trying to liberate beer from a tab without his wife hearing. Ryder had experimented with cardboard boxes by unleashing the smell off set by spraying it into the box via a flap cut in the side and then liberating it where needed by opening the box. It worked to a degree, but it lacked control, the source could be traced to the box and the impregnated cardboard could only be used just once. In fact the greater concentration of the smell was in the cardboard, not the air, so you had to waft it around. Another negative was that if stationary the physical presence of the box remained a potential tripping hazard.

An excursion to a Home Depot produced a solution of sorts, a reversal of the role of the kitchen extractor fan. Ryder had explained the concept to Ngoc who came up with a relatively quiet fan that blew air into a wide flexible dryer hose, which was connected to a three-foot drainpipe before being joined again by 30 foot of flexible dryer hose. The drainpipe was Y shaped, the shorter branch sticking out with a flap attached. You simply turned on the fan, opened the flap and sprayed in the desired smell. It would travel to wherever the hose had been placed. By the time the smell reached the target it was subtle, but worked. Ngoc, as ever, had gone one stage further and the flap was large enough to take physical items like burnt toast, oil-based paint and the neutralizing smell of onions. Its snake-like appearance gave it the code name 'python' and a silent sign of an 'S' for snake written large in the air to trigger its immediate deployment.

10.
LIVING A MILLION DOLLAR LIE

St Anthony's, Kingman, Arizona

The bedrooms at St Anthony's were luxurious and spacious. To keep people from roaming about in the communal areas down to a minimum; from day one it had been Institute policy to create personal comfort zones to such a high spec that the patients, guests, would be happy to spend most of their time in their rooms. Food too was something the Institute never cut short on. The meals were better than anything you could find locally, not that Kingman had a plethora of Michelin starred establishments. You had to go to Vegas to find their equal or better. Dent felt that the biggest area for disgruntlement was at the table, 'feed people well and they will purr like cats and sleep like dogs, give them scraps and they'll howl like wolves,' he'd say repeatedly.

There were three restaurants, one steakhouse style, one pasta driven Italian and the third fairly anonymous and subject to the changing whims of the guests. They were all served by one kitchen, but the splitting of tastes into three areas meant that people were forced into menu decisions before they sat down and that to vary their diet meant they had to abandon any thoughts of having 'their favorite seat' even though the restaurants were only divided by plants in tubs and you could smell steak and onions as you chased your radiatori around the plate. It was a policy designed to discourage the creation of cliques and allow a broader contact base for the guests. It worked.

It also worked in favor of the Experience. The constant seat swapping at mealtimes meant there was always somebody eager to stoke the fires of anticipation. The whole place was abuzz with excitement at the prospect and, unknown to Ernie, the peer pressure was such that there were probably enough ready to sign on the dotted line for EE two, three and maybe even four. The speed of information transference was more viral than networking.

At the window in his room Harley was waiting for his lunch to be delivered. The Institute discouraged room service, 'we are not a hotel, we are a community' Dent would remind everyone, but if you were ill you could receive a dispensation. They called these meals 'DP's' which was short for 'dispens' which was short for dispensation. Nothing at St Anthony's came free of implied guilt.

There was no denying that Harley had a cold that was best confined to his second-floor suite. He waited for the knock at the door and looked out of the window, for that was something that Harley could do, look. Those who walked the pathways below were trapped by the walls and circumstance; he was trapped by a lie. Harley was the only guest at St Anthony's Institute for the Blind who could see 20/20.

Harley was a nickname so embedded that no one had known him as Aaron from the day, as a 19-year old he spent every cent he'd ever earned on his first Harley Davidson. In the small Kansas backwater of Riverton, the throb of his bike was music to the dwindling numbers who remembered the clean-cut Fifties and the road that then ran through their otherwise unmemorable town. It did have one fleeting moment of fame in the 21st Century when a local store and a local character gave moviemakers a chapter of inspiration when scouting around for ideas for the mature kid's cartoon, Cars. But that was when Riverton's fame peaked. In visiting eight states Route 66 had left a passionate legacy of memorabilia pretty well everywhere, in Kansas it barely blew a kiss as it passed by. The old route stretched 2,448 miles, a very brief thirteen were in the south-eastern corner of Cherokee County. That was where 66 entered and exited Kansas, barely enough for a gear change, but they were enough to instill a desire of where to get his kicks in the young Aaron.

For ten years he kicked out westward and eastward, determined one day to do the entire route in one long delicious expedition. When that day came it was cruelly cut short by a school bus reversing out of an alley and driven by an unlicensed member of the school board. Three days into his dream, Harley was in a coma. It lasted for two months and when he came round he couldn't see. The county's education department fearful of a greater scandal settled out of court for a hefty $18.6 million and a lifetime of care which ironically turned to be 900 miles further along Route 66 at St Anthony's.

Five months after arriving at St Anthony's Harley's sight slowly came back. He was in turmoil. The extreme happiness of the shock-educed blindness evaporating was marred by the realization that he might forfeit something else. Most of the 18.6.

That was over a year ago and Harley was biding his time to free himself from the Institution and look after himself somewhere far from those whose guilt keep a regular check on his progress, or lack of it. Somewhere he could get back on a Fat Boy. It was hard. He had to learn to numb his senses. The large sunglasses helped, but he was constantly aware of impulsively reacting to that which he should never have noticed. One automatic reaction, swatting a fly, blocking an orange from rolling off the table, picking up a paper, could cost him over eighteen million. At dinner one night at St Anthony's he stood up and looked out the window some seconds after what he thought was a Harley Road Guide rumble past the gates. He noticed a nurse noticing and purposefully turned and fell over a chair.

Lights were a particularly dangerous threat. For fairly obvious reasons the Institute keep corridor and public space lighting to a minimum, so any sneaky reading of smuggled-in material or magazines left behind in the lobby could be exposed by a rogue shaft slipping out under the door. As a habit Harley kept a dampened towel stuffed along the bottom of his door. Twice a nurse had challenged him for being untidy after this shower, warning him that he'd trip over it. It was a considerable burden to live with every waking hour, so he was only too happy to pay the $8,500 for a ticket on the European Experience and nearly a month where the focus would not necessarily be on him. Out there in the big wide world where maybe he could sneak off and buy bike magazines for the first time in two years. 'What new models and colors were there,' he thought. He was so desperate that he didn't care if they had to be in German or Spanish, the pictures were all he needed.

In the next room Janne Jankowski sat expressionless in a high wing-backed chair, looking forward. Looking forward to the trip, but not looking, because she had never been able to. Thirty-one years of darkness, whatever that was, because she'd no concept of light. Thirty-one years of nothing. Of eastern European, maybe Polish, maybe Russian, maybe Latvian extraction, it depended on which branch of the family tree you climbed back up and when you drew the line in history.

In her case 1990 was an early school memory, a tinge of relief
for her ancestors being liberated from something she had only
heard about in the history class. She was 100% American, her
stunning blue eyes 100% Slavic, 100% useless, or at least the
nerve system behind them. Disconcertingly they moved in
unison, straight and true if not always in the right direction.
She didn't need to wear darkened glasses to disguise any optic
failure, but she did because it reduced the incidents of
embarrassment when people would, mid-sentence, stop and
enquire why she wasn't seemingly paying attention. She
looked forward to the trip, mostly the all too brief excursion to
Poland. If this was good and there was another EE from Tallinn
to Tirana she'd like that, but regardless, in the six years she'd
been at St Anthony's this was by far the biggest, most exciting,
most talked about, month in her institutionalized life.

The 104 current patients of St Anthony's shared one common
feature blindness, well 103 of them anyway. Many also shared
a background which had lead them to this remote dry oasis of
drier care. Money was their common bond. Either they had it,
or their families did, or their insurance company couldn't slip
out of paying it, for situational care in the States demanded it.
The bond was split down the middle. Many of those
incarcerated were locked away by rich 'caring' relatives who
just didn't care enough to want to be bothered with the daily
responsibility. Each at some point of the induction period as
they were dropped off, had heard the phrase,' 'we're doing
only what's best for you.'

Initially visits would be regular, not weekly, but certainly
monthly. Gradually they would stretch out the gaps filled by
ever more inventive and desperate excuses until eventually
they entered what the staff called BMC, the 'Blue Moon Club' –
rare and rarely the same people twice; the car would roll up

outside, the occupants busying themselves with a couple of parcels and then over the next two hours work towards an exit strategy. The thin red line of inheritance was all that kept them coming at all. It was the only thread of power over them that the patient held, that and the occasional pang of guilt. Because of that guilt the request for liberating funds for the European Experience was all but automatically conceded.

The other group were labelled by staff as the Dark Side Club; the side of the moon never seen. Some, like Valerie Little, hadn't had a visitor in the 15 years the Institute had been in operation. Now 72, the staff were sure when Miss Little died, there would be an almighty flush of weeping, concern and care right up to the reading of her will. It was something they'd witnessed many times. How they hoped she'd leave her money to them, St Anthony's or at the very least a dogs' home.

11.
FOLSOM I'M SICK AND TIRED OF YOU

Kingman, Arizona

It was EE minus 6, less than a week before the trio, now with the booster assistance of Pang and Ngoc, faced the most full-on month of their lives. Rooster had made regular scouting trips trying to match-up highlights they couldn't recreate within the locked confines of the studio. She'd spent hour upon hour combing the Internet for suggestions, with Google Earth confirming them as having potential or not. Vineyards were easy to locate and convincing an owner to allow a tour of blind people had not been an issue. Like grapes, it was just a question of picking the right one. She was particularly proud of having found the Giant's Causeway, that World Heritage gem at the very north of Northern Ireland, but on this occasion just a four-hour drive away in the Sacramento Valley. It was Johnny Cash who had inspired her. The radio had played Folsom Prison Blues and from somewhere she got the image of a chain gang returning from a day breaking rocks. True enough the Internet showed Folsom to be famous for not just songs and a prison, but also granite and Google Earth revealed vast open areas of quarried and cut stone. Never mind that the Causeway was basalt and the stones uniformly hexagonal, somehow, they would get around that. She'd already seen some six-sided paving slabs in a garden center.

The internet also showed that the real Causeway was close to a town called Bushmills, famous for the world's oldest whiskey distillery. They'd been supplying hangovers since 1608. Now there was another experience and if she could set that one up

75

prior to the Causeway then maybe they wouldn't care or notice the precise shape of the stones. Rooster loved knowledge and the hours of jumping about Wikipedia had been hours of 'well I never knew that' joy. She was amazed how one piece of research would trigger another and then another until she was so wrapped up in gathering information and detached she couldn't quite remember what the original quest was.

Ryder had been out and about more than the others, tasked with the single most important item, to buy, hire or borrow. The bus. Ernie didn't care what he got as long as it was comfortable and in pristine running order. They could not risk mechanical problems and it had to have enough room for the 15 travelers, plus the five of them and for the growing amount of ambience generators that Pang and Ngoc had already accumulated. It also had to have a beefy inbuilt sound system to cope with any unwanted exterior noise. It needed AC and if possible he was to replace the original seats with differing varieties so, like the bedrooms, the feeling of being on a different vehicle could be generated by swapping the passengers around.

Back in the studios Ernie was running Pang and Ngoc ragged with a list of requests that expanded when they did trial scenarios and they proved themselves capable of delivering even the most obscure thoughts. These were the most exciting and confusing days in the young Asians' lives yet they rose to every challenge with a growing and unquestioned loyalty to the funny man who they addressed as Mr Easy, but sounded more like Miss Teasy.

'When our important guests come, you must not talk to them, you must be invisible,' Ernie stressed, but Ngoc was already comfortable enough with English to question him. 'Invisible, why need, people cannot see you say.'

'For this secret experiment to work, you don't exist. You are here and you will be the wind in their faces, the sea in their ears, the scent in their noses, but you are invisible, you don't dare talk or even think of a fart' he said hoping that this time the message had got home. He was fairly confident and deep-down very happy with the duo, although, as he would learn, he needed to be a little less poetical and be more direct in his messaging. However, he could not have conceived a more perfect working relationship, two people for whom their continued existence in the country of their dreams was dependent on being totally anonymous.

12.
ONE SWALLOW'S SUMMER

St Anthony's, Kingman, Arizona

Ernie, Ryder and Rooster were not alone in making plans.
Patricia Swallow had left her lab coat in her office at St
Anthony's. As part of her contract she had a flat on site because
the hours were long; she worked two weeks on with one week
off. The two weeks were not all on duty, but she was certainly
on call. Two other senior nurses worked the same shift pattern
so that day and night were covered. They were a Triad, but
only one held the full attention of the director. Pat's week off
was usually spent at her own flat in downtown Kingman for it
was simply too much hassle and expense to think about going
any further afield. At holidays, when Dent was otherwise
committed, she'd grab some mom time back home in Chicago,
but for the main, her escape route from that white coat was the
fifteen-minute drive westward. Except not next month. Since
that conversation in Dent's office she'd been online Euro-
dreaming.

She was surprised to see how many misconceptions she'd
stacked up in her nearly 37 years. Europe was a lot more
complicated than she expected. Countries were smaller, major
cities closer together yet connecting between them involved an
overabundance of choice. Booking a plane was relatively
simple for one destination, but when you wanted to
interconnect flights, rare was the opportunity to remain with
the same carrier as she did crisscrossing the States. It wasn't
just a case of switching airlines, but also terminals, you could

fly to Rome with something called Ryan Air and be thirty-five miles away from the Rome airport favored by Italia, and your next flight. It was tiresome, but she had Ronnie's special credit card details and no matter how much time it consumed she wasn't going to waste a digit.

On the table was the four-page itinerary for The European Experience. If she'd followed her birth-right she could happily have stopped off at most of the names on the page and called it a homeland pilgrimage, but the sheer logistics of her and Ronnie being away from St Anthony's for any longer than seven days was too complicated to compute. Anyway she wasn't going anywhere as far as the rest of the staff were concerned. The second, and current, Mrs Dent thought her director husband would be alone in joining the EE tour as part of the agreement with the organizers and to satisfy the Institute's board that standards were being met. The board thought the same. Patricia had no need for a cover story; she was going home to mom in South Chicago as she always did in the early summer. The only person who most needed to remain ignorant of any of her movements was Angela Dent. Somehow her wifely astuteness had put Swallow high on her list of 'America's Most Unwanted'.

Taking vacation, nurse Swallow decided that one, at max two days, re-united with Mr Wilcox's groping hands would be enough. The rest of the time she and Ronnie could spend enjoying what Europe had to offer, the romance of Marrakesh, the awesome sight of the Pyramids, the canals of Venice. It was true she'd many misconceptions about this place called Europe.

What little she knew was still a higher degree of awareness than Pang possessed, or maybe not. To Pang Europe was a far-off confusion of faces and flags, of names, non-pronounceable languages. Regardless his near total ignorance was still more accurate than Swallow thinking the Pyramids were part of the package. No knowledge was also potentially less damaging than being constantly 10 per cent wrong, or 66%, as in the senior nurse's case.

-0-

Sitting at an old desktop computer that Ernie had liberated from Crawford, Pang looked at a map of Europe and clicked on an icon that played a clip of the relevant language. It was like a game where when you opened the box the 'how to play' instructions were missing. How could borders be so strong that the people on one side didn't have an idea how to talk to the people on the other side?

The differences in the Vietnamese, Khmer tongues were considerable, but then so to was the size and rugged terrain of the countries. It was only logical that those of a common means of communication would bond together into a nation. He looked at Switzerland, a country so small that its name didn't fit in properly until he'd zoomed in a bit, yet according to the fact box they spoke three languages. They had mountains and passes isolated by snow as an excuse. Then there was the Netherlands and Belgium, separated by a bump in the road but not just two, but three disparate tongues. Europe may have lead the globe in developing the daily structure of human existence, but they sure had messed up talking to each other in their own backyard. If he'd looked deeper into the mass of European tongues he might have stumbled upon the little seaside town in north west England where the people six miles away can't understand them, yet in World War II, when they sent a detachment of soldiers from the town to Iceland, within weeks they could converse with the locals.

Untangling this mess was Pang's task for the next three days. Sorting out two millennia of differences which had led to several thousands of years of land-grabbing, wars and at its mildest, mistrust, had defeated some of the cleverest people ever to breathe – at 26, Pang and speaking barely three hundred words of English, was up to the task.

Ernie had given him a hit list of locations and he'd found local stations using an app called TuneIn Radio. He was to find a station, preferably one playing music and certainly not one with frequent news bulletins. Talk channels were ok, but only if not obviously in English and even then, not for too long. They were good for color. He would record it, along with at least two others from the same country, and then cut between them into a single three-hour sound take which he'd burn onto a CD and then label with the relevant flag. Rooster online had come up with sheets of peel off, stick on flags. They were already proving invaluable, a fool-proof way of keeping tabs on where physical items were intended for use.

Pang pressed the icon 'By Location' and then scrolled down to a word that looked like Europe, gosh there were so many countries. He scrolled further to a word that according to the simple and clear instruction card that Ernie had prepared looked like Ireland. It might have been an easier task for Ngoc since the Vietnamese use the Latin characters. So to Pang it was like a detective looking at fingerprints for the most minor of differences. He hovered over Iceland for a moment and then, comparing it again to the card in front of him, clicked on the one with an 'r' in it. Now on he was on this own, Connemara Community Radio or Dundalk FM, RTE Gold or Radio Ulster, perhaps 200 to choose from. They all can't be wrong.

After Ireland he'd move to London, and then life got easier, or so Ernie had said, Danish, German, Polish radio was just a soundtrack of the incomprehensible, broken up my music that would be, more often than not, universally recognizable to those in the bus. Here Pang didn't have to listen out for the tell-tale jingle which indicated a news bulletin. These according to Ernie had to be edited out. Miss Teasy as Mr Easy sounded to them, had indicated this with a most elaborate piece of impromptu acting. He'd mimicked the jingle then picking up a pair of scissors cut around the words he'd thrown out in a mock news bulletin, grabbed them in mid-air and put them in the waste bin in the corner.

Pang smiled at the mad American and the mad American smiled back, reasonably confident that the message had got through. Beyond the shores of the British Isles, which according to the map on the wall consumed the first five days, Pang would simply tune in to Danish or German, Spanish or French radio, set the recording in progress and then disappear to tinker with loudspeakers and amplifiers. It didn't take him long to think of an easier way of achieving the same result, perhaps an even better one, but Mr Easy was Mr Number One; who was he to think of clever things? He was simply paid a simple sum to do what was simple. He'd stumbled upon a Dutch radio, what could be simpler than that? Dutch sounds like Yiddish in reverse, a constant wash of displaced vowels. He reflected back to what he'd be doing if he hadn't abandoned his life and family in a small village in northern Cambodia - God how he loved life in America.

--0—

The radio was on in Arthur J. Hilton's, west facing room. Lunch at St Anthony's had taken its course and he'd retired to pull the blinds before the sun started to cut through the room in shafts of light he couldn't see, but heat he could feel. His room had a feature shared by few others. On each side of the fine Georgian-styled windows, in constant shade, stood two bookcases that reached from floor to ceiling. They were full of books and Arthur J. ran his educated finger over the exposed spines. The titles, mostly in English, were also in braille, as exclusively was the content. He stopped at a well-used spine, Europe, Geography of a Continent, pulled it out and made his practiced way without aid to a comfortable cushioned seat. Here he would spend much of the time until the dinner gong, fueling his expectations and preparing his travelling wardroom. What was the temperature difference between Copenhagen and Monte Carlo? Would he need a raincoat for anywhere other than Ireland? The downside of this mountain of information was that most of it was as old as the hills. Arthur was mining away at data that was often past its 'best by' date.

An academic, he and his family long put down his poor sight to being a teenage bookworm. Behind it all was retinitis pigmentosa, the doctors eventually decided, but it was too late and by the time he turned 30 he was blind. His passion for reading was satisfied by his fingertips and now 48 he continued to dedicate his life to knowledge, a dedication he constantly felt the need to share. If what he revealed at every opportunity hadn't been so interesting others would have quietly slipped off away from his company. Even so some of the younger guests preferred to avoid him for fear of Arthur J. triggering a conversation beyond a comfort zone that usually peaked at the discology of Justin Beaver.

To satisfy within himself his need to create an aura, Arthur dressed like a professor, favoring checks and tweeds and was rarely without a waistcoat and bowtie, not that his fellow inmates commented on them.

Next-door Jack Megaghy was doing a practice pack. It was part of a routine built not just on insuring that he forgot nothing, but because Jack hated carrying things just for the sake of carrying. Anything that couldn't pass the pre-departure must-need test was jettisoned. Anything left behind in the process that later proved necessary could always be bought. He'd been estimating the amount of toothpaste he'd need and had used one to the point where he thought there were no more than fifty squeezes left. It could then be jettisoned before the return journey.

The hotels he was assured had laundry services so four shirts would suffice, but he was a little concerned at the stopover times. The middle part of the trip consisted of fairly rapid hotel and city movement and rare was the opportunity for more than one night in a single destination. It was a question he had raised at the introduction session where he received the assurance that the system would allow for a rapid turnaround for cleaning personal items of clothing. Rooster had immediately started a search for a launderette close to the studios where washbags could be serviced. She'd even sourced fine net sacks so that individually could be maintained in a shared wash cycle. Each sack had a plastic clasp onto which she'd later write a number to correspond with a number given to each of the tourists.

The numbers were a means of collating not just briefs and shirts, but people. With an allotted number, the intention was to confirm that everyone was present with a simple shout-out roll call or an equally quick look and tick list. The numbers were a vital tool and something of which the trio were rightly proud. They had no guidebook to follow for this exercise, no online YouTube tutorial on scamming; every situation was new, stirring up fresh problems as they occurred, so they were making it up as they went along. The numbers were a simple concept, but they would ease the more complex challenges such as making sure that they knew who was in each bedroom.

Variety and change were vital, particularly with hotel accommodation. The bedroom doors had all been sanded and given a coat of blackboard paint. Along the top stenciled white lines split into 24 small boxes, each marking a day and along the top were listed where exactly, geographically, they should be. The idea was that the boxes should have the number of the occupant. It insured that they would know who was behind the door and meant that, since the rooms were set up differently, the tourists through rotation would always feel they were somewhere afresh. The first version of 'Operation Blackdoor' looked perfectly workable until Ryder, blindfolded in a test scenario, erased most of the information in simply searching for the door handle. Mark II moved the stencil up to the top of the door.

The biggest single challenge in virtually the whole project came down to 21st Century expectations of personal hygiene. At St Anthony's everything was en-suite. Thankfully at the studio the contracts of the more demanding actors had seen a number of small bathrooms attached to their dressing rooms. There were ten in all, situated on the second floor. The converted offices downstairs had only three basic toilets, one of which contained a shower. Somehow they'd have to juggle the tourists so that they would endure sharing facilities as few times as possible. This logistical puzzle was eased by the five nights they planned to spend away from the studio, either in transit or visiting special locations they couldn't recreate on the lot.

The mathematics meant that everyone would spend about a quarter of the trip without what used to be the luxury of an en-suite, but now a basic requirement – not a killer, but something that needed keeping an eye on. Europe was old after all, and being the first with things, cars, houses, trains and plumbing meant that you had to expect that not everything was 'tickety-boo'. There are few things mused Ernie that Americans have taken too late in their development and have driven to new world levels better than the century and a half they have power showered or sat on the toilet.

In an additional muse Ernie held that there were only two types of holiday, the very good and the very bad, for they were the only experiences people talked about. A bit like bathrooms. Good was a ticket to a re-book, bad to reject. Sadly through life he'd calculated that mediocrity was the state most live in. He had to think of a way of nullifying the effect of the first floor's second-rate facilities and intended to do so by insuring that when they were using an external hotel, those who spent the previous night non-en-suite received the best rooms. He had already laid the foundations of different experiences by saying it was company policy to avoid big anonymous conglomerate hotels in favor of small character establishments. He labelled it 'soul searching'. The penalty for this being, as they told all potential tourists, was that the smaller hotels had limited space and amenities. Another way round the situation, should it develop into an issue, would be to say that over booking had caused the party to split and he could bus the first floorers to a nearby motel. It was an option he didn't particularly want, as it was an immediate draw on finances and automatically split their most pressurized resource, manpower.

--0—

Rooster had just returned from a trip to Burbank where she'd picked up several huge blue bags of furnishings. Ernie was just about to admonish her for extravagance when a moderately large truck pulled around the corner emblazoned with the initials IKEA. 'It's very European Ernie,' she said with a smile.

For the next two days Rooster, Pang and Ngoc would constantly have a silver Allen key in their hands or pockets, putting together a range of small tables, chairs or bedside cupboards which shared a design anonymity and the strangest of names. Well they were strange to Rooster, but for Pang and Ngoc letters with umlauts and crossed out ø's just seemed as odd as the rest of the language. Maybe it was an inbuilt ability to translate the cartoon-like instructions into actions that made their construction process twice as quick at Rooster's, maybe it was because 70% of what they opened and touched was last touched and packed by someone in Vietnam.

Two large boxes had also arrived filled with sweatshirts and T-shirts, forty of each and split into two categories. In the rich blue of the European flag, twenty T-shirts and a similar number of sweatshirts, had 'The European Experience' curved round in a circle, replacing the golden stars. The other set was in yellow with 'Social living experiment in progress – please do not talk to me' on both front and back. Ernie had rejected out of hand Ryder's suggestion to put Ebola Research Team on the shirts. He did however sanction two fully protective suits, in yellow and double tanked back pack sprayers. The shirts were to be worn on expeditions off site as a means of reducing cross-contact and the potential pollution of a do-gooder spilling the considerable bag of beans the EE had grown to become in just seven quick weeks. The protective suits were just for an all-out

87

emergency. The sight of two suited people spraying a bus would deter any further unwanted inspection.

They were at EE minus three, in just 72 hours they would pick up the party from the front steps of St Anthony's. Worryingly there was one major piece of the jigsaw outstanding. Ernie was relieved to feel his cell vibrate in his pocket. It was a text from Ryder 'located 30-seater, on way to pick up in SLC, back in two days.'

Relieved at finally sorting the means of transport for the next three weeks, it was the single most crucial part of the whole plan, but what was SLC and why two days? That was cutting it fine. Cutting things fine was a Ryder technique so Ernie was worried, but not surprised. It took more than a moment for it to dawn on him that Ryder was heading to Utah. Well he assumed it was Salt Lake City. He SMS'd back, 'don't they have buses in California?' Ryder came back saying that the one he'd found was an exceptionally comfortable church bus, low mileage and at a good price. It had been bought by a gospel group who'd hoped to make in-roads by setting up in the capital of Mormonism. However they had mis-calculated the strength of the Latter Day Saint's and much as they liked a good song, they didn't feel the need to clap their hands at everything they sang. The mission stalled, trembled and died as the members argued more than they swayed and chanted and the bus was one of the few tangible assets they could sell to recover losses.

13.
NOT SO EZ RIDER

St Anthony's, Kingman, Arizona

On the wall of her office nurse Swallow had a map not dissimilar to one of the ones that hung in the studio, 487 miles to the west. There were no ribbons, but the locations matched-up and each had a light blue mini PostIt with dates on it. On the fridge in her St Anthony's apartment there was another map, not the whole of Europe, but a photocopy concentrating on France and adjoining countries. The PostIt's in pale green told a different agenda, over seven days, six nights, Paris, Barcelona, Venice and Rome. Only Rome was in blue for that, for one day, was where they, or at least Ronnie, would catch up with the European Experience. It would be enough to justify the trip in the eyes of the Institute's board who'd remain unaware, like Mrs Dent, that whilst the patients were in woolens in northern Europe, she and Ronnie would be fulfilling expectations of a warm late spring further south.

Naturally Ernie had never actually been in a position to see either of the Swallow maps, but the existence of the office version he knew about and it troubled him even more than the current physical lack of a bus or the bathroom situation on the first floor. Not just because of that introductory moment with the broken zip, but he'd liked Swallow from the outset. She had a bit of Rooster in her, a slightly more educated and grounded version, but like his colleague she had a hint of mystery and naughtiness. Probably this was something evident in the bedroom, but he sensed that it went further. Classy cool rather than Rooster raunchy, but with a hint of corruptibility. She was 98% straight, it was just in that remaining two per cent that a secret lay. As with everything the two was the key to controlling the 98.

Dent had told Ernie of his plan to join the tour, 'fortunately it coincides with a speaking engagement I have in Barcelona and the chance to look up an old colleague in Paris, so perhaps only for a day or so, because I wouldn't want to disrupt, just say "hi" and give them the reassurance that we take their well-being beyond the brick walls of St Anthony's. That we care. Care is the core.'

Ernie was dumbstruck, twice over; once by the change of attitude from day one when Dent was so overprotective and once by the sheer enormity of the problem. At this point there was only one way to combat this dangerous invasion. To agree to it, let Dent lock his plans together and then change his. He noted with a flash of raised hope that Dent would meet with them in Rome at the end of their trip and two thirds into the Experience. It was Dent mentioned, the day before he was due to return Stateside. He couldn't work out the rest of the agenda and that worried him despite it revealing that he had something to hide.

Not prone to panic, Ernie was however not at ease. Every project has a watershed moment, a time to bail out, a time to cut and run like the pirates did when faced with one expensive decision, cut and lose the anchor and use the minutes gained to flee to safety. He had a mental axe in his hand, the anchor rope clearly before him when the office door opened smoothly and even more smoothly a stockinged leg dangled into the blue shaft of light from the window.

The ankle rotated as if the foot was speaking. 'bonjour mon doux,'

A look of total shock gripped Dent's face. His blue eyes went into overdrive. Ernie's knew his German wasn't great, but he realized enough to work out that he'd just been dealt twenty in pontoon.

Nurse Swallow finally brought the rest of her body through the door. She moved from a position of potential embarrassment to recovery with one line. 'Good afternoon Mr Zimmerman, we've started to tease the doctor about his trip.'

Ernie thought how good she was. So quickly she sealed the leak in her rubber boat, she could have made it as a quick-thinking television pundit or stand up. He thought of a comedian back in New York who had picked Ernie out from the crowd and mildly humiliated him. Returning to the same club a few days later the comedian came on stage and immediately picked-up where he'd left off.

'Hey look it's the little guy with the funny moustache, I forgot to ask you bud last time, what do you do for a living?'

Ernie looked at him, the rest of the audience looked at Ernie and from nowhere he said, 'I'm a talent scout . . . . what do you do?'

He couldn't get another drink, he quietly slipped out, went back to his hotel, and shaved off his moustache.

He blinked, back in the doctor's office the two medics fumbled through papers desperately trying to cover the crack. But Ernie had seen it. Dent was playing doctors and nurses. The trick now was not to show that he had.

He mulled it over; they simply couldn't be flying the Atlantic just for a day trip to Rome. 'Like fuck they care,' he thought, 'the colleague he wanted to look up was right in front of him,' Their determination to have a good time had revealed one huge weakness, any disrupted plans would mean they probably couldn't respond, but only probably. It was a worry. However, if he had ever retreated from something at the first sign of negativity then he wouldn't have scrapped a life from other people for the past thirty years.

Back at the motel as a matter of urgency he set Rooster the task of looking into who Dent and Swallow really were. He was back to that two percent, but the clock was ticking, he and Rooster were amidst the final preparations for the collecting the tour party on a fast approaching Friday. Ernie was well used to sorting out problems on the move and although the Rome encounter was major, for the time being he was preoccupied with the lack of news from Ryder and the coach.

Rooster was sourcing a back-up coach from a hire company in Kingman when Ernie's phone shuddered on silent. Not a phone call, but a text from Ryder. 'Will be at St A's Fri at 2 – need to do a quick paint job.'

14.
D DAY

St Anthony's, Kingman, Arizona

The buzz in the hallway of St Anthony's was intense, it was like a dozen Christmas Eves plus a couple of Yom Kippurs and an Eid al-Adha tossed in for good measure, and overall impartiality. In one corner luggage had been labelled and stacked. Around it, like children outside of Santa's Grotto, some of the tourists moved trying to kill time and calm the nerves of excitement before the big off. They stood out from the residents who were remaining behind, by their sweatshirts. Like a sports team, they were uniform in dress, the only distinguishing mark being the discreet numbers, one to fifteen, pressed on to the left of the EE symbol. Each number corresponded to one on the suitcases.

'Patients or guests?' Dent thought, 'now they are just numbers.' Deep in his uncaring soul he quite liked the concept and thought it had potential at the Institute. Guests with numbers, nurses with letters.

In the meantime he was making his presence felt and Swallow was marshalling other staff to insure a smooth departure. A taxi drew up and Ernie stepped out along with an exceptionally smart Rooster. She looked part secretary, part nurse, part courier, but mostly film star. With Ernie also in his only suit, the European Experience gave an air of controlled class. They looked up at an uncharacteristic grey sky.

'You've got the weather already for Europe,' Dent observed as he met them at the top of the steps.

'I've just checked, Ireland is much the same as here today, not as warm of course but we may see rain either here or there,' Ernie said rather nervously for him. He wished he hadn't been so precise for he was aware just how easy it was to keep tabs on the rest of the world. The App, an abbreviation could so easily expand to become the full truth. It was easier to find out what best to wear in London or Madrid than it had been to track down the travel plans of Dent and Swallow. Ryder had suggested that they loan Dent an old smartphone which they could program with the Find My iPhone app so they could keep track of them, but he was afraid of reverse exposure. Back to basics he'd told Rooster to keep her eyes out for anything that might give them an idea of what the St Anthony's duo were up to.

Ernie explained that he'd had a text from the coach driver, aka Ryder, that he was about an hour away and that they would be in good time to catch the flight from Las Vegas, 110 miles away, a comfortable two hours. He'd chosen Vegas at the 'departure' to avoid helping hands at Kingman airport and anyway the local airport would have meant flying to a hub and the hassle of deplaning. The direct flight had the virtue of minimal personal and baggage changes Rooster had explained. 'Where do you fly from?' she floated in at Dent with an almost casual interest – but one desperate to get some clue as to his movements. He smiled as if he didn't understand or hear her clearly, or both, whatever no reply was forthcoming, probably because in this moment of time he wasn't quite sure, that was nurse Swallow's department. He'd just pay and play, she would plan the pleasure.

Entering his office for a coffee, Rooster had hoped for a map on the wall, but Dent was wishing to remain vague, the darker the fox, the darker the night, the longer the chase. There was a map, but it only listed the tourists' movements. All destinations were in blue except Rome which was in pink.

She looked around for other clues into the life of this enigmatic man. There was no lovingly framed photograph of a family situation, or if there was it was kept in a drawer until needed. On the wall there was a small collection of photos with Dent at the center of each, usually receiving what looked like a diploma. In one he was dressed in outlandish checked trousers and carrying a golf club and cup. She moved to them and turned to Dent 'Memories, recent?'

'Oh no, they go back a while, ten, fifteen years maybe,' Dent admitted. Uncharacteristically he opened the door of the safe that was his life and went on to relate the reason for several of them, Captain's Day, conferences and awards, omitting to mention one figure common to three of the more formal photographs, a woman. 'Could this be?' thought Rooster. She floated out 'Is that you wife?' He smiled as if he didn't understand or hear her clearly, or both, whatever for the second time in minutes no reply was forthcoming, probably because at this very moment in time he wasn't quite sure, that was nurse Swallow's department. Is a wife just a piece of paper or does it require more, he thought? When the well dries up, is it still a well?

A few raindrops had started to hit the office window. It was quite a moment for Kingman since rain was not a common commodity, about half an inch was due for the whole of the month and it usually sneaked in early morning or overnight, not at midday. It moved the long-settled dust down the pane,

95

mildly obscuring the view; the view of a full-sized white, gold and silver bus pulling up well to the right of the main entrance and then reversing awkwardly down the whole curving driveway to the foot of the steps. Dent didn't notice and Rooster didn't stop to think why Ryder had made his arrival so complex, after all it was Ryder.

The sweat-shirted party gathered in the hallway as Ryder and a couple of male nurses scurried in and out of the front door with baggage. The converted bus wasn't designed to take up to twenty-five large cases so they stacked the final few in the rear two rows because the baggage hold was full of all the specialist sound gear and weather equipment the VC had contrived. When the Experience was in full-flow the luggage would travel separately – on most occasions a few meters from room to room as the party went from city to city, from country to country. It was an add-on service and one that Ernie had lodged in the back of his mind as a legitimate business idea. At this moment in time being legitimate it was quite far back in his mind.

The rain wasn't full on, but it was palpable, it ran off the front of the bus windscreen in slow dribbles. It ran down the short snub-nosed bonnet and onto the black grill, it ran down the back window and onto the now closed rear luggage door, it ran a curious pale yellow-gold into several little puddles on the gravel. Ryder dragged his foot through the colored stones to disperse them and carried on as if all was normal, which to him it just about was.

The tourists had followed each other and Rooster out to the door of the bus and even with limited hand luggage they were causing mild confusion. Ernie remained at the top of the steps with Dent, Swallow and just about every other member of staff.

He was keen to maintain a distance even thought this was a big day for St Anthony's.

'So we will see you . . . .' Ernie floated and the director was ultra cautious not to expose himself and Swallow in front of the rest of the St Anthony's team. 'Yes, I'm looking forward to catching up with you. We have the itinerary.'

'Where?' Ernie fished again.

'On the other side of the pond,' he replied conscious that there were other ears on the steps.

Ernie was not going to hang around and further chase this fox for he'd become aware of the dripping sand colored paint and the partial emergence of what it had been intended to conceal. Slowly and very lightly a crucifix tilted at about 30 degrees started to reveal itself. Some words to the left of the wooden cross were starting to appear on the back of the bus. Fortunately the back at this point was too far to the left to be noticed from the top of the steps.

'The Experience starts now,' Ernie said as he skipped down the steps trying both to be cool, in control and in a hurry. It was an exit tenser than any he'd endured during the cow plop bingo era. Ryder immediately hesitated, then placed his foot on the accelerator and let the engine sing an octave higher. In the growing rain, the party at the top of the steps waved and backed off into the dryness of the building, just as they turned, Ryder waited for the right moment, turned the wheel counter-clockwise and moved off. As an automatic gesture of good spirits Ryder pressed the horn twice. The first bar of 'The Lord Is My Shepherd' completed the bizarre exit.

Dent snatched one last view of the bus from the comfort of his off his office, as it made its way down the long driveway. 'Was that a crucifix? No, couldn't be?'

'So what's the gold paint story?' Ernie was right in Ryder's face. 'I had to do a quick tidy up. I only got the bus last night so I stopped by Home Office and picked up the closest thing I could get. I was so pressed that I didn't get the driver's side sorted. That's why I reversed in.'

Ernie glanced at the wing mirror, he thought he could make out a cross, surrounded by thorns which transformed towards the back into musical notes. 'What are the words?' he whispered.

'"The Lord's words in heavenly voices," or something,' I bought it from a gospel choir.'

Dumbstruck Ernie sat back and then lent over to the driver 'and don't press that feckin' horn again.'

Ernie sat back and stared out at the road in front. Rooster moved amongst the passengers introducing herself in the first of many roles she'd play over the next few weeks. Mr Wilcox instinctively put out his hand to stop her return progress down the narrow aisle. 'Coco Mademoiselle,' he said. For a moment she thought she was being offered a warming drink, but then it dawned and she replied yes and noted that she normally spent time on how she looked, but with this party she's need to have a wardroom of scents to create different a character. Ryder, silent, kept his eyes on the road. Ernie, silent, kept his eyes on the entire party. Harley, silent, kept his eyes on Rooster.

At a gas station just outside Kingman the whole party disembarked, keen to enjoy the freedom of simply not being in St Anthony's. This was Independence Day. Less than an hour into the adventure they already felt they'd had their money's worth. They took it in turns to visit the restroom more out of novelty than necessity and as they did Ernie inspected the now critically messy paintwork. Ryder immediately offered to sort it out when they got to base, but Ernie held up his hand and waved it in a 'hold that thought' sort of a way.

'No clean it up, take off the cheap paint you slapped on. Let's see the cross. You can do a proper cover up the day or so before we return to Kingman, in the meantime the Hallelujah Mission might just be a bonus, another reason for people to avoid us,' said Ernie before he broke into the chorus of Leonard Cohen's most beguiling song.

15.
LONDON CALLING

Route 40, Arizona

The trip to LA was a long one, but getting to HBO, what they'd labelled the studio, Home Base One, was vital. Although everyone outside of the trio was under the impression that the point of departure was Las Vegas, the party had to get to the studio and the awaiting dummy aircraft fuselage. It wasn't going to come to them. Burbank was three times the journey time.

Once on board the bus and leaving Kingman as the steam lifted from the roads, Rooster introduced herself as Millie Steel 'that's steel as in steel, not stealing, and no final e' and that she'd be their constant companion for the next few weeks. 'My new best friend' Wilcox chirped from somewhere near the back. She went on to say that there'd been a strike by baggage handlers at Las Vegas and that they would have to endure a longer journey since their new embarkation point was LAX.

'Millie can we take in a movie,' the voice was again that of Wilcox. Ernie turned to Rooster and gave a smile that was half concern that this band could be livelier than expected, or was it just that they had a sense of humor which might ease the journey.

There were murmurs from the party, but generally the mood remained buoyant. Stretching the itinerary only ate into other hours, the longer bus journey knocked four more hours off the time they would have together before the bus returned to St Anthony's. Five hundred and sixty-five in total, now 562, but who was counting? Ernie, Ryder and Rooster for three. There would be lots of plans and changed plans to fill that time. Passing a road sign he decided on his first change.

He'd avoided seeing Crippen's hometown and resisted Truth and Consequences, but he couldn't say no to a minor detour off Route 40. Heading south from Kingman, Route 40 was already a compulsory detour, needing to swing round in a huge S to avoid a range of barren hills which you could get through using an all-terrain vehicle, but not a semi luxury coach in its late thirties. At the bottom of the S, as it started to sweep left and west again, Ryder was told to keep straight and continue to Lake Havasu.

Something inside his twisted mind demanded him to make a pilgrimage to perhaps the greatest example of displaced tourism on earth. Displaced tourism is what the European Experience was all about, but to take a London bridge that was sinking into the river it was supposed to cross and place it on the edge of a dis-used military airstrip on a man-made lake in Arizona, was something Ernie could not avoid paying homage to.

Everything about London Bridge in Lake Havasu City was special to Ernie. It was opportunism and madness and it was the main reason why a 60-year-old man was able to successfully establish a community in the middle of nowhere. When, in 1967, Robert P. McCulloch bought the bridge for $1.2 million, Lake Havasu City was only known to its 8,000 inhabitants and those who sent them Christmas cards. If the residents had clubbed together it would have cost them $150 each. Not a lot, but today it would only be twenty dollars because seven times that number now live in what is home of Arizona's second most visited tourist attraction. It is only outranked by a huge hole in the ground that God created, if you read a certain book, the Grand Canyon. What particularly pleased Ernie was that, in truth, the bridge was just a façade. The original bridge was cosmetically cut up, with most of it becoming landfill, the remaining manicured blocks, the bits Londoners could see, were numbered and then shipped to the US where they were stuck on to a new concrete skeleton bridge in the right order. It must have been like online shopping for a three-piece suit and only the jacket turns up.

Regardless, they were happy with their jacket at Havasu and Ernie just wanted a moment of reflection and a photo opportunity for the party. I would be the only time in the next few weeks where they would touch a genuine piece of Europe. It would cost an hour and a half of their time, but then time was what he had to digest during the next few weeks. A few more stops, including a dining treat would break up the clock. It made sense to arrive in LA later when the locals had retired for the night, well some of them.

Sitting, nose to the window, clicking it occasionally with his sunglasses as the bus rolled along, Harley was enjoying the open road for the first time in half a decade. He cursed his reaction to instinctively follow a passing sign. He needed to be so careful he thought. Trapped by his lie, he was now more disorientated than he had ever been, even more than in the moments when he came out of his coma, even more than when he unexpectedly regained his sight but calculatedly decided to keep it a secret. Harley kept his head straight as they passed a huge sign with an image of a bridge on it and 'Welcome to Lake Havasu' and Rooster, as Millie, announced that there would be a chance to stretch legs and that they had forgotten to take the group day one photograph at the Institute that they'd promised the director, and that they would do so here. 'We should have done it back in Kingman, but with the rain . . .' she explained.

Ryder pulled the bus into a lot near the bridge itself and they walked along the shoreline for a bit before being grouped and the picture taken. 'We promised your relatives that we would keep them up to date with progress reports and photographs. Now smile everyone,' said Rooster as she skillfully displayed her leadership qualities and got the party together so that they were framed in the granite underbelly of a supporting arch. It could have been a bridge anywhere, but it would be perhaps the sole occasion when the accompanying caption didn't tell a full lie. 'The party surrounded by a bit of historical London.' She could now see the reason why Ernie had invested time in a detour.

As the party got back on the bus, Ernie announced that it would be sensible if those with watches adjusted their timepieces. In an effort to combat jet-lag they were from this moment switching to Greenwich Mean Time. Most of the party ignored the request, but several reacted, fumbling with their rather fine-looking timepieces, some of which were 'speaking watches' and they started announcing the time. For several moments a woman's voice bounced around the bus announcing variations of a time some minutes past 9am. The Experience had truly begun.

--0—

The sun was starting to annoy Ryder as they headed westward through the desert. It was three hours to it finally setting for the day and he'd have to combat it all the way. He asked a tad too openly if anyone could loan him some sunglasses and there were immediately about ten generous replies.

It was tiring for all and some had already crumbed into a travelling mess, curled up and sleeping. It was a situation the trio had mixed thoughts about. Good in that it consumed some of the drive time, bad in that they just might arrive for the 'transcontinental flight' in a refreshed mode. Rooster and Ernie each held sheets of paper with numbers on them and beside the numbers a name and short pen portrait of each of the people on the bus. They would see the number, locate the relevant sweatshirt and then read about who was in it.

Ernie was already regretting not having some logic to the numbers, it would have been easier if they had been put in some sort of order, maybe from youngest up or alphabetical even, but no, in the excitement of the idea beginning to take-off, they were based on what was his initial number one priority, who was first to produce a credit card.

That turned out to be Jack Megaghy, master of the practice pack, who had the number one on his shirt. From Seattle he'd been a dentist with a large and successful practice until in his late forties he was diagnosed with diabetes. He'd put down his increasing difficulty to focus on a molar to overwork and the growing number of gum injuries he inflicted to bad luck, but by 52 he could see nothing at all. He'd given up dentistry for the sake of his patients and to stem bleeding gums and the undoubted prospect of resulting lawsuits. His small family had found it more difficult to cope with his reduced status, so for this 55th birthday present he got a room in St Anthony's. His eyes were dead to the world, his mind as active as a rattle snake in a can.

Number 2 belonged to Valerie Little, one of the senior members of the party at 72, she was also known by the staff as one 'the dark-siders', the ones who were rarely, if ever, visited. In fact she hadn't touched a relative's flesh in 15 years. It was a savage aspect of human intolerance that she bore with a smile and a cheery disposition far out of balance with the cards of life she'd been dealt. In the hand of life she may have had low numbers in different suits, yet she still greeted them with an up-tempo glee which meant every situation was met with 'that's nice, how lovely or it's turned out OK, hasn't it?' You could not read what was behind her facial expression other than things appeared to be good. Sighted she could have cleaned up at the poker tables of what was until two and a half hours ago, almost Las Vegas.

Two further comfort stops and a remote diner dinner later, they were now descending into the greater LA area, cutting round the San Antonio mountains as the lights of what is a very flat sprawl of a city grew stronger as the drowsy sun grew weaker. It promised one last glorious orange ball farewell to the day. Ernie had toyed with the idea of diverting via LAX for an ambient moment, the smell of kerosene, sound of jets, the confusion of crowds, but it would stretch geographical logic, the busing from terminal to plane would have been through 20 miles of post rush hour traffic, which would have challenged the geographical acceptance of even the most situational unaware of passengers.

He picked up the map that was lying unused in the netted compartment behind the driver and looked at it. Ryder had been locked into Garmin for the past five hours. 'Bob Hope!'

he whispered to Ryder. 'Very funny man,' said Ryder, 'We're on the road to who knows where, but what about Bob Hope?'

Ernie looked around behind him at the static heads, 'International' he said. 'Of course he was, he was mega, super star,' replied Ryder. Unfolding the map he traced his finger along the route 210 they were on and he arrived at the symbol for an airport. 'Bob Hope International, I've been there and I can't imagine how I didn't think of it before. It's ten maybe fifteen minutes from HBO, we'll drop in there for 90 minutes, it will be total acclimatization.' It was change number two and they were still on day one. What worried Ernie was that he really hadn't thought of it earlier – how many other holes were there in his planning? Perhaps they had rushed it.

Ryder twisted his tired eyes, he was not someone who needed very much sleep, but he'd already mentally parked the bus for the day and the thought of another couple of hours was not immediately appealing. Rooster on the other hand instantly saw the benefits, the more they could cram into every situation the more exhausted the travelers would become and the easier they would be to handle. They'd already organized a shift pattern that saw one of the three on duty for the 12-hour flight that lay ahead, and for all the other nights. They could not afford to rely on fifteen people turning on and off like light bulbs. She did have an assistant for the flight to Ireland if it was needed. In her bag she had a bottle of organic sleep drops, although she wasn't totally convinced of their effectiveness. At the very least they would be a scientific experiment into their true soporific value. For any real insomniacs she had a packet of foil wrapped strips – each 'bullet' pill guaranteed to put a horse to sleep.

The bus swung round into the 'cab only' drop off section. The airport was perfect, smallish and containable, with enough activity to generate atmosphere and also human enough to accept without question a party of 15 people being shepherded through the front door and into a waiting area. Ernie had been racked with concerns since the moments before the bus turned up at St Anthony's, now he afforded the first genuine smile of contentment of the day. His decision to divert to the terminal was 'mild genius' he thought, but what triggered the smile was the connection with Bob Hope and the comedian's reported last words. When asked by his wife Delores where would he like to be buried he said, 'surprise me.'

Surprise was what the next weeks would be about, that and superb comic timing which was exactly how he felt with the party now a mixture of excitement and exhaustion. The whole con game runs on getting into a rhythm, the smoother and more natural the note changes, the stronger the flow.

Harley looked around. 'What's going on?' He was comfortable to be in a terminal, apparently going somewhere, but why here, a small airport miles from LAX? 'Where they going to fly direct from here, the planes he'd seen on the way in didn't look big enough. Now in the lobby he could see a Mexican food franchise and the thought of a cheese-topped tortilla took him towards Rooster. 'Mam, I smell something good, can you take me there.'

Rooster briefly thought it a cheeky come-on, then saw the neon sombrero sign, smiled and agreed. She then opened the invite to the rest of the party. Ten hands went up like a family of meerkats popping up in the early-morning desert sun. Methodically she said there was no choice and asked them to keep their hands up until she'd written down their numbers. She immediately relented and asked for a second showing, 'if you don't want cheese.' No hands. Cheese it was then. Tortillas, toilets and transition, the party were in bliss.

Across the lounge the doors opened and a party of Koreans came in. There were about thirty of them, lead like sheep by three shepherds, the cast an unlikely image for a massively efficient industrial national. Aged twenty to eighty they were all children. Rooster looked at them and then at her charges and then back at them, 'those poor helpless bastards,' she thought.

--0—

Ryder had driven out of the 'kiss and go' drop zone and was sneaking a half hour power nap – the journey had tired him, but it would have totally wiped-out anyone else. In reality he had not just driven from the middle of Arizona, but from Utah. The only break from the wheel was when he bought the water-based paint to cover the signage. A long time back he'd read of a technique to enhance the sleep process and sitting in the front passenger seat he'd gone through the ritual. Shoes off he'd mentally separated his toes and brought the process of relaxation right up through his body insuring that no part of him rested on any other part. Anyone looking in would have seen a man who looked as if he'd been suddenly frozen or suffered a stroke. Twenty minutes in this state topped up his sleep tank by eight hours he claimed and with his performance that day it was hard to argue.

He was awoken by a tapping at the window, the tip of a truncheon the other end in the hands of a traffic policeman who was more concerned about having a body dumped than a bus parked long term in a slip road. Ryder apologized and said he was waiting for a party of blind people who were being flown in from Denver on a private jet and he had to be on hand to immediately pick them up once his phone rang. The cop was in no way officious and the ringing of Ryder's cell towards the end of his explanation proved to be a worthy alibi. He thanked the officer, put on his shoes and moved back into the driver's seat, started the engine and headed to the second of the two adjacent terminals.

Bob Hope himself had used the convenience of Burbank airport when on the Roads to Singapore, Rio and Morocco, which like the European Experience never left the US of A. They where shot at nearby Paramount and a number of even closer locations. It was built in 1930, before Hope became a star and re-named after him when he ceased to be an active star, which he still was, even although retired. He never knew of the honour. The airport took his name after he died. So there was another surprise waiting for the legend besides his final resting place, which lay about a ten mile drive away.

If Hope were to look down on the airport today he would recognize it, but not for much longer. Dotted all around there were info boards as part of the campaign to convince the tax payers of Burbank, Glendale and Pasadena that the terminals were past their best and that a new larger terminal, but with the same number of gates and volume of car parking, would be a sensible option. Basically, it was an offer for a new pair of shoes, the color and style would change, but the size and purpose remained the same. Rooster thought, 'why didn't they just say it's a fashion issue,' or maybe it would allow more Mexican food franchises space to roll out their tortillas, more shopping opportunities before you fly. Travel today was an elongated assault on your credit card.

As Ryder made his way to the second of the two terminals, the party wandered from A to B, secure in the knowledge that after a short delay they had been called to board. There was a considerable degree of excitement and expectation combating the exhaustion that is travel. Ernie had warned them that they were being given the VIP treatment and would be bussed to the plane. There was a secondary warning that indicated that the bus would have to leave the airport perimeter and re-enter through another gate.

Outside the entrance doors Ryder had again secured an illegal parking spot, but no one challenged him when they saw the party emerge. One guy in a reflector jacket had momentarily thought about it, but he was ten minutes from the end of his shift so he did the classic see-though the problem look and moved on. Ernie noted, as he often had in the past, that people shy away from awkwardness. It was a useful tool in the conman's weaponry.

He'd once parked in a disabled bay in Washington DC with Ryder sitting in the back doing his instant sleep formula when a passing woman harangued him for not having a badge. 'Do you know you are in a disabled bay?' she asked. 'Is he physically or mentally disabled?' Ernie took one look at Ryder, hands by his side and mouth open to the flies, 'both,' he said and the woman tumbled back in retreat consumed by embarrassment which Ernie further fueled by saying it was a rental car and unfortunately they didn't supply 'dis' badges.

Something similar was happening now as the party split through arriving and departing passengers like an ice-breaker in late spring. Moments earlier Ryder had slipped a CD labelled 'airport ext' into the bus's player and they set off into the night and what turned out to be an eleven-minute journey to the plane, with the atmosphere numbed by the sound of near and distant jet engines, accelerating and humming in park mode.

Four miles away Pang and Ngoc were generating a similar sound next to a set of boarding steps that lead up to a door cut into the side of the studio and through it to a short ramp which ended at the mock up fuselage.

16.
'THIS IS YOUR CAPTAIN SPEAKING'

Set A, Typhoon Studios, Burbank - LAX

Flight EE001 was destined to be the most testing of times. They had run the hydraulics that made the fuselage mildly rock and roll when in flight and to simulate take offs and landings. They had played the inflight buzz track on a loop for hours and pumped out the ambient smells. The mock-up was the single most expensive underused piece of equipment on the lot, but it still need an amendment or two. The toilet for filming was only a door, the replacement, or upgrade, that Ryder had extracted from a written-off Winnebago worked, as did the small cabin kitchen area with two microwaves. Adequate for keeping 15 people fed and happy, but somehow it looked terribly vulnerable to Ernie, even when the starboard side of the plane, which could be removed for ease of filming, was back in place. Was it just a weird trick of memory, Ernie thought, but he seemed to think that the set up for all mock planes was the same. Passengers always seemed to face to the right. When he got time he'd investigate. When he got time, meanwhile it would remain an embryonic urban myth.

There'd been some discussion about role-play and the lengths the trio should go to. Rooster somehow felt more comfortable in her stewardess uniform as she ushered them into their seats that were starboard side and in pairs. She would only be Millie during the flight if absolutely necessary. The fuselage was for domestic flight sequences, long haul it wouldn't stretch too, even if it were to be joined back to the Boeing 727 that much of it had started life in. It was a bit like London Bridge that they had paused at – a visual hoax built on reality. Here the Typhoon management had salvaged bits from several planes and somehow made it work. Charles knew this, but economics dictated that someday if any of Typhoon's movies got on to IMDB, there would be some geek who would point out that the flip-down tables didn't match.

Rooster's uniform too was a bit of a salvage job, practical to the touch but visually dysfunctional. She was a bit United, a bit Gulf Air and partially Virgin, as Ryder had enjoyed pointing out. 'The European Experience Party,' she said in a southern drawl, 'you are in rows 25 through to 33, we will help you to your seats, but because of aviation rules you must sit in the number allocated on your ticket. Have your ticket ready and we will guide you. We strongly advise that you remain in your seat at all times unless you need to visit the bathroom. To assist we have tagged the steward request button, once airborne we'll help you find them with ease.'

Ernie looked at Rooster with continued admiration, maybe this was the career path she should have taken; she was a natural in a film studio set. The port side, left hand, seats would remain empty, save for a quartet of soft mannequin bodies for the flight with the trio using the remaining ones at random for catnapping. The chance of some Z's, but with the plus of being on-hand should the need arise and plus plus to create a sense of movement and presence.

On the other side and at the back of the studio a light cut out and shafted across the ghostly still booms and props. Shadows occasionally danced on the near vacant stage as Pang and Ngoc moved around their new domain. Their Ambient Room contained a bank of screens, mostly dead, but two showing

different angles of the activity from the fuselage. At the back of
the room a camp bed was the shared luxury for the Asian duo.
EZ had stressed that for their own security it was probably best
if they kept movement down to the times especially when they
would be called upon to contribute localized ambience.

They were two of the three most trapped people now in the
studio. The third was sitting at window seat 31G looking out at
a long strip of green material, set back from the plane. The
Chroma-key screen, when lit, allowed endless possibilities in
post-production. Harley was dizzy with confusion, intoxicated
by interest and calculating his next move. For the time being
he'd sit tight and enjoy the ride, he was already enjoying
watching the airhostess as much as he'd enjoyed the lady from
the European Experience who had been introduced rather
formerly as Miss Steel, but who everyone already knew and
had warmed to as Millie. He was caught in a twisted world,
forget the money and chance to see Europe, what he was living
was an unfolding drama. How low in morals and high in
subterfuge could these people go in the following three weeks?
Then an additional thought, one that had struck him numerous
times, how much might his silence be worth at the end of it all?

It was a mind-opening experience for others too. Ernie had
given the Asian duo a freer hand than they'd enjoyed in any
other lifetime. It wasn't hard, but he drew it at pushing buttons
more ill-defined and anonymous than the simple ones he
marked out for them. Using an old clapperboard screwed to
the wall, each day had a number, and Ryder or Ernie would
regularly visit to update the rest of the information.
Information such as whether the sound was interior hotel or
exterior, whether it was day or night, country or town. He
couldn't trust them to read any English on their own so
important sounds would be triggered by one of the trio at the

point of delivery. Some of the standard FX had been translated into symbols, fridge magnets of cars, planes, cityscapes and farm stock were stacked illogically on a metal sheet that leaned up against a water cooler. A map of the studio, hanging beside the clapperboard, had initials on it, each marking out a sound location. In general the duo had the broader background sounds, the trio the speaking parts.

Rooster picked up a small iPad and pressed the Sound FX logo. Then 'plane' and then 'captain take off' and through a small Bose speaker a pre-recorded, but permanently distorted, Ernie introduced himself and the other members of the crew who would be responsible for their safety and comfort for this ten-hour flight to Shannon.

There were other sections, 'captain update 1 and 2 and 3' and 'captain landing.' 'Captain turbulence' was in effect a crisis button designed to regain control of the passengers should they get restless start to move about too much. There were also 'Purser meal – snack' Purser meal – main' 'Purser meal – arrival' 'Purser – duty free'.

The hydraulics of the fuselage shifted left right left and the rumble of engine noise filled the cabin. In seats 29 H and G sat sweatshirts four and five. The lower number occupying considerably more space in the form of Bob Protz, a 48-year-old from Santa Barbra who before he'd lost his sight in an accident at work, had travelled extensively. For the past ten years only his taste buds had journeyed extensively; his passport was empty, but his waistline well stamped. His family, of Germanic origin, had for generations struggled with the American diet and they were, to a woman, larger than life. Mr Hamburger had married Mrs Frankfurter and the result was Fat Bob. He flowed over the armrest and into the area paid for by a blonde-haired lady in her mid to late thirties. Mette Nielsen's background was betrayed by her name, and also by the address of her family back home in California. She was from Solvang, a small community just north of LA. It was founded by a group of ardent ex-Danes over a hundred years ago and thrives today as a must-call destination for Scandinavians in need of a cultural fix, or at the very least a sugar-crammed pastry.

It was as if seat-ticketing fate was playing a historical joke the way the German had, without apology or guilt, expanded his empire into and over the border area of the trim Dane. Without protest she moved towards the freedom of the window and without comment thought of one self-promised highlight, open sandwiches in Copenhagen and at the request of those back home, a photograph of her with the famous Mermaid statue in the background. The announcement, via the iPad, of a snack meal shortly after take off, kept Protz awake. He wasn't planning to miss anything on the food front and salivated at the very thought of an Nürnberger Rostbratwurst and red cabbage on day eight, or so he'd calculated.

The pen notes drawn up by nurse Swallow were fairly inadequate, there were too many unknown origins and passions that, like time bombs, ticked in the background for the EE organizers. The simple idea that Ernie had as he'd looked over the Institute's walls had already developed into the most complex combination of contrived situations anyone had ever come up with. It made the theme of one of his favorite movies, Mel Brookes, The Producers, seen simplistic. In the meantime the hydraulics rocked semi-silently and sound systems rolled noisily as the plane made its way from taxiing to take its place in the departure queue. 'There are a couple of planes up in front, we'll be about five minutes,' the captain had informed them. There were screams of uncertainty, delight and sheer released excitement as the plane roared down the runway and up into the clear night sky. The European Experience was airborne; it had lifted from the grounds of delusion to the heady altitude of deceit, some eight feet off the tiled floor.

--0—

Outside in the distance the early birds of LA were getting themselves into work trying to get a jump on traffic before someone lost it and caused a tailback. EE001 continued to rumble on at 37,000 feet and 525 mph, in the minds of the fifteen passengers. In reality it was now at about 12 feet and the speed a rock solid zero. It was also crawling eastwards towards being eight hours ahead. The scheduled arrival time in Shannon was a little after four in the afternoon. It was good since the Californian sun would not have reached its midday peak when they got out into a rainy wet Irish afternoon. The problem might arise a little later as the clock and climate came into greater conflict.

Some of the passengers had eased into a deep and prolonged sleep that had been triggered as a result of the homeopathic drops that Rooster had stocked up on. She still wasn't sold on their effectiveness, it had been a very long and very tiring day. Tourist number nine, Janne Jankowski, had largely defeated the drops and had spent much of the night with headphones on mouthing and occasionally murmuring sections from a Learn Polish cassette. She had slipped it into her most precious possession, a Sony Walkman from 1985, the year of her birth. The familiar buttons enabled her to flick back and forward with ease and it was a source of much sadness that the format had been disappearing rapidly in the face of digital touch screens, which to her were a totally useless concept. Several other travelers had Walkmans and they swapped an ever ageing and

117

dangerously stretched collection of tapes. Advances in technology making everything slick and convenient for others had locked them all into a musical time warp. They preferred the tapes because they offered more historical stories and spoken word than CD's. It was just that the music library was wearing a bit thin. The Carpenters, the Jackson Five and then Lobo singing 'Me and You and a Dog Named Boo' and Ringo's 'You're Sixteen (You're Beautiful and You're Mine)' – life can be cruel.

Harley reached up and hit the call button in one smooth movement. It was time to play.

17.
OCCUPIED

Fuselage, Set A, Typhoon Studios - somewhere over the Atlantic

Harley's chosen sport was a dangerous game to play. On one hand, by revealing that he could see, he might most probably lose the bulk of $18 million, on the other he was clearly in the middle of a huge and very elaborate con, or a television set-up hoax program. He looked around for hidden cameras that weren't so hidden. He couldn't see a thing. So what would this funny little man, his robust side-kick and the tempting blonde pay or do to keep it a fabrication? It wouldn't be eighteen million. He himself was a total con. Not by instinct or desire, by accident and circumstance. He really couldn't see when he was awarded the compensation; it just happened that fate had been cruel and kind in equal amounts. A bit like coming back from the supermarket to find the tomatoes rotten, but that they'd forgotten to charge for the turkey breast. What do you do? Complain about the 60 cent tomatoes or keep quiet and eat the free bird.

Harley chose the turkey and admired in frozen silence the fine movements of Rooster as she moved up the aisle in response to his call button.

'Yes sir, can I help?'

The 32-year-old had a list of requests that had grown by one as he reached out and in a controlled accident stroked the red pencil skirt of Rooster with the back of his hand. It was the Virgin part of the uniform. 'I need the restroom, is it free?'

Rooster in a move of ballet-like simplicity and grace took his hand off her ass and guided him upward and out of his seat. Assuredly she lead him down the short corridor to the make-shift toilet. Although it had seen a hundred camper's bums in its life before being ripped from the Winnie, it was now closer to a version of the portable loos used on building sites. Basic for the most basic of needs. There was already as space on the old fuselage with a door with toilet marked on it. But only the vacant/occupied sign worked, it had never seen an actor in desperate need, only pretending to be. A movie fan, Ryder couldn't ever remember a scene shot inside a plane loo.

'Are you going to be alright?' she asked as Harley fumbled around getting an erotic bonus point for putting his hand full on her left breast. He was desperate to join the twenty-foot high club.

'Is that the flush button?' he asked in disguised innocence.

'The only thing that is flushing, is me,' she said as she removed his hand and with gentle force eased him into the small cubicle. The door folded shut and on both sides there was a development in situational acceptance. For Rooster she knew that she would have to stem any knee-jerk reaction to physical miss-encounters, although with this young man the accidental touch seemed a tad too accurate, and she had to admit, not unpleasant. For Harley his manly needs were re-awakened. For the second time in three years he had come out of the darkness.

With the door closed he was back in the semi-darkness now. Ryder hadn't bothered to put a door-triggered light activation switch in the toilet. He was pressed for time and it had just seemed and unnecessary extra in this situation. There was a sneaky shaft of light at the top and the bottom of the door, but not enough to do anything significant. So Harley sat, pants down with his hands wandering around the tiny compartment. For a few minutes he was restored to the same world as the rest of his party. It was a revelation moment, the point where he decided that whatever unfolded over the next 22 days, he'd do his best to help those for whom this trip was potentially the most special time of their lives. He stood up, found the flush button, the tap and basin which Ryder had squeezed in and wet-handedly pushed the door open. Rooster was still standing there, in the fullness of light, looking magnificent. He smiled a broad smile. He just couldn't prevent it and he froze as he considered the life-changing consequences of automatic reactions. Hoping she hadn't noticed and maybe put his facial reaction down to a constantly happy state of mind or bowel relief, he stuck his hands out again, fishing for something to help lead him back to his seat, but careful to avoid Rooster – resisting temptation, he was learning on the move. The stewardess, again with the grace of a dancer, grasped his hand and swooped him around 90 degrees and down the aisle.

'I couldn't find the towels,' he said.

'So is see,' said Rooster, kicking herself for the crassness of the remark. Everyone was on a learning curve.

18.
INTO THE FRYING PAN

Fuselage Set A – at 37,000 feet, somewhere 'off the Irish coast'

In the office Ernie was stirring himself after a short unsatisfying sleep. But at least it was timeout. Ryder had just returned from a trip to a diner where he'd topped himself up as the waitress helped the cook with 20 breakfasts. There's no such thing as a free lunch, but he was getting a free breakfast as they filled the small catering dishes in the belief that they were tendering for a contract to supply diner-style food to a new not-so low-budget airline. It had been another one of those thinking outside of the box ideas that just flowed from Ernie when under pressure. They could have ordered the food en mass and then decanted it back at HBO, but that would have required man-hours and a fight against time to keep it warm. Cooking everything on site was never a plausible option. It would add a whole new level of stress and the constant concern about lingering odors.

Thanks to the diner duo, all they would have to do in order to cement authenticity, would be to wheel the trolley down the aisle handing out the plastic trays and banging into the sides of the seats spilling drinks without apology. The only concern was the age of the stewardess. Transatlantic routes on American based airlines are dominated by the seniority, matriarchs of the air. The only hope was normally that the plane was in better condition than the airborne staff. Thankfully for all on board this was their first encounter with the joys of long-haul.

Bob Protz was salivating at the ill-oiled sound of the trolley wheels. Around him the others slowly came to terms of what ten hours in a cramped seat can do to the body as they untangled themselves from comfort rugs, blow-up pillows and the seat belts that had held them position for 8,230 kilometers. Soon they could stretch and step out onto the same bit of tarmac they'd left yesterday. There's no place like Ireland, except in northern LA.

It was a journey they'd repeat on the way home with two additional short haul plane trips planned, transporting them from Ireland to England and England to Denmark. The rest of the journey would be bus driven; the bus that once sang for Jesus could now well be part of the Eurovision Song Contest, the annual showbiz farce that was once about music, but now was purely a political football. More so than an UN session, it's all about bloc voting, Soviet bloc, Scandinavian bloc, Balkan bloc. The irony is that the countries that actually pay for the fiasco, Germany, France, Italy, Britain and Spain have no real friends and despite some almost worthy songs no longer have a hope of winning.

Even the most successful country Ireland was now bloc less and consequently now a regular failure. At one point the Irish actively courted failure. Winning the contest means a huge one-upmanship display for the host country. It consumed the entire Irish television budget when they won for the third time in five years. Cunningly the Irish elected to have a failsafe entry the following year. The scoured the country for the worst act they could find, gave them a hopeless song and then . . . won.

The song contest conceived to unite a continent annually manages to write chapters of inconceivable intrigue and international frustration – that's its only ticket for survival. On the bright side any advanced alien life that might seek us out and destroy us, would, if they tuned in on one weekend in May, promptly turn off their equipment and look elsewhere.

-0-

'Breakfast, why breakfast?' Protz's taste buds were not matching his expectations as kindled in the schedule. 'We're arriving in Ireland in mid-afternoon, shouldn't we have had lunch?'

Ernie's face contorted and he screwed his eyes so tight it might have taken a screwdriver to open them, but for a flash thought. 'Breakfast, well breakfast sir, is virtually the Irish national dish. They eat it first thing, they add chips to eat it at lunch and in the evening. They just can't get enough of it, so get used to it. I believe they introduce change by calling it a fry.'

'So everyday in Ireland is a Fry Day,' Protz said with such a smug smile that he quite forgot his complaint as he basked in the mild laughter he had generated.

'Very good sir, Bob isn't it?' Ernie was grasping the opportunity to bring the tour to life by introducing first names. Protz was an easy remember, the uniformity of the word Bob summed him up, his body being a few hamburgers short of a perfect orb. Bob the orb.

'Those of you who are with the European Experience can you raise your hands. Just one hand Mr Wilcox or we'll get confused.'

He did a mock hand count out loud 'fifteen, perfect, we haven't lost anyone. In about an hour we will be sampling Irish hospitality for the first time. We will have a bus transfer of about two hours to our overnight hotel. There'll be dinner, I believe it is not a fry, Mr Protz, then a session in an Irish bar, with music.'

'Day one proper takes you to some strange stones, the Irish claim and not without justification that the Giant's Causeway is a world wonder. Belfast birthplace of the most famous ship that never got anywhere and the music of Van Morrison that draws a resonance from every brick and stone like no other native has reaped. You'll walk down tree-lined streets to the sound of Cyprus Avenue, but you won't stay in the world's most bombed hotel. But don't worry, Belfast is a very safe place these days.'

-0-

Ryder had enjoyed the job of sourcing an Irish bar. It was like two night's off. There were numerous to choose from in LA, certainly more than the eight he visited, but he most wanted one within a relatively short drive of HBO and one with a music room where they could have a semi-private corner where they might not be disturbed. In the end Ernie vetoed the suggestions on the grounds of risk and the fact that even a short drive into LA would face such a challenging atmosphere that they might blow the whole EE plot on day one. Instead Ryder took Ngoc and Pang down to Molly Malone's on South Fairfax where they discreetly recorded the Thursday night céilí session. The band had been a little late on stage and Ngoc, in order to retain his cover, had had to have three pints, he was barely in a fit state to press the on button when the band let rip with Whiskey In The Jar. But he did and as he captured the right hand side of the stage, Pang caught the left. Asian stereo. Later, with a couple of neat edits under the guidance of Rooster, their night out had given them a soundtrack clean of any giveaway local references.

The Irish pub also demonstrated the plus and minus of creating live situations outside of the LA time zone. The thumping evening session would have had to kick-off just as people popped in for a snack lunch. It underlined the value of the studio as a base for controlled activities.

The area they had at their disposal was fine for their needs. There were three sound sets, one with the fuselage and a lot of extra spare space called Set A, one attached to the offices which had become hotel rooms and lobbies, Set B, and one, which when they opened the door, looked as if they'd shot Cheers in it. This third studio, Set C. would be a bar in Sligo, Dublin, Liverpool, Berlin, indeed anywhere where the local culture was driven by some form of alcohol, which in Europe is just about everywhere. It would also double as a restaurant, triple as a coffee shop and quadruple as a holding place to buy time whilst other scenarios were being pulled together. Different types of chairs and tables would be used and a moving door with frame would help create diverse entry points.

Talking of diversity. 'Good afternoon, this is your captain,' Ernie's pre-recorded and very much changed voice, broke through the sound of aircraft jet rumble. The trick was to make it as clearly inaudible as possible without totally losing the point of it, like a real announcement.

'We will shortly begin our decent. The weather in Shannon is untypically warm – the Irish will thank you for brightening up their day, but there remains the possibility of some showers.

We should be on the ground in just over an hour, we'll come back to you, but in the meantime, we hope you have enjoyed your time with us and we hope you will have a great day, if you are returning home or visiting. For landing we ask you to put your seats upright, trays up and open the window blinds.'

As Ernie listened he patted himself on his back, without one word of a lie he'd sounded like a captain, except that he'd robbed the chief steward of their moment of glorious authority. He was starting to believe in the potential of the entire project. Some of the greatest actors to use these stages employed method and mood acting. He, and he hoped the other two, would embrace the script so much that, provided due care was taken with the immediate environment, whatever they did over the next three weeks would seem natural, second nature. To help nature, Rooster distributed mini Irish coffees to the passengers, pointing out the fabulous Celtic logic that the combination of adding 40% proof whiskey to a cream-covered coffee was the perfect way for a pilot to keep on top of his game when forced by bad weather to return to Shannon airport.

-0-

In Kingman the gap created by 15 empty rooms and vacant chairs was barely discernible. Dent wondered if any financial benefit in reduced costs was worth it. He didn't wonder long for as he remembered the booking commission, a gentle tap at the door was followed immediately by nurse Swallow. She swept in as no one else could, or dared. Her lean mature body gave her latitude no others employed or enjoyed. Her lean mature body held a spell over the doctor, which was stronger

127

than his family, stronger after dusk than even the lure of the grass stained clubs in the golf bag in the corner.

'Cinque giorni cara,' She said in such a provocative manner Dent trembled. 'Appena cinque giorni fino a sei notti.'

Notti that sounded good to Dent.

'I didn't know you spoke Italian.'

'You know every part of my body, but not every part of my mind.'

True thought Dent, but if he had to choose . . . .

She placed a couple of files on his desk, turned and repeated 'appena cinque giorni fino asei notti – just five days until six nights.' The door almost closed behind her and then reopened enough for her blonde head to twist and return, 'according to my diary . . . . and Google Translate.'

19.
LAND OF SAINTS AND SINNERS, LANDED

Fuselage, Set A, Typhoon Studios – eastern North Atlantic

Ireland is a country blessed with the cast offs of everywhere. It hasn't the best of anything, mountains, lakes, rivers, weather, but what little it has, works. Even its people, down trodden and self-effacing, seem content with the perpetual role of under-dogs. They are amongst the happiest of people, content in knowing they are the world's best underdogs, so they are good at something.

As a people the Irish have punched above their weight, in politics, culture and sport. Was it an accident that the star-spangled banner was in red, white and blue and didn't contain just one of those forty shades of green? But then Ireland didn't have a flag of its own way back in 1776 and most of the world's major players opted towards red, white and blue, the tri-colors.

It was a blessing for the European Experience to land in Ireland as a first port of call. The small roads in the hills east of LA allowed driving that mimicked the country byways of the west of Ireland. A little above the city the temperature drops, not enough for a match with Ireland, but the team had prepared radio soundtracks to filter into the coach trips – announcements of unprecedented heat due to global warming. April nights in LA bounced around 14 degrees, much the same as a London day, but the west coast of Ireland could expect to knock six off that. Adjusting the eight hours to Greenwich

Mean Time meant the only real climatic danger was with the travelers' night activities when LA's temperature would rise into the low twenties.

Air conditioning would solve it, but only if they could stay within the studio as much as possible. Even the starting point for the external bus trips was inside. Ryder would park up in a corner of Set A and let the shade cool the bus down before loading up. By the time they reached day ten they would be south enough in European terms to allow more of the activities to take place in daylight warmth. Ernie just had to devise some event to enable the clock to jump back towards Californian time for the days in Italy, Spain and France. But what? His flexible mind just couldn't hit it, for the moment. He also had found and moved into position the studio's rain rig, a bulky set of curved pipes on wheels that could provide everything from mist to monsoon. Attached to a hydrant it would run for hours and Charles would be on the phone to the water company demanding an explanation and a rebate.

-0-

'Dong'

'Ladies and Gentlemen as you can see we have started our final decent, we expect to be on the ground in about 15 minutes. The weather in Shannon is a perky 15 degrees with intermittent showers predicted. Please put your tables back and make sure your seats are upright and belts fastened.' Rooster was quite enjoying role-play and that little segment went even better than the safety demo some ten hours earlier. There was nothing wrong with the safety demo, it was quite realistic for no one paid any attention. She toyed with the idea or doing it topless – maybe on the way back, just to celebrate.

There was no one quite as excited as Sean Seamus Finbar
O'Reilly. At 50 this was the homecoming he thought he'd never
experience. For the next three days he would be John Wayne in
The Quiet Man, soaking up the atmosphere that was the DNA
for his fabulously shamrocked name. The O'Reilly's had been
in Boston for six generations, they could put four greats on the
front of grandfather before they'd get back to green green grass
of home. Sean's father, Seamus, had followed his grandfather
Finbar, in his preference for the company of Afro-American
women. Perhaps as a long-term plan to develop the Boston
Celts; the end result was Sean. As a teenager, at six seven he
was a ball width higher than his teammates. His failing
eyesight from 6th grade meant that he'd never hoop a three
pointer. Now he was coming home, dignified by his mass of
grey hair, dressed in a black polo and black jeans, the darkest
Irishman since Phil Lynott, looked for all the world like a pint
of Guinness.

'Whack full me daddy oh, there's whiskey in the jar,' he sang
out loud and such was the positive response of his fellow
passengers he launched into the full version, well as much of it
as he could remember.

The plane shuddered amid screams and finally with much
more hydraulic action it came to a halt.

'Please remain in your seats until the seat belt sign goes off,'
said Rooster, merging reality with a dash of unfortunate
surrealism.

'Will the European Experience travelling party please remain
seated,' Rooster said at closer quarters and without the aid of
the mike. She shunned the use of 'de-plane' – it seemed so
impersonal. After all you don't get up in the morning by 'de-

bedding.' Miss Little, wearing sweatshirt number two, had already 'de-seated' and out of the starting blocks. A quick look at her pocket notebook allowed Rooster to match number to name. 'Miss Little, can you please return to you seat.'

'How did you know my name,' the 72-year-old sparked back.

'Passenger list, mam,' Rooster replied with the assurance of someone in control. She needed to be for this was unchartered territory for the trio. Up to this point the most crucial maneuver in any of their exploits was when she had to step forwards from an expectant crowd and claim that she held the winning cow plop ticket. The fear on that occasion was that someone in the closely-knit community might question who was this 'out-of-towner? Now the fear was different. What do you do with a party of blind people once you are exposed? Just cut and run. She hadn't asked Ernie but the gut feeling was, probably exit stage right.

One by one like oysters being de-shelled, the party freed themselves from the cramped area that had been their living space for half a day. In reality they had a couple more inches to stretch out in than if they'd been on an actual plane. The cameramen and directors demanding a little extra leeway in order to get the best shot, the seats were economy, the space business.

'Dong'

'There is a problem with the extending gangway. We will deplane by the aft door onto steps and bus you to the terminal. Please remember all your personal belongings.'

It had to be Captain Ernie's voice since Rooster was busy shepherding the flock, and talented as she was, could not do a husky male. Ryder was busy putting the bus into position, for once picking people up outside of Set A. Set A interior was the destination, the party would go out the backdoor and in the front after a brief trip to the main gate and back. It was physically unreal and confusing and Rooster was personally becoming increasingly perplexed and threatening real emotions as she fought to control a developing interest in one of the party. Harley having stripped off his numbered sweater revealed a T shirt with a motorbike on it and a very taut torso. It was her turn to flash an uncontrollable smile, it never quite reached full beam as she automatically thought 'task in hand' and reverted to default mode, moderate simmer.

Ryder had, on a rummage through the props store some days back, come across the item all fifteen of the travelers were now on, the steps from the plane, last used in a biopic about a Texan oilman and now as the entry platform to Shannon, Ireland. The props rooms had been an Aladdin's Cave of an experience for the trio. They'd stumbled across it during a familiarization walk around the greater studio area. A quick word with Crawford and half a day's lugging later, they had their very own props department, beyond tables and chairs they had borrowed, turnstiles, elevator mock-ups and for some reason never explained, gravestones and various parts of a jail set.

After a degree of wobbling caused by a host of backpacks swinging into others and the usual general chaos in liberating semi-paralyzed bodies from cramped areas, the plane was empty. The discarded rugs, pillows, headsets and coffee cups making it seem even more lifelike than it had done when occupied. At the bottom of the steps Sean Seamus Finbar

O'Reilly stopped, went down on his knees and kissed the ground. His face matched the tarmac.

'Mother Ireland your son has come home,' he said with all the reverence and sincerity of the initial moments of a Papal tour.

Three other members of the party stumbled over him, almost confirming what Ireland has always been very good at, spilling blood. Rooster picked up the pieces and guided them to the others and then onto the waiting coach.

Two large speakers some 30 meters away pumped out the first of Pang and Ngoc greatest hits, FX Exterior Airport, with hint of distant cows. Inside Set A a second soundtrack created FX Interior Terminal. The very observant might have noticed a similarity to the sound at Bob Hope some 15 hours earlier because Rooster had had the foresight to record it on her Smartphone, a precious 20 minutes of nothingness but airport ambience which seemed better than what P&N had downloaded. Amazing she thought that in her hand she held a device that could make a movie, that could tell her where she was, could inform her of the answer to any question she could think of, in fact it was so clever you could even, if you knew their number, phone and chat to somebody. That was something she rarely did since the only two people who had her number were within miming distance.

The coach pulled away from the steps and set off in an arc round the lot, eventually going from the bright sunlight into the shaded corner of Set A that was its own personal home-base. Like an automatic vacuum cleaner or grass cutter, it would find its docking station to rest and recharge. The distance driven was about a mile and a half, the distance between the fuselage and the lobby area about 30 yards across Set A.

The party was by now totally disorientated, well not quite totally. Harley could see where he was, but still had no clue of where 'was' was. It had been dark when they arrived at LAX, which was really Bob Hope Airport, which was also Set A; now it was light and he still struggled to put the pieces of this jigsaw into a picture. Part of the picture was Rooster who had now changed into jeans. 'Was there anything that that ass didn't look good in?' he thought. It was a thought that would sustain him though a turnstile and up to a windowed booth where a man talking in a strange accent asked for his passport. Nobody, nowhere walked through turnstiles at airports, but the trio liked the physical moment that logged people into a position, a moment in time and for the unknowing party, it was a punctuation point, they were in Ireland, where they do things differently. It was part of the charm.

Ernie, behind the glass, picked up an address stamper, one of those basic gadgets, eighty years old, designed to perfection with a working movement that still fascinates. The sheer simplicity of it, as you pushed down the red knob the inkpad retreated to allow the rubber stamp to make its mark. Ernie had long decided that the mark would not get a clean shot at the passport. A piece of damp kitchen roll allowed a blur to make it, but nothing you could ever read. After all, one downward movement of the hand onto an official piece of paper and goodness knows, it might be classed as fraud. 'Could you please remove your sunglasses?' The request startled Harley. Had he been sussed he wondered. 'I need to see if you are the guy in the photograph,' the official explained.

'Oh sorry, course,' said Harley as he froze a stare beyond Officer Zimmerman's left ear; Zimmerman who was not taking the deception to a fully professional level by being dressed in a Hawaiian shirt so bright it looked as if it might need batteries. Ernie didn't even give the pretense the respect of looking at him. Maybe Irish customs have a 'Casual Friday' everyday thought Harley as he struggled to hold back a laugh. Ernie stamped a sheet of paper for the tenth time in as many minutes and wished 'Mr Johnson' a fine day. It was the first time in years anybody had called him that. The disorientation process continued to hit him from every angle; it was like that fateful moment when falling off his bike, everything seemed unreal and in slow motion.

The party had somehow managed to re-assemble in a fairly tight bunch in the cooler shade of the rear studio wall. With the FX rumble of waiting taxis and buses, Rooster passed by to assume control.

'Miss Dior' Wilcox murmured when she was within two feet of him despite Ngoc having wafted a spray containing aviation fuel. Must watch out for that nose she thought and added a selection test box of perfumes to her next shopping list. He'd already correctly identified the two she most regularly used. She chose to ignore the remark this time, but she could smell danger, literally.

'I'm Sinead O'Connell.'

'Sing us a song,' requested Sean Shamus Finbar O'Reilly who had number 13 on his sweatshirt, and was determined to milk every second from his homecoming.

'Wish I could. O'Connell, not O'Conner,' Rooster replied back in a very passable Irish accent.

'Somebody asked me about baggage. Well as you know the
European Experience is using a personalized numbering
system. Your numbered bags have been collected and once
loaded into the coach we'll be off – I'm told that generally the
plan is for them to be put into your rooms without you having
to worry. However, there are a couple of smaller hotels where
there are too few staff to do this, and I'm afraid you will have
to do some carrying. That, I'm told, is elsewhere during your
trip, it is not necessary on the Irish Experience.'

The bags each had an individual schedule on them, held firmly
in place by four strips of the world's most versatile invention,
elephant tape, or duct tape, or gaffer tape, three
interchangeable names for the same thing. Well not quite since
duct is meant to be a more permanent temporary repair whilst
gaffer's role is to be strong, secure and removable, without
ripping paint back to raw wood. The schedule contained the
passengers name and number along with the room location for
the nights spent at the studio – the few occasions where they
would venture into the outside world and stay in remote
motels, were left blank. It had taken Rooster a little time to
work out, but it was the entire trip on six inches of paper.
Working as a team, Ryder, Ngoc and Pang could move the
baggage from hotel to hotel, from country to country in less
than 15 minutes.

'If you wait where you are we will escort you to your waiting
luxury coach. The journey time to Clifden in Connemara is
around two to three hours. Does anyone need to go to the
bathroom before we depart?'

To Ernie's dismay about five hands were raised. He filtered

them out of the bunch, along a corridor and into Set B and back. Better now he thought than an hour into the bus journey when they would have to make best with wherever they were.

Wherever was due to be Clear Creek Canyon, high into the hills to the east of the city where the temperatures would drop by about twenty percent during the day and could become quite chilly at night. They would drive out for about an hour and then backtrack. The first fifteen and last fifteen miles were the dangerous ones because they were the same. It was alright to head out though an urban area, in the excitement of arrival they would hopefully not notice that Shannon was a lot more congested than might be reasonably expected. However, that same congestion would face them for the last thirty minutes as they entered remote Clifden, Co Galway, with a population a little over two thousand. It would be an early test for the ambience system inside the bus. Built on the promise of a night's Irish music, Ryder would play the Dubliners Greatest Hits several times whilst Rooster would break in to give a talk about the history of the west of Ireland, gleaned from Wikipedia. She'd used the online knowledge facility so often that already she felt guilty for not donating to it. But she comforted herself by labelling it sustainable guilt, some of the facts were dubious.

At about two hundred years old, Clifden was a new town in Irish terms, but it had grasped enough significant moments in history to make it interesting. Home of the Marconi's European base for the first transatlantic wireless communication, a bog outside the town was also the unscheduled landing spot for the first transatlantic flight. Well semi unscheduled, the aircraft had enough fuel left in it to reach at least London, but recognizing the Marconi mast, Alcock decided they'd done enough after sixteen hours of flying. His sandwiches were starting to dry out. He picked out a flat piece of land and glided in only to find that Connemara, even on a June day, can be a tad damp underfoot. The former World War I plane ended nose-down in the bog peat. On the plus side they had done it, and in the process had also made the first Transatlantic air mail delivery and picked up a small fortune in prize money. It was a double whammy for Clifden. The history books could now add the mail achievement to the wireless one and quiet remarkably, both within a matter of feet of each other. At the mention of Alcock and Brown, Reilly chipped in 'that's me', a joke that flew over most party without response, as they assumed him to be a carrot-headed Celt. Clifden had also had endured enough obligatory Irish historical moments of famine and civil war, to make it historically marketable.

It was a bit of a detour, but Ernie had already planned a strategy that involved as much movement as possible. Apart from sleeping, static was dangerous, a chance to breathe in and think. Sitting on the bus was the most cost-effective use of consuming time as the party was confined and controllable. He remembered a trip he'd taken when he was younger and had decided to see the world. He headed west to Hawaii, where he picked up his taste for shirts that glowed in the dark, and then on to Australia. Inspired by the image of Linda Kozlowski bending over in her G-string by the lagoon in Crocodile Dundee, he'd reached Darwin and was taking a four-hour bus trip to the Kakadu National Park, the location for much of the movie. There were no Linda's on the bus and by fifteen years he was the youngest tourist. After about three hours in the middle of nowhere the bus stopped so the party could snap some photographs of a collection of giant termite mounds. It was fascinating, an insect high-rise city with perhaps eighteen mud 'sky-scrappers', some reaching ten feet high.

He returned to the bus to find one elderly American lady still firmly in her seat. He enquired if she wanted help down the steps so she could see the wonders of nature.

'Fuck no,' she said 'I just spent $1,200 getting rid of the bastards from my backyard, why would I want to see them now?' and she returned to looking out at the long straight road that lay ahead, another two hours plus of driving. That evening he'd add a new measure of time to his vocabulary. The slab. To some Australian's a slab is a flat-pack case of tinned beer, 24 of them.

His fellow travelers had dined and it being eight o'clock most had retired to bed when Ernie found himself in the bar. It was a classic Aussie outback location, what if lacked in comforts it multiplied in color and two bits of color were at the bar. They said it was their local, and it being Friday night, after work they'd driven over for a few beers. What is local in the outback is transcontinental travel to some and Ernie asked the guys 'how long did it take them to get home?'

'Usually two slabs,' was the reply with the added information that since there were no roads, if they felt emotionally exhausted from the night's activities, they just stopped until they woke up again.

It had stuck with Ernie that there are people for whom sitting on the move was some kind of therapy, like Sunday drivers who tootle about analyzing the fuel efficiency for a journey they never had to make. To them just the sensation of going somewhere totally unnecessary was better than sitting around. A bit like yachting. He hoped this party of 15 embraced moving ambitions rather than being incarcerated in St Anthony's waiting for the next dinner gong.

The five had returned from decanting the wine, beer and soft drinks that had been generously available on board EE001. There would be a lot of sleep-inducing alcohol available on this trip, but there was a payback factor, the constant need to find restrooms for the more elderly members.

The bus set off with Rooster picking up a microphone – she seemed so natural with it in her hand.

'Now, any of you looking for a sparkling Irish colleen?' She flinched, she'd done it again, looking for, another 'don't mention the war' incident. But she needn't have worried, the party were long-term comfortable with their private situations.

Two hands went up, one from the illustrious O'Reilly, and the other . . .

'Mr Wilcox. Really. If it were September we could have headed to Lisdoonvarna instead of Clifden. The west of Ireland is all about farming and fishing. When everyone was forced to go to school the bright young girls, knowing they won't get a life out of the kitchen, packed their bags and took their educated heads to the city. Dublin is crawling with single colleens, the west with bachelor farmers, too busy to find a wife until the harvest is in. That means that in September they head to a small town in the Country Clare where the girls available and ready for a life in the kitchen meet and dance with the farmers from dawn to dawn.'

Rooster had already decided that her role over the next few weeks was not to be the heart and soul, but the eyes of the party. The more interesting every passing mile would be, the shorter the journey. If they were going to ask questions, was it not better that they were guided into an area of relative

---

neutrality than to sit there and listen to the world go by and think, 'that's strange.'

-0-

Ryder had skillfully driven the bus through Glendale and at La Canada, the Angeles Crest Highway. It was a mixture of freeway followed by a brief residential section and then into the clean air and sounds of the mountain road. The first two sections had only taken 20 minutes, a good sign for the return journey. He held back from driving into thickening traffic in the hope that it would have cleared by the time he hit it, which in most cases it had. The journey was therefore slow but smooth and without the added danger or pulling up alongside a convertible full of teenagers blasting out some very non-Irish music.

The highway into the mountains was well maintained and ideal to induce the slow side-to-side movement that lulled many of the party out of excitement and into sleep. Seventy-five minutes into the journey Ryder found a scenic spot, empty of everything except a crude wooden picnic table and a view.

He pulled up and announced that they could stretch their legs. He would then turn the bus round and they would head back, two bits of information he didn't relay to the party. If he hadn't turned around it would have taken half a day to return, at one point the road they were on meeting up again with Interstate 40, the highway that had brought them much of the way from Kingman.

Broken sleep and travel weary bodies, the liberated party took about twenty minutes to reach the point where the legs were now back in default working mode. It was not a moment too soon, for Rooster could see in the distance a couple of cars making their way up the twisty road, perhaps they would innocently pass by, but she was nervous that they might stop to enjoy the view and express how surprisingly fine LA looked from this vantage point. She'd already lifted the pump-pressure garden sprayer from the back of the bus – in a minor emergency she'd use it to flick water up into the air and then announce that a heavy rain shower was on its way.

There was no need, the party was already back in the coach by the time the two cars had disappeared into the last hidden bend before re-emerging and arriving at the scenic spot. They were keen to reach Clifden, change clothes and get ready for some lively singing.

20.
DRUMMING UP BUSINESS

Reception, Typhoon Studios – Clifden, Connemara

Roger, in the outer office at Typhoon, picked up the phone for the third time in as many minutes and pressed a two-digit number. This time it got a response with Ernie at the other end of the line.

'There's a guy with a guitar here Ernie and says you have booked him. But because you're a closed set I can't send him up. Does this make sense to you?'

It made perfect sense to Ernie who was comforted by Roger's policeman-like diligence in maintaining the projects secret status.

'Just a guitar?' asked Ernie so loudly that the question broke free of Roger's ear and went across the room.

The guy in his late twenties shook a 'no' and nodded down to a bag that looked as if it contained a spare wheel for a small car. His backpack also seemed crammed with items that to the ex-basketball player looked like the leftovers from a plumbing job.

'No, he seems to have other things, bits of pipe' Roger conveyed and Ernie, a little confused, said he'd be right down.

Five minutes later a tattered golf buggy rolled up to the Typhoon reception and Ernie stepped out. The guy with the guitar and 'spare wheel' and 'piping' was an inspiration and insurance ploy that Ernie had insisted on after hearing the music 'borrowed' from Molly Malone's. Clifden would be the first night and first impressions are lasting and with that in mind Ernie wanted some more genuine contact and atmosphere right from the outset. Rooster had found the guy, Michael, on the wall of a musical instruments shop. He was pinned between someone giving an electric piano away under the heading 'Organ Donor' and a photograph of a curvaceous lady offering cello lessons, a photograph that took a second viewing to determine which was which.

Michael made bodhrans, the taut-skinned Irish drum, and gave lessons in how to play them. He was also offered himself, and his guitar and his tin whistles, the bit of plumbing, for party entertainment. He had Irish blood in him and had visited Dublin as a kid on a whirlwind family holiday. He wanted to use the Gaelic version of his name, O'Suilleabhain. It proved too problematic for email and although there were several Michael O'Sullivan's who had risen to fame in the worlds of sport and entertainment, there already was a distinctive Michael O'Suilleabhain too strongly identified with traditional Irish music. He'd just have to stick with his birth name.

Ernie drove him to another disused part of the studio, the choice for a quiet spot being just about anywhere, and stopped the cart.

'Thank you for coming at such short notice,' Ernie started. 'I can assure you that you that you will never have had such a strange gig – a strange gig that must remain a secret. Do you have a girlfriend or wife?'

Michael nodded and was about to launch into an explanation that sort of fell in between the two options when Ernie cut back in.

'Whichever, whatever, you can't tell her anything once you have signed this piece of paper. You can't tell anyone. You can say you had a gig somewhere usual, maybe a try out for a job, but leave it at that. If you don't sign the piece of paper, I drive you back to the gates and you can only speculate what might have unfolded – all I will say pre-signature, is that national security is part of the issue.'

Michael didn't mind, he was more interested in the tax free $300 that the hour or so would put in his pocket. It was a figure he could multiply by two or three if he took any orders for a drum or a tin whistle, should that become a possibility. He signed.

Ernie explained the clandestine nature of the whole project saying that Michael's part was to help convince a party of blind volunteers that they were in Ireland. There were, Ernie said, other volunteers in other locations facing a different geographical deception and once all parties were firmly in the belief that they actually were elsewhere, they would start a series of related psychological trials.

'Michael, for the purposes of this exercise, you are an Irish/American on a study tour of Ireland, here to develop your musical ability, which includes making the drum things. You must not convey any information beyond music and the instruments and for the purposes of this trial scenario you are in Clifden, County Galway. If you can get them to sing along, that would be brilliant. You can show them how to play the drums and whistles, you can even sell them if you want. You have just arrived, you don't know the area and you are playing at O'Brien's, a bar in the town.'

A totally intrigued Michael was then driven back to the reception, given a sandwich and a beer and left to work out his 45-minute musical set. He was also handed a sheet of paper with a mini outline of 'his' first impressions of Clifden, but marked, "Only to be used if conversation provoked." Ernie looked at the clock and anticipated the party's arrival in about an hour. He felt fairly comfortable about Michael, but not totally, that's why he opted for Typhoon's reception, Roger had left for the tennis club and Charles was out scouting for work, or so he said. 'I'm landing a big one,' he had promised as he left. Ernie was left to guess if it was a carp, a crap or a contract.

It would be perhaps three hours before he was on stage. At reception he would be free to head back out for a couple of hours and if he suddenly got cold feet he would have nothing greater to recall than meeting a strange man in a golf cart.

The fewer who saw inside the studio the better. Less is more in terms of security, look at the Islamic State and the IRA, those cells where the insiders were so inside they didn't know who anyone else in their hijacked car actually was. The more air in the balloon, the more likely it would go bang, but having the third dimension of a living breathing musician was a risk worth taking. The additional bonus was that if he sold just one drum thingy then the souvenir would be a constant reminder back in St Anthony's that a great night's craic was indeed held in Ireland. The bobhran would drum-up business for EE2. Ernie made a mental note to peel off any manufacturing details that might be a giveaway. Safer to slap on a 'Made in China' sticker.

21.
ON THE ROCKY ROAD TO CLIFDEN

Glendale, LA – the bog land of Connemara approaching Clifden

Ryder had the AC up to max and the onboard music system not far below. The syrupy harsh tones of Ronnie Drew, like concrete mixed with honey, and the rest of the Dubliners cut through the AC and suppressed the drone of the early afternoon traffic. As they travelled back through Glendale, Rooster outlined the joys of Clifden from the seat behind Ryder. Normally she would have taken the pole position of the seat by the front door, but the first two rows of the bus had been sectioned off, leaving Ryder in isolation. When they reached Copenhagen Airport the acrylic sheet would be removed and Ryder could stop pretending to drive on the right and the front door of the coach would be used for the first time since the tourists were left off at LAX. But for the present they were driving on the left-hand side of the road, or so it seemed.

Right hand or left hand drive the coach was one of a kind. The original owners had sung for Jesus all over the western and southern states, and to help the free movement of the choir, they'd taken out four seats on one side and custom installed a second door. To match it, on the left side they removed six more seats and replaced them with a large sit around table onto which they'd placed an electric organ so they could sing the miles away. For the British section of the 'tour' Ryder had removed the table so the bus might feel different when on the Continent when he put it back in. One of the choir had owned an engineering works and eager to please had done a good job.

The alterations reduced the normal carrying capacity by sixteen, but with the table seats occupied it came back up to 25. The choir had cared for its bodywork by keeping it undercover at the engineering works when not on the road and because they weren't particularly good at singing, the lack of demand for their tortured tonsils had kept the mileage down. So, although from 1989, the MCI coach was much younger in real running terms than a quarter of a century old. It was just that on this sunny day in LA, with the raw paint job by Ryder almost washed away, it was a bit of a sad sight.

Ernie had decided not to invest in a re-spray and had followed up on instructions to restore it to its Christian choir condition. Ryder now saw it, along with the T-shirt warnings, acting as an additional noisy-parker deterrent. He'd noticed other drivers trying to avoid eye contact. The money that the paint job would cost could be invested in hiring a true luxury coach on the way back for the last leg. Ernie simply couldn't live with the thought of a repeat of the departure scene. Not even Ryder could arrive back in reverse and make it look normal.

-0-

Back unexpectedly from his search for a script the unproductive producer was at his desk, his attention drawn to the window as a crucifix passed by to the strains of 'you're drunk, your drunk, you silly old fool, still you cannot see, that's a lovely flower pot, me mother sent to me . . .'

As the dust settled behind the disappearing bus Charles tried to console himself that 'Project X', as he had labelled it, at least had a soundtrack. A bit tasteless, but still a soundtrack. Michael had also returned from killing time at a mall. Charles walked through to what they called the planning office when Roger was in, and reception when someone from a local media college did work experience for a pittance wage.

Looking at Michael's wrapped-up bobhram and his shamrock label-covered guitar case, Charles ventured into a conversation.

'You part of . . em,' he was unsure how to describe the back lot.

Michael nodded yes, but added, 'Can't say.'

'Of course,' Charles replied, putting a finger to his mouth and then one into each ear. 'Same boat. Heard nothing.'

-0-

With suitcases already in their rooms, the party had not taken that long to move from transit to tranquil. The peace of having individual space for the first time in 30 hours was for most, blissful. Harley wondered how he would ever get to sleep in his. The former office had been functionally furnished as a bedroom, but there were tell-tale signs of its previous existence on every non-windowed wall. One of Typhoon's few lucrative areas had been in cheap and cheerless horror and around Harley's wall where posters tagged with slogans like, 'The Mummy's Tomb, you might never sleep again!' and one with a huge cracked gravestone promising 'there is no escape from the darkness.'

Thankfully there was escape from the room. In half an hour they were due to meet in the hotel's reception. Rooster had promised to knock him up and he was looking forward. Disappointingly she was also going to knock on everyone else's door and lead the party in small groups to a rendezvous in Set

B. From there, in crocodile fashion and along a covered corridor used to keep actors clean, dry and out of the Californian sun, she'd take them to Set A where they would once again team up with Ryder and the bus. A fifteen-minute drive round the studios would end with them back in Set C and walking towards 'O'Brien's Bar' and the promise of food, drink and conversation, what the Irish term as craic. To qualify as craic, the drink has to be free-flowing, the chat has to be up to a scintillating standard, and when you waken the next day you're unable to remember a word of the conversation and you wonder where the bruises came from.

Ryder had created four stop-off points within the bus pick-up and set-down area. Each was twice as wide as the bus's door and stretched for fifteen feet into the studio. Individually they contributed a different surface experience, cobbled stones, rough ground, concrete sidewalk and gravel so that arrivals and departures would generate and atmosphere through the soles of the souls. As the bus swung in through the opened entry doors, a series of colored ping pong balls, suspended from the ceiling would hit the windscreen. Ryder knew that if the green one rested on the window, the doors were perfectly placed at the sidewalk, blue for gravel, red for rough ground and yellow for cobbled stones. On this occasion he hit the blue. He'd save the yellow for Templebar, Dublin.

A small wind machine gave the party a breezy reception and Ngoc pumped some moisture into the air as they crunched through the gravel and up a couple of steps, through a doorway and after a maze of turns into O'Brien's. A general bar atmosphere track was slowly mixed into the scene and once all were within the zone, music started to play from a jukebox.

From behind the bar Ernie moved a few glasses around and shouted out in a very fine Irish brogue, 'Now who put that on – don't be feeding that jukebox too much tonight, we have live music form Michael O'Somebody,' he paused and added, 'and you won't ever want to waste your money on your ears – save it for the mouth.' He paused again 'and talking of drink, what can I get you folks?'

Rooster explained that they were a party from America and that they had rung in advance to book a private area of the bar.

'Indeed you did, indeed you did. We've a couple of fine snugs over there, you'll be as comfortable as kittens in a closet.'

'What's a snug?' The question came from #3 Ben Nelson, one of the younger members of the party.

'A snug, young man, is a brilliant invention of the Catholic Church. They taut it improper for a woman to be seen drinking with men. So they insisted on these lovely little boxes where they could be out of sight. Sorry.' Ernie bit his lip and then thought he was being over sensitive. 'The fact is that the privacy was the perfect ticket for naughty goings on, if you get my drift – many a priest was conceived in a snug! Many's a priest enjoyed a prolonged communion, many's a guard conducted interviews through a glass. As I said, a brilliant invention.'

With that Millie shepherded two groups of seven and eight around two huge tables. She was very relaxed in this role for it was the most consistent of all those she'd be called upon to play over the next three weeks. Here she was one of the party. As Millie she'd be at the front of the bus in Belfast, Berlin, Barcelona, in fact everywhere. She'd be in the hotels championing their complaints, in restaurants clarifying menus and, as in this case, a bar getting together everyone's food and drinks. Millie was the soul of the party and already on day one proper they all loved her.

Ryder had just returned from the Typhoon front gate where he'd picked up a huge thermo box from the trunk of an old sedan. On the door it had a faded transfer with a gold large harp on it with Sweeney's Irish Bar written large across it in green. He'd also picked up Michael from the unmanned reception. His period of enforced isolation and perspective thinking was over.

The fact that he was clearly in a film studio had prepared him to a degree. He'd never been in one before, but all the trimmings and trappings matched those of expectations taken from television and movies. However, it was a surreal moment to go through a series of doorways and suddenly be in vast studio, devoid of cameras or the usual paraphernalia and to find a group of people huddled together round two tables. Two tables penned in by what looked like high quality garden fencing. It was like a huge manila envelope with one colorful stamp in the corner.

Between the bar and the two crowded tables there was a small raised island of a stage. 'That's all yours,' Ryder said as he turned to whisper in Rooster's ear that the food was here. There were fourteen Irish stews and ten fish pies with three portions of a vegetarian version of Irish stew – basically potatoes, carrots and onions boiled to the point of unrecognizable pulp. Basically it was the Irish stew with the lamb lifted out, well most of it. Rooster would distribute as best as possible under the guise of a local waitress with 'Millie' standing by in case there were any issues. What was left over was for EE crew and Michael, if he was nice enough.

As the party tucked in, the music recorded earlier at Molly Malone's sound-tracked their meal. Michael looked on. It was quite amazing how much these people were putting into enjoying themselves, like long-term prisoners given a night out in a bordello. Turning down the offer of the veg Irish or a fish pie, he sank a comforting second Guinness and stepped onto the small stage.

'I'm Michael O'Sullivan, Irish American, here in Clifden to sing for my supper. I hope you enjoyed yours.'

He launched into a melody of the most commonly badly sung Irish songs, Galway Bay, When Irish Eyes Are Smiling, Danny Boy and Molly Malone, but he sang them with a clarity that froze the party in admiration. Twenty feet away, in a corner, Sean Seamus Finbar O'Reilly lent back against the garden fence and cried, 'I'm home.'

Looking on Ernie was reminded of a night in Chicago. Everyone was at the bar, heads tilted back an extra 20 degrees to watch a quartet of large screens all showing the same images. On each the Bulls were in full flow, basket following basket. They didn't notice someone stopping off at the jukebox on their way back from the restroom, until that was Van Morrison's Brown Eyed Girl cut through the speakers. The barman immediately muted the screens and the whole bar sang along with Van the Man. When they'd finished shal-la-la-la-te-da-ing, the TV's were turned up again. It stuck with him as a fantastic example of the power of music. Here was another and he was so pleased to fork-out $300 - the decision to hire him had softened the con in Connemara.

Michael had fully embraced the task in hand and had stepped down from the stage after a session with the bobhran. He handed it to the closest person, 'try it out, it is called the bow ram.' One by one the party tested what Miss Little described as a giant tambourine, 'but without the tinnie things.' After a little coaching the party were able to pass it on without Michael's tuition and he returned to stage and picked up a penny whistle to accompany their efforts – sort of Irish jazz.

An hour and a half later, Michael's repertoire exhausted, but with orders for five bobhrans and eight whistles, he was driven by Ernie to the front gates.

'Thank you Michael, that was special,' Ernie said, surprised by the degree he'd been humbled by a young man with a guitar, and a talent. He handed over an envelope 'As agreed, and as agreed, the matter ends here – you have in the document you signed, a clear exemption from declaring this as taxable. Tonight never existed. It ends here at the gates.'

'Not quite,' said Michael, Ernie flinching as if he'd heard a police siren. 'I'm back tomorrow with five drums, eight whistles. Your assistant was to collect $480 dollars for me. Dollars not Euros.'

Ernie's smile was so natural it concealed his anxiety. 'Not a word about it, this experiment is,' he raised his finger to his lips, 'we have a unique dispensation. The tests come before tax. Anyway, any tax in this situation would be an in-house economy, like moving money from one pocket to another.'

As Michael strode out to his car in the parking lot, Ernie shouted 'Not even to the wife or girlfriend.'

'What about a boyfriend?' came the laughed reply.

With the music still ringing in his ears Ernie turned his car around. 'I hope his mother's dead,' he thought a little uncharitable and then found himself replaying his last remark and analyzing if he might be a friend of Dorothy's.

On his way back to HBO Ernie passed Ryder with a coach full of very happy travelers who had on day one come face-to-face with the European Experience. 'Fuck it was hard work,' he thought, but never in his career had he been responsible for such undiluted joy.

Ryder would drive around for another ten minutes, or so it was planned, but a weak voice from the back of the bus pleaded for him to stop. At least two of the party had enjoyed at least one glass too much of the Irish spirit. There was generally no alcohol available at St Anthony's apart from the occasional celebratory glass of wine, so the concoction of beer, whiskey, Bailey's and an Irish coffee had been more than the academic Arthur J. Hilton and the shy and retiring Miss Temple's constitutions could take. If Ryder didn't get back to base quickly he'd have to clean out the bus. The fifteen-minute outward journey was done in less than six on the way back. 'Funny how coming home always seems shorter,' Protz had observed out loud. Ryder took the reasonably sensible step of abandoning continuity when he got back to Set A, stopping the bus on the green ping-pong ball. The sidewalk would be easier than gravel to clean puck off.

An hour later Ernie, Rooster and Ryder sat round a table in Set B, 'just 21 to go,' said Ernie. Rooster and Ryder stared at him, a vague blank into the distance stare; already they hadn't the energy to reply.

22.
FAIRYTALES IN STONE

Bouquet Canyon, California –Giant's Causeway, Co Antrim

It was midnight in Clifden, four in the afternoon in Burbank. Between them the trio would get a fitful sleep before it was eleven pm in Burbank and breakfast in Clifden. In the office storeroom Ernie wrote upon the whiteboard – Day 2 'Today Bouquet Canyon, you are the Giant's Causeway.' Rooster was upset that the gem she'd found at Folsom was rejected because it didn't fit into the geographical logistics of getting to the second or third locations marked on the schedule. She'd started to keep a log of potential visiting places, like a good location manager she now looked at everywhere with wide open eyes and an even wider open mind. At Folsom there were huge chunks of discarded granite, enough to create their own causeway, but Ernie was adamant – perhaps, she thought, it was the association with the volunteer granite masons housed in the famous not-local-enough prison.

So now after breakfast, which meant two full fries for Protz, it wouldn't be the granite of Folsom and the coach would make the same journey as it did on day one, but ignore the chance to turn back. Destination was Bouquet Canyon, an artificial reservoir, but more to the point, birthplace of many, if not most, of the sidewalks of downtown LA. It had several disused quarries and going on information dug out by Rooster, Ryder had found one with significant quantities of discarded or rejected slabs. Rooster had also found something with a very different brief, an old stone building a bit of drive away, but important to the EE script. Both would feature largely in the first night-time operation, one as Northern Ireland's oldest and one as its newest tourist attraction. After a four-hour drive they'd arrive at The Giant's Causeway and a couple of hours later Castle Ward, better known to Games of Thrones fans as Winterfell. Winterfell on this occasion was known to the people of Pasadena as 'that spooky old house you wouldn't catch me dead in,' an abandoned mansion with a courtyard, outbuildings and a bleak history that kept it shut and perfect for one slice of the European experience.

Neither had held out great attraction to the fifteen tourists. The Causeway they'd heard of and it would be nice, cool and breezy, but the castle meant little to those who couldn't ever watch the mega series. They were merely following one of the basic rules of tourism – ticking the 'Yeah I've been there,' box. They were more excited about the prospect of another night in an Irish pub, this time in Belfast. That would happen after a trip to the quay where the most famous of all ships never to complete a voyage was built, the Titanic.

It was a busy day so Ernie would also be on board the coach, he couldn't drive, but he could fill in the gaps by taking the party on little 'breather walks' and let Ryder do some of his express sleeps.

Cities are different at night. Less noise, more sound. Without the constant blanket of traffic smothering most other sounds, those that survive, cut through, harsh and strong. Distant ambulances and police cars clearing the path in front of them. The bus was leaving Clifden. To find an American departure that was in anyway similar you would have to have gone to Oregon or Washington State and Ernie was acutely aware. Ryder had loosened the exhaust to create a distraction and

Ernie wanted to be sure there was no side effects. Purposely sitting towards the rear he cringed every time the exhaust dipped and he heard something in the distance. Up close noise was okay, they do have ambulances in Ireland, but in the far west sound doesn't travel, the mountains, the trees, the twists and turns in the road killing what little mechanical motion there was after dark. On most nights the wind in the trees and rain on the windows is all you might expect to hear.

Ernie had read that so quiet are the roads in two of the countries of Ireland that an attempt was made to allow drink driving, in fact encourage it. The logic was that enforced temperance had killed life in the traditional village pub and threatened the very core of the Irish way of life. It was argued that the country roads were so empty, a drunk driver was unlikely to cause any damage to anyone other than themselves. It didn't make it as a piece of legislation. It lacked a catchy slogan, he thought, something like 'Country roads, take me almost home . . . .'

Ambient countryside noise would cease to be a big issue after tonight. Belfast, Dublin and then London before several busy European cities. Ngoc and Pang had already sourced some more continental sounding sirens to blend into the Californian evenings that lay beyond day six.

-0-

Ryder eased the coach up the two-lane mountain highway and mile by mile away from the sleeping, but mildly snoring metropolis. The road was already familiar to him through yesterday and the recce trips he'd made to confirm that the destinations were made-to-measure. Much of the area had been quarried, stones crunched up to create the concrete that created the city, so in a strange way the silent mountains were the mother of the sound they'd just tried to disguise and leave.

The Giant's Causeway is a No1 global tourist attraction, but fortunately today, at four in the morning with sunrise a good two and a half hours away, the party had hit on a quiet period. The high mountain air held natural moistness at this time of the night and in it a hint of salty sea-ness. Ryder had rigged a garden spray kit with the nozzle reaching six foot about the bus like a shortwave aerial. A thin tub lead down to a ten gallon plastic barrel attached to a compressor tucked beside the driver's seat. The little engine was overly noisy so when the button was on Ryder preferred to run it with the bus's diesel ticking over. Anyway the compressor drew its power form the cigarette lighter socket and he didn't want to risk a battery failure. The degree of success was dependent on wind conditions, but in the stillness of the quarry little stirred and the bus itself was being slowly dampened in salty water.

The 'atmos kit' in the bus's hold was part of a growing eclectic collection of items. The hold itself looked like a student's closet that had been hurriedly crammed with DIY and sports gear to make the apartment fit for a surprise landlord inspection. There were two more garden sprayers, hand pump action ones, each filled with ordinary water and the nozzles pre-set to long-range. Fired high up into the air, the jet would split and with a gentle rocking of the sprayer, fall like the first splatter of raindrops. Added to the weather machines there were battery powered mini-speakers which could be Blue-toothed into action using sound effects from any of the trio's phones. A large sub-woofer near the hatch was connected to five small Sony speakers that were rather crudely clipped onto and along the roof in a spaced out line. From them the gently rolling sounds of distant waves emerged. They had replaced the bigger Marshall speakers, which were quite frankly, a disaster in waiting. They were not secure enough when in transit and caused the whole body of the bus to vibrate when on. The hold also temporarily contained a Giant's Causeway kit – ten hexagonal paving slabs from a garden center. There were to be lifted out and, at 15kgs a time, placed securely on parent rock. They would not be retrieved, and for years into the future they would become a geological black hole for visiting school groups.

The party walked around feeling the rocks and listening to Millie telling the tale of Finn McCool the Irish giant who built a causeway to Scotland purely to have a bash at a Scottish giant and then thought better of it when he saw him. Academic Arthur J. Hilton couldn't resist displaying his knowledge on the subject, despite being a tad hungover from the night before.

'The Scottish giant used Finn's causeway to come over to Ireland. He was huge and the smaller Finn decided it better to scare him off rather than fight. He climbed into a bed and with his wife's help pretended to be their son. The Scot, Benandonner was his name, took one look at the infant and said "if that's the baby I have no quarrel with the father" he then went back to Scotland ripping up the middle of the causeway as he went to make sure the baby's father wouldn't follow.'

'Is that really true,' said Wayne Kerr, the penultimate sign-up member of the party with a 14 on his shirt. 'Cool, cool story.' Everything was cool to the ex-surfer who was unique amongst the Institute's guests in that he'd self-inflicted his blindness through years of cocaine abuse. 'They don't write legends like that anymore.'

'McCool story,' Protz said with an extra emphasis on the 'cool' from a rock platform some six feet above Kerr's head. For a moment it looked as if, half a step further forward and the portly Protz would tumble on top of the suntanned prune of a Californian.

Millie rushed up and guided Protz to a lower level and safety. 'Seems like that McCool geezer was a quick-thinking conman to pull the wool over Benny McDonald's eyes.'

Protz settled on a large rock and did as many portly people do, sat with his hands entwined across his chest twiddling his thumbs as if it was an athletic achievement, but it was simply because his barreled body made that the only possible form of hand to hand contact. Harley looked at him thinking, at least being that large you can get a decent slogan onto your T shirt, like half of the Ten Commandments, or a recipe.

'Benandonner,' blurted Arthur J, who couldn't ever escape years of marking exam papers.

The party were drawn back towards their waiting transportation by the sound of bobhran music coming from the bus's stereo, an echoic rhythm that bounced off the sides of the quarry walls. It made the most compulsive of soundtracks, but not to the two pairs of fearful eyes looking up from the back windows of an old Chrysler Pacifica. It was a great cross-over to bring up a family and now the owner of the car and of the older pair of eyes had just crossed over the marital touchline and taken down his secretary. The haunting drumming had shocked the tongues out of each other and scrabbling away from decadency they fumbled around gathering their clothing whilst trying to work out what exactly was happening. There was a bus, perhaps twenty people and what seemed like Native

American music. It was four in the morning. Was it a satanic ritual? Whatever, next time he'd fork out for a motel. If this was having an affair, his nerves needed some protection.

The party drove off, the music slowly following, the cross on the side of the bus, freezing in the mind of the disheveled secretary. Mamma had warned her and now Jesus knew. She recalled the story of a deeply puritan family of Cooneyites, an obscure Irish protestant sect, where the eldest daughter carried out a secret liaison with her more elderly boss – in a remote location he turned off the road, turned off the car and in a moment of total ecstasy turned off his heart. Even if, and when, she managed to liberate herself from under him, she hadn't a clue how to drive a car. One imagines that the cell call to get assistance was a gem.

In the Chrysler the secretary adjusted her clothing and re-booted her mind. There would be no motel, no second night. Love is as fickle as raindrop in the wind. One minute you are up there, flying through the atmosphere, the next splat and you are an anonymous part of a puddle, then a stream, then an ocean and then maybe a cloud and a raindrop again.

The coach moved gracefully through the darkness. An hour and three quarters later and about a thousand feet closer to sea level, Ryder pulled through the broken gates of the old mansion, the early morning sun picking out dirty window pane by window pane as it started its daily journey across its south-facing facade. The sun was the house's only visitor. Some said it was the scene of a horrific family murder, some that because of that it was haunted, whatever the stories it had been enough for the considerable house to fall into considerable decay.

'How many of you have heard of The Game of Thrones?' Millie enquired as the bus bumped over discarded brickwork and in and out of dried potholes. It was a book and then a major television series stretching to many series and it was perhaps a modern telling of the types of stories that Finn McCool generated. We're only stopping here to let you stretch your legs, in an hour we have an appointment with the birthplace of the most famous ship in history.'

'Is it Noah's Ark?' The voice was male, from mid bus, but Ernie couldn't pinpoint the source. He chose to ignore it, but did give it a star for its amusement value.

That hour was a very long one for Jack Megaghy, the 55-year-old former dentist from Seattle with teeth so bad you had to wonder how he ever got clients, classic bare-footed cobber's son.

Since he was a kid he had been inspired by all things to do with the Titanic. He'd researched it at length hoping to find some family tie with the 713 survivors. There appeared to be no connection although he did find an aunt who lived in the same street in Queens, New York as a woman who said her stepmother was on board. It was not the stuff to generate a book, but the hook was buried deep into Jack's mind. The 20th Century had turned up more major events in history than any other, yet that one night in April 1912 was a defining moment – it was the human-interest story that had everything, love, greed, ego, envy, heroism, class segregation, gross cowardice. Within an hour he would touch the Titanic's very soul. Almost.

The sign on the fence defiantly said, 'Private Property – Keep Out' but the half ajar gate creaked to fully open as Ryder gave it a gentle nudge with his front fender. A little tired, he'd given up caring for the bus's paintwork. The place seemed familiar and that was because for a movie goer like Ryder it was. The Bethlehem Steel Corporation's former Southwestern Shipbuilding yard was a much-used location for Hollywood productions. Mr and Mrs Smith, Charlie's Angeles, Barbed Wire, Gone in Sixty Seconds, and Live Free or Die Hard had all used the now derelict works and warehouses on Terminal Island.

The sun was now up and doing its Californian best, which on most days is hard to beat. 'Bit chilly earlier, but it's turned out nice,' observed Mette Nielsen, a 36-year-old from Solvang, the small town a whole hour and a half from where she now stood. Of Danish origin Mette was looking forward to day six, Copenhagen and getting that photograph of her to send home. It had escaped Ernie and Co's attention that Mette was from Solvang, the overly cute little Danish community, because if they had noticed it, they wouldn't have planned Day Six around it. That was four days away. In all likelihood had they noticed the link, she would have been bumped off the passenger list as a potential disaster.

Now standing on an abandoned slipway, the party listened to Millie as she unfolded the story of the White Star Line, picking facts out from her iPad as they went. Jack Megaghy assuming the role of subject matter expert and trumping any Arthur J facts in the process. Upset at being reduced to a secondary level of knowledge, Arthur J comforted himself by thinking this was more hobbyist than the serious subject matters he normally lectured on. Ernie and Ryder meanwhile had taken the larger mobile 'atmos speakers' into the shell of an old welding building. They pumped out the noise of heavy machinery bringing the factory back to life for the first time in over thirty years – it was a sound mixture of atmos and commentary, the sort you get in exhibitions. The party would wander through the building and then onto the bow section of an old coaster left high and very dry in a dock. It's life story was one of taking goods and people to the islands off the LA coast, but for a few brief minutes it would become the Nomadic, the feeder vessel that took the First Class and Second Class passengers on their last journey from Cherbourg to the waiting Titanic. The Third-Class passengers, as Millie explained, were ferried out in a smaller less luxurious vessel with a very un-early 20th century name, Traffic, along with all the baggage. 'Please don't wander off, the vessel is still in the process of being restored.'

The questions flowed and Millie skillfully dealt with them with a combination of some basic notes she'd written and quickly searching on the Internet. There was also the odd bluff or two. On several occasions Megaghy chipped in and for ten minutes held the whole party in rapture with his description of the last moments of that April night. It was a magical experience which lifted the few blonde hairs on Rooster's neck up. Surreal, everything about the environment was foreign, nobody had the remotest connection with the tragedy yet the moment was tangible. They don't write disasters like the Titanic anymore.

Tour over, the party scrambled back into the bus and it left, Ryder stopping outside the gates to haul them back to nearly shut – he figured they might need the location again so there was no point tempting the responsible agents to put a chain lock on the gates. The LA traffic was up and about and the journey back to HBO took well over an hour – 'Belfast's bigger than I thought,' commented Arthur J stepping onto the sidewalk stretch in Set A. Millie replied, 'not really, it's just because of a traffic accident we were diverted, not once but twice. It's just been identified as Britain's most traffic-tied city.'

The walk from the bus to the Crown Bar was a short one. Out of a side door in Set A and across to a side door in Set C. The furnishings had been moved around and the party came at the bar they'd sung in the previous night when in Clifden, but from a totally different angle.

Ernie stepped forward. Amidst the hum of bar chat, he asked for everyone's attention. The FX continued humming in the background as he did the first of a series of headcounts. 'Please raise your hand as I call out your tour number . . . one, two, three . . .' he went as the party smoothly anticipated their moment to raise an arm. How much easier was that than calling out names he thought?

'And now another chance to raise an arm, if you want. We have a dining choice tonight. Would you like to eat here, I believe it is an Ulster Fry followed by apple tart, that's a thin version of a pie to you guys, or would you like to eat back at the hotel. It's democratic, the majority decides. So who wants to eat here?'

Slowly three and then four hands were raised, including that of Protz.

'Okay, ten, so it is here,' he announced as the majority of the party shrugged off the disappointment. The Ulster Fries, or the closest they could get were already at the front gate – a mixture of bacon, sausages, toasted soda bread, hash browns instead of potato bread and an ominous dark something, the black pudding – an essential element mad of blood and traditionally moved to the side of the plate and left there. It was minus the eggs. The eggs would be fried to order by Ngoc on a small double ringed camping stove behind the bar.

'I just want to get to bed,' Miss Little announced.

'Don't worry we won't be long, we understand it has been a tiring day for you,' said Ernie.

'But good,' Megaghy threw in to the general agreement of those around him. They spontaneously clapped.

From behind the bar and with a line of settling Guinness in front of him, Ernie looked to Rooster. The sort of look that said, 'hell shit, we must be doing something right.' Her looked reply was "hard feckin' work, but it feels good."

'Anyone for a Guinness?' he announced and several of the party stumbled and felt their way through a maze of barstools towards Ernie's voice. The Guinness was from cans and had to be poured outside and quite a distance away to kill the tell-tale sound of the released hiss. The pouring of Guinness in Ireland is not a job, it is an art-form. The barstools, like all furniture, had become vital aids in blocking off no-go areas. Beyond them the stage ended and an excursion into the world of pain. 'What if?' was a constant worry for Ernie. What if someone needed hospitalization? How would they cover their tracks? In the meantime he continued to produce Guinness and for the first time in this entire exercise, and possibly his life, displayed an ounce of consideration for those he was now responsible for. He looked at the dark cloudy greyness as it separated and settled into a sharp black and cream. What a pity he thought, what a pity these people cannot enjoy even this one simple pleasure of looking at the world's most beautiful drink. He reached out across the bar and put one in front of Harley.

23.
A DENT IN THE PLANS

Set B, Typhoon Studios - Belfast

Night two after day three away from Kingman and the party had all been shuffled into different rooms. Ngoc and Pang had pretty well had the day off once they'd moved the suitcases from room to room according to the plan that was on the doors and matched up with the large numbers on the luggage. Looking at the itinerary gaps in their duty schedule was something that Ernie had noted and he was considering taking the risk of bringing them more out into the open, possibly even having them on board some of the excursions. Their ability for stealth was quite remarkable. No wonder Ngoc's forbearers won that war.

With the sound of increasing slumbering echoing down the halls, Ernie and the two R's were taking a break in the large reception area and deciding who would do the first watch. Their low-key, low-level chat was interrupted by Ernie's cell as it rumbled on the glass coffee table. From departure all their phones had been on silent when they were within half a mile of the tourists. The name on the screen caused Ernie to snatch at his breath. He caught it again, took another to settle and pressed the dot at the bottom of the screen.

'Ernest Zimmerman'

'Hi Zimmerman, how goes it?' said Dent.

'We're enjoying all the delights the Emerald Isle can give us, the party are now in their rooms, exhausted after two day's traveling and,' he hesitated over the word sightseeing, 'days full of experiences.'

'No, problems?' said Dent who just wanted to hear what he was hearing. For him and his curvy assistant there were just six days before they departed for him to 'help' for a solo day at the end of their week-long tour. Dent didn't want any issues arising that might disrupt both their passionate itinerary and rock hard alibis. He too realized that an unhappy or sick traveler could just wreck everything.

'None whatsoever,' Ernie replied to Dent's relief and he delivered the good news across the desk to Swallow with an uncharacteristic uncool gesture, a raised thumb.

'What's the time with you and how's the weather?

Ernie glanced at the wall the first of three clocks, under one it said LA, under the middle one Kingman and under the third it simply had "HERE" written in large letters. It was the only clock that would change, moving an hour forward when the party 'arrived' in Denmark and it would stay that way until the end of the trip. Kingman needed its own clock because it was in the Mountain Timezone. When Ryder put them on the wall in March it differed from LA by an hour.

What Ryder had failed to notice was that Arizona doesn't use or need Daytime Saving, so when the coastal states moved their clocks forward a month later they came in line with Kingman. The clocks read 14:14, 14:14, 22:14. The extra clock Ernie, pragmatic as ever, pointed out would be useful if they took another trip in late November. Anyway, it wasn't worth taking back to the store and it would probably help in the time transition he planned for the latter part of the adventure when the European Experience moved south of the Alps.

'It's a little after ten in the evening. Weather-wise we've had a fairly warm day, a bit misty at the beginning. They seem pretty lagged so wanted to crash out.' He held back from mentioning the pints of Guinness consumed in case there was a medical or even a puritanical backlash. Dent's coldness could cover so many traits. He could be religious, some kind of fanatic, or both.

'I'll experience that next week, so I've planned a couple of days to readjust and I've a conference to go to in Barcelona before I catch up with you in Rome.'

The very thought of it caused Ernie to shudder, he hated the word catch and in response he offered a very weak 'Okay, looking forward, must go now, things to attend to before tomorrow,' and sat down.

'Fine, I'll be in contact,' said Dent as the screen hesitated and then restored the home page. The word contact caused another shudder. And a further shudder for the use of 'I'. Had things changed? I was much more dangerous than we.

The cell phone has been the driver of the biggest social change in the history of communication. With the traditional phone you knew exactly where the end of the line, and the caller, were placed. With the cell the opportunity for mischief is unleashed by freedom of movement, but curtailed by the trackable trail you leave behind. In Kingman Dent marveled at the cleanness of the sound over all those miles; in Burbank Ernie thought of the number of people whose torrid hidden lives had been exposed by the smartness of the phones. Affairs blasted open, jobs lost by over robust messaging, families ripped apart by truths exposed. The cell phone is a loaded gun. Its main casualties domestic bliss.

Ernie's rang again. A very different tone. He picked it up to see a request for a FaceTime connection. This was not the time to show his face. He ignored it.

Again it rang. A familiar tone, a familiar name.
'Forgot to mention,' Dent started, 'can you send some photographs. Relatives have been asking.'

'Sure thing, pretty busy, but I'll ask one of the team to see if she can get them to you.'

'Excellent. By the way just tried you on FaceTime.'

'Oh did you,' Ernie replied in surprise.

'Suspect it is the coverage over there.'

'Suspect you are right, it isn't great on my phone, just one dot, talk later,' Ernie clicked the screen for the second time in as many minutes.

He looked up to find Rooster already looking at him.

'One of my team, she,' Rooster looked at Ryder and back to Ernie, 'suspect, that's me.'

'But FaceTime, what a bummer that could be. Just don't answer any requests unless the location you are in is perfectly anonymous or generic. We can do the photos, they may be awkward, but at least we have some control.'

Ernie smiled to reassure them he himself was in control and the smile expanded as Rooster explained that she'd seen this coming. She went into side storeroom and emerged a minute later with a large circular black bag. Bigger than a bicycle wheel it was the thickness of the world's biggest pizza, only black and made of cloth. She unzipped 180 degrees of the bag and pulled out a second bit of cloth, only this time vivid blue. She let go of one part of the supporting frame and the whole thing wildly went out of control before settling into a huge oval the size of a dining table, blue on one side, green on the other.

'Chroma key,' she said, 'with this, my camera, Google Images and Photoshop I can make you travel the world.'

'Rooster,' Ernie said, 'I do love you.'

Ten minutes, a lot of laughter, cursing and sore wrists, the two meter wide Chroma-key was bent and buckled and finally back in its black sack. It was like trying to force the genie back into the lamp. But it could conjure up illusions, it was magic in a bag.

'I suspect there's a technique,' Ryder muttered before offering to take the first six-hour shift of the night.

24.
POUNDS AND CROWNS

Set C Typhoon – Belfast hotel

Day four away from St Anthony's started with a breakfast not dissimilar to the dinner the night before, but without the huge steak fries. Ernie had promised the Land of Fries and Ryder had delivered. Contrasting meals styles were the key to the feeling of change. Here little had come out of anything other than a frying pan, the principal work tool of the Northern Irish kitchen, but with the addition of orange juice, tea, toast and coffee, a whole new day was set brilliantly in motion.

'There are no quiet days on the European Experience, but this is one of our two international air travel days. We head from here to taste Dublin, and then on to the airport and the London flight,' Ernie announced to the entire breakfasting party. Then added 'What's confusing is we, at some point on the road heading south, switch from miles to kilometers and from pounds back to the Euro. Up to this point you haven't had a real chance to spend any money.'

Ernie was interrupted by several reminders from the tourists that bobhrans and whistles had been bought from Michael. Since they'd left Clifden before he could deliver, they'd neither received, or paid for them, in pounds, euros, or dollars.

'Yes, Michael said he would get them sent to the Irish tourist office at the airport and we could pick them up there. Regarding payment, there is a delivery charge, but if the

European Experience pays and then you pay us in dollars, there will be no delivery charge.'

Money wasn't something that the EE team had really properly thought out. They assumed that the party had little need for it when in St Anthony's and probably didn't have credit cards.

'How many of you have credit cards with you?' Ernie asked.

All of the hands went up.

'Fine, since there are only several of you it is perhaps best that we take away the need for changing from euro to pound to euro to pound to kroner, to euro, to zloty, to euro. It would be financial chaos. We can run a tab, similar to the one we have for drinks and extras. Millie here will respond to all your shopping needs and keep a cash log book with the daily rate alongside. Ask at any point and she'll tell you where you are. We can tally up at the end. We will always seek the best exchange rate. Good idea, all happy.'

No one was happier than Ernie, a huge potential pitfall removed with no likelihood of someone visiting a cashpoint in 'Berlin' and receiving dollars and their family back home a transaction slip for a withdrawal somewhere in downtown LA.

As Ernie spoke Rooster logged on and searched, her curiosity pricked and driven by the fear that any minute one of the party would ask what did the Euros look like. She knew she could lie, but already she felt responsible for her charges and they deserved the truth. She took grabbed snapshots of sterling, the Euros and the Danish Kroner, which turned out to be the simplest of the currencies, as it was uniform. The zloty she'd ignore since the Polish part of the trip was no more than a brief detour.

The Euro notes were the same across the entire continent, but the coins differed from country of origin. The notes she found out were made of cotton and she decided to try and get the hold of some as an additional prop. It would be nice for them to feel, to have a Euro Experience she'd tell Ernie later. In the United Kingdom the notes were also standard, but because the Scots and Northern Irish can print their own, there was a miss-mash of color and design with the Queen not always featuring. What was novel was that across Britain and Europe the notes differed in size, the larger the note the greater the value. It had always been so. The Europeans are such a logical bunch of miss matches. Rooster wondered why the dollar was such a sight-driven currency. It smacked of a lack of care. How did a blind person differentiate between a one and a fifty? She asked the party.

'We fold them differently,' Wilcox perked up. 'At St Anthony's they've a small shop, cigarettes, candies, cds and bottom range perfumes. We can buy what we like. We have a common system, the dollar bill is never folded, the $5 lengthwise, the $10 width and the $20 length and width. We don't use anything bigger. Like I said, the perfume is cheap.'

He moved towards Rooster and sniffed. 'Millie, Obsession'

She jumped back, 'what?'

'Calvin Klein, Obsession.'

Angry at her knee-jerk reaction, Rooster, smiled and conceded that he'd got her latest purchase in one.

'Very good Mr Wilcox, bang on the money.'

'I think you'd need at least two folded length and width-wise for that one,' he chirped back.

'$40, you'd get two unfolded back, I got it Duty Free,' she replied.

The party of fourteen damaged, one trapped, two fugitives and three manipulating souls was starting to mold into a group. It was a development that caused Ernie mixed feelings. It was good to feel comfortable, but they should never relax. Taking the foot off the accelerator and eye off the road is when accidents happen.

Harley looked on as only he could. Behind the thick-rimmed Ray-Bans his eyes were filled with a new torment. This lovely lady, he'd heard her called upon to do different roles, but she was changing more than her name and her perfumes. She was an object of raw beauty. Each day her smile grew more genuine and caring, each day for Harley she grew from an obstruction into an obsession, and not the Calvin type. He didn't know how much longer he could hold back. What was worse he had no idea how to break free from the illusion that trapped him. He felt like a counterfeit bank note. One day somebody would notice and he'd be taken out of circulation.

'Can I feel a new five pound note?' chirped up Jankowski. 'I heard they are made of plastic.'

The trio froze. The request melted. The tour moved on.

-0-

Bags packed and left outside their rooms, the party had made it down to the reception area, which was beside a lobby area beside a restaurant, beside a kiosk. Set B was a busy place. The clocks on the wall behind a long, raised desk read 00:20, 00:20, 08:20. Outside the clear night sky had brought the temperature down to 14, a reasonable spring morning for Belfast. Within 12 hours it would be kissing 30 and if things went to plan they'd be back in HBO in time to disguise the Irish heatwave. The decision to see all temperatures in Celsius, was an early decision to confuse Kingman yet add a touch of Euro realism. The only events outside today were a proposed walk through St Stephen's Green, a tour of Temple Bar and crossing the River Liffey on the Halfpenny Bridge. The Guinness Tour had been voted off the itinerary in preference to just drinking it.

The plan was drive south through LA for about two hours, then loop round to end up near the Union Bank Plaza. At three in the morning it would be nearly deserted. There were green spaces, water and they could decide which of the raised pedestrian-ways, pedways, would best become the famed Halfpenny Bridge over the River Liffey. As a late additional precaution, Ngoc and Pang had been elevated from illegal immigrants to a mini Hollywood crew. Wearing vests and carrying a camera and lights borrowed from Charles, they would alter the identity of the party from 'what the hell's going on here?' to 'Oh it is just another B crew picking up shots.' They would also be carrying the mini 'atmos' speakers. Ngoc and Pang were having the time of their lives.

For the first time since leaving Kingman the party were asked to dress in something of their own choosing. To any late night onlookers, it was after all, a movie shoot. The ward-off T-shirts and sweaters with their 'experiment' warning and worn for three days, had gone to the wash. It was an all-round good solution. Some of the tourists were beginning to leave a vapor trail.

The Temple Bar tour remained a problem. They had trawled the Internet and there were numerous Irish bars to be found, but none that stayed open beyond 2am. The simple reason being that hip LA just doesn't flutter to a halt at two, it slams itself shut, mostly by law

The benefit for Ernie and his team was the relative freedom to roam about at what was mid-morning to mid-afternoon European time, the disadvantage being that when you needed a bar scene you had to be back in the studio. With a map and a limp you can make it on foot from the Halfpenny Bridge to Temple Bar in 20 minutes, but somehow they had to get back to HBO, potentially some 45 minutes away. The solution was to go on a mini historical tour with Millie highlighting half a dozen moments in Irish history – the Easter Rising at the Post Office, the blowing up of Nelson's Pillar in O'Connell Street, the Guinness Brewery, Joyce's home, the warehouse where they shot Roddy Doyle's Commitments, Croke Park, home of Gaelic Football and then Temple Bar, a walk round an old outdoor set at Typhoon, a drink in Set C and then back on the bus for forty minutes before arrival at Set A to prepare for embarkation and the one-hour flight to London. It was all talk no action. 'As easy as pissing and writing your name in snow,' Ernie remarked. Rooster looked at him, 'not for me, and one who has to do all the talking for three hours!'

25.
BURNING ISSUES

Set A – Aer Lingus Dublin to London

They'd passed through customs and three of the tourists had received questions and warnings about hand luggage and the bobhrans they now proudly possessed. Tour chameleon Rooster, in a further development of her characters, offered to store them safely; the mad un-rhythmic beatings from the new drummers causing her to curse Michael's talent, not musical, but sales. The whistles too were an issue, but telling the tuneless musicians that other passengers were complaining usually quelled that tide of enthusiasm. But tides do come back. Only Harley had seemed to pick up anything like a tune, perhaps because through his sunglasses he could still read the finger patterns on the back of the whistle's hard plastic-wrap pack. 'Will Ye Go Lassie Go', a Scottish lament simple enough to sound like something, even if your timing was dubious or your fingers got into a muddle.

'Where did you pick that up Harley?' Rooster enquired. A little perturbed that he'd blown the cover he so wanted to blow, he said he had 'eyes for darkness, ears for music and lips for kissing.' He paused a moment and added slightly under his breath, 'lied about one.' Rooster did a quick calculation with little chance of getting it right.

Back on board the fuselage in Set A the party had been seated in B, C and D, E as a variation allowing for cross aisle communication. The flight to London would take them to

Heathrow and an adjoining hotel and there would be no need for coach transport until the next morning when they would be driven around the city with several notable stop-off points. Afternoon tea at Fortnum and Masons promised to be a highlight. Rooster was already on the case having found table settings from a Victorian period drama that included three-teared cake stands. In the fridge there were about 20 plastic see-through packages with a variety of sandwiches, in pairs. These would be cut into delicate triangles. English afternoon tea is a triumph of presentation over content. Researching it she'd found that there were two schools of thought, triangles versus soldiers, the straight cut fingers. She'd remembered the conversation from the previous day about distinguishing between dollar bills. Unable to find pre-made cucumber sandwiches she had opted to make them herself, cutting the crust-less squares of pan bread into three long fingers so the guests could easily select them if they wanted. Was she turning soft? There was no doubt that the harsher Rooster was taking a back seat, but she was not a new person, it was just that the current environment had brought the best out of her - there was a lot to bring.

Finding cupcakes that were small enough to match the refined appearance that the tea required was a greater problem. She'd planned to cut brownies into quarters and find some mini-muffins and then joy of joys she stumbled upon the British Wholesale Imports company over at Westlake Village. It wasn't quite what she had in mind, but the store offered treats that would sustain the party in raptures for their entire time in England. Biscuit tins in the shape of London buses, mustard to take the top off your mouth, British chocolate, Scottish shortbread, HP sauce, and then a tarlike substance you spread on toast just so you can talk about the single greatest divider of British public opinion. Not whether they should be or not be a

181

part of Europe, was Diana's death really an accident or where the Stones a greater contribution to modern culture than The Beatles, but do you love or hate Marmite? Unlike the other queries, there is no middle ground.

Rooster, organized as ever, had taken a corner of Set C as a storage area, but this had developed into a studio feature and along with specialist goods from Denmark, Germany, Italy and France had become a mini-mart. Ernie had cringed at the cost, but the snacks and treats had a dual value since the party could use the mart as a walk-through as an add-on to the coffee shop or the main reception. It even could double as Duty Free if necessary and all the time it would be readily available to fill a void or create a taste diversion. 'Have you tried these, you must, they are a local delicacy,' words that Ernie noted, were the most dangerous phrase in travel.

-0-

Back in the real world, LA, some yobs had opted to borrow a car to get to near home, sort of Uber, but without the driver. Not home all the way, because that would have been too much of a giveaway. The car they abandoned close to home on a quiet unmarked road. Not knowing who owned it, often not even taking notice of the make or model, on this occasion they would seal the anonymity by torching it as a nice gesture of thanks for borrowing and then set off on foot. The torching was necessary because one of the party had experimented with too many cocktails and had dispensed his DNA all over the back seat. The perimeter road was a back entrance to Typhoon for heavy vehicles carrying props and scenery that couldn't cope with the sharp turn at the main gate. There were several abandoned burnt-out wrecks, apparently fairly regularly they struggled to hold on to their drinks. So frequently in fact that they referred to the whole procedure as 'taking a Zippo'. The new glow developed along the back seat and then into bang as the gas tank exploded.

The bang was loud enough to break through the heavy drone of the sound FX in the fuselage. It was a 'what was that sound?' not a 'what the fuck was that sound?' and only two of the passengers noticed it and without comment. A potential unseen crisis over. Or maybe not.

The car had a set of extra tires in the trunk and when the resulting blaze broke through the back seat and popped the latch, it sent up what looked like a black tornado. That itself was not an issue for the travelers currently in mid-flight, but the wind was blowing the tower of smoke directly towards Set A and Wilcox was, not surprisingly, the first to pick up the scent.

'Burning, I smell something burning,' he said in a remarkably cool manner. It was as if he wanted to diagnose it further and be first with a precise conclusion. 'I smell rubber.'

That was enough to trigger moderate hysteria amongst several of the passengers, most noticeably Protz and Perry, neither of whom found the concept of flight an easy one to grasp. Not unexpectedly since they were amongst a minority at St Anthony's in that they had been blind from birth. A car they could understand because they could walk round it, sit in it and feel it and the wheels seemed a logical option to move it, but they'd never quite understood how tons of steel could suddenly go up in the air and stay there. They were not alone.

Several shouted out that they smelt something and it woke Ryder from his catnap and brought Rooster down the aisle.

They were right something did smell of burning rubber. Ryder stepped off the fuselage and picked up a lip mike and said.

'Co-pilot here, you may have noticed a smell of rubber. Nothing to worry about, all is ok up here in the cockpit. We think it is something in the air con, but relax we'll be down on the ground shortly.'

'It's how we get down onto that ground that worries me,' Protz shouted not helping the situation. Ryder continued to do a quick inspection inside Set A and then stepped out, saw the glow, the pall of smoke and put two and two together. In the meantime Rooster had tried to neutralize the smell and situation by spraying some perfume in the air. That failing, when she heard from Ryder what the true source was, she rushed back to the small galley and threw a rubber glove into the microwave, pressed 90 at full and searched for some tongs. She then entered the main cabin and announced that it was all her fault, she'd put a rubber glove in the micro by mistake, and she wafted it around to create both proof and a stronger smell than the grand auto thieving Zippos had managed.

The party settled back into an uneasy mood and Ryder pressed the pre-recorded captain's message from Ernie announcing the near immediate arrival.

The landing at Heathrow was a bumpy affair with several shrieks from the passengers. It was Ngoc's first go at the hydraulics and, all in all, considering his previous biggest mechanical achievement had been mastering a scooter carrying 15 chickens in cages, quite laudable. But they were down. Ryder had moved a high-level walkway normally used by the lighting technicians to the rear port door of the fuselage. In Ireland they had deplaned using exterior steps, but hey this

184

was London, they needed covered walkways and with the smoke outside, staying inside was an extra bonus. Using a guide rail they trickled up the slight incline to a viewing gallery and then into the second-floor office complex. Here in groups of five they were escorted up and down corridors until it was deemed far enough to have reached customs. That was the booth down on the first floor of Set B. Inside was Ernie and behind it Ngoc and Pang who each sat in the driver positions of two battery-powered passenger assist carts. They'd noticed them two days earlier parked behind Typhoon's reception, presumably for the exclusive use of visiting VIPs or saving actor's legs. Consequently they weren't used a lot and the batteries had to be put on trickle-charge for a day.

'Will you please wait here and the transport will come back for you, it will take you to your hotel reception,' said Rooster in a mildly acceptable English accent. Was there anything she couldn't do thought the customs officer, who was also a pilot, barman, tour organizer, wine grower and potentially a father confessor.

The party was broken up into small groups and they were driven from Set B, briefly out into the open air and round to Set C where they could put their feet up and wait for the rest of the party. The problem here was that Ernie only had a matter of minutes between checking the last passport at HM Customs before he needed to pick up the whole of the party in Set C to get them back to B and hotel reception. He made a mental note to re-instate the bus as the preferred method of transporting the tourists from plane to terminal to hotel by the time they got to Copenhagen. That appointment was three very long days away.

Gathered together in C, Ernie did a quick headcount. Fourteen! One missing, but who? Without their numbered sweatshirts the process of elimination was considerably hampered. He detailed the two R's to make sure the fourteen found their rooms, but first he called for a mathematical count. Jack Megaghy started with his number one followed by Miss Little and so it moved up to Vernon at ten and Harley at 11. Then it stopped.

'Number 12?' Ernie said, eyes flashing across the room. 'Number 12?' in a weakening plea.

Rooster had the list in her hand.

'Miss Sander,' she said in a strong stage whisper.

Ernie picked it up and repeated it so it filled the entire studio. He repeated it three times before he realized that he was transferring his anxiety to the remaining party.

'Not to worry, suspect she's gone to the restroom,' he said waving at Ngoc to check it out, but the Vietnamese's English couldn't workout what he was on about and he stood smiling at Ernie with the helpless expression of a third violinist with a broken string looking at the conductor in mid-symphony.

Ryder picked up the instruction and quickly did a restroom check, when he returned Rooster ran up and around the offices that were now bedrooms in Set B; the doors were all open which meant she had to poke her head into every room. She returned to find Ernie a little stressed but trying to cover it over by explaining that after a brief rest in their rooms they would be called to dinner, here in the hotel.

The two R's started the settling in process as Ernie grabbed Ngoc and Pang and desperately tried to convey that they needed to find a lady. The two Asians, bewildered by the event, just nodded and smiled.

'I want to find lady, please yes,' said Pang.

Ernie turned his back on them, threw his hands in the air and set off on a one man, one woman search. There was no sign of her at Set A and as he moved into Set B he realized that there were several of the party he couldn't put a face or name to, or in some cases both. Ms Sander was one.

The clocks on the wall read, 11:20, 11:20, 19:20, it was approaching the hottest part of the day, if she's not in the building where could she be thought Ernie, his shirt now stained with the exertion. He heard a cough and turned to see Ngoc smiling at him; he was about to lose it, when Ngoc did a half turn and pointed out the window. In the distance there was an old western façade with all the traditional fronts, from saloon to jail, grocery store to undertakers. About twenty buildings in total, all with roofs for cowboys to stand up, grasp their chests and roll off into the street onto an airbag. On a raised wooden sidewalk, leaning against a post, was a blonde headed woman, or boy. It was over 300 yards away and the person was in denims, fittingly for the cowboy nature of the setting.

Ernie jumped into the electric cart. He didn't drive bigger things, but had found the device designed to take the exercise out of golf, wasn't that difficult. He turned the key, pulled the lever on the steering wheel, hit the thinner of the two pedals on the floor with his foot and reversed back into a large trash bin. Maybe I should have pushed it he thought, turned a switch from R to F and grabbing the lever again and he set off in the direction of the one-dimensional Tombstone.

Sander looked up at the approaching noise as Ernie tried to work out what she held in her arms. It was the missing Miss for he now recognized her. In his life he'd been in a number of police identity line-ups and thought it easy to be on the other side of the glass. He was having a brief re-think before he pulled the cart to a relatively smooth halt. He got out.

'Miss Sander, we thought we'd lost you, we were a little worried.'

'I didn't know that I'd wandered, I was listening to music and suddenly I felt alone. I shouted and there was no response apart from this little thing.' She tilted her head down to her arms that held a purring cat.

'I shouted out European Experience and she replied. I've called her Europuss.'

'How do you know it is a she?' Ernie said anxious to build on a second scenario and get as far away from the obvious western scene they stood in. This was just too wildly west for West London. Would Ms Sander question the London sidewalks or footpaths, not for their labelling, but for being made of wood. But no, her mind was on the feline.

'If it had been a boy it wouldn't have talked to me, they never do.'

Ernie smiled a sympathetic response that he realized was lost on her so he added the line, 'I'm sure that's not the case. Shall we say goodbye to kitty? She won't be allowed in the hotel.'

'It's a pity, she's been in a fight, bit of her left ear is ripped. But I suppose so,' Sander replied, 'I like animals,' and placing the cat on the ground said, 'Goodbye Europuss.'

Ernie gently led the 32-year-old to the cart and they sent off back to Set C. Europuss, did a euro piss and licked where his balls used to be before deciding to follow the nice lady. Halfway across the lot he gave up, lay in the sun for five minutes and then returned to Tombstone.

26
PRIDE AND NO PRESSED JUICE

Set C, Typhoon Studios – The Stag Bar, London

The party, now reunited, enjoyed dinner at the hotel and retired, again it had been a long day. From one of the rooms the sound of a bobhran drummed a not unattractive beat. It was picked up by another and then another until four of the five were giving a free concert. Harley had the fifth one, but he resisted the temptation and returned to the reception area driven by a greater temptation and if that failed to materialize, maybe a beer. Rooster was alone cleaning up the plates, putting them into plastic box racks for them to be cleaned down in the canteen area which boasted a huge industrial dishwasher.

'Shit,' she muttered as the remainder of someone's steak and kidney pie tipped onto her white blouse. She looked up as Harley carefully navigated with the help of a stick his way into the restaurant and bar area.

'Sorry,' she said, 'just spilled something on my top.' With one movement she unbuttoned the three top catches and slipped it off and over her head. She wasn't hugely breasted, just perfect he thought, the black bra doing the job it was designed to do.

Harley tried desperately to control his head, neck and loin movements. Two out of three wasn't bad he thought considering the sight that smoldered in front of him totally unaware of the display she was putting on.

'Harley, isn't it? Can I get you anything?' then a pause as she waited for a reply, 'Orange juice, beer?'

He struggled but managed to get the word beer out thinking the performance deserved something stronger than an OJ. Rooster turned to the glass-fronted cooler at the back of the set bar. On the side of the door magnetic flags indicated the origins of the beers inside, stacked in rows.

'English, Danish, French, they've even got American.'

'When in Rome.'

'I'm not sure we have Italian,' she said before she realized. 'Got you, London Pride, or Tetleys, or Suffolk Ale, or . . .'

'When in Rome,' Harley repeated.

'London Pride it is,' said Rooster happy that that was his choice since it was in a bottle and she felt that opening a can in a bar was un-natural.

'Do you get much call for American beers over here,' Harley asked, unable to resist the tease. After all she was teasing him to distraction.

It was a distraction due to come to an end as she went to a corner of the studio and returned pulling a sweatshirt over her. Harley wasn't the only one sad to see the end of the unwitting performance. In their control room, Ngoc and Pang had been viewing it on the cctv screen.

'Lady shit,' said Ngoc as he turned to Pang. He was up to three hundred and one words.

27.
MUCH ADO ABOUT ENGLAND

Typhoon Studios, LA – London bus tour

The English Experience was due to stretch over three days. After London the party would move to the Midlands and the birthplace of Shakespeare where they would have a picnic lunch at an open-air performance of Much Ado About Nothing. That was to be followed by a drive further north to the birthplace of those other great British bards, the Beatles. The Cavern and leaving Liverpool for Copenhagen via John Lennon Airport, from Love Me Do to Imagine. There promised to be no problem with the soundtrack. Except that Ngoc or Pang had never heard of the Fabulous Four.

But first there was the historical coach trip around the capital in a big red London bus, not that the color mattered. You can pick-up just about anything in LA, and then buy the cure for most of them. It only took one phone call and a bit of convincing about the unsocial hours to book a proper London bus. It was even red. The pick-up point was agreed as the Robin Hood British Pub on Burbank Boulevard. The tourists were to have a late brunch breakfast there at 1am local, followed by a five-hour trip around the city. Although the iconic Routemaster bus would come with a driver, there would be no night/day off for Ryder. He was to follow in the Hallelujah Choir bus to provide FX atmosphere and just to be on hand should the need arise, which they already knew would be at precisely 4am local time.

The route was to start at an early morning market pub, the Robin Hood and to take in the south of the river crossing Tower Bridge disembarking to walk around the walls of the Tower of London. Then a spot of shopping in Selfridges, which bore a striking resemblance to the 24hr Walmart on Sunset, down to Westminster to hear Big Ben strike twelve times and on to Buckingham Palace. In the evening they would take in a show.

Rooster had had the presence of mind to do some pre-planning. Using Typhoon Studios as a leaver she'd rung both Harrods and Selfridges to get them to send over some bags for a movie about an English model trying to break into Hollywood. With an assurance of preview approval and that the model was not playing the role of a hooker, both companies had dispatched enough bags to start an outlet store. She'd got the idea of the bags from an article about Japanese tourists in London. Strapped for time, not cash, they arrive and do a tour not dissimilar to the one planned by Ernie. It was remarkably similar for although the Japanese could see, they never saw the prestige stores. Arriving at breakfast in London and due in Paris for dinner they didn't have time to stop by Harrods, Burberry, Selfridges or anywhere else with a nice label. So, some enterprising guy got the franchise to move all the small-sized raincoats, light sports gear and handbags, along with a delicatessen and a whisky outlet, to a one-stop location in Hanover Square. They are in and out in a flash. It is the shopping equivalent of a Formula One wheel change.

Although shopping wasn't a big wish for the party, the odd green Harrods or yellow Selfridge bag lying about in homeward bound luggage was a subtle confirmation that they'd been somewhere. Now with Dent's request for photographs they would be extra precious. Rooster had packed the Chroma key along with several powerful LED lights – the secret of making it work was to have the background as clean as possible and for that you needed no shade changes or shadows. If it failed or they hadn't time on this expedition, she'd get the party into a pre-lit part of the studio and somehow concoct a reason why they should pose in various positions.

-0-

Back in the Union Bank Plaza area there was a strange 'Groundhog Day' feeling for the couple cuddling on the same bench as they did each night after their bar shifts had ended and before they headed home to their respective partners. The number of people seemed the same, the camera team were the same, but the dialogue, what little they had picked up from a distance on the previous occasion, was very different. Stories of Vikings, giants and great writers had been replaced by Romans, jewels and grotesque public punishment. Whatever the film, when it came out, they'd take the time off the bench to catch it, if only to work out what they were on about.

'Harrods' was blissfully empty, although Protz was disappointed in the layout of the food section. He'd heard of the tiled floors and walls and glass-fronted cabinets and his nose had drawn him to the cheese section. It seemed as spacious as he'd expected. He was eager to have some White Stilton Gold, at $420 a pound he was very keen to have just a couple of ounces, grams even, maybe thirty bucks worth, so he could say he'd had it, but after some ten minutes none of the famed Harrods service had materialized. In front of him the combined cost of the cheese might have bought little more than a few ounces of the precious White Gold. Rooster spotted Protz and moved in to ease the wheels.

'I've been here since I came in, not a soul, is this British service at its best?' he announced as one of the few local shoppers passed. Protz explained his needs to Millie. 'It says closed due to a refrigeration problem,' she offered.

'But I can smell the cheeses, surely if the fridge has gone they wouldn't leave them out.'

'What is it you are looking for?'

'White Stilton Gold – one of the world's most expensive cheeses, I just wanted a slither.'

Rooster looked around, Walmart apparently didn't stock it. The stock of multi-flavored Cracker Barrel would be a miserable substitute. She hadn't time or she would have mentioned the omission at the customer desk. The girl there attending her nails looked like she would immediately locate it, not.

'Maybe we can get a moment to check in Selfridges,' said Rooster as she guided him away and straight into a parked shopping trolley.

'Never imagined they'd use these.'

The shopping opportunity had been close to a disaster, suddenly liberated into too big a space and the party had spread out like mercury spilt on marble. Human nature being what it is had helped avoid moments of contact that could have terminal. The late-night staff were, in the main, shy retiring characters for whom English was not yet a second language, stocking shelves before sunrise because that was all that was on offer. Avoiding answering questions because there were questions they didn't want to answer.

It took twenty minutes, but eventually all the tourists were back on board the big red bus. They had to rush if they were to get down to Westminster in time for Big Ben's busiest time of the day, not that they were ever going to miss it. The distinctive chimes were on a CD waiting to thunder out at the press of a button from the speakers on the top of Ryder's bus.

The driver of the big red bus had taken many parties on many trips, but had never quite had one as strange as this in the middle of the night. But heck he was on double decker double time so why should he care? Parked up on Clyde Avenue, he waited in his cab as the fifteen people were carefully lead off and on to the sidewalk. The pretty female tour guide was giving them a colorful breakdown. He could hear words like gunpowder, Winston Churchill and Queen Elizabeth. He'd been told by the same rather attractive guide to drive to Clyde, but he couldn't work out why since it was blocked off at the eastern end. It was just a typical mid-LA middle-income residential area. Across the road beside a palm tree the strange vehicle that had been following them all night was already parked up waiting, like a sulking child – but it wasn't. It was a bus with a crucifix painted on the side and something about a choir. Somehow there was a connection, but it was neither his job or desire to find it out, heck he was on double. It was not exactly blasting out noise, but from somewhere there was a constant hum of passing traffic that was out of context with the surroundings.

The tour guide pointed to her wrist and the choir bus driver immediately responded by turning his attention to something low down on his dashboard. A huge clang rang out followed by another. The party jumped up and down in excitement and by the seventh clang, lights were starting to come on in the houses scattered amongst the trees. By the eleventh some residents were looking out the windows, but they were well used to odd goings on in LA and since the red bus and the party looked innocuous, they returned to bed, marking it down as yet another B crew catching footage. But that if it happened again, they'd complain.

Even so, Rooster and Ryder didn't want to invite any police attention and as quickly as possible, without seeming hasty, hustled everyone back on board after the twelfth bong and headed off. Somewhere up the road they would repeat the exercise, without the chimes, outside Buckingham Palace as the band of the Guards, passed through the gates. Then it would be goodbye to the red bus and its totally bedazzled driver and back to the studio.

Ernie had booked the viewing theatre for a matinée. Rooster had checked what was on in London that week the list was impressively long, but she'd narrowed it down to three, Guys and Dolls, Les Miserables and Mamma Mia. She'd got hold of all the stage dvds and in a bit of nudging over the past few days had pushed popular opinion towards bouncing along to Abba. It was a good choice for the more songs the better. They would have to be in their seats by just before four.

-0-

The next morning the party set off early at midnight and the busload was in particularly buoyant form. Abba are like a bad head cold, once caught they are the devil to shake off.

Destination, Stratford-Upon-Avon, a little over a hundred miles from London. The bus was heading to Lancaster, California. A shorter journey by about an hour, but by taking Route 5 north and then turning off towards Neenach, Ryder could eek the journey out. Ernie had decided to twin Lancaster with Stratford simply because of its very Englishness of sound. He'd originally marked the Oxford Inn as a possible overnight stay, but it threatened to be too busy. Lancaster would do as a stop off point and its famed poppy park could become Anne Hathaway's garden. The location for their first night away from Set C had to be quieter and more controllable.

Online Rooster found a motel in Rosamund fifteen minutes further north, which had the convenience of being able to accommodate the entire party and was close to the home of the Roadrunners, the local high school baseball team. Since they played their games in the middle of the afternoon, Ernie saw no harm in using the tiny unlocked stadium to put on an open-air performance some hours earlier. The memories of seeing footage of the Beatles at Shea Stadium lingered. Baseball grounds offered a natural American amphitheater, even when it was the Little League. Here it would be a stage performance, just voices recorded at an outdoor venue somewhere by an educational website and offered as a free download, one of Ernie's favorite words, free.

It was midnight in LA as the bus navigated the avenues and minor boulevards parallel to the freeway. The driving experience had to be more staccato, representative of the famed London traffic. The party had got through Waterloo and Thank You for the Music and were now in full flow with Dancing Queen.

The bus pulled up at stop-go lights and waited. A group of middle aged drinkers had emerged from a bar and were looking for transport home when the sound of
'Friday night and the lights are low,
Looking out for the place to go'

cut through the mildly smoked-glass windows.

The drinkers looked at the sun-glassed singers, looked at the signage on the side of the bus and looked at themselves, turned round and went back into the sanctuary of the bar. 'Must be one of those strange new religious sects,' one muttered.

The lights turned low and the music drifted off into the night. Ryder had logged in the final destination into the GPS and muted the sound. The navigation system worked well until on Route 5 it became a bit confused. The silenced lady had recalculated the journey several times asking Ryder to turn around. He couldn't hear her, but the screen kept offering big yellow U turns. He knew that if he ignored her, eventually she'd come around to his way of thinking. That thought was a turn-off about 50 miles out of LA. Thankfully some engineer had the presence of mind to call the tarmacked route, Lancaster Road. If he missed it the next option would be in Bakersfield, another 50 miles north.

On the screen it was more of an intersection than a turning and even if he messed it up, there was no one on board aware of the distances needed to get from London to Stratford to Liverpool. It was just that from an EE scripting point of view it seemed more natural, it helped the trio get into their roles. What was totally unnatural was the timing driving along in the dark just having had breakfast.

Rooster had struck a special rate with the motel in Rosamund. They only needed the rooms early morning to just after lunch – they wouldn't stay the night. They promised to vacate the rooms by 14:30 for they had a long drive in front them. The guy at reception, well used to even shorter daytime bookings, was intrigued. The normal 'quickie' bookings were for one room, here they wanted twelve! He thought, what were they up to, was it a swingers' convention? Rooster had explained that they were a very special group, with special considerations and one of them was absolute privacy. A request that confirmed the arrival of a strange religious sect.

They could have taken the entire motel and booked eighteen rooms, but Ernie had said that he'd prefer, and not for financial reasons, if they could double-up for this one occasion. With two in a room the party would be easier to control; fewer doors to keep an eye on. They'd requested that the rooms would be in the same block.

Strangely it was the first time that the organizing team had to consider the make-up of the party, nine men and six women, a bit of an imbalance which Ernie couldn't work out since he seemed to remember that females dominated at St Anthony's. Perhaps it was the nurses, for it was an optical illusion, there were more male guests at the Institute, a statistic possibly down to the families being more tolerant with quiet ladies than grumpy old men. Or maybe the men had better insurance policies. It was an interesting human equation that he'd look into, but not today.

The party had been told that because of the Shakespeare performance rooms in the town were at a premium and that consequently they would have to 'rough' it for this one night. He asked them to try and settle amongst themselves who they would like to roommate with. In a self-congratulatory way he was pleased with the way they had developed solutions, not into problems, but into situations. Little things that made life easier, like the personal numbers, the warning on the T-shirts, the acceptance of initial financial responsibility for buying souvenirs and taking photographs. To this they had just added the buddy system.

From now on everyone would have a buddy; they would be responsible for each other, checking that they were where they ought to be and that they felt fine. It threatened to make morning get-togethers noisy, but be part of a greater bonding. It was the sort of thing companies pay huge sums for in the name of teambuilding. If Miss Sander had had a buddy maybe she wouldn't have wandered off to the not so OK Coral.

As the bus swept along the smooth highway, Rooster, as Millie, tried to log who was with whom. She started with the ladies who were quite easy. The eldest two, the Misses Little and Temple, were already best friends, and Mette Nielsen and Janne Jankowski we kindred spirits in searching for their genealogical roots. That left the shy cat-loving Jill Sander to team-up with Joyce Reed, a boisterous Afro American lady from somewhere in Florida, but who had travelled the world as a marine before an accident robbed her of her sight. What grated her most was that she'd seen so much action in Afghanistan and Iraq, she might have expected a battle wound and a medal, but her life-change was from a car accident back home on leave.

Jill and Joyce were a bit of a miss-match, but generally Rooster liked the pairings, there was a mild logic to them that would make life easier, age and age, Slovak and Scandi, salt and pepper.

The men were a little trickier to allocate to each other. Former dentist Megaghy and Wayne Kerr, the ex-junkie, were an unlikely match, but they came together because they knew so little of each other, and they were sitting side by side on the bus. Ben Nelson one of the younger members at 26 teamed up with Vernon Wilcox largely because they were also sitting side-by-side and the younger man couldn't get out of it. Protz and Perry came together as the two P's. Back at the Institute they were commonly alphabetically linked. That left Sean Seamus, the loner academic Arthur J. Hilton and Harley to sort themselves out. Harley was determined to maintain his independence and sitting at the back of the bus he held the advantage. Thankfully he thought, he hadn't taken a front seat and been forced into some means of turning around without causing suspicion. When Millie asked, 'so who's yet to find a buddy,' his hand stayed firmly down until Sean Seamus and Arthur J. had raised theirs and were buddied and bunked together. He then lifted his half way up in belated mock innocence.

'Oh Harley,' said Millie, 'there's no one for you to room with.' Harley knew there was, and that she was speaking. It just mightn't be tonight.

-0-

'Can we stop at a roadside café?' the voice had come from mid-bus and belonged to Wilcox. 'I need a restroom.'

Ryder looked ahead the and in his rear view mirror. He wasn't sure if they'd passed Neenach, whether it was up ahead or they were actually in the middle of it, a scattered array of homes from which only the odd light shone. There appeared to be no center, only outskirts and certainly no service station with a toilet. Ryder told Wilcox that they were in the middle of nowhere running alongside a river.

'If you don't mind going au natural, you could use the countryside,'

Ernie offered, 'we have hand-wipes here in the bus.'

There were four or five yes's, thankfully all male. In the darkness they stood in a line peeing into what was now the longest urinal in the world, outside of India, and had been, up to ten minutes earlier, the pollution-free aqueduct serving and keeping Los Angeles alive and green. Ernie couldn't help wondering how long it would take for the extra liquids to get back to Burbank, the pee might make it back before they did.

Headlights cut along Lancaster Road toward the static bus from the direction they were due to head in. Ernie sucked in a long breath as it passed, the patrolman inside not as bright as the lights on his car. Minutes earlier and those lights would have put the five decanting passengers into a lot of trouble. Was peeing in the aqueduct a State or Federal offence? He suspected State since the initial action and the final consequences were both in California. However, he was only too happy to avoid any contact with authority. A busload of what looked like pilgrims possibly stranded out in the middle of scrub at nearly two in the morning should have tickled the interest of any policeman worth his badge, except it appeared, the Lancaster-based patrolman.

Back on a road so straight Ryder hardly had to touch the steering for the next twenty minutes, where eventually he would need the brakes. Failing to stop at a T junction would have resulted in a lengthy bumpy ride across the Mohave Desert to Las Vegas. The sensible option of stopping and looking at the signs placed them on a tarmacked highway, halfway between Lancaster and Rosamund. It was just coming up to three and in the clarity of the star-filled night he half expected an extra-terrestrial moment to occur in front of him. He waited longer than was necessary at the deserted junction. Then he turned right, for Lancaster's poppy garden was the next port of call. Half an hour wandering around, hearing a potted history of the Shakespeare family, would set them up for As You Like It, or was it Much Ado About Nothing, he couldn't remember. It was a performance for tonight and for one night only, at the Roadrunners. The performance was again a matinee kicking off at 5am and finishing an hour before the first school buses might start to roar in.

There was no gate at the school sportsground. Well there was, but you could drive round it. Ngoc and Pang were already there. They had set off on a MetroLink train in the early LA evening reaching Lancaster before the party had even left the studio. They should have reached Rosamund, however, although the track runs west of the town, the trains don't stop. Thankfully the one they were on went no further than Lancaster. Confused they got on a bus for the remaining miles and then more confused they got off again, still four short of the town. They needed time to set up the speakers in the arena. Rooster had given them a map of the town and a grabbed snapshot from Google Earth of Rosamund's baseball pitch. She'd drawn a stage area and stripped in where the audience would sit.

Carrying five mini speakers and a sub-woofer with yards of wire and a small mixing desk in two huge rucksacks, they looked like a Vietcong unit on maneuvers. This was probably the principal reason why they failed to get a lift from where the bus put them down. It took them a little over ninety minutes and they had only just finished setting-up and were waiting for Ryder with the power source, when he did. It was a risk not to test on site, but they had done one back at the studio. There was an element of confidence and more than an element of physical exhaustion. The party were on rugs scattered in the central outfield having a picnic lunch. In the middle of the night, in the middle of a baseball pitch, in the middle of a small remote desert town, this, thought Ernie, was probably the safest moment he'd enjoy in the three weeks.

The odd bit of wah wah feedback confirmed that power had reached the speakers and for the time being Ngoc and Pang could sit back and relax. A bit of Shakespeare might do wonders for their English. Picnic finished, the party were escorted to some terraced seating just behind the home dugout.

There was a lot of hustle and bustle coming through the speakers and then a strong male voice broke the night air:
'As I remember, Adam, it was upon this fashion
bequeathed me by will but poor a thousand crowns,
and, as thou sayest, charged my brother, on his
blessing, to breed me well: and there begins my
sadness.'

Protz turned to Perry in a loud stage whisper, 'he sounds American' there was a 'shush' from Ernie which gave the stalls a feeling of authenticity and then Miss Little chipped in 'It's Orlando.' Another 'shush' was followed by Protz closing the issue with 'sounds like he comes from Orlando' with half the party unable to hold back a chuckle.

Ernie wasn't chuckling. He looked at the laptop that was generating the performance, why hadn't he noticed before? Blinded by the word free. It had been recorded in Oregon, in a natural amphitheater in a forest; so here they were in the heart of England, listening to the mother tongue being spoken by the

Portland Players. Maybe it would be, as they like it, he hoped so.

No one had noticed an additional member of the audience. In the bleachers lay the partially picked body of a fellow traveler. He, like the trio some weeks back, was heading to nowhere and the stadium bench was all he could afford after the bottle of rye he'd picked up at the local store. He wasn't quite sure where he was and further confused by what was going on below him. Picking up the brown bag he took one last look at the play without actors, took a slug of drink and slipped back into his alcohol induced slumber. It was more Midsummers Night's Dream than Much Ado About Nothing, but it was just as he liked it.

Three of the tourists had fallen into dream mode by the time the sun started to come up and the curtain, if they'd had one, due to come down. Ryder would transport them to the motel, dump the luggage in a pile and then double back and pick up Ngoc and Pang. By which time they should have de-rigged.

One by one the tourists responded to Ernie as he called out the numbers on the luggage and once both buddies were bagged, Millie directed them to their rooms. For the first time it was of no consequence which room they had. They were all exactly the same and all had double king-sized beds. Millie filled up the rooms on the second floor by each time going a little further along the external railed-in corridor. Once all were anchored, she further secured the party by tying the children's safety gate they'd brought with them, shut, protecting them from the stairs, cutting off unwanted visitors and allowing the trio to relax a bit more in their rooms on the first floor. The sign she placed on the gate was the final deterrent, 'Rodent Infestation – Keep Out!'

-0-

Perhaps it was the beds, but when Ernie looked at his watch he'd slept for seven hours straight. He jumped up and pulled back the thick curtains to let in the light. It was blisteringly sharp, almost painful. He had fallen into his own time-trap; he felt disconcerted and then comforted by the fact that they had managed to beat the body clock so effectively.

The 3 S's, a shit, a shave, a shower and he'd be up to face Day Five. He was excited, they were going to Liverpool, or at least Griffith Park.

He was halfway through the third S, the most difficult of the three. Since as a kid he'd a phobia about taking showers in motels. Why couldn't Janet Leigh have just run the bath? He'd still to do the final rinse when the door knocked. It was a blend of emergency, impatience and discretion. It was Rooster. The chickens were already up and they needed to go. Most of them were outside on the upper balcony, penned in by the extra railing and eager to get on with the trip.

Rooster, who could have been a dancer, an actor, a tour guide, could also have been an ace researcher. She'd been chasing the Cavern in Liverpool to see what possibilities and problems it would offer. The original one was long gone, but there was a mock-up next door that seemed to satisfy the thousands of pilgrims to this musical Mecca. When she told Ernie that the original didn't exist and that there was an artificial substitute, he said, without a hint of irony, that he was disappointed in the lengths people went to in order to pull the wool over innocent peoples' eyes and make money. The three-hour drive was a bit much just to go down some relatively insignificant steps and hear canned music. But then it ticked another box and that seemed to be the most important reason for some people to travel.

They'd already earmarked Griffith Park as the best location for the copy of the copy of the Cavern and in her research Rooster had come across a story which could easily take up several hours of day five. It also involved going underground and again Griffith Park was ideal. She stumbled on a Joseph Williamson who for some reason decided that tunneling under a city was a fab hobby. His wealth had allowed him to create huge interconnected caverns all around his hometown, Liverpool, miles of them. Unknown to anyone except the miners he employed for thirty years, he dug out enough soil to create an island and the labyrinth of brick-arched tunnels included a banqueting hall 70 feet long by 20 high. To this day no one knows where the soil went and Rooster had an image of an elderly man walking about Liverpool depositing earth down his trouser leg like she'd seen in an old prison camp movie

The speculation about why he ever did it still exists and Rooster thought that since they were 'in the area' the party could wander around the man-made and often filmed tunnels of Bronson Canyon. It as a dawn-to-dusk operation in real time, so from after lunch to bedtime for the tourists. The morning was to be filled with a Ryder organized boat trip, which meant he had to find a vessel and some water. There was plenty of water on hand, it was called the Pacific, a little wider than the Mersey, saltier but still water. Fittingly still, just as it appeared to the guy who first gave it a name.

What he'd come up with was nothing like the photos he'd seen of the green and white ferries that zig-zag across the River Mersey connecting Liverpool to the other side, that isn't Liverpool. Liverpool is one of those city's that has a river running through it, but doesn't. The Mersey is so wide that it defeated the Victorian bridge makers who would have 'captured' the southern bank and let it merge into the greater metropolis. Though they did come up with a tunnel. Perhaps it was that Williamson guy again. The ferry trip, Ryder noticed, only takes ten minutes, so he'd opted for a mini cruise and an old fishing boat. The captain had long given up looking for fish and was only too happy, for a few hundred bucks, to get up early and go up and down the shoreline for an hour to the strains of Gerry and the Pacemakers.

Los Liverpool had potential for an attractive day out.

-0-

The party were still singing . . .
'So ferry 'cross the Mersey
'cause this land's the place I love
And here I'll stay,'
. . as they entered the derelict remains of Griffith Park Zoo.

Once a popular day out for the locals, but from this coachload only Miss Little or her buddy Miss Temple could ever have had the opportunity to visit it. It had been closed for over fifty years, but the park reopened as a hiking area and one much used by Hollywood producers. The only animals you might ever see other than dogs, look like deranged mutts, but go under the name of coyotes.

'She Loves You' seemed suppressed, it was sing along music until deep within the cave where the reverb gave it an edge that George Martin would have adored. Here they stood in awe, worshipers in the Temple of Change, the music that shrunk the world. The loop that Pang had made contained three songs and there was some discussion amongst the Beatle aficionados as to whether they were the real thing or were they listening to cover versions? Arthur J finished it with the pronouncement 'that is was probably a copyright issue.'

Arthur J was the sort of man who as a boy would have been molded at the hairdresser and outfitters to look and sound like his father. The sort of kid who stood no chance because he was out of his and his piers' time. In the school photograph of 1960 he stood out as the immediate target of teasing and bullying. Thirty years later and he would have stood out as the nerd, the guy who's worth millions for a fingernail's worth of software.

Back on the bus and a short trip around Griffith Park brought the group close to another hole in the wall, not a cash machine, but a cave. Fittingly the cave, like the considerable digging efforts of Mr Williamson, had been man-made. Those responsible weren't looking to get anywhere or for anything valuable other than the rock which today forms much of old LA. The cave was on a half-mile hike over undulating and rough ground, which the tourists accepted as being the normal terrain for Liverpool. 'There's a lot of development and regeneration,' said Arthur J, so it must be true. Ryder was keen to see the old rock mine for himself. A huge Batman fan, he knew that in the real life that is Hollywood, this was the home-base for the dynamic duo, Bat Cave. Where they kept the Batmobile and Robin his extra pair of tights. Griffith Park itself is a place with a history as strange as the tunnels of Liverpool. Rooster found it hard to hold back the information she's come across and America's Mr Griffith seemed as much an oddball as England's Mr Williamson. Just his very name intrigued, Griffith J. Griffith, what kind of parents did he have, she thought. The same as Arthur J's she concluded.

Her voice echoed off the cave walls and responded to an ever-increasing number of questions and remarks. Whatever, she was in her element, she'd never had so much fun with a bunch of adults, with her clothes on. She felt for her current reading material, not that she had much time to read, but this was part-work, Here, There and Everywhere, a European tour by Bill Bryson. 'Without her clothes on,' it was just the sort of line he would have come up with.

28.
A SLICE OF DANISH

Solvang, California – Copenhagen, Denmark

Three hours later and back at HBO, the party were gathering themselves together to go to the airport. Destination Copenhagen and for tourist #5 Mette Nielsen, her spiritual homecoming.

Heading to Denmark was a logistics conundrum. It involved taking the party back to Bob Hope, now in the guise of John Lennon Airport, for an hour or two of travel atmos, then find a reason why it takes the same time to return to the studio set and the mock-up plane. They would then get the party on the plane for the 90-minute flight to Copenhagen's Kastrup, where Ryder would then pick them up in the bus that he'd converted back to left-hand drive. This was a ten-minute removal of the partition behind the front seats, restore the choir's table and then to help the illusion of a fresh coach, place covers over the other seats. There was also one tricky technical operation, changing the dangly fir tree on the mirror to vanilla. Ryder had quite taken to his last-minute purchase. The MCI bus didn't look that old until you parked it next to a 21st Century coach. Not a deep thinker he still found the resources to wonder what sort of adventures this bus had had compared to the ones that slipped off the production line half and hours before and after. He'd even, with the help of Ernie, given it a name, Daphne, borrowed from Jack Lemmon's character in Some Like It Hot. Like Jack's Daphne, the coach was living a lie.

Meanwhile in the lounge of Bob Hope/John Lennon Airport, Harley had cornered Rooster. They were laughing and the encounter ended with a soft hand on Harley's broad shoulder. He placed his on top, removed hers and gently kissed the back of it. With controlled grace he stepped backwards, turned and re-joined the queue to board. Rooster, a little flushed, immediately powered up her iPad and was logging on to Amazon when Ryder came up to her.

'What was that about?'

'He asked me a favor,' she admitted.

'Bet he did, what was it?'

'He's a soccer fan, likes Liverpool and asked if I could pick up a jersey if there was one in Duty Free. But it has to be someone called Gerald.'

'Give him any jersey, I've a LA Galaxy shirt someone gave me, never fitted, never liked, never worn.'

Ryder had always been the strong silent type and both Rooster and Ernie put that down to personal low esteem. She had never prepared herself for what was to follow.

'You're getting too fucking close to them – never forget they are numbers, not names. They are marks, not people!'

She dragged him physically into a neutral corner. 'This may be a con, but they are not marks – they are people whose care, passion and ability you would love and they only thing they'd wish for from you, is your eyes!'

From managing the head of the queue Ernie had spotted the rift and he waved Rooster over. They hadn't time to discuss it, he needed help getting the party back into the Daphne, down the road and into the fuselage. Today's seat plan was for both sides to be utilized. Change he said is the key to progress, variety the spice of life.

-0-

After a pre-recorded cabin crew announcement, Rooster stepped up. 'Hi it's me, Millie, your constant companion and tour guide. When we arrive in Copenhagen we'll be bussed directly from the airport to our hotel. We should have you happily fed and in your rooms by ten o'clock. Remember we lose an hour. Tomorrow we have a short two to three-hour drive to learn about Denmark's most famous son. Later we visit a Danish furniture museum, walk out to the spot where the mermaid lives, I'll take some pictures to send back and then we experience what Tivoli offers. You've all heard of the Tivoli Gardens I take it?'

'And smørrebrød, plenty of smørrebrød,' said Mette.

Millie had to do a double take before agreeing and made a mental note to take the top slice of bread off the sandwiches still in the fridge and left over from the afternoon tea they'd had two days earlier.

Ryder had taken over the steward duties and once the hydraulics had levelled out, rattled down the few seats offering snacks and drinks.

'What beer's do you have?' asked Protz adding, 'Jez this is the trip of a lifetime.'

Ryder racked his brains and tried to think of those in the glass-fronted fridge in Set C. 'We've Heineken, think that's Danish.' He was still thinking of a second option when Ben Nelson chipped in 'nope, that's Dutch.'

'Danish, Dutch, ain't they the same?' It was Joe Colino, a Sicilian from the Bronx who didn't speak any Italian despite being in an age group where he might have heard it daily from his grandparents. Joe never heard it from anyone. Abandoned at birth he'd been brought up by a couple from the Dominican Republic in a house full of Puerto Ricans with a Russian landlord. He spoke like a middle-aged rapper, taught himself guitar, thought he was Jose Feliciano and considered himself American to the core, which with that demography, he was.

Ryder then remembered 'Carlsberg' and Protz, Nelson and Wilcox immediately put in a request. He reached into the blue trolley, pulled back a tray and handed them three beers at random, but all locally brewed. The Carlsberg were in the glass-fronted fridge in Set C, it would been improbable and time-sappingly dangerous for him to go and get it.

In quick succession there was the sound of two tabs being pulled. Wilcox raised the plastic cup to his lips, sniffed, took a large slug and announced, 'Tastes like our American shit!'

As the third tab was pulled Protz changed the conversation. 'Bright fella the guy who invented the built-in tab. No litter, you just throw the whole can away. But he missed a trick. My ex-wife could hear the hiss of the tab from 40 feet, through two lounge walls. Couldn't he have made it silent?'

With that stunning observation, the plane itself went into cruise mode, as did the passengers and despite the shortness of the flight, most dozed. Colino had a Heineken and felt he was totally in the groove.

In the quietness, Rooster rebooted and re-joined Amazon. These soccer shirts are not cheap she thought, but then he'd a lot of money. Wonderful, it could be here in three days so she'd tell Harley she had to order it and get it delivered to some location down the line. She went through the list of players, there was no Gerald, first or family name, but there was a No8 called Gerrard, perhaps that would do. For some unexplained reason it was on special offer. She'd take a risk, she wasn't going to ask Ryder's advice.

-0-

Copenhagen is an attractive and compact city, a plus for most tourists, but not for the European Experience. There were a number of must-do things. Must do in the sense that you could live without them, but the 'didn't you see?' accusations once back home made them more important to tick off, than miss.

Ernie had earmarked Solvang, the self-styled Danish capital of America as rich in opportunities, but it was two hours away. Then there was the eating and drinking of Tivoli, which could be covered by visiting the Castle Park or Pacific Park amusement centers. LA has several of the world's most famous and fabulous wonderlands, but Ernie wanted something more intimate and less label driven. One guffaw from Goofy would be hard to logically bury or explain. His final choice would be based on feasibility, Pacific Park being at Santa Monica with Castle to the middle and east of the city on Highway 91 at Riverside.

Then there was the mermaid, who God bless her, could be anywhere. In 2010 visitors to the real thing were disappointed to see a bare rock as she'd taken a holiday to China to promote Denmark. To say that the statue itself is fairly unremarkable is unfair and an insult to the sculptor and his wife. After all she agreed to get her kit off because the ballerina it is modelled on, wouldn't. So, the body is that of Edward Eriksen's wife Eline. The ballerina Ellen Price contributed her head, which has twice been crudely sawn off by vandals, who were presumably not ballet fans. The price of fame.

A little more research offered a way out of the driving logistics. If they added a trip to Hans Christian Andersen's birthplace that would account for the drive to Solvang, and bless them they even had a statue of the famed writer, about the size of the mermaid, but with clothes on. Strange he thought how H.C. never married, just wrote for children, a bit like the guy who wrote Peter Pan and then there was the unmarried Lewis Carroll – all raving hetros he thought; thank goodness Ernie's favorite J.K. Rowling had found herself a man.

Sourcing locations in California, as film-makers continually prove, is not a problem. There was however, a more basic inconvenience to sort out, in just over two days, Dent and Swallow would head off on their own EE, but this time it was Erotic Exercises. The day before, as he slept deeply in Rosamond, Ernie's phone had briefly lit up the ceiling with a further request for photos 'for the staff and families.' When he opened it at breakfast in a very confused coffee bar, he could see another reason hidden in the reminder. They would be proof of him being in attendance. It didn't matter that nurse Swallow was missing, in fact she had to be omitted so it was a big plus. Perhaps Mrs Dent would not have appreciated the thought of the two of them working so hard together in Europe.

Perhaps. Timing is the greatest gift given to comedians . . . and conmen. Without it the first die on stage, the second go on the run. The suppressed relationship between the doctor and the nurse was Ernie's big line. In how he delivered it hung the whole caboodle. It was the master thread the spider uses to catch its prey. If broken the whole web of intrigue and deceit would come to a sticky premature end.

Ernie calculated that if he were to expose the tryst now, there would be only two potential outcomes. Firstly that Dent would explode, leave his wife and carry on the holiday as planned, but more openly. Secondly and best, he could be forced to abandon the trip. Then a third hit him that made him retreat from pressing the Dent destruction button. Panicking, the director could ditch Swallow and, in order to save his marriage and cover the tracks he had already disguised, he and Mrs Dent would join the European Experience for the entire six days. Ernie shuddered; it was all about timing.

There was another issue also regarding time. As Rooster had announced to the entire group, they were losing an hour's sleep by moving further east. The nights being days had been a bonus, but there was a growing concern that the feeling wasn't right. There would be increasing pressure to match weather and events to something closer to the actual time of day. Not exactly, but maybe if Tour Time was just four or five hours ahead, instead of nine, they would have added flexibility to control cool and hot, calm and hectic.

Somehow. they had to do it and before they left Berlin, four days down the road to head to the warmer south. The bonus

218

point in the time shift maneuver was that when back in Arizona the party would have their body clocks so confused that it would take the nursing staff two weeks to get them over the 'jet lag' and further support the whole illusion.

-0-

The call time was crucial for the start of the Danish Experience. Ernie had eventually chosen Pacific over Castle Park as the location for the LA Tivoli. The amusement pier closed at midnight. It meant leaving the hotel at six-thirty to be there for seven, that is 22:00 LA time. He'd called it 'Breakfast at Tivoli,' which Miss Little had confused with a favorite movie of hers and told everyone on the bus journey to the coast just how much she loved Audrey Hepburn. It was the last movie she ever saw.

The Pacific venue held the additional advantage that, being on a pier, the party could be kept together with ease, providing no one overstepped the promenade. That he just didn't care to think about, he just hoped the actual Pacific was as pacified as the day it was given its name – a rumbling sea might just be a dead giveaway for anyone who knew of Tivoli's central city location despite all the canals. If it became a crisis, he could claim they'd come to Bakken, the other, and older, Danish fairground from which you can see the sea, only just and only from on top of the big wheel, which no longer really deserves the word big. Bakken's claim to fame is as the world's oldest fairground, a fact that would help in an emergency explain why it had replaced Tivoli. People love extremes, touching the edge of the biggest, smallest, oldest, fastest.

Calm it was and the cloudless sky brought a chill which sent most of the locals back early to their late-night movies. The

Pacific proved to be perfect for shepherding the party. The rides were neither expensive or excessive, the thrills very much confined to the 1950's. The tourists looked like eggs in a carton, packaged in twos and fours in each of the rides and in rows on some of the more adventurous, the party were in seventh heaven. One last ride before the management flicked the on switch to off and Rooster was placing the couples in their buddy format into a series of sea planes. Harley had stepped back and was on a stool at a hotdog bar leaving Mr Megaghy alone. 'But you shouldn't be alone, where's your buddy Wayne?'

Megaghy just raised his hands and shoulders in a single movement of non-commitment or care. Rooster flashed her head left and right and left again. She caught something disappearing in and out of a world of motorized chaos. Above the chaos the sign read Sig Alert EV, but she knew it only as dodgems. In the middle of maybe eight cars bashing the hell out of each other Wayne Kerr was gliding gracefully through the mayhem without a nudge or a bruise.

'Stop the ride,' she shouted at the operator who was sitting in a control cabin the size of an aeroplane toilet. 'Get him out!'

'Why?' the youth responded. 'He's the best driver there!'

-0-

Rushed at the beginning to get to Pacific before it closed at half past midnight, they needed to eat time so that they'd reach Solvang just before it woke up. They didn't need any buzz of human life in order to walk the parks and feel the statues; they could even drop in on the Danish church, the single most authentic thing on offer.

The time-killing could at least solve Dent's photo call requests. Rooster had split from the other two and with the help of Pang had set up a huge green screen, eight meters by three, in a corner of the car park just down the road at Paradise Cove. They'd a bank of borrowed lights that were far in excess of what they needed for the screen and when they tested them, several of the parked cars quickly started up and drove off, an anxious hand or two wiping the steam free from the windows. Waiting for the bus to arrive they tested them on several occasions and each time the few cars that had just arrived, would be knee-jerked into leaving, some having never got out of gear, the people that is, not the car. It was the exact counter reaction to the number of flies attracted by the intermittent brightness.

The bus drew up at a quarter past two, a little ahead of the projected half past, but a walk along the promenade ate some minutes and got the party into the mood to do something they didn't normally do or care for. They had been wearing their numbered 'please don't interfere' sweatshirts for the amusement park, but somehow Ernie thought they might give the game away on camera. In case any had forgotten to bring the requested change, he'd turned up with a couple of spare neutral windcheaters and some heavier weather gear, it was Europe, it was summer, after all.

Rooster explained what was going on, skipping the part about the green screen. One by one, and in small groups they made-up themselves, they gathered and giggled, posed and pointed out to an even green sea of fabric. When she got a moment, Rooster would open Photoshop and place the famous mermaid in the background. She clicked like mad realizing that the photos could become useful for other dropped in backgrounds. The number of lights, that at first seemed excessive, were fully utilized by Rooster to get rid of the killer shadows. It was tricky and she decided to try it again elsewhere if she got a chance, hopefully in sunlight, defused by light cloud cover. Least that's what it said on the website she'd found. The secret was constancy of color and no shadows.

The analogue clock on the bus's dash moved to 3:21. Solvang was another hundred miles away and the Sat Nav estimated arriving at 5:32, which should mean just before sunrise, a sunrise that was pretty certain since Solvang gets 365 days a year, 350 of them without the hint of cloud. Perhaps that's why its founding fathers called it 'sunny view' – solvang - in 1911. One of those founding fathers was Mette Nielsen's, great grandfather and the family name was dotted all-round the small town. Danish to the core, most of them now congregated together, the Jensens beside the Olsens, the Mortensens beside the Johansens, the Larsens beside the Kristiansens – they don't talk, they just share a common heritage, and graveyard.

Not quite dotted around, but certainly present, was a familiar image. After an hour of taking green-screen pictures and a two-hour drive to Solvang, the bus pulled into the market square and the familiar mermaid looked in on each passing window. Of course they would have one here. Rooster laughed inwardly, perhaps she should have taken the pics here? But then removing the pancake shop from the background would take longer than starting clean and from scratch. Anyway, if the mermaid in Copenhagen seems smaller than anticipated, this was definitely mini-me. With a saw and a suit case you could have grabbed it, and not just the head.

Rooster transformed into Millie and started their tour in the
small park over the road from the Kong Frederik Hotel on the
opposite side to the huge windmill that the founding fathers'
sons, being a further generation removed from reality, thought
most symbolized their roots. There were a number of classic
sailed windmills in Denmark, but as a national identity they
are emphatically Dutch and the source of the single biggest
confusion in European geography, something that challenges
both national tourist boards, the mixing up of the Danish and
Dutch cultures. Colino's stab on northern European culture.
Mette Nielsen new better and had picked up on one of Millie's
rare mistakes. Denmark and the spring tulips she was referring
to in the park, did not come together as a travel cliché.

Helping Millie out, Ernie asked Mette, softly, how come she
knew so much about Denmark.

'Well I'm from a small town in the Santa Ynez valley, called
Solvang.'

It was already silent and still in the park and you could sense
the energy generated by Ernie as he looked left, right, left,
turned around and repeated the action. Was anyone looking
on, anyone who knew this woman? He hadn't taken her to
'Europe' he'd brought her home.

Mette was still going on about why Solvang was established
whilst Ernie scanned the immediate area to see if there were
any locals up and about. Mette's condition made the whole
party more obviously approachable. Friends, relatives or even
just generally caring people could come round any corner at
any time. Seeking the sanctuary in the church didn't ease
Ernie's anxiety attack. Every other name on the wall seemed to

be a Nielsen. They at least, were the ones he didn't have to worry about.

The main street, Mission Drive, at six in the morning seemed like High Noon, Ernie already aware that the town wasn't big enough for both of them. They were heading to the bakery to tap on the door and see if they could get something piping hot and fresh out of the oven. Targeting a bakery was a bit of a selection problem. In most small towns of 5,000 people you'd expect maybe a single traditional bakery struggling to compete against the monster stores. A custard pie last stand. Not so in Solvang, Olsen's, Mortensen's, Birkholm's, the Danish Mill, the list of pastry purveyors was a long as the variety of sugar-basted tasties in the window.

Rooster grabbed a couple of bags that just about covered the spectrum of expectation that Protz had been banging on about since breakfast. Kringles, cinnamon and chocolate rolls, snails and figures of eight made up the bulk of the order, and to top it off there was type of cake so rich in sugar that it made an accompanying glass of Coke taste like water. The cake, the baker had informed his first customer of the day, was called 'Brunsviger' and it came from the island of Funen where Hans Christian Andersen was born.

Happily Rooster ordered enough for twenty people and was presented with a tray full, one gigantic slab of sticky caramelized sugar – if they didn't like it, at least it would catch the flies that several of the tourists had been complaining about. Anything that landed in this sticky caramelized molasses wasn't going to take off again without a power-nap and a shower. Stickiness excluded it would also be a valuable part of her H.C. historic walk, a slice of local color. She brought them back to the bus where the morning delicacies were gulfed down as afternoon treats. Mette, thinking the cake superior to that at home, was in raptures, but at least she to Ernie she was now in the relative safety of the choir bus. The problem was how to do the Hans Christian walking tour without her or with her, but in such a way that no one would recognise her.

As they progressed through the Danish, Millie snuck beside her to do a mild cross-examination of Mette's roots.

Her family had indeed been amongst the first to sign-up to the concept of a sun-filed, religiously driven, culturally encrusted existence as promised by a group of clergymen. Europe in the 19th Century was a tough place to call home and tens of thousands of Scandinavians, down to their last pickled herring packed their bags and followed their spiritual wanderlust to the west. Only this time, unlike the Vikings, they stayed, were deeply pious and generally, outside of weekends, evaded a life of rape and pillage.

Some of them didn't stay that long. Mostly they'd chosen the Mid-West because it said in the brochure, 'virgin farmland as far as you can see. Come and grab it! PS no Brits'. It didn't take them long to understand why the prairie land was so expansive – after two and a half generations and about sixty winters as cold as the Ice Age, some of them picked up another brochure promising sunshine. Mette's great grandfather, an ultra-conservative who had just fallen out with his "radical" neighbour, 'that darned Mennonite,' was one.

The Nielsen family had re-planted themselves for a second time, from Jutland to Wisconsin to the Ynez Valley. They, like those around them, prospered, grew and dispersed. Now, she said, only her widowed mother and elder brother and his family lived 'back in Solvang'. 'I get home every September for

225

a week, they have a special Danish Festival with food, music and talks.'

'What does your brother do?' Rooster probed.

'He's the local chief of police.'

Ernie at the front of the bus shuddered and dropped his Copenhagen slice, landing sticky side down – life sucks. Now being on the 'continent' Ryder felt more comfortable justifiably driving from the left-hand seat. The raised seat on the right had now become the default base of tour guide Millie. Ernie had parked himself on it to munch the now discarded Danish and think. He'd penciled in Solvang for a return trip in two or three days as a Bavarian diversion en route to the Alps and Italy. They'd scanned the Internet for a Germanic version of the town and could only find one up in Washington State. Too far to the Fatherland, so far in fact he referred to it as the Further-land.

He'd been keen to find a Berlin, of which there were many, he counted eight, but the closest was over in Wisconsin, perhaps it was familiar to Mette's forbearers. But it was the current generation bearing the Nielsen name that concerned him. He saw the name everywhere he looked, on advertisements, mailboxes and the occasional store. That was because Nielsen is the second most common Danish surname. If they removed all the Jensens, Hansens, Pedersens, in fact anything ending in 'sen' from Solvang, the remaining population would fit on the bus. The top nineteen Danish family names are all based on being someone's son, until that is you hit number nineteen and the first name based on an occupation, the miller. Of the Møllers who left Denmark very few arrived on the US mainland, their proper names usually Anglicised or

Germanicised during their brief induction, were discarded on Ellis Island.

'But did he hear the 'c' word? Chief of police.'

Maybe it was just 'chief' and he had imagined the last two words. He picked up Rooster's iPad from the pocket on the side of her seat and typed in 'Native Americans, California'. Maybe there'd been some intermarrying. He glanced at Mette, she was not the classic Danish blonde, but maybe she didn't go to the drug store often enough. Immediately up came 'Chumash' and he breathed a sigh of relief at the newly found knowledge that the Santa Ynez valley was the heartland of the Chumash tribe. The rest of the article was not good reading. Spanish missionaries and disease had decimated the indigenous population before they'd got around to thinking of marriage. 'Police' it must have been, he deduced.

The Danish pastries had done their work and many of the party were taking an afternoon snooze before the much-awaited cultural tour. They were only disturbed by the number of flies that had invaded, lured on board by the high sugar content of the dropped or surplus delicacies. They were becoming a nuisance, developing into an issue.

Ernie was always observing that God moved in mysterious ways. At one hiccup in his professional career he'd spent a week in a Boston cell, sharing it with an Irish-American who put down unexpected misfortune to 'Murphy's Law' and unexpected luck to 'God's an Irishman'. Ryder had resumed his place in the driver's seat and was running the bus through town, up and down streets, giving the tourists value for money and by creating a breeze trying to get rid of the nose-landing insects.

'Stop,' said Ernie, 'God's an Irishman.'

With an unfamiliar athletic ability, he skipped off and across the road to a small general store, the sort of fabulous American establishment that sells everything except Danish pastries. Worryingly over the door it said "Proprietor: Carl Nielsen. In the window there were hoses, spades, lounger chairs, gun-racks, rat-traps and a bee hive, complete with protective gear. He dived past the plastic laundry bins and through the half open door, emerging ten minutes later with an armful of beige wide-brimmed hats and a large brown paper bag which contained a cheaper option.

'I'm sorry about the flies,' he announced to the slowly wakening passengers. It is the first real blast of spring here and they are a bit of a problem, they've just flown in from the Swedish lakes. Who is most annoyed by the little feckers?'

The response was slow so he added the rider that some of them bite. Of the fifteen, eight or nine immediately raised a hand, including, he was relieved to see, Mette.
I'm sorry, but they only had six, so we'll have to share,' then realizing that they didn't know what the six were, and with Ryder struggling to work it out, he said 'sorry, six lightweight beekeeper's hats with a fine mesh and the rest will have to use some purpose-made things which go over your head and tie round your neck. Not fashion statements, but perfect protection.'

Twenty minutes later the party were marching down Mission Drive, it was nine in the morning and the locals were up and about. Half a dozen of the party looked positively alien. The first tourist buses hadn't arrived, but the over-nighters had emerged from their suitably named and themed accommodation eager to grab breakfast at an equally suitably named eatery. Some turned into Paula's Pancake House and Rooster couldn't understand the thought of diluting the Danish experience. 'When in Rome, eat Chinese,' she thought.

She turned up an alley between a clothes shop and a year-round Christmas shop. 'Jule' as they call it, must be big in Denmark she thought. Here she encouraged the party to touch the gable walls and as they did Ernie snapped away with a small digital camera.

'These are called "bindingsværk" and they are very common in northern Europe, especially Denmark. They are basically a wood-framed house, peasant but pleasant. Very pretty. The wood is usually oak and as you can feel the beams are pretty thick. The gaps between the beams took windows and doors and where you didn't need them, the gaps were filled with a mucky clay which over the centuries has often been replaced with brick.'

'In America you call a house old if you are the second owner. When you are in a bindingsværk house you are living in a bit of history, maybe three hundred years of it, as old as the America we know and love.'

The party were in raptures and even passing locals could not fault Millie's description or, more importantly, question it. They might have, if they'd stopped and listened to the next bit.

'Hans Christian's house was on the corner. A single-story house out of which a hundred stories grew,' the line had just

229

come out of her and she stopped for a second to bask in it. Rooster could have been a writer. 'It was here he picked up a needle and thread, an apprentice to a tailor. What a loss to literature if he'd been good at making pants.'

'When Hans was born his father was just 22, a shoe repairer and his mother a washer-woman. He slept in the workshop and 5,000 people then lived in the town of Odense.'

'That's the same number as live in my hometown today.' The voice came from behind an anonymous mesh, but it was recognizable as Mette's.

Everywhere the party went held a strong Danish atmosphere; unknown to them many of the buildings would not have looked out of place in Odense and only the lack of cobbled stones in the pedestrian streets were an immediate giveaway. Several of the buildings proudly flew the Stars and Stripes, beside and on equal terms with the Dannebrog, the flag of the Danes.

Millie took a break from tales of the Ugly Duckling and Princess and the Pea to talk about 'the flag that flutters overhead. It is the oldest flag in the world and it has been constantly flown, without change or alteration, for nearly 800 years.'

A couple from Atlanta, who'd passed several times in an attempt to hook onto a free tour and glean some information to finally explain why they'd driven for four days, stopped and looked up at the red, white and blue flag that flapped above them.

'Do you hear that George?' she said, 'That flag's been up there for 800 hundred years. Makes you feel proud to be an American.'

It was eleven o'clock Solvang time, eight in the evening in Odense.

'Time to get back to Copenhagen,' Ernie interrupted.

There was time for one more astute observation from George's wife, Joanne.

'Copenhagen, that's near Denmark George, in up-state New York. Remember we stopped there on the way to the Niagara Falls.'

For once in her life, Joanne was right.

29.
PINING FOR IT

IKEA, Los Angeles – Design Museum, Copenhagen

The last night in Denmark, ended back at the studios and a late snack, a smorgasbord of freshly made open sandwiches and a mug of asparagus soup. Millie explained that at Danish parties the hosts, under the guise of the utmost care, give guests a tasty hint to go home by feeding them for a second time. Just in case you thought it was not subtle enough, the asparagus soup was as emphatic as 'now go home'.

'The sandwich was invented in England,' Sean Seamus offered as a water-cooler moment, 'but the Vikings, when taking them back, weren't careful enough, it was pre-Tupperware, and the tops blew off.'

No one laughed, unsure if it was fact or fiction.

Rooster remembered being puzzled as a child why two rectangles of Egyptian white cotton, sewn together on three sides was worthy of a red and white flag sewn in and a note that said 'Danish Design'. The attachment of which must have been the most awkward and costly in the entire process of making a pillow case. She thought she'd chip it in but, didn't know if to interject. Surely someone would. That someone was Arthur J. 'I believe it is symbolic of Danish design, putting presentation ahead of practicality.'

Together they chanted 'skol' and knocked back snaps, even Miss Little, before they put their heads down for the night. Skol, Arthur J. pointed out, coming from the Vikings who used the skull of a vanquished warrior to drink from, perhaps it was too far to row to the shops. Tomorrow promised to be a long day, the highlight a couple of hours experiencing Scandinavian design at first hand, functional or fabulous or both, before the long drive towards Berlin.

The Design Museum in central Copenhagen, Rooster had read, is a three-hour visual feast of simple wooden furniture and the art of hiding knobs on electrical equipment, re-inventing the dustpan and where you can finish with a designer coffee. If you like chairs, this is a wooden, cloth, plastic Valhalla where the only confinement was that you couldn't touch, let alone use them for what they were created. The Design Museum in Burbank is a two-hour walk round where you can pick up and sit down wherever you like and finish with meatballs. The locals love it, they call it IKEA.

During the night Ernie and Ryder contrived to create a time machine. On a ladder, Ryder lifted off the clock in the middle, the redundant Mountain Time, and moved the hands round and round, backwards, taking five hours out. The trio of clocks read, 23:00 03:00 08:00. They now had LA, Tour Time and HERE, which they changed to Central European. It was going to be a short night, but blaming the snaps Ernie would claim they'd slept in. A brunch breakfast at 11 and leaving at 12 they would arrive at 'the museum' at lunchtime, about one, just as the doors opened.

Perfect, except in executing the schedule they pulled up into an empty car park. Ryder just thought that the locals where taking their time, but when he got to the door he saw that it didn't open for another hour. Back on the bus he announced that they had time for a drive round Christiania, the famed free zone where three generations of Copenhageners had grown up, including its now most famous son, singer Lukas Graham. Famous, of course, if you had heard of him.

For Christiania read Compton, they would drive, stop, get out, have a talk, get in and leave. Hopefully the sheer extreme difference of the party would give them a pardon in the one of LA's hottest areas. Hot in terms of, you don't hang around. They did 'Christiania' with two stops, it was a breeze, the atmosphere considerably authenticated by a blast from an aerosol called Caribbean Melody that Pang had bought for cents in his quest for scents. In its complex recipe, it had a very distinctive whiff of simulated weed.

Back in Burbank the IKEA experience was to prove to be the smoothest exercise so far executed. The key to the globally adored innovative store selling clean simplicity, is the way they leave you alone to guide yourself round; you know IKEA staff, they are the ones with five people following them around holding tape measures and lists. Once on the grey lino you follow the arrows, passing temptation left and right. The biggest challenge, after a three-kilometer hike, is to get out with only what you came in for, and no jumbo bag of tea-lights and a shelf that looks easy to put up, but when home you can't figure why you bought it or where to put it. Rooster and Ryder shepherded the party to avoid kitchen appliances and bathrooms and said they were in another 'don't touch zone' when they hit glassware. They re-assembled in the café for Swedish meatballs and chips. It was possibly a first for the super store. Eighteen people spending two and a half hours without carrying a single yellow bag, pushing a trolley or paying for anything at the checkout. But they did sit down a lot and discuss the furniture.

It occurred to Ernie that he'd now found a center to his empire. Every big corporation needs a headquarters, IKEA would be his. Here in future exploits he could sit all day, access to free Internet, meeting rooms, cafeteria, toilets and parking. All he needed was to have a yellow bag at his feet. He's read that there were 56 in the States alone and approaching 300 in Europe, should he ever get there.

The bus headed out and southwards. For two hours Ryder would just drive then turn and head back to North Hollywood and Berlin. He drove like a skilled taxi driver, avoiding delays and effortlessly putting miles on the clock. Destination number one was the Portal of the Folded Wings Shrine to Aviation, a fabulous archway with all the ambiance of the Brandenburg Gate, just none of the traffic. For Ben 'Charlie' Nelson it was to be a pilgrimage. Son of a diplomat, he was born in Berlin on November 9, 1989, the day the wall came down. He'd one request he'd held back until he got there, he wanted some time by the old wall, if there was any still standing, somewhere he could sit alone and listen to the entire soundtrack of Roger Water's The Wall, the last true musical masterpiece of the 20th Century, if you can forget the musical contribution of New Kids on the Block. Oh you have, well done.

He approached the right person in Rooster, for she was quite touched, loved the music and asked if she might join him. Then Harley, eager for any contact with Rooster, wanted to be there and as Charlie's wish became wider known the chances of solitude weakened. He too was moved by the way the others wanted to mark the moment and agreed to share it. The day ended with Ryder taking just a few of the party back to their hotel by taxi in Set B with the remainder, eleven in all, sitting in the arched memorial. Rooster, driving Daphne for the first time, could bring the rest, it was suggested. 'No' she said putting her foot down, 'you taxi back and drive that monster,' she said to Ryder, who rather than be upset was quite chuffed at her recognition of his value.

On rugs and picnic chairs they sat listening to a CD of the live concert coming from a mini Bose speaker that defied its diminutive size to create the most wonderful of moments. The speaker was designed to use solid objects to amplify the bass sound. What better than the Berlin Wall? It was, Rooster thought, the defining moment of the tour to date. She wished Ryder had been there for it was so good it might have melted his often times insensitive heart.

She looked at the embedded panels on the floor of the monument, the names of Californians in the main, who had contributed to the world of aviation. She searched on her iPad for details of the only married couple mentioned in the plaques, Mr and Mrs Smith.

James Floyd Smith died 21 years before Hilder Florentina Smith, so it wasn't together in a plane accident, unless she'd been in a particularly long coma. What tickled her most was the fact that James was credited with inventing the parachute and Hilder for trying them out. They must have been the most trusting of couples and most gamblers would have bet on their deaths being in reverse sequence.

Rooster wanted to share the story with Harley, after all he'd been kind enough to share his blanket with her, wrapping the two of them together, warm in the cooling evening air. But circumstances keep Mr and Mrs Smith in their place.

236

The concert ended with the new local time approaching nine. It was one o'clock for real, time to recharge the Bose, and the bodies.

Getting out of the bus, Harley lent forward and with unashamed accuracy placed a kiss on Rooster's cheek. She didn't flinch and she moved her head to the other side of his and returned the compliment.

'Night Millie.'

She almost spoke and then she did.

'Guten Nacht.'

30.
ICH BIN EIN DOUGHNUT

Chinatown, LA – Berlin, Germany

'You're booked through, New York, Paris,' the girl at the check-in assured them. Dent and Swallow had arrived in good time for the flight from Las Vegas and a good job too since a fair slice of the 42 million each year who visit, what Dent, without a hint of self-deprivation, called the "City of Sin' seemed to be traveling that day; the one's with full pockets in arrivals, the near empty pocketed brigade in departures. Broke, but not broken. Dent gave off the air of a seasoned traveler, which compared to Swallow he was. This wasn't to be her first time outside of the United States, but she looked upon it as her first true international trip, since she didn't count several Mexican expeditions or a week in Puerto Rico as being international. This was real travel.

It promised to be so good, Dent had cashed in his frequent-flyer points and topped them up with some Institute funds, for seats in Business. Patricia Swallow felt superior, that glow that Business Class gives before it is blasted away when getting a glimpse of First Class and the resentment and envy flows in. At least it was better than at the back of the plane where the real people sit; they would arrive in Paris fit for purpose. For her the purpose was romance in the top league, for him it was sex with the added sparkle of knowing he didn't have to put his pants back on afterwards and drive home.

He texted Zimmerman to update him on their progress.

Amazing, a few words and they flash eastwards across 5662 miles from one phone to another. The words 'At Vegas, NY then Paris eta tomorrow 07.00' had in fact shot 229 miles westwards. Ernie shuddered, but like a poker player with a hidden ace, held back from replying. It was one of his little unwritten rules – responding immediately makes you subservient. It was like in the eighties when pagers first came out. To have one moved you up a league, until it was recognized that you were a slave to someone else's commands.

Whatever the distance or direction, he'd decided against trying to stop Dent and Swallow from leaving, he planned and gambled his single ace on causing enough disruption so that missing each other on that one day in Rome would seem to both parties like an unfortunate mishap. He'd spent his life reading people and thought in this duo, that meeting up was a necessity that they would love to live without. Dent was such an aloof character back in Kingsman that he never featured in any conversations. Not to be mentioned in the wave of aftermath joy was better than to hear a reference to having 'joined us in Rome for a day' and both Dent and Ernie deep down inside knew that. Dent and the 'inmates' moved in different circles, and for the doctor that was his comfort blanket.

Ernie looked at the new clock formation and estimated that the party, out with Rooster and Ryder, would have been to a building site where the foundations and concrete walls had been laid and erected, the twists, echoes and turns creating the feel of a stone maze not unlike the Holocaust memorial and then onto the steps of Schoneberg town hall where they would hear a recording or JFK's 'Ich Bin Ein Berliner' speech and enjoyed a cream-filled donut, which in fact is what a Berliner is. What the natives of Hamburg and Frankfurt did with on-the-move, in-the-hand savories, the Berliners did with sweet deserts.

It was the last stop of the day, and the last stop for hundreds of household names, the Hollywood Forever Cemetery, that caused Rooster to halt in her tracks. The graveyard at the back of the Paramount lot is a permanent collection of 'Who Was Who' from more than just the world of entertainment, but it was the planted mega stars that were the pull. The tourists target had been Marlene Dietrich who is humbly interred in relative obscurity in Städtischer Friedhof III, a small cemetery almost lost in a quiet urban corner of south western Berlin. At the very start of the whole sales pitch for the European Experience, Ernie had asked for specific requests based around the draft schedule and the detour to Marlene's plot was Gerald Perry's. His grandfather had always claimed that he had met her, or knew somebody who had. The exact degree of contact expanded in decades of retelling the story. For the rest of the party it was a walk in a park, but still a welcome relief from being on a bus or a plane.

What caused Rooster to stall midway through the walk was not the hours she could have spent wandering around ticking off famous names, but Harley. They'd parked up and were gathering themselves together when he commented 'F40, a red Ferrari F40'.

'So what,' said Ernie when she relayed the story back at base. 'I'm no car freak, but don't they have a very special sound?'

'Maybe so, but this one was parked, 40 feet away, engine off, driverless. . . . and he knew the color!'

240

Ernie came up with several more maybe's that Rooster put down including his belief that saying red Ferrari was as automatic as a red London bus, before suggesting. 'Maybe we ought to keep an eye on that one.'

-0-

Their eyes and minds were getting increasingly busy with the biggest potential problem, now 37,000 feet in the air. The original intention was to leave 'Berlin' in the morning and drive south, taking a long eastward diversion to Poland and Auschwitz, but multiple factors showed how impractical and dangerous it was. It added 300 miles to the trip and Jankowski had been heard practicing Polish. Added to that Jack Megaghy had been complaining of nausea and chest pains.

'Confuse and conqueror,' Ernie said, and launched into a plan which touched on each of the issues.

'We're going to have another night away, not Poland, but Bavarian Alps, ski lodge and a dash of snow. I've checked there is plenty of the white stuff still lying up at Mammoth Mountain and I've got a large lodge that was due to host a surprise 90th birthday, but the central character surprised them by not getting out of bed three days ago. They come together to bury him tomorrow apparently. No, it's double up again for some of the tourists, but it is so much safer and less tiring than the slog to Auschwitz. And Ms Jankowski won't need to find someone to practice her Polish on.'

'Where's Mammoth?' said Ryder, ignorant of Californian geography and keen to know if he had to drive hard or doddle.

'It's five hours north of here, perfect since that is exactly the drive time to Munich and then five hours back gets us through the Alps and into northern Italy.' Ernie added that he'd shortly send Dent a text indicating the change in plans, 'it'll make him aware that we are flexible. I might even suggest that we head to Paris and meet up with him there. Be proactive. That would ruin his private party.'

'You can't be serious,' said Rooster. 'You are courting disaster.'

'We won't hit Paris, we will threaten and then say we couldn't change the hotel booking, or it wasn't logistically feasible. It's just that we will be more in his face with such a suggestion.'

'But what about Rome? How do we avoid him, not that avoiding is a problem since we are 6,000 miles apart?'

'These itinerary changes are just foundations. I don't suspect it will break Dent's heart if we don't meet up, as long as no one knows back at the Institute, or more importantly, back home. We are nothing other than an alibi to him. What he doesn't realize at the moment is that if he fails to meet us, which we know is a cert, then the power switches to us when we meet up again at Kingman.'

'But if he wants an alibi. Surely he'd love a photo of him and us together,' Rooster said thinking it through.

'In a perfect world, yes, but I suspect he'd forget about the photo because he'd be more afraid of us capturing one of him and nurse Swallow. Something tells me that Mrs Dent would be uncomfortable looking at it. It wouldn't go up on his office shelf.' Ernie paused, 'I might just . . .' and then paused again.

242

31.
FOURTEEN FOR DINNER

Mammoth Mountain, California – Austrian Tyrol

The next day the party, excited by the prospect of getting into
the snowy Alps, were fumbling their way on board the now
familiar Daphne. Millie ushered them to seats, keen to make
then use alternative ones; life back at Kingman was all about
routine and familiarity, on tour change was a vital ingredient it
to be an experience, in order to disguise the entire fragile
situation. She aimed to do the by now regular head count, but
it never started. There was no #1, no Jack Megaghy. That was
very strange she thought, he was always up packed and ready,
usually first, it had become his trademark.

Before she checked with the rest of the assembled party she
asked buddy Wayne Kerr, if he knew where he was. He hadn't
spoken to him at breakfast, so 'no'. She continued to see if any
others were missing and the number count went smoothly
from two to fifteen.

Ryder clambered out of the driver's seat and with a degree of
urgency set off through Set A and along the corridor to Set C in
case he was still eating at the café area, but no. Then back and
up the stairs a quick look at the first door. The entire schedule
was there, the only difference between it and the next door was
the highlighted tour day and the number of who was in the
room. It was Day 9 and tourist #1 was in Room 2, one of the
rooms on the first floor, the rooms where they had to share
bathroom facilities.

The door to Room 2 was ajar; a suitcase lay against the bed, but no sign of it being ready to go. Clothes were laid out on the bed and personal items in neat order on the small table. This was very 'un-Megaghy' Ryder thought.

He tracked along the corridor to the communal bathrooms; there were two. He tapped one and then the other door without response. The second was locked. Ryder remembered how flimsy the lock was and put his shoulder to it – enough to gain entry without a massive repair job because he knew who would have to do it.

Jack Megaghy didn't look up. He was sitting on the toilet, dead to the world.

-0-

Ernie had filled his mind for the past two and a half months with just about every conceivable scenario, but a stiff wasn't one of them. This one required thinking time and he needed Rooster's Internet searching skills . . . and possibly more. The bus was already loaded and the tourists were getting a little restless so Ryder set out to drive around the lot for a while and kill time, which seemed extended by Wayne Kerr reminding the driver that his buddy was not onboard. However, this left Rooster and Ernie to come up with a solution. For a flashing second he felt like Hitler in his bunker with Eva. He'd never been big on the concept of Plan B, he believed it was the default setting for mediocrity, although he had once said that he'd like his grave to be marked with the inscription, 'Ernest Zimmerman III – at last, a Plan B'.

The question was 'how do you get someone to die in Europe when they were lying prone in a toilet in California?' Busily they looked into what the state laws were in both California and Arizona. The second seemed quite lax. Head buzzing, he was easily diverted, 'lax' that means slipshod and careless, funny name to give to an airport, he thought before getting on with the matter in hand.

There was no estimate as to the precise moment of Megaghy's passing. If they got a doctor in that would open many doors that might later be difficult to shut.

'Hank Williams!' Ernie said with the glee of someone troubled by a quiz answer as they were being pressed for the last time.

'No, it was Elvis who died on the toilet. It's the second most common place to die. Anyway, this isn't the time to go all C&W, Ernie,' said Rooster.

'No Hank Williams died in the back of a car on his way to a gig, it was never ascertained when exactly he actually stopped breathing. The driver just said that he'd been very quiet for the journey. So, if Ryder were to drive back to Kingman he could report the death there. He could say they left San Marino and had been driving all night. San Marino, California that is. It's only around the corner from here.'

'He leaves him at a funeral home, reports it to the police and hopefully in the sad chaos the word gets about that he died on the way, somewhere outside San Marino. In the meantime we inform the Institute of his sad death and to expect him back in a day or so, from San Marino, Italy.'

Rooster looked at Ernie in awed-reverence, mad, improbable, unlikely and yet brilliant. It was so simply unbelievable that it just deserved to work. It was out-of-the-casket thinking.

'He can take Pang, he might need some extra muscle power.
He's like an ant.'

'But who will drive the bus?' said Rooster aware of Ernie's
inability and her limitations. She could drive, but she'd no bus
licence and didn't at all fancy the challenge just as she'd
refused on the journey back from the Wall. She would not shirk
most things, but the thought of the bus on twisty mountain
roads was one turn too much.

They looked out the window. Ngoc was scooting around in the
golf cart like Lewis Hamilton on speed. They looked at each
other.

-0-

Charles had been distracted on several occasions as the
Hallelujah Choir bus passed the back window of his office.
'Wonder how they are getting on?' had morphed into 'What
the fuck are they up to?' Anyway that was their business, he
had an important meeting to prepare for, a visitor and potential
work.

Ryder had been summoned back to base and was being
detailed for 'Operation San Marino'. Aware that Megaghy was
from Oregon, it seemed unlikely that Kingman would be his
final destination, but as a devout Christian it could be assumed
that he'd already arrived where he thought he'd end up, it was
just a case of back-filling the route. A family plot in Seattle was
a plus since every additional stop-off point to get there would
help conceal the truth from the reality. There was no time to
squander, the warmth of the bathroom might have delayed the
onset of rigor mortis, but things were going to change in the
physical state of Megaghy and Kingman was five or six hours

246

drive away. Ryder was given the number of a funeral home and told to phone it, in a state of mild distress. But that was only once he was about half way there.

Charles was on the veranda awaiting his visitor when Ryder passed with Pang in the front passenger seat of the rental. Slumped in the back, Megaghy's head rested against the window. 'Shouldn't he have a seat belt on? That's dangerous,' he muttered as he moved out to intercept and deliver his caution. A caution built on years of fraudulently filling out risk assessment forms after the incident had happened and the injured crew member was en-route to hospital.

Pang smiled and waved as if he was off to a day out at Disneyland. Ryder swerved to avoid a rogue trash can and regained his exiting line. Megaghy rolled over and on to the floor.

Charles had just regained his composure when a bus jumped and lurched towards him. As he retreated he spotted the diminutive Ngoc, wide-eyed and beaming, at the wheel. 'Boy I love America, land of opportunity' he was thinking to himself in Vietnamese.

On board Millie informed the remainder of the party about Megaghy. Not that he'd died, but that he'd been feeling unwell and that they had taken him to the doctors. Once restored to full fitness he'd re-join them.

Harley couldn't quite work out what he'd seen. It was pretty evident however that Jack Megaghy would miss out on the evening at the beer hall that was now the promised replacement for a walk around a concentration camp. He for one wasn't complaining about the change although the thought of the evening up of male numbers might give him Wayne Kerr as a buddy was disturbing. He'd work on it.

After a few rather robust gear changes and the odd toot of a complaining horn, Ngoc had managed to get the hang of the bus. For a moment as they headed north on 5, Ernie broke away from his thoughts about Megaghy and Dent, to realize what a blessing the two illegals had been. What would the world have been like if there wasn't a land where people could get a second chance? You are only born once, but for Ngoc and Pang, this late spring in California was a re-birth. He looked at the beaming Vietnamese at the wheel – only some misfortune and subsequent red tape could awaken him out of his New World dream. With that thought, a highway patrol car passed and he could see the officer was considering asking a few questions. A driver with no license, no id, no passport, no nothing, those weren't the questions, but could become so. The patrolman pulled in front and put his flashing lights on and, window open, was asking the bus to slow down and pull in.

Ernie was ashen white, everything could end here on the highway verge in 27C degrees of midday sun. Everything that was until an old open-topped Mustang roared by, 20 mph over the limit with four young people in control of their parents' finances, but not of themselves. A discarded beer can, aimed at the bus, but due to pure physics, travelled on and bounced off the hood of the patrol car. Within seconds the youths were being pursued and what seemed like Ernie's third major problem of the day was evaporating into the tarmac haze in the distance. 'God is an Irishman,' Ernie muttered and indicated to the oblivious Ngoc to turn off towards Bakersfield.

The Sierra Nevada Mountains were a considerable barrier to the early settlers and no more so today. The route to Mammoth

Mountain was a choice of heading to Fresno and Sacramento and then turning right and east before heading south again, or to take the roads round the southern part of the range and approach from the other side. Ryder had programmed in the western route since, on paper, it felt more like the drive from Berlin. The change just meant that they hit 'the Alps' about three hours earlier than was physically possible by road. But hey, Ngoc on a twisty mountain road for the first time in a bus, no sweat.

-0-

Ryder and Pang meanwhile had cleared the geographical barriers that immediately faced them and were now approaching the most dangerous hurdle that the early gold rushers had to overcome, Death Valley. In their situation it was the most southern tip and in truth Ryder didn't know if they were in the valley or not, it all just looked the same, straight roads through a sun-blistered environment. It was a road they shouldn't have been on at all. They missed Route 40 and now stuck on 15 they had to bear it out and endure an extra hour and a half's driving. They would kiss the outskirts of Vegas and then turn towards Kingman. At least near Las Vegas the chances of getting a strong signal on the cell would be better, he needed to talk to the other two in order to sort out the story. Rooster had been putting some time in creating one that was logical and open to misinterpretation. She'd found one or two options.

The trio in the rental had set out from San Marino, California, a city within a city. Somewhere in heading to Kingman they became a duo and that was it as far as they were concerned, almost. Ryder was to tell the funeral parlor that they'd met Megaghy who was on holiday and who, hearing that they were heading to Arizona, asked if he could grab a ride back. He had, they believed, fallen out with the rest of the party and wished to return to somewhere in Kingman. He being blind and they being kind, they had agreed to drop him off. They would not go into too much detail but say that he was very quiet, 'in fact he didn't say a thing from the time we tanked up in San Marino.'

Ernie had chosen San Marino since they could detour to the small country as an extra treat, and there Megaghy could briefly re-join them. They'd tell the party he'd 'had a little turn' and had gone to hospital. Sadly however, after a relapse he would not make it. Paperwork for the tiny independent country, famous for its stamps and not much bigger, they hoped would be brushed aside in the immediate grief and since Dent wasn't there, by the time he came back to the Institute, Megaghy would already have been flown to his family in Oregon.

The second option was to buy a flight casket in Vegas on the pretext of a bachelor party practical joke, put the dead dentist in it, and somehow leave it at the airport at Kingman, along with some Italian vague paperwork covered in the words Megaghy, Seattle, St Anthony's and San Marino. The assumption being that whosoever found the casket would put two and two together and wrongly make the right assumption.

On Route 15, the AC on the rental was up to max, the local radio station saying that the outside temperature was 78 degrees Fahrenheit, but for the driver and navigator the worry was just how much longer to the funeral parlor. It didn't matter where they were in this heat, with Megaghy in the back, nature was taking its accelerated course. They were the trio that put the death into Death Valley.

In the considerably cooler and fresher Sierra Nevada, Ernie, thought perhaps he was pushing the concept of luck a little too far. He would inform Dent when he was in mid-Atlantic, and inform the Institute at much the same time, saying that 'Dent knew and that Mr Megaghy was dispatched overnight from San Marino, all repatriation costs are covered by European Experience insurance'. He could only hope that no one went too deeply into paperwork or examined the logistics of where and when. He was hopeful that the general lack of care on the part of the Institute and family continued.

It had taken over six hours, but by the time the party arrived at Mammoth, they were only too happy to walk in the snow and get some fresh Alpine air. German beers and a hearty Swiss fondue were promised to follow, after all this was Austria. Snow is a wonderful leveler. Within minutes of de-busing the average age had dropped to thirteen and they were all out there, totally underdressed for the conditions but screaming with happiness as they gathered up handfuls of snow and flung them who knows where. Just the gathering and flinging process seem to satisfy them. All bar one. The snowballs traced through the late afternoon air like a meteor shower that had lost its way, except those released by Harley. With uncanny luck he managed to hit Wayne Kerr twice and Arthur J, once in successive thirty foot throws.

Rooster picked up a handful of snow, squeezed it into a ball and waited. Once Harley was within range and full on to her, she flung it at him. He ducked to the side. She said nothing, she didn't want to go into this confrontation without Ernie. Timing was important since Ernie, she had noticed, had been close to the edge during the whole of the day. Party off piste, Dent en route, Megaghy off planet, Ngoc on roads, but without a license and now Harley on site, but not unsighted. They would, she decided, meet later, all three of them. For the time being she'd carry on and take a few photographs, surely this was the easiest location to snap and dispatch images from. Over the hills lay San Francisco, but here in Mammoth they could have been in the Tyrol.

-0-

The ski lodge too had a strong feeling of the Tyrol. That's what you get, thought Ernie, when you make everything of blocks of wood and create furniture so heavy that moving a dinner table and chairs is a team sport. It was an enigma how the Italians designed furniture with a chisel, and, just across a border, the Germans with an axe.

The lodge was large and semi-manned, but Rooster had explained the 'defined complications' of their mission and the owner and his wife had agreed to play along, not wishing to face a second end of season cancellation. In fact, they were very happy to take a back seat and add the cash Ernie gave them to the 60% deposit they retained from the non-90th birthday bash. This lot seem so quiet and easy they thought. Dinner, bed and breakfast, thank you and goodbye, or 'Abendessen, Übernachtung mit Frühstück, danke und auf Wiedersehen,' if they had to speak at all

-0-

The temporary undertakers had opted for the second plan. Rooster had emailed a document she'd hastily grabbed off the Internet – it seemed Italian and with a little Photoshop she'd injected the necessary details with the added elaboration of routing the remains through Rome, Rome Nebraska, as if it were an error. Ryder was at reception of the motel waiting for a printout and making sure that the note was neither read nor copied. He need not have worried so lack-luster was the receptionist's approach. Outside Pang sat in the car, the tailgate half open due to the tarpaulin covered box that jutted out a good 18 inches. They'd advertised the station wagon as the ultimate 'family getaway' but the luggage of the ad, a few flexible personal bags, hadn't included a rigid casket. It was no family go-away.

It was hot, but darkness had put its shroud over the whole operation. It needed too. The last maneuver was the trickiest. The airport at Kingman had just said farewell to its last flight of the day, there were about a hundred planes on the tarmac, where they'd been for years, waiting for their recall to duty. In the rental, parked about 50 yards from the locked gate, were the only living persons at the airport apart from the night security guard. Ryder was having trouble explaining the reason for why they were here to Pang. Through fairly elaborate and ineffective sign language Ryder tried to show the problem to his Cambodian comrade.

'You, me, big box' and he pointed to the small arrivals area where they needed to deposit a departure. He clapped his hands together close to his face, 'gate, gate.'

Pang smiled and opened the door and slipped out into the night. The last Ryder saw before he was engulfed in the darkness was of a slight figure on hands and knees rummaging through the uncollected trash bins. He jumped as the door reopened and Pang slid back on to his seat.

'El fant' he said, 'El fant.' There was a pause 'Duck, Elfant, Duck.'

Ryder was just beginning to think the activities of the last weeks had finally got to the Asian now talking animals, when Pang resorted to sign language. It spoke it better than Ryder, a swish noise and the motion of wrapping and suddenly the message stuck home. Elephant, Duct tape. By more than luck Ryder had a roll, the one he'd bought to hold the tarpaulin in place and stop it flapping on the journey from Las Vegas.

It was under one of the seats and once shown to Pang, he revealed the results of his bin search, a strip of plastic, about eight inches long. Suddenly all three were out of the car, the plastic, the tape and Pang. Again Ryder could only look on as he saw a diminutive figure walk, crouch and then crawl to the main obstacle between them and completing the drop off, the security gate. Pang slipped the bit of plastic onto the bottom of the pole on the opening side of the gate and then secured it with the tape. He then came back.

It was nearly two hours before the security guard did his hourly walk around in his Jeep. They'd caught this action just as they had arrived. The guard returning from a drive round the perimeter fence to ensure that none of the TriStars had gone AWOL. It was amongst the most predictable and boring schedules in working history. But tonight was different. The guard emerged from the building, opened the personnel gate, the plastic flicking into the gap, just enough of gap to stop the spring-loaded gate from becoming a barrier, but close enough to fool the ears of the security guy who was already pressing the remote to open his vehicle and carry on with the most boring of routines.

254

The way clear, the two struggled to get the casket out of the car and then onto two luggage trolleys placed head and toe. Through the gate and round the side of the building to a set of moving rollers where the normal luggage was transferred from outside to in, from plane to passenger. One push and Mr Megaghy rolled through the rubber flaps, out of sight and into a world of confused bureaucracy. Hopefully. Mr Megaghy, who practiced packing before every trip, was now dispatched without little more than a plan that relied totally on confusion.

-0-

The party had retired to bed wonderfully early, it was just approaching six and normally their guests wouldn't have returned from the slopes. In a corner sat Rooster and Harley and three beers. Ernie was on the phone out on the veranda. It was Ryder.

The departed Megaghy, he was told, was now at Kingman arrivals. How the rest would unfold, only time would tell, but there was certain timeline that the authorities, St Anthony's needed to follow, one driven in part by the wishes of his family in Oregon and by the airport's desire to avoid any press coverage that would suggest an uncaring, disorganized body. Confuse and conquer, Ernie thought, but more with an added little hope this time.

Mr Megaghy's connection to the Institute would be revealed once Ernie had talked to Dent's office reporting that the body was on its way. The fact that it was already there he hoped would skip notice. It wasn't perfect, but so far, seemed to be okay.

What seemed to be perfect was Harley's eyesight and when Ernie sat down to his beer he addressed it.

'So, we are in an interesting situation Harley.'

Harley wasn't quite sure where this was going to go.

'It appears that you are not what you seem. We've suspected it for a few days, but now it has been confirmed. You are a fraud.'

'I'm a fraud,' said Harley half shocked to be outed, the other half shocked that such an accusation could come from these people. 'What do you call this?' he flung his arms around as if to gather in everything. 'One word from me and where would you be? Forget this façade, inside a real prison.'

Ernie had had the benefit of presuming several reactions. He didn't know whether to expect remorse, embarrassment, indignity or anger. It appeared that Harley wanted to attack his way out of it and Ernie had prepared a block.

'Eighteen million. I believe that's what you got for losing your eyesight. We could be in the same prison, except I'd leave as poor as I went in, you wouldn't leave as rich.'

'Believe me, I was blinded by the accident. I don't know what caused me to beat the doctors' prognosis, but it just happened. Since then I've been living a lie wondering how to get out of it.'

'How to get out with the $18 million I suspect, or you would have revealed your miracle earlier!' Ernie nudged.

Rooster opened her mouth for the first time and the mood changed from a potentially explosive aggressive one to that of calm consideration.

'Harley, we know that what we have started here is morally wrong. We started by thinking it would be an easy way to make a lot of money. We were wrong, but I don't now see us as morally wrong. What we are doing is providing a service. More than anyone you must feel the change in the way everyone here reacts and does things. Forgive me, but you can see it. We have taken them from what is a morally shady institution where they are dumped by families and brought them to a world that is exciting and stimulating. It may be a false world, but it is real as long as they don't burst the bubble.'

'Or someone bursts it,' said Ernie.

'Disneyland is a collection of dreams, transporting you to somewhere that doesn't really exist. Do they complain, or do the visitors take part and contribute to it?' Rooster added trying to get a two or three-way conversation.

'There are lots of "I don't wants". I understand what you have given my friends. I sought the same, a break from routine. By touring I hoped to get a glimpse back of what I've been missing. In truth, I had a plan. I was going to give life in the Institute another year and then sign myself out to fend for myself. I'd quietly disappear from everywhere and somewhere pick up life again, and a Harley, or maybe two.'

'There's nothing to stop that happening, you have a secret, we have a secret, we cancel each other out,' said Ernie reaching down to the table, replacing his glass of beer and picking up the cell phone reached it out to Harley. 'Here, make a call. Ring

257

the police . . . . and become poor.' There was a long gap, 'or don't.'

Rooster reached out and put her hand on Harley's leg and instantly hated herself for doing it. It took three seconds for the hate to melt. 'I started off this thing, thinking it was just another Ernie idea, but it is more than that. It is the first time we have done something that has a truly positive side. Just look at the joy they are experiencing.'

Harley knew he was in a boxing match. Had it been physical it would have been over in seconds, but there were two of them and one he would never ever think of touching other than tenderly.

'What's your real name, Millie, steward, guide, bar lady, receptionist?'
The whole tone had changed. Five minutes ago they were on the verge of a confrontation that could have blown everything out of the water in a storm, now if seemed like they had entered a quiet calm bay. Rooster was quite taken aback by the simple question. Even Ernie didn't know her real name.

'My friends call me Rooster – it's an old nickname.'

'How did you get that?' said Harley, something that Ernie had asked and never had a reply too.

'Too private to tell.'

Ernie was keen to get back to the core issue. He had other things to sort, Megaghy and Dent, he wanted to be sure there was no ambiguity from this point on. Was Harley with them or against them or might he remain neutral? 'The way I see it is that we all have things to lose if we burst the bubble. So what do you say?' Ernie moved the phone towards him. Do you want to use it or not?'

All cards were on the table, along with three more beers. Harley reached out to the phone and pushed it back, 'it's too expensive to phone from Austria.' The team that was three, then five with Ngoc and Pang, was now effectively six.

-0-

There was one more phone call to make before he called it a day, or night, he was no longer sure. Ernie made his way to the bus to pick up a briefcase crammed with papers, some of which nurse Swallow had insisted he took, 'for insurance purposes.'

There was a small folder with about thirty sheets in it, and these pathetically short notes summed up the lives of the fifteen tourists. People who had been in the Institute's care for years, but only merited one or two hundred words to sum up their lives. It was mostly photocopies of passports, lists of allergies, health insurance details and a point of contact outside of the Institute. It angered Ernie just to see the shallowness of care.

There it was, Megaghy, Michael Johnson, known as Jack, diabetic, qualified as a dentist in 1987. From Seattle, Oregon. Next of kin, ...and there it was, he had a brother William and a sister Joanne still living in the north west and beside William's name a telephone number.

Ernie braced himself and from the privacy of the front seat of the bus keyed in William's number. He counted six rings and was half expecting it to go to answerphone when William spoke, a mellow sounding voice reassured Ernie.

'Can I just confirm that I'm speaking to a William Megaghy,' said Ernie.

'Yes, but I don't want to buy anything,' came the crisp and immediate reply.

'I'm not selling, my name's Ernest Zimmerman, I'm with the European Experience, can I confirm that you are a brother of Michael Johnson Megaghy.'

'Yes, what's he done now?'

'I'm afraid that I have some sad news. I have to inform you that he passed away two days ago.'
The other end of the phone was silent.

'I'm sorry, did you hear that?'

'Yes' the sibling said quietly.

'His remains are now back at Kingman. I believe they were flown in from Rome this evening. They were to be flown to Seattle direct but there was a hiccup, Italian hiccup. He died in his hotel room peacefully of natural causes and I'm ringing you because he was in my care at the time. We were in San Marino. After I've spoken to you I will talk to St Anthony's, but I'm sure you would want to deal with this as a family.'

Ernie talked on and William confirmed that he should like Jack to come home to Seattle and that armed with the details he would organize it from his end. William said he was shocked and needed time for it to sink in. He then thanked Ernie for his kindness and consideration and hung up. By Arizona law the burial decision rights rest with a spouse and then a pre-determined order of the immediate family. Bachelor Jack's brother had all the authority that was required.

Immediately Ernie phoned St Anthony's and told them that the Megaghy family had been informed, but that there had been a bit of confusion. Instead of flying the remains directly to Seattle they had been sent to Kingman. He said he believed they should arrive later today just to add another layer of confusion to the trail. He asked if they could ring a rest home when it opened in the morning and inform them about Jack's final destination and to tell them that his family would be in contact. He said he'd contact Dr Dent and nurse Swallow.

'There's no need to contact nurse Swallow, she's on leave in Chicago with her mother, but isn't Dr Dent with you?'

'Aah, not yet,' said Ernie trying to untangle somebody else's subterfuge. 'I believe he also had to address a conference somewhere.'

He thanked the receptionist for her time and pressed the red button.

Ernie starred out the front of the bus as a few of the last flakes of snow landed on the windscreen and slide down onto the still wipers. 'Interesting, so St Anthony's doesn't know of the Euro tryst,' it was a gem of a fact that made the doctor very vulnerable and opened-up several options to solutions for the proposed Rome meet up.

He reckoned that Dent and Swallow were, by now, enjoying each other in Paris. It would be past midnight. He could be mischievous and ring and imagine the scene at the other end with Dent fumbling for his glasses and Swallow, naked on the same bed, trying to piece together the picture from only hearing one side of the story. There was a timing issue. Why would he, if he is in the same timezone as Dent, have waited until the early hours of the morning to ring? He settled on a text lie.

'Tried to contact you earlier, but maybe you were still in transit. Sad news I'm afraid, Jack Megaghy died peacefully of natural causes in his sleep and is in the process of being repatriated to Oregon. Family and Institute informed. Sad, but all else good, we have changed the schedule to inject another level of conversation and diversion from the genuine grief, currently in San Marino. Zimmerman.'
He pressed send.

On the thick carpet, under a quickly discarded pair of crumpled chinos, a pencil slim skirt and a bra, the phone vibrated. On the bed two spent characters were in an oblivion caused by the twin energy sappers of travel and passion. The phone stopped vibrating, Ernie had played his first transatlantic card.

He waited for five minutes knowing that if the message had been read he'd have and he would have to make an immediate response. Ernie left the bus and headed to his room estimating that at around 8 am Paris time he'd get a call and that he should be in the same mental zone as Dent – even though it would be eleven in the evening in Mammoth, or three in the morning according to the new Tourist Time that they were running on.

-0-

Ernie woke after a disturbed sleep half expecting it to be his turn to have missed a call or text, but no. Perhaps Dent and Swallow were playing what they were best at, doctors and nurses, perhaps the message hadn't got through, perhaps he mislaid his phone. Whatever, there seemed to be a feeling that what went on with the European Experience was secondary to fulfilling the desires of the duo in Paris. By the time they got to Rome they might be a little more focused on the need for an alibi. But then according to the receptionist at the Institute Miss Swallow was in Chicago – Dent could not risk exposing her to a photographic opportunity, so would he turn up on his own?

He remembered a story about a journalist who told his wife he was off to a financial conference in Geneva. On his return he moaned about how boring it was and that it was fruitless in terms of stories. He did have a tan that covered more of his body than you might expect from sitting on a veranda overlooking a Swiss lake and reading annual reports. It was a good year later when at breakfast his wife again brought up the subject of the trip. He repeated that it was a waste of time. She then broached the subject of dopple-gangers and passed a holiday brochure across the table to him.

'Doesn't that look like you,' she said pointing to a guy stretched out on a sunbed beside a pool. He stalled and admitted that from a certain angle there were similarities. 'And the woman beside you, doesn't she look like Jane, your secretary.'

Frozen he took in the scene and the implications, in the slow-motion effect of a car crash. 'And the bitch is sitting on my fucking beach towel!'

He believed they were no longer together. How would Mrs Dent react to such a situation? Ernie had one mad idea, but he couldn't afford the time or personnel to do it. In a counter-attack he could dispatch Rooster and now possibly Harley, to capture a picture of the lovers or even bump into them, whilst at the same time explaining that the rest of the party had headed on to the next location. It would take a minimum of four days and two air tickets. It would confirm once and for all that the party were in Europe – but it was strictly a last ditch move. Rooster, as Millie, was too vital to the smooth running of the rest of the operation.

32.
LITTLE REPUBLIC, A GREAT REPUBLICAN

Bruno Street, Pasadena – Republic of San Marino

The Alps had proved a major hit. The snow, fresh air and beer had combined to give the tourists a refreshing change and at six in the morning with the sun coming up, some late-season ski fanatics were already out making the most of the slopes. It all added to the atmosphere as did the plaster on Mr Wilcox's upper right cheek. After dinner the previous night they had had an impromptu 'um pa, um pa' session drinking some imported beers from the steins that were part lodge decoration, part guest functional. Mr Wilcox's dexterity had let him down and he'd stabbed the half-opened lid into his face. A brief moment of pain, but a long glow of the notoriety that he continually sought. He could use that story again and again.

'That little scar, when I was in the Alps, skiing accident . . . don't talk to me about steins . . . even before you taste it, Austrian beer hurts!'

What probably wouldn't bear examination was what part of the Alps, German, Austrian or Italian they were actually in. The trio had decided that if quizzed they were on the border, not far from Germany or Italy, but probably in the Tyrol which was a little vaguer in that it crossed national borders. If they could keep the location unclear then any subsequent questions about the photographs Rooster was constantly snapping couldn't be attributed to any one place. It was remarkable just how careful you had to be thought Rooster. Checking for vehicles in the background, tell-tale branding and innocent looking mail boxes. She'd made sure the camera didn't have any smart GPS system to reveal where exactly they were. The pictures were labelled Tyrol, Day Twelve. By lunchtime they'd be in Italy for sure and as a bonus they had changed the itinerary for a second time. The only mildly disgruntled passenger was Janne Jankowski whose months of learning Polish had been to no avail. Having missed Poland, they would skip across the Po Valley and head to one of the world's smallest countries, San Marino. Little bigger than a postage stamp, fittingly so since that was its lasting claim to fame, and even that seemed fragile in the letter and postcard free 21st Century.

The landlocked micro-state was less than 200 miles south of where they were supposed to be, two hundred that is, if you flew. The twists in the road would take up most of the day and they would arrive there in the early evening. San Marino had taken on an additional significance and it was important to plant this destination into the minds of the now remaining thirteen 'true' travelers. Jack Megaghy, as they'd been told, had been flown on ahead and was waiting to re-join the party there. Jack was now permanently sleeping in Seattle, but to tie some of the story together he had to have one last European experience. On arrival the party would be informed that Jack had suffered a relapse and sadly had died peacefully in his sleep the previous evening.

There would be one genuine reunion. Ryder had returned to LA with Pang and there was a lot for them to do. They had borrowed a Typhoon Films truck and along with a substantial amount of props, had driven to Bruno Street in Pasadena. The small street boasted little other than a supply shop for beauticians and a few non-descript facades. It was relatively easy to section off a corner and put up signs saying, 'Quiet Please' and 'Filming in Progress.'

Bruno Street's other attribute was the granite cobblestones that marked it out from just about everywhere else in the city and maybe California. San Marino is famed for its cobbles and with the portable flats and sound FX, they would create a walking maze. Ryder had also been to a deli and picked up kebabs and pane rolls, Parma cheese and ham. The kebabs were sitting by the small Cobb grill ready to waft out atmosphere and sustenance in equal portions. They were smell props and would most likely end as a frazzled mass of cat food. The studio also had an outdoor set with cobblestones, used for period dramas set anywhere east of Pittsburgh, and that would be utilized the next day. This was only a taster.

The coach meanwhile had cut through the Sierra Nevada a journey that kept Ernie, Rooster and now Harley, in high anxiety at Ngoc's relatively relaxed approach to cornering. On the highways from Fresno they felt more comfortable and were deeply relieved that they hadn't opted for Route 1 and the Big Sur. It was a combination of Ngoc's pubescent and developing driving skills and the fact that the Pacific, playing the role of the Adriatic, would be on the wrong side of the coach that caused Ernie to go for the more direct route. They would divert around northern LA and dip their toes in the sea at the quietest beach they could find. Miss Little was amongst those to express dismay and not going to Venice, but Ernie assured her that all they were missing was continuously and perilously hopping in and out of overcrowded gondolas. Venice, he said with a degree of statesmanship, would go down in history as the first city to be killed by tourism, unless someone dug up a flyer for 'Atlantis – Visit Once, Stay Forever.'

'My father spent time there in the war, Venice, not Atlantis,' Wilcox muttered from mid bus, 'he said a lot of the guys came back with gondolas. Least I think that is what he said.'

Arthur J said nothing, wondering if the comment was down to ignorance or humor. He was too busy to get involved with tittle tattle since he was about to give one of his impromptu, but well-rehearsed, lectures. It came as a revelation to all that their beloved homeland, the New World was actually nearly a century older than modern Italy. He didn't include anything about the substantially older San Marino, which had been a republic since the 4th Century, because he didn't know he was going to go there until some hours previously, so he'd never made a study of it. The new destination left Rooster surfing on the bus and building up an impressive list of trivia that would help sustain the guided tour. On some earlier instances, poor Millie had to bite her lip as Arthur J would contradict or take over. Here she had a clear home run. Her particular favorite snippet was that the great Republican President Abraham Lincoln was an honorary citizen of the 24 square mile republic. He never visited, but they must have sent him a letter to give him the good news, so the very least he would have got out of it was another nice stamp for his collection. History would later put him in the runners up position, behind George Washington, for the number of times he appeared on a stamp, so philately will get you somewhere.

-0-

The whole European Experience was now into its second half and Rooster and Ernie were together in the front of the bus and being fairly philosophical. There was plenty of free space behind them allowing a few moments of reflection, many of which, if overheard would have caused no alarm. This was

268

turning out to be the sting that put the 'con' in conscience. They were discussing the added value of the trip being not in what they did or where they went, but in what lay ahead. The expectation factor was measurable and the party eagerly awaited the next couple of days, a vineyard in Tuscany and then Rome, the Eternal City and for the party organizers, the infernal, for they knew not which way the deck of cards would deal the next hand.

Ernie asked Rooster to pass his briefcase and he dug out the personal folder that had contained Megaghy's details. He was agitated that he hadn't thought of it earlier, but was there a list of people's denominations? They were heading to the Vatican, so how many practicing Catholics were there on board and what might be their needs? He looked down the list, Megaghy was formally one, Jankowski, O'Reilly, Wilcox and Little all came up as Roman Catholics, but how devout? He'd been downtown with Ryder some weeks back and marked out an area in Chinatown that had space and fountains. It was the perfect Trevi, a passable St Peters. The idea of going to the Cathedral of Our Lady of the Angels for a Mass went out the stained-glass window when they popped in to gauge the potential. Closing their eyes the ambience was more concrete than cloistered and opening their ears the priests were more Ventura than Vatican. He just hoped the tourists wouldn't ask for a confessional, although given the degree of deceit they had generated, getting someone into a box to hear their sins and concerns would be easy. Maybe he should provoke it since it would be an opportunity for honest feedback.

There was one event that Ernie had put down as a lynchpin of the whole operation. The Vatican website showed a healthy workload for the Pope with a Mass on the Sunday that Dent and Swallow would be in the city. Ernie had scheduled St

Peter's Square as the last stop in Rome before heading to Monte Carlo.

Plan A was to tell Dent that they would meet up in the square and that he had, in a moment of rare genius at the beginning of the planning stage, acquired tickets for the service. He'd booked the touring party's tickets online and paid extra to have them shipped to the States, because he thought they would provide a useful talking point and proof of actually being there should relatives visit St Anthony's. There was no way of getting the tickets for or to Dent, but why make it easy for him. Rooster had ordered two for him to be picked up at source. If he wanted to see them he would have to get his own tickets and then look for them. It shouldn't be too difficult, normally with the popularity of Pope Francis, there are about 15,000 in the square, marshalled and penned in for their convenience and overall security.

Plan B, and Ernie couldn't quite believe that he had one so he called it Situ 2, was more brutal. Even more than brutal, it was positively explosive. He would wait until an hour before the Mass and then ring Mrs Dent with 'a word from a friend' that the doctor was in Rome with a certain nurse. The resulting chaos would put Dent into such a flurry that it would be easy for the party to move on whilst he tried to cover his tracks. Ernie had also calculated that this might backfire as Dent could urgently need the party as an alibi, however the doctor had made the mistake of getting his proof too late. He and Swallow were due to fly out that evening. Swallow was, after all, in Chicago and for her side of the story to gel needed to be back at the Institute on Tuesday morning. If she didn't turn up, questions would be asked.

270

If he made the phone call more questions would need answers. The decision was who should make it. An anonymous male or an anonymous female, who carried the greater punch? Or more to the point, which seemed more natural and couldn't be misconstrued as spite. Dent had been purposely vague about his arrangements, so Ernie correctly estimated that Mrs Dent would be as much in the dark as him. Maybe she had a section of the European Experience schedule, a version of the timescale those back at St Anthony's also believed he'd be spending.

Ernie didn't want to attach the management of the European Experience to any malicious act, so he decided to come at it from the side of a caring airline, a potential flight change for both parties. Rooster would make the call.

That, if needed, would be in two days' time. For now it was a Millie moment, a brief guided tour around Bruno Street whilst a small crowd, mostly of real tourists snapped away at the end of the street. It was a thrill for them to stumble upon an actual Hollywood shoot – Ryder had erected a large green screen background, initially for some stills, but realized that chromakey was such a common tool for the industry it added a very cheap bit of authenticity to the whole procedure. To the seasoned LA eye, well used to shoots, it did look more like a school project than George Lucas on location.

Behind the small crowd of more inexperienced onlookers, a rather tatty bus appeared and tooted its way through.

'Must be a prop,' suggested one of the bystanders.

'No it's a choir, they are going to sing,' said another as he fumbled for the button to switch his digital camera from stills to video.

271

In all there were about a dozen onlookers now gathered and without any official restrictions beyond the Typhoon signs, they had, as crowds do, gradually encroached further and further forward. Ryder was about to panic when Ernie put out his hand and in a very calming way indicated to leave things be. One of his other guiding principles was the ability to turn setbacks to his advantage. Ernie crossed the remaining feet to the eager faced tourists.

'Hi, as you can see we are about to do a little 'B roll' here. Would you be interested in being voluntary extras? No talking just walking, and we're low budget, so I'm afraid no dosh, just your fifteen seconds of fame.'

Quicker than a flash they were all on board and Ernie outlined 'the script' creating something which he thought quite plausible and with potential. They were in San Marino in Italy for the purposes of the shoot and this blind choir was on tour, but the tour operator had gone bust so they needed to sing their way home. He asked that they simply moved in amongst the actors as they walked around the cobbled street. 'Please no photos whilst doing this and the actors are mood actors developing their own lines and roles.'

Having been isolated for so long inside the Institute and protected from external contact even when on the trip, the party immediately picked up on the close proximity of other humans. Smells, bustle, just the joy of tripping over other people's feet, brought a new life to the experience and through it all Millie guided and conducted so effectively that even the sighted tourists were transported into a new world.

She batted questions from the party, the spontaneity and variety of which deeply impressed the "extras". 'Are they

Italian or something else? Have they a flag? Do they have to buy everything from Italy, like oil and electricity? Do they drive?'

That last one was from Arthur J. recovering from his enforced banishment into an un-researched area. 'As you can hear,' said Rooster, taking a cue from a police siren some way off, 'they do have cars and motor-bikes so be careful, they come through these tiny streets without any care or sense. The bikes that is, the cars are mostly outside the inner city, although there are small delivery trucks. The distant hum of traffic is coming up from the plains below us, we are some 400 feet up.'

'Planes below, I don't understand,' said Perry and from the nodding heads of half the party and most of the extras he was not alone.

With iPad in hand she brought up the San Marino Grand Prix before realizing that it didn't happen in the republic, but just a short distance away at Imola. In fact, it didn't happen at all any more. She recovered by saying that's where many people had heard of the state, that and it is famous for stamps.

'May I purchase some stamps for my grand nephew – I think he's the only teenager left in the world who collects them,' said Miss Little who then went into a mutter with Protz about why the simple things in life were fast disappearing.

One of the extras turned, whispering to his wife, 'boy they are good, so fluent and natural. So totally off the wall!'

For Ernie it was another, impossible to explain, sublime moment. Dangerously close to life-changing. But not that close, so he snapped out of it, there was work to be done, ten more days of it. Perhaps, he thought, the trio could relax by actually experiencing Europe. The idea had many virtues. They'd be walking on solid ground. Not a tightrope. They could recharge, get background photos and pick up souvenirs for EE2. The very thought of EE2 stopped him. This had already been the most energy draining twelve days of his professional life.

-0-

It had already been the most energy draining two days of Dent and Swallow's lives. The flight, even though they'd 'turned left' and sat almost up front, was tiring. The first night's 'sleep' even more so. What was it about Paris? They'd got up, showered and headed out to a small café in the 2nd Arrondissement for breakfast. Dent's phone was without power and lay silent half hidden, half under the bed. It was only when a local on a neighboring table was disturbed by his phone that the doctor fumbled in his pockets and felt under dressed, unarmed. Instinctively he went around his trousers, jacket and shirt until he remembered, he hadn't lost or forgotten his phone, he had just down prioritized it. He wasn't overly keen in being controlled by the slim slice of technology, but he did want to have an overview, albeit very distant. If Mrs D phoned he would ignore it, unless he was alone. The most terrifying tone to him would be the soft ring of FaceTime. Anyway, for the time being he felt in a safe zone, it was something after midnight in Kingman. He'd pick up the phone before they went sight-seeing.

Swallow had made out such a detailed-filled itinerary that it almost listed the number of coffees he could consume. She had printed it out, one for her and one for him; it was like he was a schoolboy. He didn't mind and she seemed happy, the number of references to 'Relax' time indicating the number of times he'd probably enjoy her naked body. There were two, sometimes three, a day. He might need a wellness break after this he thought, and then wondered what was French for batteries.

Back at the hotel 'Swallow Tours', as he was now calling it jokingly to her face, had only time for a comfort break. He picked up the phone without glancing and shoved it in his jacket, the rest of the morning promised a walk along the Seine to the Eiffel Tower, popping up to the top, and then lunch in a bistro in Montmartre, back into the city for Place de la Concorde and nipping into Notre Dame, getting on their knees and then back to the hotel to get on their backs, well one of them.

The perfect plan, except that springtime in Paris is wait-in-line time. It only took forty minutes to get a ticket for the Tower, but it took an hour and a half to reach the first level, and forty more minutes to reach the next. All around in they could see weary tourists throwing in the towel in the effort to get to the top. Climbing Everest in a vest is easier. 'Hell, I'll just say I got to the top,' said one New Yorker who turned around and reduced the wait time by 20 seconds.

Swallow was not a quitter and if it meant a total revamp of her precious schedule then it would have to be. She wanted her moment on top of the Tower with 'my dear Ronnie', for it would be an anchor point in their relationship. The Eiffel Tower one of the world's most recognizable and used images, CNN can't report from France without it in the background, and what Swallow wanted was an unconscious eternal nudge in Dent's mind that every time he saw it on the news or in movies, he saw her. Whether he chose to see her in the jeans and sweatshirt she now wore or as she was curled round a sheet some hours earlier and again later, it didn't matter. The Tower would be their own very public, but private, symbol of their commitment to each other.

Halfway up the erect symbol of their love, frustrated by the progress, Dent took out his phone.

'Fuck it,' he said to all, including the smiling Japanese behind him. 'It's dead, battery flat.'

Swallow smiled and reached into her substantial handbag. A sucker for gadgets, she pulled out something she'd bought at the JFK stopover. It looked like a girl's toy, but it was a battery booster. 'I'm not sure if it is charged enough but it says on the back that you should use it fully first time round before re-charging, so it must have some kick.'

'Pat, you are just too much,' he said and she acknowledged that he was right with the subtlest move of an eyebrow.

It took ten minutes, not to re-vitalize Dent's phone, but to get the plastic sealed packaging off.

'This has got to be the world's most frustrating invention,' Dent fumed as he changed techniques from ripping to biting open. Eventually, with a USB cord connected, the phone slowly came back to life.

'There's a message from Zimmerman,' he said.

He didn't speak further, he just showed it to Swallow and they stood in-line, in silence. Swallow was devastated. She knew every time he saw the Eiffel Tower, he would think of a mal-practiced bridge job, Jack Megaghy.

-0-

Although it was four in the morning Ernie had been up for an hour. In another they were due to leave for the vineyards of Tuscany, at nine o'clock Tourist Time. The phone rang and he desperately fought off the automatic reaction of saying 'morning' – the caller's name jolting him into a 360-degree spin in order to see who was about.

'Doctor, I was getting worried, you hadn't responded to any of my calls.'

The doctor thought that he'd only missed a text, but two-thirds the way up the Eiffel Tower and surrounded by photo-clicking Japanese he was not on the most comfortable debating platforms. Ernie in no way could envisage the swing in the balance of power, but he sensed he was riding a wave of good luck and to increase that fortune he immediately told Dent the line wasn't great and he was breaking up.

'Can you hear me?' Ernie inquired again picking up the initiative. 'It was sad about Mr Megaghy, but all is in order, I believe he is back with his family. Have you been in touch with the Institute?'

Dent shuddered, on seeing the text he'd intended to call both, but one had to be first and he figured that he needed 'on site' information before he talked to St Anthony's. After all the staff there knew where he was . . . almost. So he lied. 'Yes, indeed. And sad we don't like losing a guest at any time. You said it was natural causes?'

'Yes,' Ernie was quietly enjoying this, 'he'd been complaining of tiredness although he was eating well. We were about to go on a tour of San Marino and he didn't come down to breakfast. We found him in his room, on the toilet.' Ernie thought the odd true fact might not go amiss.

'He'd like that,' said Dent and uncharacteristically added, 'he was a big fan of Elvis.'

Ernie put the flippancy down to a nervousness he'd never seen before in the doctor. He'd have been worried if he'd mentioned a connection of Hank Williams.

Swallow consumed by curiosity asked, 'who is it?'

'It's Zimmerman, Mr Megaghy's died,' Dent replied automatically before realizing he'd just revealed his hand in this game of poker.

Opportunity is chance meeting timing, another one of Ernie's guide rules, and he grabbed it again this time it passed.

Ernie took out the knife, 'Is that Nurse Swallow, is she with you?'

There was a pause and then a cough.

'When do you arrive in Rome?'

The pause was even more protracted and Ernie was enjoying conjuring up an image of Dent and Swallow somewhere in Paris, dressed or undressed, but in total flap-out. The hunters hunted. The fox was cornered.

'I've a conference in Barcelona in two days and then Rome and back to the States on the Sunday, 'Dent detailed his schedule

'So Rome will be the Saturday afternoon and or the Sunday morning.' Ernie detailed his problem.

'I think I got that,' he lied, 'we've made a couple of changes to facilitate the group's wishes' he lied again, 'and the intention now is to be in Rome Friday thru to the Sunday, so will catch you there.'

With a sense of temporary relief, Dent said his farewell and prepared for the next call, 'the I'm on top of the situation' chat with the Institute. He wasn't on top of the Tower, or the situation, and he knew it. He looked at Swallow, resplendent, and thought, I don't really care, there are some things I am on top of.

33.
KING OF THE WINE FRONTIER

Mulholland Highway - Tuscany

There were more potential nominations for a suitable vineyard within a forty mile radius of the Dolby Theater, than there were actors for the Oscars. It was just a question of getting one that was quiet yet open to the public with private tastings. Rooster also wanted one that would be prepared to open their gates a couple of hours earlier than the eleven o'clock favored by most of them. A personal appeal on behalf of these very special tourists would most certainly find a kind responsive ear. She was finding people more caring and understanding than she'd ever thought and personally, with each passing day, feeling a little more uncomfortable about the deceit.

Wherever vineyard it was to be, it required two hours plus of driving time. Ngoc sat quietly in row three with Ryder now restored to driving live people about. There was a quiet sense of relief, and an even quieter transmission. The target was one of the medium sized wineries that had grown up on the northern suburbs; they could have returned to Solvang, Ernie had been tempted by a sign to Fess Parker's place at Los Olivos. Davy Crockett, King of the Wild Frontier, was Fess's biggest part and both were Ernie's heroes, but the vineyard established by the action actor wasn't continental enough, should any chatter slip out from a third party. On the website it looked like a cowboy ranch to get pissed at. Also, he was still missing sleep from the Mette Nielsen revelation that nearby Solvang was her hometown. He couldn't ask her to put the beekeeper's hat on again. Anyway his hero Fess wouldn't be about to share a tipple with, he stopped drinking wine in 2010. Sadly, he stopped drinking everything in 2010.

Rooster had found a bunch of vineyards up off the Mulholland Highway and then stumbled upon a gem about three hours north. Just west of the very Spanish sounding Paso Rambles was the Pontiere Estate, family run and specializing in Italian wines. Rooster had clocked that Mr Wilcox's passion for identifying perfumes, usually only when freshly applied and from close-up, was matched by his ability to nail a grape and wine and on a good day, the year.

The website of the estate was a strong indication of people who cared. They used words like 'custodian' rather than ownership and on the phone they seemed happy to help, 'and if helping is by keeping out of the way, that's cool for us,' the lady had said. It also saved them from bringing in any staff two hours before normal opening time. She herself would man the shop next to the tasting rooms, but Rooster had warned her that the 'special circumstances' meant that the tourists wouldn't be able to buy anything. However, if she could set aside a case of the 2014 Viognier and one of the Zinfandels, she herself, or their driver, could pick it up.

The wines came to close to a thousand dollars, but she thought Ernie would see the twin logic in oiling the wheels at the vineyard and the fact that they could always use them over the rest of the trip. They were fairly punchy in terms of alcoholic kick and a glass or so with the evening meal would shorten the transition from social to slumber. Anyway Ernie liked what he called cross-over wine, anything over 14%, which bridged the gap from beer to spirits. He'd already bought a couple of bottles of imported Barolo and Barbaresco, which he'd intended to use as an emergency if anyone was sharp enough to question the origins of what they were sampling. Even that was a risk if sampled by a true connoisseur, since the Barolo and Barbaresco were from Piedmont, in real terms the next region up. However, he thought the comparative lack of wine at St Anthony's would have nullified any ability to distinguish between any two good wines. What he hadn't considered was Mr Wilcox's nose and Arthur J's passion to be a smartarse. Thankfully these two abilities were un-connected.

Driving north on the 101 Ryder took the turnoff for Templeton and then cut left onto Vineyard Road. He smiled to himself, who needs a GPS? Rooster, as Millie, was giving a lecture on Tuscany and explaining that lunch today would be a picnic from goods bought in the local market. In the back of the bus two seats were heavily occupied by several large manila grocery bags, all bearing the name Rock Eagle Italian Bakery and Deli on them. As she talked she kept an eye out for a likely open space, quieter than a layby, but with the same attributes, a couple of bench tables and maybe even a toilet. She hadn't seen any but was loathe to take up the offer from the vineyard to use their facilities. They'd calculated an hour and a bit for the tour and tasting and then an hour and another bit for the picnic; that would clash with the real time opening of the vineyard tours and the arrival of the first uncontrollable elements.

Of these wildcards the potentially most alarming was a seven-seater SUV with a three-generation family getting out. The trio were well used to gauging human strengths, weaknesses and likely outcomes. Many a con depended on understanding the most obvious movement of 'the mark'. Third party interventions like an SUV spanning the human lifecycle had become one of the many social observations that lead them to reconsidering locations when planning anything outside of HBO.

Most couples getting out of a car quietly go about their business, even two couples a generation apart seemed able to communicate perfectly well through actions and smiles. Introduce a third generation and all hell breaks loose before the car is even locked. The parents try to marshal the children and protect the grandparents, the grandparents are eager to get as much out of the grandkids as possible in such a short period and vice versa. The kids with an inherent ability to see a weak point, jump in and utilize it. The result is a cacophony of care-driven chaos; something that would blow the cover of any illusion. Just one extended family from Pasadena could open a floodgate of reasonable questions. 'Why are there so many Americans in the Po Valley?' could be a starter.

In the mountains there were plenty of opportunities to marvel at the bench placing ability of the National Parks. Ernie dozed and woke as the bus pulled off the country road and up a dusty drive. They parked up as far as possible away from the old farm that had been converted into a winery some two or three decades back. After a brief 'hello' Millie took the party on a long loop down one side of the vines and up the other. They stopped every thirty yards to re-group, for the ground was uneven and although using sticks and holding on to buddies, they found it tough going. Occasionally the line would break and a fraction of the party shoot off in a different direction, like a train splitting on route, except there were no tracks to hold the carriages back. They could just wander off anywhere. The vines however, acted as an effective coral and providing they kept on moving the train could be regrouped at the next turn. In regimentally tidy rows the vines were well trimmed back and only the first shoots of leaves distinguished them from dead wood. 'We're on the Deadwood stage,' Protz chipped in and waited for immediate laughter. He waited. Then he moved on.

Millie had several pre-recorded instructional audio files about wine-making and in the heat of the morning sun they would stop and listen to one emanating from the small Bose speaker in her backpack.

Ernie meanwhile was in the shop chatting to the owner, and a little nervously. The conversation was mostly about wine, but when it drifted towards the visiting party he felt un-comfortable. He maintained the line that it was a Government experiment in awareness, but through it all he was uneasy about being somewhere where he had no real control. He enjoyed tasting the wine, but looked forward to later that day when they'd be back in the safety of the studio. After all what would he do if Dent were to ring him now? He'd have to do the default setting: ignore the call and then ring back when the conditions were more in his favor. If the cell phone is a modern-day weapon, you need to know if it is cocked.

-0-

In Paris Dent was thinking along similar lines. He'd spoken with the Institute about Megaghy and was a little surprised that they had played such a minor role. A phone call from the sheriff's office, triggered by the airport manager that had alerted them to Megaghy's temporary resting place. Thereafter William Megaghy had flown down to collect brother Jack and to do a quick pack and empty his room at St Anthony's. The sad thing was that it took so little time and effort. There wasn't much in the room and two removal boxes were brought up from the cellar, full of little meaningful trinkets from Jack's sighted years, but left untouched since he moved in to the Institute. William took them home knowing that 90% of the bric-a-brac could have been dumped there and then. He just couldn't bring himself to do it and back in Seattle he and their sister could go through it. One by one the little items and photographs would trigger memories for all of them and then flicker out and into a black plastic bag. They were a bit like the stub end of a candle, the last inch and a half. You know it is not really worth lighting, but you can't bring yourself to throw it out. So, you light it and then twenty minutes later you need a knife to get the wax out. There were a lot of small candle ends in the boxes.

Dent reckoned that with Megaghy the European Experience team had had their slice of bad luck. There must have been a mountain of paperwork, particularly at the Italian end and he quite admired the slick professional way they had dealt with it. Back at St Anthony's all was running smoothly, although the buzz of the death had dominated every conversation. The doctor struggled with repeated uncertainty when asked how the rest of the tourists were dealing with the situation. He kept all his observations vague because he was scared a good 'sound-bite' would linger and then come back to chew him. He wanted to avoid circumstances where down the line a conversation would spin around 'the doctor said you were very upset,' and bounce back with 'how did he know, he wasn't there?'

He decided he wouldn't ring Zimmerman until they left Barcelona for Rome. They were two modern day Scarlet Pimpernels trying to hide from each other. The longest game in the world is Hide and Seek, where both parties are hiding.

'They seek him here, they seek him there
Those Frenchies seek him everywhere
Is he in heaven or is he in hell
That damned elusive Pimpernel'

That Baroness Orczy knew something about being evasive, thought Dent as he glanced at Swallow, reflected on the bathroom mirror as she stepped out of the shower. He looked at his schedule. It had been a disruptive day, but there was still time to relax.

34.
VIVA LA FAVOUR

Typhoon Studios – Greve in Chanti

The party had fallen into a semi-comma for the return trip to the studio. The sun, the wine, the picnic, the fresh air had all combined to put them into a communal form of blankness – when they woke up they wouldn't know where they were, but that's the way it had been for the past two weeks. They were, to a man and woman, happy.

The only people about to be upset were the EE team when they returned to the studio. There seemed to be more activity than usual and as the coach slipped by Charles rushed out in a futile attempt to stop it. Having failed, Ernie and co carried on before Ryder instinctively put on the brakes. Two police cars sat outside Set A. Two uniformed officers were resting their butts against the hood and smoked as they drank coffee.

'Are they waiting for something, like us?' said Ryder.

'Who's waiting for us?' Protz chipped in unhelpfully from mid bus.

'No one, I think it maybe a DHL package I'm waiting for,' Rooster said quickly.

'My Liverpool soccer shirt?' Harley added to bolster the thought process. He too was alarmed, was this the end of the road for his $18m journey?

In the wing mirror Ryder could see a golf cart approaching as fast as a golf cart can, but since they had stopped it had a reasonable chance of catching them. It was being driven one-handedly by Charles, the other hand waving as sort of 'don't go there' type of wave. If it were a choice between Charles and the cops, the producer would win, so Ernie indicated to Ryder to remain where they were.

Charles was alongside and just about to scream something when Ernie motioned to him to be silent and to wait for him to come to the cart.

They walked out of earshot. 'I'm so sorry I didn't get a chance to say this to you, but a last-minute ad came in that needed a shot in a plane. You were away and honestly I wasn't in a position to say no. . .'

Ernie looked at him, the anxiety melting enough for him to wipe out the worst-case scenarios, 'but the cops . . .'

'That's another scene. They said to me they'd be through an hour ago, so it can't take too long.'

Ernie looked at him, the anxiety total melted, but he maintained an outwardly frozen persona. Never bet or bargain with a smile, it was another Zimmerism. 'We had an agreement. This is a lab experiment and you have contaminated it. You could have blown many months of work out of the ocean. I'm thinking a reduction.'

'A reduction in what? You're paying nothing as it is!'

The freeze couldn't hold back the inner smile. 'Okay, but let's just remember this moment. We'll take the volunteers out for another hour, but then we have to come back to our previous status quo, if that makes sense?'

'Total, and thanks. How is it going, dare I ask?'

'You've dared, but I dare not say anything other than.' He stopped and put his hand to his face and with a twist of the wrist turned up a vague hint of a smile. Happy Charles got back in his cart and drove off semi silently towards the smoking policemen.

Back on the bus Ernie silently signaled that everything was okay and whispered into Ryder's ear the news that they had to somehow find a detour. Detours are easy when in mid journey but when you've got to your destination, they are somewhat tricky. Before they'd got to the gate, Ernie tapped Ryder again and pointed back to the sets. Why not use that exterior Victorian street scene? Some of the unused exterior lots were not in the agreement they had with Charles, but hey, he owed him one. He whispered Sienna to Rooster who tapped it into her iPad. The image that came up was too huge to cover at this short notice. Far better a small Tuscan village, she started searching. Greve in Chanti seemed interesting, small rural market town with a name linked to a wine bottle half hidden in straw.

Greve on the web and Google Earth turned out to be surprisingly featureless for a very picturesque part of the world. That quite helped, maybe less to talk about, but also less to try and respond too. Pisa wasn't too far away, but the thought of trying to match the Leaning Tower at such short notice was not worth brain time. Perhaps the spiral ramp of a disused car park? He logged that thought. In the meantime, Pisa was off plumb, and limits.

On the Victorian set the party had moved up and down the street half a dozen times before being finally shepherded into a mock tea house. There was enough left over from the picnic to open an instant café and Ngoc and Pang moved some tables and chairs out into the street. Food and tepid water were not an issue, they could even do wine, but at the first stop most wanted cold water or coffee, Italian coffee.

Millie took orders and dispatched Ryder to a coffee shop about 10 minutes away. Harley went to help, and to get away from sitting around observing without being able to make observations.

'Why do the Italians do coffee like no one else?' The question came from Joyce Reid, the large noisy lady from Pensacola. There was a general muttering of 'good question' and 'I wonder'. Arthur J pretended not to hear. He was sure there was some logical reason, it was just that he couldn't quite think of it and until he did, he would remain silent. Unless that was, someone else's suggestion needed to be put down.

'It's like God decided, "Hey you French, you do the wine, you English the tea, you Americans the Cola, you Belgians the beer, you Irish, you Irish, you drink it,"' said a surprisingly sparky Miss Little.

'Easy,' said Sean Seamus, 'that's a sweeping damning statement condemning an entire proud upright nation. I could sue, or you could buy me a pint.'

'When God woke up and wanted a coffee,' interjected Protz. 'Hey Mario, he shouted, coffee, no milk, no sugar.'

'You can say black if you like,' Joyce chipped in.

The party laughed, all that was except Arthur J who was still wondering, 'why is it that the Italians do it so well? That, and clothes, and cars. The odd ceiling and organized crime too, but with other things they do fall apart. Politics and war and mammas over the age of 45, to name but three.' He knew then and there that when he got home he'd stop reading books and write one. The whole concept as to why some cultures do things better and differently was a gold mine of mental opportunity. Why is left wing, left? Why do Republicans have an elephant and the Democrats a donkey? Why do Danish and North Korean audiences clap the same way? He could talk about it forever. What a potential joy.

After twenty-five caffeine-free minutes there was the obligatory comment, from Protz. 'Where's the coffee, has she gone to Brazil for it?' It was followed by the obligatory laugh and obligatory thought, someone had to say it . . . and that someone was most probably going to be Protz.

Harley came through the back of the mock up set, the tea house was open to the world beyond the flat concreted pathway for tracking shots. They'd multiplied the order by 1.5 to compensate for mind changing and re-ordering. And there they sat in the mid afternoon sun thinking it was closer to late evening. Miss Sander let the cooling froth of her Cappuccino roll over her lip and drip of her chin. Across the street a cat came down from the crude ledge it had been using as a sun lounger. In front there were nearly twenty people, but it had one target, the nice lady who had shown a couple of moments affection some days earlier. The cat wasn't sure if it was four or five days because cats don't have watches, listen to the news or generally care about anything other than feeding one end and licking the other.

They also adopt people. The cat purred round her legs and Miss Sander felt down for it. Like someone tickling a trout out of the water, she swooped it up and on to her lap. Ernie and Rooster looked on in horror. Her hand stroked the cat's head and she announced, 'how strange, this cat has the same tear on her ear as the one I found in England, Europuss!'

There was a huge prolonged silence. It was only five seconds, but to Rooster and Ernie it seemed forever. It was broken by Harley. 'What color was the English cat?'

'How would I know?' said Sander.

'It was a tabby, this is a ginger thing,' said Ernie so happy that Harley had pointed the way to the escape exit.

'What a coincidence about the ear,' Miss Sander added.

'I'm not a cat person,' Ernie cut in, 'but I think they are all like three-year old cars – they all have a dent on the driver's door.' As he said it he made a mental note for Ryder to put the cat in a bag and drop it off next time he was out on an errand. Preferably a trip that required two bus changes. He'd once heard of an Irish terrier that wasn't abandoned, but left in the house whilst his family viewed their next home. He got out and still managed to locate the new house ten miles away whilst the family were still looking around. That trip was easy, it only took one bus change.

Ernie didn't want to see the cat again, they might run out of colors.

Over at the locked-off studio they could see that the police patrol cars had gone, and the ferry bus had removed the crew and actors. The set might be the same, but Ernie still felt violated even though the whole thing was built around an impossible promise. However, it was a Government promise and Charles should have respected that. He'd pop by in the morning when on the way to Rome to confirm the latest contribution to the favor-owed account. He loved moral high ground. It's where he wanted to be buried.

The next few days promised to be the most hectic of the entire trip. More than anywhere they had to create a presence, one strong enough to fool Dent and Swallow into believing that they had just missed the party, again.

They were about to enter the Lion's Den.

35.
A SNATCHED OPPORTUNITY

Typhoon Studios / somewhere in Italy

His phone vibrated for several seconds with St Anthony's coming up on the screen. 'What could they want? He thought.

He picked it up.

'Mr Zimmerman?'

'That's me,' he chipped in.

'It is Shelly from St Anthony's. I need to talk with Dr Dent. Is he with you?'

It was not a missile he'd expected to duck and he replied that 'at that moment' they were not together. He played the vague card.

'He said something about research and a congress.'

'Okay, it is just that he rang last night and left a message that his bag, with phone and wallet had been snatched off him.'

'God is an Irishman' that quirk of uncalculated good fortune struck Ernie, who then paused to genuinely thank God profusely, promising all manner of devotions. He tried to piece it together. If his 'man-bag' had been snatched it would been when they were in Barcelona. Swallow would have hers, but she couldn't ring from Spain when she was supposed to be in Chicago. He must have used a hotel or payphone.

It was a point that needed some geographical anchors and Ernie said that Dent had detoured to Spain to a conference and that they were due to see each other in Rome.

'Did he lose his passport?' Ernie inquired, worried that Dent might be stranded and seek them out. Although he didn't know if it was possible to move across Europe without one. He suspected that for a European it might be, but for an American, probably not.

'The message just said phone and credit cards, no mention of his passport, but we have heard so little. When do you next expect to see him next?'

'We were to have met up tomorrow. I can't remember what he said about the conference.'

'At the moment, unless he calls back, you are the best way of keeping in touch with him. I'll keep in touch.'

Ernie pressed the red button and looked upwards. Would it be too cruel to phone back with the details from the airline? Yes. He went looking for Rooster to brief her.

-0-

The trio sat outside Set C, the late evening sun still had its worth and they shared it. They also shared a six-pack of Sam Adams, the wine was too soporific, and occasionally shared glances at Ryder's phone. It had an image of a corridor, still life, or at least they hoped it would stay still. It was beamed from a small camera, their electronic night watchman. Megaghy's demise and Harley's revelation had eased up the pressure on the second-floor rooms with en suite. Now only one person needed to walk to the communal bathrooms on the first floor, so it was no longer communal, just very off suite. From where they sat they could hear any movement in that area. All was quiet.

Ernie was still in a mild spin from the news of Dent being mugged. In his mind it had started as just a simple misplacement, it developed into a full-on loss and now he could imagine Swallow and Dent, arm-in-arm strolling down the Ramblas and having his man-bag ripped off his shoulder by a pillion passenger on a motor bike. Whatever the circumstances he had to evaluate how best to use them. Despite his chosen profession, Ernie was not a mean person, but Dent's misfortune had the potential to give them a relatively free ride home. Unless, and it as a big unless, Dent saw in Zimmerman his own and only emergency escape route.

He tried to put the doctor's hat on. What would he do in such a situation? Dent's salvation and obstruction were one and the same thing, Patricia Swallow. In her handbag he presumed there was a means of immediate financial survival and communication. Her finances and where she spent her money were between her and her bank, the phone was another thing. If it were hers, again it would be fairly private, but if Dent had organized one paid for by the Institute, the foreign calls would show up in the accounts department. Anyway he couldn't phone the office or home on her phone for fear of caller ID. After all Swallow was with her mother shopping for summer gear in Sears. If he were Dent he'd stop and take a deep breath. There would be things to do in Barcelona, police reports, extend hotel booking, change plane reservations, get

296

emergency funds. Perhaps even a passport. Throwing a coin into Trevi and making a wish, would have to wait, although the list of desirable requests had just dramatically expanded. Dent was so in need of a bit of luck, would need to throw in his Amex, if he had one.

So in the mind of EZ, the doctor was temporarily out of the game. But how should he play it? Turn the screw or stand back and take his hands off the gas? Shelley, the receptionist at St Anthony's was the unwitting and unlikely controller of any pressure. She'd promised to keep in touch with Ernie since he was the only person in Europe she had a number for. The phone records of Ernie and Swallow over the next few days could be 'the black box' should this particular mission come crashing down. With one phone call he could crush the arrogant doctor, but then all future EE's would implode. On every level he was unsure if he could face an EE II. Maybe they could go legit, come clean and just run experiences. Maybe this was his last con. He detested the word, the concept of blackmail, but he now had a tool, not to use it would be a sin against his chosen vocation.

-0-

Back in his hotel room Dent could barely sleep for the conundrum he was in. He tossed, turned, dozed and then stared out the window. Things must have been grim for him to ignore the prone but stunning semi-naked body of Swallow, partially wrapped in a loose white sheet. His side of the bed was wet from nervous perspiration.

The wallet had contained a huge amount of cash. He didn't want to flash hospital plastic and leave a trail, at least until they met up in Rome, so he had ordered €5,000 from his bank. Some had gone in Paris, but most was now in the back pocket of an anonymous and very happily occupied pair of jeans. His phone had already been recoded and sold on; the man-bag was in a green wheelie bin, waiting to be recycled. It was too middle-aged for the seventeen year olds who had had an otherwise very profitable night. Oh yes, there was the ring. In a small zipped part of the wallet they'd found a man's white gold wedding ring. They'd shift that somehow.

Dent stared at the ceiling, a shaft of light from the bathroom revealing some fine plasterwork around the over-elaborate central lamp, modelled to look like candlelight, but not capable of matching the wax version, more powerful, but real candles don't get so dusty. He always kept the bathroom light on in a hotel, a beacon to relief. Slowly he raised his torso from the damp sheet. He began muttering in near delirium. Sweat dripped along his eyebrows, he could feel it on the back of his neck, running down his spine. He felt his left hand and looked at the fading white band of skin. He only ever exposed it to the sun when he did his other favorite hobby and even then it was covered by a glove until he grabbed his putter. He then began to uncontrollably shake and this, along with the strange sounds, broke Swallow free from her sleep.

'Ronnie, what is it? Are you okay?'

The mumbling persisted and Swallow assumed he was having a bad dream, God knows his mind had enough material to play with.

Eyes wide open he turned to her, 'the ring, my wedding ring was in the wallet.'

He'd removed it in part deference to her that this was 'their special trip' and that it shouldn't be blurred by any connection to the realities of a life that they would have to return to. This was their free time and they wanted it free of any considerations other than themselves.

He couldn't think, but she could. She got up, wrapped on a gown and went towards the half open French window, even though they were totally in Spain. She took a cigarette from her bag and walked out onto the small Juliet balcony.

'You've told the police that it was a snatch job. We can't change that. We can't say now they demanded your ring, it just wouldn't work like that. That's not how we portrayed it. They wouldn't have stopped there for they would also have taken your watch.' It was her Joan Crawford moment, elegance meets menace.

She turned back to him. 'you only left a message at the office?' He nodded in the affirmative. 'have you spoken to home?' He gave the opposite response.

'Now try and recall the wording of the message.'

Dent was still a mid-bed zombie, but he slowly delivered the facts. He had been vague, but he thought he used the expression, 'taken' not 'lost or snatched'.

'Whatever, it's early evening so pick up that phone and call home, the story can differ from the police report that will never reach home and even if it does you can put it down to lost in translation. So you were robbed at knifepoint, they took your phone, your wallet, your ring, your watch.'

Dent looked to the bedside table. He loved his Breitling Navitimer, it was number four in his possessions coming after his two children, Patricia Swallow and his golf clubs. At this point in their frayed relationship, his oscillating electric toothbrush had just nudged the current Mrs Dent out of the top ten.

'That has got to go.'

It was like being mugged for a second time. He'd bought it second-hand for $4,000 as present to himself to mark his 40th birthday. He could see her logic, it was his alibi; without it on his wrist his wife, and anyone else, might just accept the missing ring.

'We can't sell it because that will start a trail. But I can't just throw it away.'

'There is one solution. It is not as foolproof as tossing it, but it is a compromise. Give it to me and I'll put it somewhere safe. Hide it away. I'm not here after all. If you can bear to be without it until this blows over, you can then "buy" a similar one, second hand, but really this one with maybe with a strap change, you are back to . . .' the final words held themselves in the thin trace of smoke that hung over Swallow and were lost to the balcony's breeze.

'I could always say I 'd left it in the hotel.'

'You could, but without losing it, the ring is an isolated incident, and open to more dubious questions. That watch, much as you love it, is more valuable lost than . . . .' Her calm direction had already sunk in.

Dent got off the bed, picked up the Breitling and dropped it into her handbag. He held her from behind and kissed her on the neck. 'You're a special cares nurse.'

He released her and walked over to his side of the bed, he always took the left when with Pat, it made everything seem different, which it was. He picked up the phone.

-0-

It was seven in the evening in Kingman. Angela Dent had skipped making her new island-based kitchen untidy by not cooking for the fifth time since Ronnie had been away. It was the perfect arrangement, the kitchen remained pristine and teenagers Rikki and Toni were only too happy to comply with another night's ordered-in pizza. The menu was on the fridge, next to the itinerary the European Experience dad was religiously following.

As a family they'd never been further than the statutory pilgrimages to Disney and Universal in LA, a handful of Nationals, including Yosemite and a fishing holiday in Washington State. So the opportunity to match up the names on the menu with real travel destinations was a glorious one. Today dad was in Rome and they'd have a 28" Roma pizza to mark it. Thank goodness he joined the party after Poland. Travel broadens the mind, but in the case of stay-at-home thirteen-year-old Toni and elder brother Rikki, the constant dough diet was broadening their waists.

Angela's phone vibrated on the polished steel worktop. There was no number, no caller ID.

'Hi darling,' Ronnie started, 'all well?' Before she got the opportunity to answer he told her the sad tale of being mugged and how he lost everything, wallet and phone 'and bastards took my watch and wedding ring. I'm still a bit shook up.'

They didn't have the closest of relationships, but adversity is a bonding element and she went straight into the care and repair mode. Dent would have preferred a more indifferent response. Like 'serves you right for being out walking alone.' Beyond the mugging he'd barely thought out his storyline. Where, when, how? According to the fridge he was somewhere in Italy, if she offered to ring back how could he explain Barcelona? Best to be vague and quick, but there was the opportunity to throw in a tangible fact that would tie him to the party.

'It's annoying and I will sort things out with the office. I have to ring them anyway to check on the progress of Mr Megaghy. You remember him?' without waiting for a reply he explained the dentist's demise and how it had upset the party and travel arrangements.

'We're relocating, gotta go. Love to the kids.' They were scrambling towards grabbing the phone when the line went dead.

Dent lay back on the bed, back in the zone of uncertainly that had dominated his life since halfway down the Ramblas. He had to get to Rome.

One more phone call from the hotel. He didn't know who was on late duty at the Institute, it didn't really matter, all he needed to do was to expand on his earlier message and turn off a potential offer of assistance to him at the hotel in Rome he wasn't at. He definitely had to get to Rome.

36.
THREE COINS

Chinatown, LA – Trevi, Rome

'Has anyone a spare coin?' asked Miss Temple. Ryder reached forward and with the aid of a nylon-meshed fishing net, scooped up one from the rough concrete base bringing it up through the eight inches of water into the full morning light. He shook it free of droplets and handed it to Miss Temple.

'It's wet,' she pointed out and Ryder explained that most of his coins were wet from the mist of the fountains. She tossed it in.

'Not like that Miss Temple,' Millie interjected. You throw it with your right hand and over your left shoulder. Within seconds there was a burst of tinkling sound as coins went in every direction with only a few landing in the water of the fairly anonymous, yet impressively big fountain in LA's Chinatown. Rooster thought it a nice twist that Chinatown was that great movie about bringing water to the city and that Trevi Fountain marked a similar feat in Rome, albeit over two thousand years earlier. She then had a Monty Python flash, 'and what did the Romans do for us?' before getting on with the job in hand with a secondary thought of what would people do to tempt good fortune in a cashless society. Was there a Trevi Mobile Pay? There ought to be.

The few onlookers who were up this early, kept well clear of the party, preferring to observe rather than be drawn in. They watched as Ryder starting to help the coin throwers with some individual tuition. He looked like a golf pro trying to correct a learner's swing, but it worked and more and more of the coins ended with a satisfying plop. Millie continued with her history lesson.

'It is an offence to take the money out of the fountain. Each day about €3000 is thrown into Trevi, each with a wish attached. We don't know how many wishes come true, but for the hungry of Rome, every coin represents a bite of food.'

Harley turned his back on the fountain, and flicked a coin high up into the air. Looking directly into Rooster's eyes he had time to make his wish before it broke the surface. She wasn't throwing any money away, but she was, as each day passed, more in tune with Harley and somewhere down the line, time and opportunity might prove that his coin may not have been wastefully discarded.

Ernie had missed the early morning tour of Trevi and the Pantheon in order to be ready for the next unpredictable chapter in the life of Dent and Swallow. He wanted however, to be with the group by the time they got to the Colosseum, he'd never been inside the Hollywood Bowl before. They had booked an adult self-tour when the doors opened. The place was huge and full of potential for a Roman walkabout. With additional sound effects from Pang and Ngoc, they could easily spend much of the day there although there was always the concern of bumping into a school group, a fate worse than the three generation SUV. They had marked a point to retreat to should any third parties threaten, a bank of seating high up on the top left, U2. The code word for the emergency move was 'Bono'. From there the Bowl itself was an eggcup, any gladiatorial killing could be done with a sword or sub-machine gun as far as anyone without binoculars would know. Rooster had told him she'd 'seen' Gloria Estefan there in 2011, but only noticed her three costume changes when she later saw pictures in the papers. There was an issue between the stage area and U2, the middle rows of plastic seating. The Colosseum was ahead of its day but not that far. Even the wooden seats at the back might take some explanation.

There'd be no performance today. They'd checked in case the Philharmonic had a rehearsal on, but Rooster had booked music for later when they got back to the studio bar. He wasn't a Pavarotti, more what she called a 'lounge lizard crooner' from a Venetian-themed restaurant in Monterey. He'd do for Italy what Michael had done so splendidly for the west of Ireland in what already felt like a lifetime ago. So many days that it seemed like forever. Only occasionally was that memorable night rekindled by the spasmodic outbreak of a bobhran coming late at night from a bedroom before being silenced by near universal disapproval. At least this guy didn't have any instruments to sell. He was just sing, grab his money and go, preferably with, as requested, no chit-chat between numbers. Rooster had heard him and was comfortable that at least some of the performance would feature a classic. His highlight was melody of Leonard Cohen numbers, in Italian.

-0-

His phone rang and briefly he was admiring the acoustics of the Bowl before the thought of answering. He then thought again. Better not to answer. If the acoustics were good for the ring, he'd no desire to turn his reply into a one-man show. The awaiting audience were a block away, but this was a perfect amphitheater. The number had no name, but he recognized it as probably being nurse Swallow's, the first digits being similar to the phone Dent used to own. 'So, it's a company deal, he thought,' adding another telling detail to the bank of knowledge about the couple. He made his way to an exit and waited for it to ring again, assuming quite rightly that Swallow would think she'd misdialed. It rang.

'Ernest Zimmerman,' he said on pressing the red dot on his screen.

He instantly recognized that it wasn't the nurse, just three words, but the voice was new to him.

'It's Angela Dent.' He nearly dropped the phone, but with years of practice recovered.

'Hello, Mrs Dent, is there a problem?'

'It's Ronald, as you know he's lost his phone, wallet, watch, jewelry? How is he'

'Of course, and how devastating. He's not here at the moment, there is so much red tape.' He then threw in a little color to emboss the image she held in her head in the kitchen beside the bottle of Pinot Grigio which still had a glass left in it, but not for long, 'we're enjoying a Colosseum moment, fantastic.'

'Can you get my husband to ring me?' she requested without saying if the purpose was support or a screaming match.

'Of course I will, whenever I next see or speak to them, we're due to meet up later today or tomorrow. It'll probably be after they've sorted things out with the police.' he replied hopefully planting a seed of a plural relationship in Angela's mildly-sozzled mind.

The line dead she hung up, tipped the last of the Grigio into her glass and looked at the clock on the oven. It was the only part of the equipment she felt confident to use. It was early morning. She'd wait til lunch before opening another bottle. 'Did he say "speak to them"?' Putting it down to a transatlantic miscommunication she went out onto the patio to await the gardener. Life was so hectic.

The phone rang again before Ernie had barely emerged from the dark exit tunnel into the full light of the stadium. He turned on his heals, the number was again familiar, but again unrecognized. Was it Angela ringing back to ask about the 'them' he'd mischievously slipped into their very brief chat? No, it was a different number, although similar.

'Ernest Zimmerman,' he offered, half suspecting it to be a male voice. He was 100% right, though the phone turned out to be registered to a female, one Patricia Swallow.

'Ernie,' he was completely taken aback by the informal nature of the opening. 'It's Ronnie.' And even more derailed by implied buddy-ness. 'Ronnie Dent, at the airport about to board.'

'You found your phone?' Ernie floated, attempting to buy time and information in one simple question.

'No this is borrowed, but you can get me on it anytime, day and night,' the words were already out of his mouth and lodged firmly in Ernie's ears. It was at moments like this that Ernie wished he taken up a lifestyle course that would have lead him to the other side of the law. A lawyer would have had such fun with this in cross-examination. The open question flashed 'and if we should want to contact nurse Swallow?' He didn't get the time for Dent was already into the call's main purpose.

'The plane won't get into Rome until nearly ten. That means we can't meet up for breakfast, can I see you at your hotel?'

It was the single most worrying sentence that Ernie had been living with since Dent announced his intention of 'popping over and helping out'. Preparation is the key and Ernie twisted it in the lock of Dent's plans. What was jamming it was Dent's attempt to expunge Swallow from the script.

'Of course, you won't have got our last couple of texts! Some of the senior members of the group expressed a desire to be a little out of the city in a slightly cooler environment. We didn't want another fatality and can you believe it, coming from Arizona, they found Rome too hot! It hasn't been quite so, but it was the lack of A/C that triggered the move. We found a charming little hotel about 50kms up the Tiger valley, it only takes us an hour and a bit to the center – depending on traffic, which is pretty horrendous as you will find out. The plan is to leave this hotel after an early breakfast and head to St Peter's for the Papal Mass we then leave for a late lunch at a little restaurant on the road to Genoa. Are you going to the Vatican?'

It was actually on Swallow's now decimated holiday tour schedule. 'Yes, I'll text you once there.'

'And I'll text you the restaurant details,' offered Ernie as gesture of commitment. They then returned to their respective fake environments. Ernie to the Colosseum, Dent to the airport flying to a city where, to everyone else he'd never been, never filed a police report, but where he had lost anything.

Ernie had the restaurant details to hand. Days earlier he'd got Rooster to look one up and to book for a party of eight. He just needed the Experience on the reservations list, not seats for everyone and he didn't want to disrupt the finances too much of the small restaurant. They were perhaps the longest distance 'no shows' in history, but at least if Dent turned up, their name was on the table. If there were to be no need to have the chef waiting anxiously, then she'd cancel. No card details were requested or offered. Ernie liked the simplicity of the ruse and wondered where he might employ it again.

The party had finished hearing tales of emperors and gladiators and had made their way back to the bus. Down on stage a kid from Orlando decided to try out the acoustics of the famed Bowl.

'Good Morning Hollywood,' he belted out, 'today I'd like to run a melody of Justin Beaver songs past you,' blissfully he didn't follow up the promise and signed off with 'thank you Los Angeles, you've been a terrific audience.'

Colino turned to Protz, 'sometimes I'm ashamed of being an American. Some don't travel so well.'

Ryder had been away on Mission Gelato, with instructions to come back with as much Italian-style ice cream he could get without going beyond the melting zone. They were enjoying the Roman sun and commenting on the ice cream being another example of something the Italians do so well, when four large coaches appeared on the approach road. They seemed to contain the entire scouting community for Orange County and the sound of sing-along campfire numbers pierced through the combined emissions of the four diesel engines. Ernie looked over at a sign-post displaying a concert that evening, Rooster had got it wrong – underneath a list of unknowns was the line 'backed by the Massed Choir of Southern Californian Scouts.' The side of their little bus would be like a magnet to them. Ernie quickly signaled the Double X to Pang and within seconds there was the sound of distant thunder and with Ngoc's assistance rain was spraying from on high. It was a tropical moment the Asian pair had been looking forward to for weeks.

The spectacle of people in sun-glasses eating ice cream whilst being sprayed with water by a little man in shorts, was too much for the singing scouts and the four buses passed by with the silent spotty faces glued to the windows in confused awe. Before the mass choir could pull up, the Hallelujah Choir were back in their seats and Ryder was rounding an island of broad-leafed plants and pulling away.

'Wonder if they are performing tonight,' said the scout choirmaster to his number two.

'That's the first rain we've had since Ireland,' said Wilcox as he nudged the last bit of ice cream into the tip of his cone and then crunched it in one bite. 'Boy that was good, you don't get it like that at home.'

Rooster made a mental note to get more, maybe tomorrow on the way to the Vatican they could stop off and try some new tastes. She offered the idea to the entire bus to a very genuine positive response. She liked these people and liked making them happy.

-0-

Back at the studio the party were shown to their new rooms by

310

Millie and Ryder and told to take it easy for an hour. 'Have a practice siesta.' They'd be called for dinner and then the evening in the bar with Fabio. There was general agreement that they'd enjoyed the Italian food the most so far on the trip – the French would have to go some to top it and the trio realized that. Italian food is the best traveler of all European cuisines: the four days in France would test the local restaurateurs. The two countries share a passion for food and cars, yet their roles are totally reversed. The French make very good mass produced Peugeots, Renaults and Citrons, but can't come up with a single luxury car in the range of Lamborghini, Ferrari, Maserati or Bugatti whilst the Italians make the most perfect food without ever reaching into the stratosphere of Michelin stars at café level. It was a conversation that car-loving Ryder could have had time and time again with food loving Protz, if they weren't as mismatched as the Italians and the French.

It was a topic the trio would touch on as they later took a coffee break once back at the reception area in Set A. 'Why on one side of a red and white stripped pole do they speak French and on the other Italian or German or Spanish,' questioned Ryder. The only other place where the demarcation was so exact was where they'd been a week earlier, Liverpool. Liverpool has its own tongue which ceases immediately you pass the 'thanks for surviving' sign.

In the States you can notice a slow difference as you drive north to south, east to west, a bit like going down a piano keyboard. Europe is a concert orchestra of variation and difference - you change instruments at the border and this is all the more remarkable now that you can't really see the border, there's no man in a hat with an up-and-down barrier and a little hut to shelter in on wet days. Even in Ireland where boundaries are to die for, there is the subtlest of signage.

Driving from Dublin to Belfast you think you've suddenly slowed up until you realize that the distances on the same road switch from kilometers to miles.

'The political changes of the past forty years have ruined movies beyond repair,' Ryder contended. 'You no longer see cars crashing barriers, going from escape to freedom. It's boring,' he said summing up the European Union's single least impressive advancement. 'Look at James Bond, he's now got to go to funny countries ending in "stan" to do it – there, or in some private industrial estate.'

Rooster and Ernie, couldn't argue, even if they'd wanted to. Ryder, they correctly surmised independently and silently, was gaining the least from this particular European Experience. But he did have a point, why do European languages change so dramatically rather than melt from one into the other. After all they've been at it for thousands of years, he observed. You'd think they'd haven emulsified into a common tongue by now.

Ernie and Ryder sat on two sofas, Rooster in a high-backed chair with narrow cushioned arms. Bored with the confinement of his room, Harley joined them, not taking a vacant place next to the gentlemen, but sitting on one of the cushioned arms. Rooster raised her elbow to rest against his firm butt. From the on-line radio station that Ngoc had tuned the public speakers into, Rod Stewart belted out 'Tonight's the Night.'

37.
THE ROOSTER CROWS IN ROME

Set C Typhoon - Rome

The scream was uncontrolled, it was not one of horror or pain, but still it was one over which the source had no ability to govern. Liberated, it was out there, repeated five or six times from the room next door but one to Ernie. It was female pleasure mixed with ecstasy, but to Ernie, disturbed and rolling over to see 4 am on his local time clock, it was like a cockerel, marking his territory at dawn. He rolled onto his back and looked at the ceiling as one more shriek cut the stillness.

A smile of enlightenment mixed with envy broke across his face. He muttered the end to four years of wonder, 'Rooster'. He wouldn't need to ask her again.

38.
EVERY iCLOUD

Central Los Angeles - Vatican City

There were no shrieks coming from Room 432 Hotel Admiral della Santa. The mental pressure of the past few days had taken their toll on the doctor. He felt he had aged ten years, the bathroom mirror was cruel enough to confirm it. Aged in Eternal. Here he was in Rome, where he was supposed to be, but the route had been one of pleasure followed by pain followed by more pain and he wondered just what the next 24 hours would bring. They should have had more than two full days, now it was a smash and grab, a bit like the Barcelona bike incident that had him awake most of the night.

Not having his phone was such a handicap, more than money or cards, but at least he was released from the constant concern of seeing Angela's name pop up on FaceTime. Pat and he could go to St Peter's together, but dared not be caught together in person or worse, on camera. Zimmerman and his team perhaps aware, perhaps guessing Swallow's presence, but the tourists could never know, it would get round St Anthony's like wildfire.

Swallow had applied for tickets, but they had to be picked up before ten. It had been a messy week, but Pat still had a little raw emotion to vent when she saw two tickets booked in the name of Dr and Mrs R Dent. Maybe, she thought. For years they'd lived the lie, now they were lying to the Holy Father – how could she avoid that at her next confessional. The couple, married only in name in the eyes of the Vatican, split to avoid any confrontation having agreed on a pre-arranged spot to meet afterwards. They would just have to rely on the arrangement because the doctor would need the nurse's phone. Without it he would never track down the touring party. If asked why there was a call from Swallow to Zimmerman she could put it down to professional care. When he eventually found the party, he'd use the old philanderers trick of creating enormous presence by fussing with everyone and shaking every hand in order to grasp an alibi for the past six days. The luncheon was out of the question since the restaurant was in the opposite direction to the airport and anyway Swallow would have to hide somewhere whilst it all happened. Her holiday of a lifetime had already turned sour. If not sour, potentially bitter sweet.

They'd ask the taxi driver to drop them off at the bottom of Via della Conciliazione, near San Pio X and they could walk up towards St Peter's double checking the meet-up point for later as they went along. The nurse showed one of her innocent gaps in education by asking why did they put the sign up there when they knew it was a mistake, marking it with an X, or was it a crossroad? The concept of Roman numerals had by-passed her.

In the search for a rendezvous they settled on two, a café on the east side and another further down on the west, almost directly opposite the Brazilian Embassy. It was ten o'clock and already the place was abuzz. It reminded him of the scene from Angels and Demons where Tom Hanks was cutting his way through the Vatican in pursuit of a cryptic clue. His progress seemed equally difficult, the square had been already sectioned off and the chances of being allowed to roam in Rome already seemed limited. If he could meet Ernie, he could discard his seat and have Megaghy's ticket to join up with the rest of the party. Pat would have to listen to the Papa unaccompanied, apart from the other 15,000 in the square.

Finding Ernie would only take an hour or so, or so he told Pat who had disconnected herself from the physical side of the holiday and was swept away by the surrounding spiritual influences. She was free to be a tourist. Dent was harvesting alibis. All he needed was one photo full of anchor points. The other earlier photos that Rooster had fabricated would be part of his collection back home which were stored in his email, though now he did have the advantage of saying many had been lost with his phone. Although every iCloud . . . .

-0-

There weren't that many clouds in the sky over Rome, but the few that there were had started to cause Dent visual chaos. A slight smattering of rain and umbrellas magically appeared from backpacks and handbags and within half a minute turned a sea of heads and faces into a wall of waterproof nylon, an ocean of moving greens, blues and greys. He would never see the group as a single identity, it was like looking someone dressed in black in Mecca. The rain, what little there was, stopped, the umbrellas came down and then another tinkle and a repeat of the exercise. It was very hard to follow who was where.

He pulled Swallow's phone from his front right pocket, he was taking no risks with this one wanting the constant reassurance of its continue existence with every leg movement. He noticed that Pat had already put in Ernie's number. Typical of her efficiency. It rang.

Ernie's phone responded and he again noticed the growingly familiar first few digits.

'Ernest Zimmerman,' he said, checking on the time both in LA and Rome.

'Hi Ernie, Ronnie here,' I'm in St Peter's, hell of a lot of people here.'

'We haven't arrived yet, stuck in the bus,' Ernie wasn't lying, he was in the bus, alone. It was after all three in the morning local time, but approaching wake-up and breakfast for the party.

'You'd better hurry, the big man's on in 25 minutes.'

'There's nothing we can do from here, but hope it frees up,' said Ernie making a mental note to include a long traffic delay in the process later that morning of the party heading into their St Peter's and to arrive just in time for the show. For that event they'd decided that it was too risky to commandeer a corner of some public space and then play a recorded Papal blessing out over speakers. It was sure to arouse the religious passions of the Hispanic Americans that marked a huge percentage of the LA population. There were about five million and much as Ernie would have liked some third-party participation, the prospect scared him. Better to take the bus for a loop tour of the neighborhood coming back to an exterior set where Ngoc and Pang had set up the largest speaker system they could find in the widest open space.

'What area have you been delegated?' Dent asked. The question could have been devastating had Ernie not got Rooster's fact pad at hand and an example of a ticket in his hand. It contained a map, the seating arrangements for Papal moments and a grabbed photo from Google Earth of the Vatican. On that Rooster had listed and numbered several landmarks, not just historical, but fairly trivial. Ernie played it with a vagueness that was neither seeming elusive or overly helpful. He was in the middle of this when he said, 'can you hear me? I can't hear you. Are you still there?'

Dent responded, but realized they'd lost each other and hung up. He wouldn't ring back immediately, he'd give it ten minutes until they perhaps had more information, got free of the jam and had better reception. He looked around, perhaps the problem was at his end. There were 15,000 people in the square, about half of them seemed to be phoning home or broadcasting the event on FaceTime. Surely they can't keep their arms up that long, he thought. From a certain angle it looked disturbingly like a Bavarian rally in the Thirties.

From the front seat in the bus, Ernie saw Harley and Rooster emerge and go into the reception area. They kissed each other, affection and connection rather than passion and then Rooster looked around and seeing no one, kissed Harley firmly on the lips. That was passion. Ernie desperately needed Rooster's talents, but held back for a moment to allow a decent passage of time that would preserve their secret; the secret that everyone within earshot was party to for the past six hours.

Out of the bus he doubled back to come around a corner and into the lobby.

'I need you to make a call to Kingman.'

318

'But it is three in the morning!' Rooster said twisting her head as if to say 'why now?'

'I know, but you will be calling from Europe where it is midday. You can apologize and somehow it makes it more real.'

Ernie was about to play the ace he'd held for some days, but thought circumstances had been trumped and made redundant. If this was the shoot out at the OK Coral, Ernie was down to his last bullets, they had to count. The wounded fox was in the henhouse - Dent was too close for comfort.

'We need to ring Mrs Dent, apologizing for disturbing her and saying that we need to confirm some flight details with her husband, but we'd had no luck in that we couldn't get through on either of the numbers we had.'

-0-

'Either of the numbers?' a sleepy and confused Angela Dent said.

'Yes, we are getting no reply from Dr Dent or his travelling companion's cells,' Rooster revealed.

It would take more than a bottle and a half of Pinot Grigio for that one to slip by the mildly-tolerant and long-time suspicious Angela Dent. Shocked out of her sleep, she wasn't totally dumbfounded.

'Okay, my husband's phone was stolen three days ago. Do you have the number of his travelling companion's cell? I'll check that I have here on the fridge door.'

Angela wanted to more than check, her second thought was that it might be Zimmerman's phone. That was her second thought. Nobody, not even Tiger, could play that much golf. She fumbled for a pen and a block of PostIts, and jotted the number down as Rooster read it out, slowly and with unmistakable clarity.

'That number isn't on the list.'

'It should be, the passenger name is a Ms Patricia Swallow,' Rooster offered. There was no reply. The line went dead.

-0-

There was a huge roar as Pope Francis, a dot in the distance like a wasp on a window across a crowded room, appeared high up on a tiny veranda.

Swallow's phone vibrated, but there was no caller identity.

Dent was presumptive. 'Hi Ernie, it's started, where are you?'

'Where are you, you fuckwit and more to the point where's that bitch Swallow?'

The phone never had a chance, Dent's hand was semi-paralyzed by the voice, totally dysfunctionalized by the words, and now the only remaining means of communication bounced off the floor of St Peter's in several bits. Not that he was in a chatty mood.

Angela was still screaming down the phone, but nothing was coming out the other end. Both ends of Dent threatened to reveal something. He looked up as the Pope appeared to be pointing out where the four pieces had landed. Bending down he picked up the pieces of plastic and circuitry and wondered if it could be repaired, not the phone, but the situation, his marriage, his life. Maybe this was a message from God.

Like a man broken by a last desperate gamble on Wall Street, he turned his back on Christianity, and made for the first of the agreed meeting points. He hadn't felt this hollow since he four putted the last green when three shots ahead at the Kingman Invitation Championship.

There was no way on the planet that Ernie could have realized what devastation one phone call could make. It was like Oppenheimer waving goodbye to the planes carrying Little Boy and Fat Man. He knew the purpose and the menace, but not the true destructive ability that would, nearly eighty years on, be the byword for devastation. Ernie allowed himself about ten minutes and then rang Dent to gauge the consequences of Rooster's call. Would his wife have rung him? Sure as hell she would.

There was no reply.

Ernie texted a message, making it less formal now that he and Dent were mates.

'At Vat now, we're sitting near the front, EZ.'

39.
PAPA MIA

Back lot Typhoon Studios - St Peter's Square, Vatican City

The party had dressed up, this being a Sunday and their destination, RC HQ. The feeling of it being special was marked, on more than one occasion, as the coach drove past the odd church or two which occasionally beckoned business by ringing a solitary bell.

Back after a tour of mid-central LA and a stop off for coffee-to-go at an Italian deli, the coach pulled into Typhoon and stopped well short of the closed lot. Ngoc and Pang were already on hand standing in the middle of nowhere, each looking like a combination of golf caddie and sandwich-board man. Attached to their chests they had some electrical gadgetry they'd earlier enjoyed sourcing from Radio Shack. Above them, on a high pole, were attached two small speakers. A third speaker along with a mixer accounted for the gadgets in front of them and they had backpacks containing a subwoofer and a lawn tractor battery.

The party got out of the coach, and now again as Millie, they were led by Rooster in a line with numerous sideways diversions towards an outdoor set. Ngoc and Pang zoomed in and out of the party, emanating street, crowd and traffic sounds. Ryder in the meantime had driven on to the set and was standing by a large mixing desk, protected from the sun by a triangular canvas shade. He raised the tone of an expectant crowd and an accompanying choir as the party came towards him and then lowered it if and when they turned away. Hearing is believing, or something like that he thought.

-0-

Aching with angst, Dent and Swallow had moved to their third café, each time trying to distance themselves further from the goodwill to all men being Tannoyed in four languages.

More broken than dented, more gulping than swallowing, the two tried to piece together a survival plan. Patricia Swallow knew this was a watershed moment. She couldn't push Ronnie, but she needed to get him to the edge, to look over the precipice and see the futility of life with Angela. Ronnie was trying to work out pennies, not passion. In his golf club his partners would probably pat him on the back in that vulgarly sexist lads' way, but he probably couldn't afford to put his hand into his pocket for five years and friendship as hollow as his club wouldn't tolerate it. Especially on the few social occasions where wives were actually invited. Angela had quite buddied with the golfers. She was good with a drink in her. Miserable without. On the other hand Pat's attractiveness was an instant mood killer when with other competitive females.

Pat's apartment downtown was cosy, but there was no stay-over space for Rikki and Toni, and how would they take it? Wicked dad destroyer of family and social standing, probably. He could take a suite at St Anthony's but then he would be just another inmate.

The immediate issue was, did they go back that evening and face the music, even if he didn't want to dance with Angela? Or did they stay on, join the touring party openly, building a platform by showing their new found professionalism. To do that the news of Swallow not being in Chicago would blow open another front in this battlefield. The Institute's board would quite rightly ask questions and the tittered murmurs of the rest of the staff would be prolonged and unbearable.

He ordered his third Bourbon in forty-five minutes and realized that he had to decide. They were due to check in at six. Time and money were running out. Could he afford to stay, no. It was a decision that would go to the line, the line most likely being the one marking the floor between him and the passport control booth. There was only one route, not to just go back home and face the music, but to return home and march right through Angela's and the Institute's band.

40.
MONTE OR BUST

Eastern California – Corniche

Miss Little was on her knees, enduring the intense heat thrown up from the concrete that had one time been a small landing strip before it welcomed film strips. She was in row two of three rows of seating, isolated from the rest of the vast open space and separated from it by four roped bollards that Ryder had found in the props room. Around her the other tourists listened with varying degrees of involvement to the loudspeakers.

It was Sunday and Charles would never normally turn his key on his office door, but he fancied giving Roger some overtime and the two of them stood, semi-naked, looking out of the second-floor window and across the vast space of nothingness to the three rows of seats, the small gathering of people and the array of electrical sound equipment.

'You've got to hand it to that Zimmerman, when they test, they test,' said Charles as Roger dressed explaining as he did that he'd an afternoon session at the tennis club.

'Isn't it too hot for tennis, Rog?' Charles hinted.

'Not for coaching,' said Roger as he picked up his tennis bag, which was, as usual, strangely barren of things, like a racquet, but full of interesting oils and rubs. Charles thought he must be a great inspirational coach.

-0-

After the Papal Mass, the party made their way, elevated to new spiritual heights but at ground level on foot, to Set C where the oft-used bar was now a Roman café. Again the local deli's had come up with a super buffet. Ernie briefly wondered how much all the food was eating into his profit margin, but the party seemed very happy and that was now, even to him, the most important thing.

'We have a bit of travelling to do over the next few days,' he announced to the party as they sat down to eat.

'Isn't that all we ever do?' said Protz with Ernie again thinking profit margins, why couldn't it have been him instead of Megaghy.

He carried on, 'today you had a divine moment, we travel west now for a very different experience. We move to the world of the high rollers, where you can spend a few Euros if you like, in pursuit of even more.'

There was general murmuring around the news and a discussion broke out between several of the tourists as to whether it was called Monte Carlo or Monaco.

'Names don't matter where we are going and I'm sure Millie,' he paused, 'or Arthur, here will answer your query at some point over the next couple of days. It's a long drive, up the coast and west, plenty of time for explanations - it will take seven hours.'

For possibly the first time in the trip, the 'ghost journey' exactly mimicked the reality trip. The driving time from Rome to

326

Monaco was, almost to a minute, the same as LA to Carson City, Nevada. Again they had located an out –town-motel, but on this occasion they had booked a private room in a casino for a session of Black Jack and roulette as well as having access to a bank of slot machines. The casino deal was in on the same lie as Charles', only there was less need to elaborate or sign papers. The two croupiers were instructed to just call cards and numbers and would be playing, with the tourists' huge approval, with marked decks. Rooster had ordered half a dozen packs of braille playing cards and the whole trio had marveled at their potential misuse. Getting the feel of the Mediterranean was going to be a little more problematic, the nearest decent sized bit of open water, Lake Tahoe, was nine miles away and nice though it was it lacked a refreshing salt flavored breeze. They had opted for the less fashionable Carson City in preference to going 25 miles north to Reno just because it was less fashionable, less brash, more manageable and in a strange way more Monte.

The Carson City trip would be the last occasion the party would 'sleep over' at an external location and the EE team looked forward to it, half in adventure, half in anxiety.

Within an hour they would be on the road.

-0-

In the back of a rather shabby and dubious taxi, Dent fumbled through his papers, which were now entrusted to Swallow's monster-sized handbag, the cross-over version between a clutch bag and a carry-on. Thankfully he'd earlier kept his passport alongside the European Experience and the Swallow Experience schedules inside the tour organizer's bag. They were heading to the airport. He'd made a preliminary decision;

the paper trail was too strong to deny Angela her moment in
court. With no wallet, he'd had to abuse Pat to pay for the hotel
in Barcelona and again in Rome. Along with cash withdrawals
she was reaching the limits on her two cards and her one
relationship. Dent was card-less, but his two relationship
accounts differed greatly. His current account with Angela was
severely overdrawn, his investment account with Pat held out
the prospect of better long-term interest. For both Dent and the
touring St Anthony's party it was a case of heading off to
gamble. For him it was all cards on the table, and the stakes
considerably higher.

'Stop, stop, or whatever you say,' he shouted tapping the
driver on the shoulder. He pulled over and Dent sprang out of
the cab and back down the road to a phone shop. Repair was
out of the question, but he still had the chip from Pat's phone.
The cheapest possible replacement was outrageous, he didn't
need a six-month contract with free texting to make a few calls
from the airport, but the guy was prepared to let him have an
old hand-in for fifty euro.

He beckoned to Pat and she stepped elegantly out of the cab
and walked down the road as if she owned it. It was Rome
after all and in her final moments he couldn't deny her an
eternal moment's chic. She was a head turner, that was an
undisputed fact, and he needed her credit card.

The guy behind the counter smiled as she walked in. He would
have charged her €20 and given a free contract just to get her
phone number. As she tapped in the four numbers, Ronnie's
birthday, the taxi slowly pulled away and headed off. Dent,
catching it out of the corner of his eye, sprinted out the door
screaming and swearing like Pat, or no one else in the street,
had ever heard. He pursued it in ever-increasingly

disappearing hope. It turned left, he stopped running. He didn't stop swearing and took out his intense frustration on every post and poster he could find. Across the street a woman wondered about calling 112 and if she should be for the police, the hospital or both.

Previously he'd thought of being like Tom Hanks' in Angels and Demons, now he was Jack Lemmon in The Out of Towners. Pat was not dissimilar to Sandy Dennis, but what was absolutely the same as the film script, was that all their luggage was now in the back of the cab. The cab he could no longer see. His nerves were shredded and he'd just about finished kicking a lamppost and a hairdresser's sign and been joined by Pat when the cab re-appeared on his right. The driver wasn't so shabby after all, he had been on a double yellow, forced to move by a passing police car and simply did a loop around the block.

It was however the moment that pushed Dent beyond the point of no return. His European experience was over. America was home no matter how vile the homecoming. How was he to know that back in Kingman the early morning sun was glinting off his golf clubs, dumped in anger on top of his dozen suits, his fitness gym equipment and the high-end fishing gear he'd only used once on that family holiday in Washington?

Back in the taxi and using tweezers from Swallow's monster bag - that girl had everything he thought, 'I bet if I asked for a corkscrew she'd dig down into it and pull one out' - he prized the chip out of the remains of her phone.

He pressed the on button for several seconds and the screen lit up. The battery had only time to wink. There was a text from Zimmerman and another from Angela. He was too shaken by the events of the past four hours to click on either. Controlled ignorance is near measured bliss, or the coward's way out. Swallow dug back into her bag and brought out the battery booster for the second time, she never thought it would be so useful. She eased the phone from Dent and plugged it in, placing both electrical devices in the monster bag for safety.

She noticed his hand still trembled and Swallow picked it up and placed it on her thigh, with one movement covering it with her other hand. He looked at their clasped hands, another decision made. When he got home, he'd have a pedicure.

-0-

Unaware that his greatest perceivable obstacle had thrown in the towel, Ernie dozed as they headed up eastern California. A couple of comfort breaks had been requested by Wilcox and enjoyed by all. Arthur J had come back on form to give a brief historical tour of Monaco and explain that 'the tiny principality had four quarters, the richest of them being Monte Carlo, so in fact they are not the same thing.' He then went on to expand a theory as to why the state, once threatened to be engulfed by France, was still there. 'It was all down to the popularity of our American beauty, actress turned princess, Grace Kelly.' He went on about her life and times unaware that they were closer to her place of birth than her untimely death.

'Charlie' Nelson, the young guy born on a historic day in Berlin, had a growing passion for the past, particularly the morbid, and asked if they could drive the same road as Grace did on her fateful last trip. Ernie considered it, said it might be a bit dangerous for the bus, but that he'd look into it and maybe it could be put into the next day schedule. After all any twisty road would do.

330

In the meantime they would arrive in Carson City when the gamblers were just starting to think about getting into full swing. They would however not rush to the tables, but just to get the feel of things, stop for a late beer and some slot machine action. Rooster had thought after a long day they would only be too eager to get to bed. She was right and no one more so than Harley. Ernie noticed that the two had been constant companions for the entire day and wondered, being ever economical, if he could get a refund on one room.

It was a relationship that crossed the professional divide and put the project in jeopardy by going outside of Ernie's Zimmerism rule #17, never mix pleasure with greater pleasure. It was however a more solid situation than Harley sitting, brooding and clocking up the events that slowly unfolded across Europe somewhere between Nevada, Arizona and California. He was onboard and one positive aspect was that they now had someone 'planted' in the opposite camp. Any rumblings of discontent would be flagged by Harley and they could head them off at the pass. As long as Rooster and he were happy, the problem would be a bonus. As long as. He had no track-record to gauge its lifespan.

The coach pulled into the parking lot behind a building that from the back looked like a warehouse and from the front a gambling palace. In its time, it had been both. Ernie went in ahead and almost secured the promised private corner with machines on either side. Almost, because an elderly lady was perched on a stool like a stuffed parrot, locked on to a machine and feeding it $5 notes like fish to an obese sealion. He tried to break her concentration to get her to move, but after a couple of nudges realized that she'd probably been installed with the machine and it was futile. This was her spot. Anyway, she had a hearing aid on. He put her down as an acceptable risk.

331

There was a bigger risk, one that they had never considered. How do you gamble in Monaco with American slot machines? Millie had even gone to a bank and got Euros, kroner and sterling to use as props but not dollars. Back in the bus Ernie explained that Monaco, like San Marino, was a micro-state and not part of the European Union. They did however use the euro, although in casinos the chip was king currency.

Seated in the bus he asked those interested in playing their luck to raise their hands. He was amazed to see the first two shoot up, the misses Little and Temple, and they were followed by most of the party.

'OK, it is late I think we should set the same limit for all of you. I will get one hundred and fifty chips for each of you, that's $150, and Millie here will keep a log book. If you spend it in five minutes, tough, if you win, lucky you.'

The ten gamblers were lead into the slot area and each given a small plastic food bag with chips and a brief instruction on what to listen out for. The machines had audio with a limited language choice, English, French, Spanish, and several had headphones for the hard of hearing. A couple were lowered down for wheelchair access, but there were no other concessions. Back in 2002 Ray Charles successfully campaigned for slot machines for the blind so that they wouldn't be deprived of the opportunity to squander money and further ruin their lives. One company listened, made them and won an award. They didn't however sell very many and now you were more likely to come across one in a lock-up than a casino.

It didn't really matter to the ten gamblers; it was the atmosphere they wanted to tap into. Within half an hour the fistful of dollars had gone the way of so many millions. Except for one machine. Miss Temple was somehow dancing her fingers round the machine and it was responding to her touch. Millie looked at the tally in the top right hand corner – she was €355 up!

'Fantastic Miss Temple,' Millie said. 'The others have all finished.'

'Oh good, I was getting right bored,' she said and turned and walked away from the machine.

Millie looked back and forth and pressed the button to release the winnings.

'Miss Temple, you won something, a lot. In American it's nearly $400!'

She stopped, 'and what would I do with that?' She paused, 'Give it to charity.'

Rooster was happy she'd been given the instruction and would respectfully follow it through. She thought, what would Ernie have done? For him charity had always begun at home and on extravagantly good days maybe reached the front gate, but never beyond the mailbox. Or had she seen him mellow over the past two weeks? Better not risk it. She'd say Miss Temple had won a few bucks and donated it to a charity. She wouldn't elaborate and once in the hotel she'd look up a local charity, hopefully one for the blind. What happens in Carson City, stays in Carson City.

-0-

Dent and Swallow had repaired their stress-educed differences. They weren't there yet, but the nurse believed she'd finally got her doctor. There would be challenges and embarrassment to face back home, but the prospect of becoming Pat Dent was one worth chasing. All the signs were in her favor, Ronnie was at her side in business class, it was her business to keep him there. Life for a while would need to be in economy, but the long haul was surely to be first class.

She'd one last European hurdle in front of her. They had a three-hour stopover at Charles de Gaulle, the final opportunity for Ronnie to flip and decide to meet up with the tour party who were due there in four days. By restoring his professional status and role, he could perhaps contrive to conjurer up an argument for her to have also been there. But again, when asked, as surely he would be, how and why did he pay for hotel nights in Paris and Barcelona when the tourist group was elsewhere and moreover how, if it was on Ms Swallow's card could he conceal that they paid for only one room? Normally she wouldn't have thought twice about a few more nights in Paris, but she'd rather get him stateside and be proactively supportive as she helped destroy his marriage of seventeen years.

The seatbelt sign came on again and the plane dipped. She was about to endure three of the longest hours of her life. Above all she hoped United were flying on time. 'United' she thought 'that's a nice omen.' She certainly wasn't flying Virgin.

-0-

The neighbors had begun to put two and two together as the pile of clothes and boy's toys grew taller on the driveway. They kept back and observed from the safety of their own, outwardly portrayed, happy homes. There was such daytime crap on TV that this was a show and a half. When would the star turn up?

Or maybe not, Angela seemed to be having second thoughts. She was out there making order out of the mess. A couple of tables had been dragged from the garage and with some logic the piles were being split into clothes, formal and sporting, books, formal and sporting, equipment, just sporting. After about an hour it had taken on what it was to be, a yard sale. So maybe the early, disorganized vigor was just the way she approached things like spring cleaning.

It was when she put a $100 ticket on each of Ronnie's three fully-clubbed golf bags that the watching males broke their cover. Angela didn't know that each club was worth the price tag. Ronnie had mumbled about spending $500 on a new set and she thought even that outrageous. That's why she put a hundred tag on them and that's why every golfer in the road was now making his way to the yard. This wasn't just better than afternoon TV, this was the US Open Sale of the Century. The clubs were worth around $1,200 a bag.

Suburban envy feeds off suburban greed and here was the carcass of a very substantial beast. The vultures were digging their beaks into Ronnie's years of selfishness. There must be a catch. Was it worth exposing the years of envy as watching on they'd seen Ronnie lift his better-than-theirs clubs into and out of the trunk. Sure as hell it was. It may be the second mouse that gets the cheese, but here it was worth the risk. First into the trap or nothing.

By the time Ronnie went through Gate 26 and settled into seat 11B, he'd be a golfer who'd last all his balls. A golfer with a club, but no clubs.

Well almost. Bradley Weston, who was something in insurance, a prat, and the buyer of his most expensive set, put himself in what he was supposed was Ronnie's situation. Inwardly he promised that if normality was restored, he'd sell them back to him. Members of the same club, he wasn't quite sure he had the balls to tee off in front of the former captain with his favorite driver. If in a tight corner he could explain that he was simply securing them for Ronnie's return. However, if Ronnie had done a runner and left the state, that was a very different matter. Ping, straight down the middle.

41.
CHIPS WITH EVERYTHING

Carson City - Monte Carlo

Day two in Monaco started with the bus taking the tourists down to the shores of Lake Tahoe, which was standing in for the aqua blue Med. Pang had a pump action garden spray filled with two gallons of seawater. It gave a misty start to the walk and had the positive effect of putting a fine hint of salt on everyone's skin. He just had to position himself upwind and would, every so often, scurry off to pump up the pressure, to avoid the sound being a bit of a giveaway.

There was one hint of Europe the tour organizers had thankfully escaped. The headline in the local paper had read 'Go Home Europeans - WASPs Out'. Intrigued about this open racism that was not limited to one particular country, but all the Anglo-Saxon members of a continent, Ernie picked up a copy of the Gazette. The headline had done what a good headline should, it sold the paper. It revealed that the previous year had been the worst in Tahoe for attacks by the European paper wasp. Thankfully they only competed for the Stinger of the Year Award with the local yellow jackets in the late summer. It had been a prolonged contest with the Europeans just edging it and the locals weren't too excited about the prospect of a replay.

Not a problem today, but down by the lakeside, Rooster, Ryder and Harley had been told to keep a special lookout for any stinging insects. One zap from a hornet could open a whole bees nest. A picnic lunch was followed by a return to gambling. This time the cards were very much in the favor of the tourists. The croupier had been encouraged to give her performance a mild French twist and she went at it with glee – a glee hampered by not being able to count above five in French. The tourists didn't seem to mind and they split up, some asking for more of 'des chips' to play the machines.

The venue was a lot glitzier than the slot machined warehouse they'd stopped in the night before and was relatively quiet in the mid-morning with just the odd regular holding on to their favorite bandit, eking out time and making sure no one else withdrew all that they had just invested.

In the center there was a single machine, highlighted by a roaming spotlight that slowly moved its attention from it to the metallic blue Chevy Corvette Z06, which, along with an ever-increasing cash prize, was the reward for getting the five bars in some sort of order. The cash prize currently stood at $643,320. It increased by ten dollars a minute. Ernie tried to work out in his head how long it had been going unclaimed, but gave up, it was moving at $14,400 a day or maybe not. Perhaps they turned it off at night, or in the morning, since the place didn't seem to close, but must have had a lull at some point. He put five tokens into the slot. It was complicated, but hell, worth a try. The first four goes did nothing. He pressed for the fifth time and the symbols rolled round and finally stopped. Nothing. He went back to the semi-private room and the Black Jack and roulette. Harley was near the wheel and doing a splendid job commentating without calling out a number or color.

At the Black Jack, Protz was a couple of hundred of 'checks' up and feeling like a big roller, which he was physically to start with. Rooster whispered in Ernie's ear, 'going good, but we might have trouble pulling him away.'

Ernie looked around, day 16, country experience number eight, number of fatalities one, Dr Dent nil, yes it was going good.

He had made one decision, which involved a schedule change, not a location, but a means of getting there. Once they reached Barcelona, which was another long drive, they would fly on to San Sebastian, bus journeys of over seven hours were just too much for everyone to hack. Anyway, the old Ernie wasn't totally lost in his new philanthropic suit. The emperor may have new clothes, but he'd charge them an extra $180 for the flight.

He checked the time on his phone. He'd an offer for a new tariff and missed a call from Dent. He'd resorted to a text.

'Missed you in St Peter's and would have changed schedule. On way back to Institute to sort out an issue. Leave Paris for NY shortly. Will phone. Safe journey. Maybe next time. RD'

'Yes, safe journey,' Ernie muttered, 'An issue, you bet it is an issue!'

Rooster heard him. 'What are you betting on now?'

'Today, the way things are going, I'd bet on anything.' He walked back to the Corvette and slipped another five chips into the slot. Nothing, nothing, nothing, nothing and then, nothing. 'Maybe Lady Luck is somewhere else for an hour, she's been with me for a day or so. She deserves a break.'

'She can have my room number if she wants,' said Rooster opening the door to a world of remarks.

Ernie surveyed the potential. He'd go light. 'three in a bed . . . .'

Rooster stared at him through a growing glow, turned and went back to the roulette table.

Ernie shouted after her, 'Hey blusher, put your money on the red.' The other option was too obvious and offensive, even for him.

-0-

The buzz of Monte was slowly wearing off. Protz was back to zero plus ten and most others had given Millie back their chips, if they had any. She looked at the logbook and with a rough guess thought the night and day had cost the tourists about $75 a head, on average, because some didn't risk it. She'd tell them individually precisely what later. It was round up and go time and how she wished getting the party together was as easy as the croupier's graceful sweep to pick up the cards.

Seven of Millie's cards took up the offer to go to the restroom. She'd agreed with Harley that he'd chaperone the gents making sure that no locals passed a sideways comment along with their redundant water. One 'how's it going buddy?' remark could break the house – the House of Zimmerman.

Outside it was quite breezy so the party were keen to get on the bus even if it were to be hours and hours before they got off again. Rooster started a head count. It was something they done less and less since they had lost the number one, because starting at two seemed a little crass, but here it was important.

'We can't afford to leave anyone behind here with all this temptation,' she said as they found the seats that had become their private docking station.

The numbers bounced along quite effectively until eight and a pause. Millie said nine to kick start the process already having logged that Janne Jankowski was missing. It stopped at fourteen. 'So we are missing two Janne and Joyce.'

The spotlight moved from the Chevy to the prize that was now kissing $650,000 and on picking up a bit of the back wall as the two 'J's emerged from the restroom. They were making their way to the exit so Rooster left them to their own good selves and went back outside to signal to the Ryder with a double thumbs up that all was ok. By the time she was back inside, Janne had made it to the reception area.

'Hi Janne,' she said in her Millie voice, 'wasn't Joyce with you.'

'She stopped to use up her last chips,' Janne said and Rooster could just see her outline, backlit every ten seconds or so by the spotlight. Then she could see all of her, and all of the casino as all manner of lights blazed and the ceiling opened up to fill the air with slivers of silver paper. Automatic cameras flashing to capture the moment. The horn on the Chevy blasted, the headlights flashed and people were running towards Joyce from every angle. One person blasted past Rooster shouting, 'she's won the bloody jackpot!'

-0-

Across the American continent, the wheels of the flight from Paris hit the hard JFK tarmac. Good and ill fortune United. For

Dent the homecoming had turned sour, for Swallow, bitter finally tasted sweet.

-0-

Rooster froze and grasped her options. She needed assistance, but she couldn't leave the building, Janne Jankowski could stand there on her own, isolated, but she had to be the first line of defense between Joyce and the growing crowd. She swept down and cut through the wall of envy that had engulfed her. Thankfully she got there before any of the staff.

'What have you done now Joyce? You've just won the jackpot,' she looked up to see the frozen digits, $650,060. She was about to say how much, but realized she couldn't convert instantly to Euros so she lead her away from the fray and sat her down ushering others away and to stand back.

'This lady has just had a shock. She's uncomfortable in this foreign environment.' Later on in a moment of reflection she'd be particularly proud of throwing in the 'f' word, but the appeal had failed to have full effect. A man in a tired business suit, that close-up revealed how hard he worked and how personal hygiene had been nudged out by diligence, was fast approaching, hand out and smiling.

'Congratulations mam, you've won the biggi!

There was no sense of loss on his part. Someone winning big was the best advertisement and he knew just how much had gone into that machine to get it there. 'Blind lady wins Chevy' he could see the headlines nationally now.

In the background, scurrying through and putting two and two together and coming up with 650,060 was Ernie. His feckin' five dollars were the last ones in the machine before Joyce's. 'Lady Luck what where you playing at?' Worse still was the fact that he'd given Joyce the chips.

Joyce was in a state of shock and in no state to make any rational decision. Ernie quickly convinced her and the manager that she needed to get outside and into the air. No photos, just for the moment. No photos period thought Ernie. Rooster, quick as ever had used her Smartphone to do a lightening calculation. She was ready to break the news.

'Joyce you have won 570,614 euros,' she told her. There was a very long pause. Ryder looking out the bus window couldn't work out the fuss.

'What's that in real money?' she eventually asked.

'That's $650,060. And you also won a car.'

There was another agonizing pause before Joyce spoke.

'It's been a nice day, I like Monaco.' She then added 'but I can't drive.'

-0-

In the manager's office Ernie was in the unique position of being able to leave somewhere pretty well legally with a huge sum of money. The money wasn't his although it had technically been generated out of his pocket since he funded it up front. The manager said he felt comfortable if he had all Miss Reid's personal and bank details that he could sign a form to enable the casino to transfer the funds. Under the circumstances, they proposed making a cash offer instead of the Corvette, if she chose not to take it. 'She could of course give it away as a present. The cash redemption is not as much as the car in a showroom,' he explained 'because they had promo deals with the companies.'

Joyce's knees had given in at the realization of what she'd done and she was wheeled into the office, cane in one hand, glass of champagne in the other. Drinking and gambling were fighting her deep religious principles. Losing to her was OK, then she won and the wheels of guilt and betrayal of her beliefs rolled in. Harley was rolling too, pushing the chair, perhaps with his eyes on the other wheels, what would he have done with the Corvette? Given it to a non-existent relative and stashed it in a lock-up was his immediate feeling. Even with his money, a win is a win.

'We need a little time for this to settle in,' said Ernie with the major understatement of his life. 'If Joyce can sign, we can celebrate Spanish-style tomorrow.' Thanks to nurse Swallow the list about each tourist gave them the details of Joyce's bank. There were several sheets full of legal jargon and Ernie took time to read them. They seemed okay; he was more worried about follow-up paperwork that might find its way onto the wrong desk or that there might be nationwide promotional commitments attached to the good fortune. Joyce signed and Ernie witnessed. As he did he neatly and quietly, as if it was a blind instinct, ticked the 'no publicity' boxes. For the casino it was a good story, but it wasn't as if she'd won millions. Had she won it the next month, when it was in seven figures, then they would have argued for the right to tell the story. Still the whole jackpot investment was about publicity so the management reluctantly agreed to release the win in

344

anonymous terms. 'A blind lady' rather than 'retired public sector employee Joyce.'

The EE trio thought they had got away with the departure of Jack Megaghy, however ticked box or no ticked box, Ernie wasn't quite so sure they could keep the lid on this one. He thought he'd phone Kingman once he got over the shock of all that money being won with his $5. That call might be a long way off. He really just couldn't do it and an hour later Rooster rang the Institute. In a possible French accent she said that a Miss Reid had had a sizable win and that they would be transferring funds via their Nevada-based holding firm.

'How much is sizable,' asked Shelley.

'Around six hundred thousand euros – there are some final calculations to work out.'

Shelley put down the phone and typed into her search engine, what is 600,000 euros, is that like Mexican pesos? For a single mother living on a receptionist's salary the answer bore no connection to reality. 'Life's not fair,' she thought before asking herself, of the two situations, hers and Joyce's, which would she rather be in? She looked at the photo of her six-year-old. Point six million bucks wasn't enough.

In the bus Ernie had yet to come up with that question of himself. He was still in shock. There was no way when he looked over that wall at Kingman for the first time that he saw this coming. The mood on board was of communal delight, by comparison the east Germans were miserable when the Wall came down. The mood was helped, some might argue generated, by the dozen bottles of champagne the casino manager had insisted they took with them. That wasn't enough for Ernie, champagne was the only drink that keeled him, so he got Ryder to pull over at a liquor store, got some beers and two bottles of Jack.

He and one of the Jack's now sat in the front passenger seat looking out to long straight road ahead. What was round the next corner he wondered? Where was the next corner? The answer, according to the schedule was Dent's dark nightmare, Barcelona.

42.
NO REMORSE, JUST REJOICE

Santa Monica beach - Barcelona

Barcelona promised much. A bit of Gaudi, a tour of a repro Santa Maria, a bit more Gaudi, dinner at one of Picasso's old haunts and to round it off, a bit more Gaudi. Gaudi does well in Barcelona and Barcelona does well thanks to Gaudi.

When outlining the daily itinerary Gaudi came up so often Wilcox observed 'they really like their cheese' before getting a twelve-minute lecture from Arthur J, who was immediately angry at himself for doing it there and then because he'd put that particular performance aside for the visit to the Sagrada Família. He recovered when he realized he had so much more to talk about. He was just a little concerned about the timescale for the interesting information was only really valid in the Catalonian capital. Next stop San Sebastian was a very different kettle of fish. How could he be an authority on the European people with the most confused and unidentified origin?

-0-

The adventure in Monte would take a long time to fade, for several it was the highlight, not just of the experience, but their lives. The trip had already changed the make-up of the party. From a group of individuals who shared something they wish they didn't, they were molding into a unit. A unit with edge, honor and wit. Characters had evolved and the passing of

Megaghy had served as a reminder that whatever cards you are dealt in life, they are only on the table for an uncertain period of time.

Even in a world of shifting improbable stories, no one could have guessed or even suspected the next development. It started just outside of 'Nice'. The champagne had taken its toll and only a few of the travelers had resisted the temptation to nod off. Joyce Reid was sitting fairly near the front of the bus and she could hear Ernie talking to Ryder.

'Mr Zimmerman, how many are we?'

'What do you mean?' Ernie replied.

'How many of us are on the trip?'

'You were fifteen and now fourteen.'

'Yes. but in total with your team. I've bumped into one or two or maybe three funny little men who won't speak to me. Are they with you, us?'

Ernie thought for a moment, Jack was half empty beside him and was causing his normally agile brain to trip over even the simplest of thoughts.

'Ah our baggage boys,' he said wondering if that would help explain Ngoc and Pang who had clearly been more evident than intended. 'they are our silent heroes who transport your baggage and most everything else we need. The picnic today for example. They don't speak very much English.'

'So there is you, the driver and Miss Millie and the two baggage boys.'

'Yes,' said Ernie growing ever more anxious at the line of questioning.

'Okay, was just thinking,' said Joyce and then with a late request for conformation added, 'so we are nineteen.'

'Yes,' replied Ernie with just a mild hint of growing frustration.

Another 'Okay, just thinking,' finally ended the two-way.

The journey then fell into its now near normal routine. Ryder happy up front driving, Ernie tucking in behind him and Rooster and Harley on two seats, but really only needing one and a half. Ngoc and Pang were prone on the back seat, sleeping toes to head in amongst the baggage. They would have slept in the overhead luggage rack if requested. In fact, given the option they would have preferred it. The idea of being stopped by the police still disturbed them when outside the Typhoon gates.

Maybe it was Jack doing the talking, but Ernie, alone with only the headlights of the Californian traffic to punctuate the darkness, was more reflective than all the tailgates now in front of him put together. What had gone wrong? This had started off as the simplest of concepts, take a party of blind people on the experience of their lives, don't go anywhere and then bring them back. How difficult could that be?

What he hadn't put into his presentation portfolio in the Walmart coffee bar was that they'd be doing it with a thoroughly nice bunch of people, who might not have his eyesight, but had much more backbone than he had. They cared, they looked after each other and they held no grievance against life. God, he would have been bitter in a similar situation, but not these people, with the exception of Harley. And Harley he liked. He'd been dealt a really bad card, but the next one was an ace and he had bluffed his way to keeping the $18 million, so far. Again here was a change. The Ernie of old would have lit up with the idea of being able to scam some of the cream off the top. But no. Even today when Joyce won a huge nest-egg, he resisted from being a cuckoo and tossing her out. It took a little time, but he put the fact that she'd won $650,060 via a five-dollar note he'd given her as pure fate. If he'd used the same note on the same machine, he probably would have pressed a different button or something. Easy wasn't what it was meant to be for Ernest Zimmerman III.

He didn't know if there would be an EE2, but if there were, it wouldn't be a sham. This had been life-changing for most of the party now numbering 14 and at least two of the organizers. For the two Asians on the back seat the only anxiety was when the rollercoaster would come to a halt and they would have to get off. Well they would have wondered that, Ernie thought, if they'd ever seen a rollercoaster. He put it in his mind to take them to Disney when this charabanc finally parked. If they were subsequently deported they could tell tales of seeing the real America.

He was about to say goodnight to Jack, when a rustle, a scent of old perfume and finally a considerable physical presence forced him towards the window. It was Joyce. Or since she returned, re-Joyce.

'Mr Zimmerman, I've been a thinking, now don't talk my sweetie.'

Ernie didn't talk he was too scared; the most fearful of thoughts flashed through his mind, holiday romances. Next to 'you must try this, it is a local delicacy' they were the single most dangerous aspects of travel.

'Now my family is, forgive my English, a shit load. They dumped me in St Ant's at the first chance they got. They ain't been to visit me in three and a half years. So, I'm there on my lonesome, paid for by my former employers, the state of Florida, because I'm below the line. To them I'm a token they can hold up and say, "see we care". They are worse than my family. If they knew I'd more than a hundred bucks, they'd claw it back out of my sickness allowance.'

Again thanks to Jack, Ernie wasn't quite sure where Joyce was going.

'What I'm saying man is that money's no good to me. I'd like a little, stashed away, to do nice things like learning to sing big time, but if them people at County Hall heard I'd nearly seven hundred grand under the mattress, they'd have the legs offa ma bed.'

'That's a why I was asking how many are we a little while back. You said 19. Now the car I'm going to give away to the only relative I mildly like, a young cousin. He can do what he likes with it, but he has five kids, so I suspect the Corvette doesn't fit into his garage of life. He can sell or exchange it. Whatever he does will piss off the more uncaring members of my family, and that's the rest of them,' she paused, '. . . the money, I'd like to share with us all.'

Ernie was about to speak and made a couple of odd noises, but Joyce put a clumsy finger towards his mouth and poked him in

351

the eye saying 'Hush honey, I was a bit slow coming up to you, but I calculate it as 19 people but some, like Harley, don't need it. I've done my own means test and I have come up with ten who are young enough to enjoy or need it, plus the three of you. I wondered about the two bag boys. I don't know them but it seems wrong to exclude them, so I made them into one man. That means 14 parts of the ticket, and this is important, the voucher you gave me, is shared. I work it out at $46,432 and 85 cents per person.'

It as the finest, most generous, speech Ernie had ever heard. It was as if all the thoughts he'd handled alone a few minutes earlier had crystallized into something special.

Ernie in a rare moment of physical commitment, stretched over and awkwardly kissed Joyce on the cheek. She flinched for a second before realizing that anything less would have been a tad rude and ungrateful.

He looked back down the bus. He couldn't accurately calculate what the money would do for the lives Nelson and Grotz, but for Rooster is was a chance to put an anchor somewhere, for Ngoc and Pang it was more than they could ever comprehend. He couldn't work out what it meant to him other than a deep feeling of guilt for even considering claiming the money on his dollar bill.

Joyce thanked him again for being so understanding and exhausted and elated he and Jack dipped into a deep sleep immediately unsure of what had just occurred. She'd just one request, to keep it a secret between them until the next time everyone was awake and receptive.

-0-

Ryder had looked it up and the actual drive time from Monaco to Barcelona. It was six hours and forty, about the time it would take him to get to Burbank. The three time zones where frazzling the minds of the three tour organizers. They'd left Carson City at three in the afternoon, that was midnight Monte Carlo time and seven in the evening tour time. The drive through the night knocked another day off the calendar. For the past ten days they had been trying to marry weather conditions and external outings. The clocks were getting closer to being in sync but sheer travel fatigue of the homeward leg final would be put down to the consequences of jet lag. The tourists then taking days to re-adjust when back at Kingman was added proof of the trip. 'Confuse and Conquer' This was a bit like a cocktail, the heady mixture of excitement and exhaustion had to be spot on. The better condition the goods were on arrival, the easier to recruit for a second trip, should they have the energy and mental willpower to attempt one.

It was ten in the evening when the bus pulled into a parking bay close to the beach at Santa Monica, which should have been seven in the morning in Barcelona, but was in fact now designated as midday. The chill of the night hadn't yet bitten, but it was such a contrast to the day that the locals had long abandoned the sand for bars and cafes. Thank goodness for the siesta-loving Spaniards, they would paddle and then have breakfast at a Hispanic run café which was only too happy to stay open an extra hour. Then it would be in the bus and back to Typhoon for an afternoon snooze to help get over the uncomfortable night they'd just had. Life hasn't always been so nocturnal for the Spaniards. Spain lies in the same logical timezone as London, but in 1940 General Franco moved the clocks forward an hour, to show solidarity with Nazi Germany. The clocks moved, but the Spanish body-clock remained governed by their stomachs as it does to this day.

In the café Ernie announced he'd some good news for them. Remarkably he'd forgotten the moment with Jack and Joyce, probably because of Jack. Somehow it was so surreal it had to have been a dream. But it wasn't and Joyce had reminded him of it as she stumbled around the furniture in search of an eating space.

Earlier Joyce had chatted with Harley, Wilcox and the misses Little and Temple. For various reasons they either didn't need the cash or it would adversely affect their standing in terms of medical funding. She'd decided that forty-six thousand dollars for singing lessons was more than Rod Stewart would have paid and was happy to rely on the Lord to accept her voice as it was. She'd take nothing from the moment in the casino. She'd also decided that the bag boys that she'd never met were probably too young to handle such a windfall. She reduced them to sharing a half share, which the nice Mr Zimmerman would administer. That had the twin virtue of taking the dividing number of those to benefit down from thirteen to twelve and a half. She was religious and superstitious in equal measures, which on this occasion was quite fitting since much of the bad press the number after twelve receives, comes from the table setting at the Last Supper. She'd also settled on a flat figure of fifty grand. The remaining $25,004 could go to a charity, or maybe a second-hand coach so that the rest of St Anthony's could enjoy day trips away from the Institute.

Ernie tapped a coffee mug with a teaspoon and was about to launch into changed travel arrangements, the flight to San Sebastian, when 'Thank you Mr Zimmerman,' said Joyce. 'That mad moment in Monte yesterday came as a shock to me. The Lord don't abide gambling and I must say I feel guilty for the bad words I said and for using the Devil's Mouthwash, champagne. I don't know what came over me.'

354

Two young couples cuddling in a corner looked up in curiosity and stopped their fondling.

'I've talked with some of my lovely companions and they too have no need for the money. I could give it all to charity, but which one, why and how would they miss-spend it? It's really not a lot of money, $650,000, but I want you to help me distribute it.'

The four fondlers did what all young people do today in such a situation, they acted calmly and looked around for hidden cameras – this had to be reality TV.

'This trip has been the best two weeks of the past 10 years of my life and that is down to Mr Z and his team, especially Millie, and to you, my dear friends from St Anthony's. I want to give you all $50,000 – each - you can re-connect with your families.'

One of the young lovers thought he'd worked it out. 'I've seen this before, it is Undercover Boss, it's great.'

'Or you can select your own charity. And this includes Mr Z's team. But it is your choice. This way the money flies in the same direction, but ends stopping on different situations, a bit like the slot machine barrels that created it.'

Rooster looked at Ernie in disbelief. Ernie could only muster a smile that said, 'I really don't understand this, but it is really happening.' Outside Ryder and the two Asians were sharing a smoke unaware that they could now buy and awful lot of cigarettes.

'We are drawn together by a common condition, but it is one

that has many causes, perhaps we can help in some little way to eradicate them. You can open eyes around the world. Eyes or minds, you chose.'

There was a general murmur of surprise mixed with huge admiration for the gesture. In the corner the four anxiously waited for the big TV moment. It didn't come, 'It must be the way they edit it,' the sultry brunette observed, quietly adjusting her disturbed blouse in case she was on camera.

'Thank you everyone for helping me with this problem, let's enjoy Barcelona,' said Joyce and sat down.

'I didn't know that this bar was called Selona,' said the girl in the corner.

Ernie thought that if that was problem solving, count him in every time. His good news of the plane replacing the bus for the next leg would be lost in the buzz of life that was Ricco's Café. Behind the bar Ricco wondered who to hand the bill too, 'and what was it with Barcelona?' It didn't really matter, at that moment anyone in the room would happily have paid, except the four in the corner.

-0-

Joyce Reid's unique method of redistributing wealth created an interesting sociological experiment. In the bus on the way to Typhoon, and what was certain to be a dream-filled siesta, there was a broader range of the acceptance of the good fortune than might have been expected. Those who had opted, for various reasons, not to accept the gift, were composed and silent. Arthur J was upset that he should be seen in need of the cash, but thought of the library it could create. Nelson was ecstatic and could imagine a room and life full of sound-based gadgetry. Janne Jankowski thought of her family and what it would do for them, maybe a private trip to Warsaw. Jill Sander thought of the cats that had been attracted to her in England and Italy and tried to calculate how many she could make happy again, quite a lot. Protz was just going to attempt to feast himself to death. Food from around the world, global gluttony, what a way to go.

Across the EE team, the sphere of reaction was equally broad. Pang and Ngoc didn't know what they could or would be allowed to do with it, for a start they couldn't walk into a bank and open an account. Their first real encounter with consumerism had come from the visits to Radio Shack – they'd seen a huge karaoke screen with speakers, but they'd need to take the side wall off their caravan to get it in. It was a problem they were happy to try to solve. Rooster wasn't as into money as she was, through necessity, some weeks earlier. She didn't know where she and Harley were going and in this fickle world dared not think of what was around the corner, $18 million, $50,000, or a police van, or two police vans. An insignificant amount compared to Harley's, at least it was hers, an opportunity not to ask for everything, for a while. Ryder had already earmarked it for a red Ducati Monster on which he'd do Route 66 – it would piss off so many Harley fans he thought.

Ernie was mellower than the others expected. The evolution from two-bit crook to quality conman to a decent paid-up member of the human race had been too quick for his mental metabolism to keep up. There had been one flash of anger at the six hundred not being all his when he first heard of Joyce 'getting rid of that token', but that had gone and he had put what to do with the fifty grand aside in his mind until they had got to the end of this project. It could after all blow away with the exposure of the whole experience. The fear of discovery was being suppressed more and more each day by the genuine feeling that the party were having a great time, getting value for money. This whole thing had been a sham, a falsehood, again he thought maybe it might be fun to do it for real. It would certainly be easier.

The people had been the revelation. His normal scams were based on human greed and he was only too happy to harvest it. But here the people where real. Sure there were jerks like Arthur, pains like Wilcox, timid mice like Miss Little, but they we real and contributed to the color and flow of the group. There were too few Joyce Reid's in this world and perhaps one too many Ernest Zimmerman's – 'did I really just think that?' Ernie said to himself.

-0-

Rooster had enjoyed the nap, largely because Harley hadn't let her sleep, and arrived down in the lobby to find Jankowski and Nelson playing cards. There was no one else about and Rooster reprimanded herself for letting things get a little lax. The dog must always watch the sheep Ernie would say and now, even if this burst of lust with Harley failed to mature long-term, there was still a fifty-grand bonus to be had. But even that was at risk when the tourists were allowed to roam freely, especially here were a matter of feet could transport you from one environment to another.

As it was Jankowski and Nelson were so wrapped up in their game that they didn't hear Rooster approaching. They were using the braille cards she'd bought and had been used in Carson City.

'Now I take off my bra,' said Jankowski in reply to Nelson's claiming he had two pair.

The game continued and with an 'ace high' Nelson said he'd removed his shirt. They were both fully clothed.

'Hi guys what are you doing?' Millie asked having seconds earlier moved a chair to announce that they were not alone.

'Playing strip poker,' said Janne, 'we have a great imagination and no need to bare the flesh for real. It's a blind plus. We started last night in the bus and so far I've got him totally naked four times!' Nelson retaliated that Jankowski had great nipples. Or so she claimed.

Harley looked at Jankowski and for a second wished the game wasn't so surreal. Then he looked at Rooster and felt guilty for even thinking such a thought. He'd played his cards to perfection.

Millie laughed and said that they'd better get their clothes back on because they were heading off to the Sagrada Familia and although it was an only half-dressed cathedral, they should show some respect. Several others of the party were now emerging from their slumbers and picking up on the back of the conversation, couldn't quite work out what they'd missed. They were sure of one thing, this was the trip that had everything!

-0-

During the communal siesta Pang and Ngoc had re-arranged the café area into a small restaurant. Heavy wooden tables and chairs replaced the light seating and several big bushy plants were pitched in to break up the floor-space. It was to be the 4 Gats, a favorite eating haunt of Picasso and just about everyone else in northern Spain who owned a paintbrush and little else at the end of the 19th Century. The artists obviously ate and drank more than they paid for; it closed in 1903 and somehow the history was mothballed for 80 years. Today it is a place of homage and tonight for the 14 tourists a place of high-class tapas and beer.

Millie asked if they had had tapas before and several hands were raised. 'Where?' she asked. The answers didn't really matter, New York, San Fran, Walmart, what she wanted to expand on was how the Spanish did it, after all it was their idea.

'Tonight, and,' turning to Ms Sander, 'Jill you will like this, we are in the Four Gats, which is Catalonian for Four Cats. You find tapas all over Spain and nowhere better than tomorrow when we hit San Sebastian where we will do it properly by moving from bar to bar'

'Then why are we having it tonight?' Protz chipped in menacingly. He hadn't yet put tapas into his global gluttony game, it seemed too delicate and small.

'We wanted to be here and we have much to achieve this evening. It's quick and we can take some with us to snack on later. We have tickets for Park Güell and then the Sagrada Familia. But Mr Zimmerman has some good news. Some more good news.'

Ernie stepped forward. 'We've made a few changes during the trip and we have learned that, maybe in terms of miles we were putting you through too much. Tonight we will stay here.'

'In a restaurant?' said a hopeful Protz.

'No, no, in Barcelona and in the morning we will fly, not drive, to San Sebastian tonight – the flight tickets are about €200,' said Ernie, 'and the hotel an extra 125' having calculated that they were now cash rich. Looking on Rooster thought, a cheater can't change its spots.

There was general approval after the draining trip the night before and everyone got up to go to the buffet. Chairs and people were going in all directions until Millie said, 'please stay in your seats, the tapas are on big trays they'll be brought round to you.'

-0-

It is amazing how Hollywood uses and reuses locations and the European Experience was doing the same on a return visit to Griffith Park. Ryder had bought some mosaic kitchen tiles, several square yards in fact held in place by a plastic backing mat. He had also picked up three vulgar statues from a garden center. One was a large lizard, one a Venus and the third a huge turtle. Only the lizard needed any adjustment, he'd put thin lines of sealant all over it so, to the hand, if felt as if it was made from hundreds of small pieces.

Park Güell, according to Rooster's research, was crammed with modern bits of art and mosaic seating. It was light and five in the morning and the dog walkers would have screamed if they were anywhere other than LA. Pang and Ngoc could be seen carrying the garden statues from bush to bush as a party of people went around being encouraged by an attractive blonde lady to touch things. Occasionally they'd be encouraged to sit on a bench that looked like someone had tried to hide under kitchen tiles. But hey this is LA.

Mitch Groubner, had been walking his spaniel in the park for ten years. Both were slower and greyer now than when they first started their morning ritual, but never in 3000 mornings had they seen anything quite like this. Sixteen people perhaps, standing in line, waiting for nothing and then being lead to a disfigured garden ornament.

At 6:30 local time Ryder re-set the satnav to 621 W Adams Blvd, Los Angeles, CA 90007. It was just about as central as you could get in the sprawl that is California's biggest city and it was uncomfortably close to an overhead highway, but it was still a perfect location. 'Today St Vincent de Paul you are Sagrada Familia.' They had ninety minutes before the church opened, but they were facing the morning traffic and the extra time on the clock was consumed statically.

In researching Rooster had become fascinated by the Spanish cathedral and loved the fact that the LA church, that for one day only, would take its place. St Vincent was built the year before Antoni Gaudi died, and had passed its 90th celebration with Gaudi's Sagrada still years from completion. She wondered how much of Sagrada's attraction lay in the fact that it had taken more than 130 years not to build. Then again would the Titanic be the Titanic if it had missed the iceberg?

She held a picture in her hand to enable her to fully describe the scene. The party moved freely in and out of St Vincent's since business was slow this early in the day. It was a convenience church, sort of God's answer to 7-Eleven, although it was more like 8-Ten. The caretaker, busy getting the hymn books in order, looked on, and listened.

'The sixth tower, when finished in 2026, will be the highest religious structure in Europe, and if we come to this wall here, I have to describe a fairly gruesome sight. This was Gaudi's city, he was a kind of superstar and could get away with anything. High above you are the moldings of bodies of real children. Taken from the hospital immediately after their deaths in childbirth and modelled into the archways.'

The party looked up instinctively, not all in the same direction, but up. The caretaker followed their lead, shook his head and got on with his business, thinking how come there were so many books to rearrange each day when there were so few people, particularly on a Thursday? Millie meanwhile carried on bringing in all manner of trivia. The caretaker would not contradict the tour guide, he couldn't, his only tongue was Spanish and it was only Millie's odd attempt at the language that first drew his ear's attention. He hadn't a clue what she was on about. Thankfully she'd run out of facts by the time the priest arrived. She couldn't avoid a meeting and she discreetly thanked him as she opened an awkward lid and stuck a $20 note in the vase that he was carrying. He looked a bit surprised and turning back for a second glance she did think the vase looked rather like someone's ashes.

'Who says you can't take it with you?' thought Fr Michael. The ashes were destined for internment, a local guy who died abroad suddenly and his family opted for DHL rather than filling the hold of a plane. The urn would be placed in a plot alongside his grandparents, although he now had pocket money to flash at the gates, ash cash. The father certainly wasn't going to poke around and retrieve it.

In the bus, Protz tucked into his tenth tapas. He'd by now embraced the concept and was taking it to a whole new level.

Normally you are encouraged to eat one or two small tapas and then move on to another bar, ensuring a constant flow of different conversations. It is the total opposite of British pub culture where Barry comes in at seven thirty gets his 'usual' handed him in his own embossed tankard, gets upset if someone is on 'his' stool, reclaims it and then sits to closing time talking about the train timetable and why there is now nobody in English national rugby team with a name he can spell or pronounce, provoking mild racism by pointing out that it was 35 years since someone called Smith played. He then sips his pint at near evaporation speed, or lack of it.

Protz's solution to tapas was to move from location to location, but keeping the tray with him.

They were approaching Typhoon at the end of the day when a rogue tapas struck him. He liked just about everything that ever went in and out of a fridge or on and off a cooker, but anchovies he couldn't take. Tapas eleven nearly ended him. He coughed and spat the morsel he'd tasted into a piece of kitchen roll and tucked it into his pocket to dispose of later. The remaining two inches of tapas was another issue. He wrapped it in a second piece of paper and quietly slipped it down the side of the seat on the coach.

By way of innovation, Ryder stopped Daphne 200 yards from Set A. He, Ngoc and Pang had been chatting at Ricco's about additional FX and it being Spain had come up with the idea of the two Asians on wheels. As the party disembarked the two on mopeds shot in an out between the walking tourists with alarming closeness and no little skill. By the time they'd reached the lobby they were quite relieved, but the air was full of exhaust fumes and atmospheric anecdotes about 'the mad bike riders of Barcelona'. Miss Little was even convinced one of them had tried to snatch her bag. It was a story that would grow and grow and unwittingly cause so much reflected pain when back at St Anthony's.

The party seemed to have a new life, the adventures of the past few days lifting them in spirits and attitude. They had achieved so much and there was just enough left to look forward to without going into the down mood of preparation for home.

Ernie clapped his hands. 'Time for bed everyone.' And so it was.

43.
BASKING IN THE SUN

Sandwiches in Set C, Typhoon - Tapas in San Sebastian

'The flight time to San Sebastian will be one hour and ten minutes. Sit back and I hope you enjoy your journey with us.'

In seat 14B Protz was still going on about the anchovy and that he wouldn't need salt for a week. 'Mouth like an empty crisp packet,' he said. Gerry Perry beside him, his buddy, was only too happy to be away from sitting on the bus, seven hours of anchovy chat reduced to one.

'Seventy minutes, Mr Z said it would have been at least six hours by road. I would have liked to have gone to Pamplona though.'

'The bull run?' Protz said proving he was listening.

'I think that's later, like summer, and kinda suspect we might be at a bit of a disadvantage.'

'It's in early July for a week,' the voice came from row 15 and could only have come from Arthur J.

To add variation and create the feel of an authentic travel experience Ryder was to act as a taxi driver to take the party in small groups to a central meeting point, a café. The excuse offered was that the rooms weren't available until midday. With one car at their disposal it would take him four trips, each of eight minutes, the delays adding to the true frustration of travel. No proper trip, especially one lasting over three weeks, ever went off without a hiccup and Ernie repeated that he had read that there were only two types of vacation experience worth talking about, the good and the bad, look at Trip Adviser he said. Preferably, very good or very bad. This was just a minor disruption, but it would give them something to gripe about. More color for the hours of reminiscing back at St Anthony's.

The San Sebastian tapas session promised to be the most hectic meal scenario of the tour. One bar had to become five in quick succession. The party would go on a tour and approach the café bar area in Set C from just about every angle. During the short walks between the bars some furniture would be moved and the food shifted around and a combination of steps and doors employed. Some would have music, but very low key. In essence, most true tapas bars have the same feel, less seating, more standing in sawdust to eat on the hoof and it can be quite a struggle to get access to the bit of Bayonne ham you want. To ease their way The European Experience had 'asked' each bar to free up some space for them. Planning, Consideration and Constant Care, it could become their slogan Ernie mused.

Once they had re-grouped, the party en masse went for a walk around the old town with Millie giving a very passable description and helping them gain a feel for the place. Narrow streets with just the occasional car parked, delivering goods to the shops and bars. Ngoc had found a couple of old cars from another back lot and had enjoyed placing them in the already heavily used Victorian street setting. He was getting quite into driving. The set had been many things in its life, even before Ernie fell in love with it. In role-play it had crossed the Atlantic more times than the Ryder Cup, but this was its debut as a gem of a Basque city.

Pang had placed a couple of really neat barbeques safely round the corners, out of harm's way, the Cobb model with a lid which used about five bits of charcoal in as many hours. When the time was right he'd put some chorizo on them so they wafted a sense of 'come and get me' from the tapas.

The Cobbs had been an investment for the picnics on the external Typhoon days, but what he had found for free were several old postcard racks and they were in position doing what they always do, blocking a sidewalk. They would be moved around as nudging barriers. Sadly this party of tourists were probably the last on earth to know that the age of the postcard home had passed into travel history. Pang had painted an 'X' and some funny squiggles on the next three locations the card racks could be used for. Ryder assumed it was his numbering system. He was right.

San Sebastian has two of the best city beaches in Europe, one for the sun and one for the surf. Rooster chose to delete that fact from her notes fearing that someone might trigger a desire for a paddle. Santa Monica was just eight miles too far of a walk to dip toes in the sea. Instead it would be tales of the British navy blasting the place, ETA and the struggle for Basque people to break free of Spain and a bit about the gastronomic societies that were a feature of most men's lives once they had given up sunbathing or surfing.

Elsewhere in the world men meet to hit a ball as far as they can and eventually into a hole or clandestinely come together to roll up a trouser leg and do things too mysterious too understand to those who haven't been invited to join. But enough about golf. Here in San Sebastian, or Donastia if you are talking to a true Basque, they roll up their sleeves and get stuck-in in the kitchen. In surroundings that many a hotel or restaurant would envy, they take turns to show off to each other, but only male to males. The men only clubs where they like to out cook each other are unique. Basque men are not totally sexist. They allow women into the club, to do the washing up. For them it is a buy-off, for a few it means extra cash, for the over tolerant wives at home, extra peace and a clean kitchen at home.

Sadly, being a mixed bunch, they couldn't visit such a club, even if they'd split the duties and pleasures. Not that Rooster would have let it happen, the research alone offended her justifiable streak of feminism before she'd got to the second paragraph. Anyway the clubs are harder to get into than the masons.

The Basques are a unique bunch and academics to this day argue over their origins. They have developed, or as is the case failed to develop several strange sports. The Scots have tossing a tree trunk, the Irish throwing a medal ball hundreds of meters down public roads, the refined English croquet, the unrefined chasing a cheese down a hill once a year, but the Basques have an Olympic-sized collection of physical oddities. Most of them involve tempting hernias carrying stones too heavy for a wheelbarrow and too misshapen to handle with ease. The consequence is that the true local males all look like sumo wrestlers dressed as farmers.

'Stumbling' upon a tournament, the party were refreshed with some excellent local wine whilst several were enticed to take part. Rooster and Ryder operating as eyes and guides as buckets of water were hauled and splashed from one rain barrel to another.

San Sebastian was treating them well, weather-wise. In fact, several had remarked on how fortunate they'd been. 'Europe must just get a bad press,' Perry commented, 'it's been almost as good as back home.'

'Anyone hungry,' Millie asked, and in response to several 'you bets' the bar onslaught began. Ryder had sourced some Spanish tapped beer, a keg of San Miguel, and was struggling to get the head smaller than the body. In tapas bars they use small 25 cl glasses as part of the process of stopping you from having a full-on drinking session, this is about snacks and snippets of food and conversation. The first half dozen poured glasses were an inverted disaster, but that didn't stop Protz from fingering his way along the bar, and, sensing the coldness, believed he struck gold. Most of the golden brew going on his shirt as he failed miserably in his haste to judge the distance between the froth and liquid.

Perhaps by the time they arrived in bar five, Ryder would have mastered it. But then he didn't have to. Looking on Ngoc took up the challenge and within minutes, the beer flowed from keg to glass just as God meant it. 'Was there anything this little Vietnamese couldn't do?' Ryder thought in growing admiration with just the slightest hint of irritation. What a bonus they had been, he couldn't imagine the project without them and he was right. If he, Rooster and Ernie were the big wheels, they were the oil. Without them the whole thing would have ground to a halt or fallen apart by Liverpool.

Rooster couldn't help but observe the different ways people eat. People don't look like their pets, they couldn't for this bunch had never had any, but they did eat like animals. It was not a totally negative thought for there was an attraction in the way Miss Little hovered and pecked at her tapas like a canary, though Protz was more definitely a bulldog. His lower jaw extended and amplifying each bite, each bite was accompanied by a self-satisfied smile that made her want to put a spiked collar on him back to front and jerk the lead. Wilcox, as was his wont, sniffed everything from every angle before delicately putting it in his mouth. His lips then confirmed or rejected his nasal interpretation. He was always the last to finish a meal, a very annoying trait.

Drying out and now happily in command of a Ngoc special, Protz, touched the edge of each tapas platter and asked the same question. 'Any anchovies?' Behind the bar Ryder had assumed the identity of one of his comic heroes, the little Manuel from Fawlty Towers. 'Na fishy,' he said in a very fishy accent. The night, like so many before, was going swimmingly.

As an interlude in the drinking and munching down of larger than bite sized snacks, they 'stumbled' upon the remnants of a second Basque sporting event. The competitors, Mille explained, had retired to a nearby bar, but had left the equipment. She added that Basque rural sports fall into the category of showing off at work and were all about strength with very little finesse. Two 20 kg stones were just lying there and Ryder guided volunteer Nelson to the point. He picked it up and then was guided round a course which wasn't so much of a race track but more like thirty yards to a pole and back. 'Sporty fuckers these Basques' he remarked as he dropped the stone on the ground, somehow missing five pairs of feet and a really awkward explanation at a casualty department. Basque origins being what they are, or might be, there seemed a strong likelihood thought Ernie that the games were all invented by a farmer who induced the gullible into clearing his field of rocks.

'First prize goes to the goon who can move the heaviest, most misshapen in the fastest time. Broken backs, blisters and bleeding hands to the winners.' There was then something a little less dangerous, tossing hay bales and the only game that seemed to have any international appeal, a tug-of-war.

With five on each side, Millie captaining one and Ryder the other, it turned out to be the perfect event for the tourists who just couldn't get enough of it. From best of three, it extended to five and then best of nine and ended with Ryder's team winning five two.

They were still laughing and in high spirits when they were given a breakdown of other strange Basque sporting facts. Like the goose game where a dead bird was hung from a hoop suspended over water and the winner was the one who managed to hang on long enough for the goose's head to fall off. Great fun, but again with limited attraction as a potential television audience grabber. It was back to tapas.

'One more bar perhaps?' suggested Millie. She could gauge from the slowing response that they were getting to the end of the trail. 'Maybe just a quick nightcap, can we go back to the second one, I liked it' said Protz and they all headed out one door to come back in another.

'Can we go past that shop with the postcards?' the simple request came from Miss Temple. 'I'd like to take some home to show my family.'

'Not a problem,' said Millie, wondering just what the subject matter of the prop cards was. She'd noticed they were real, but whether they were images of Paris, Moscow or Bangkok she couldn't recall. 'I'll nip out later and get you some,' she offered. There was an immediate response from several of the rest of the drinkers wanting something similar. As long as they had something in their hands by the end of the trip, thought Rooster, noting she had three or four days to sort it out. eBay where art thou?

In small groups Ernie, Ryder and Rooster escorted the party to their rooms. On odd days they approached from one way down the corridor and on even, the other direction. This again broke up the geography and helped create a feeling of continual freshness, along with rolling out different types of carpet. The trio noted the room plans for the entire trip on each of the doors. Mercifully the list was now all but complete. Only two more changes of bed linen for Ngoc to fit into his cramped timetable, three more baggage moves. In front of them was only a night in central France with the remainder of the tour being spent in Paris. Then it was back on the plane and home.

Ryder had already booked a 'proper' coach in Los Angeles for the very last part of the trip – the choir bus simply wasn't up to the expectations of those seeing faces at the Institute. But the bus that he had picked up for a song from a choir had done them well. In the 19 days so far, it had done nearly 4,000 miles in ten countries and in the process driven on both the left and right hand sides of the road. He did realize that for the homecoming they couldn't risk turning up with the roof showing signs of where the speaker system was and the ever-fading crucifix on the sides. Ernie's decision to keep it seemed to have paid-off as it had been quite clearly an additional busybody repellent. If the European Experience were to turn into a museum, the MCI bus would be the star exhibit.

Never once had it refused to start and in truth Ryder had become quite attached to Daphne. The decision to fly across the southern Pyrenees hadn't meant saying goodbye to her. Ryder, in his role of taxi driver or barman, had never identified himself. He had for eight hours of the schedule, been written out of the script. That was to allow for him to bring the empty coach across so that it now stood outside the hotel in central Sans Sebastian – a journey of about six minutes. Rather than pretend to pick up another coach it was Ernie's idea for he felt that the party had also grown too accustomed to the interior of the vehicle. It had changed three times on this trip with a couple of seats taken out and closing off the front door. It had carted everyone from the Institute to the plane and then from Ireland to England and finally to Denmark. It was a good decision not to risk another change.

Protz struggled on board and put his hand baggage on the seat before pushing past it and settling at the window. Instinctively he nestled into the area that was now his and in doing so touched upon a piece of kitchen roll. He smelt his fingers, 'Anchovies!'

Watching on Ernie grabbed the moment to explain that the bus had followed them, but that they hadn't had time to valet it. He apologized and then settled the issue, 'I don't know what kind of person would put half a sandwich down the side of a seat . . .'

Protz did.

-0-

374

The cab pulled up outside of 233 Arlington. It had already deposited Swallow at her downtown flat where she busied herself in the early stages of converting it from a tryst location to home for her and Ronnie.

There was no one looking out the window of 233, but there were a few eyes behind blinds looking towards 233. He went up the now cleared driveway, stopping to pick up a couple of golf tees from the side kerb and wondering how they got there. The front door was closed and as he reached to pull out his keys he saw a crudely written note stuck against the glass from inside.

'We've gone to mothers – you go to hell!'

He tried to put the key in the lock, but like Angela herself, it was not receptive. Thank goodness he had Pat's new old phone. He sat in the sun on the front step and re-called the cab. Across in 242 Arlington, Bradley, looked out from behind a curtain and wondered if he'd ever get to play openly with his $1,200 golf clubs that cost him a fraction of that. This was perhaps not the moment to offer them back.

-0-

All on board and all happy, the party had just a two-hour drive to their next destination. They would briefly pop into Lourdes, pray and pop out again. 'Well it's on route,' Ernie explained to the mild protests of the younger section who by now had had one church experience too many.

From the studios, Ryder would set out northwards and then cut east to arrive back at the location they first used what seemed a lifetime back as the Giant's Causeway, a disused granite quarry on the road to Acton. They would, after a walk around, then head further east and at some point loop round to arrive back at the studios where the much-used bar had transformed into a small rural French inn, or auberge as they say there. Rooster had found a real French chef and he'd been induced and programmed into thinking it was a reality TV game show and that he'd cook for this party as if he were somewhere in the middle of France.

In the meantime Rooster was in the back of the bus, changing from Millie into Sister Kris. She'd got a full habit from costumes as she felt that there might be the need more physical contact at this location. Anyway, she was a mood actor. Harley looked on as the fine underwear he was now well used to seeing coming off was covered in black religious gear – she made a super nun he thought and added the outfit to his growing list of now achievable fantasies.

As ever to do her best Sister Kris had been online looking at Lourdes and trying to work out what to contribute. She'd sourced a lot of photographs with the idea of adding to the travel memories with a new green-screen shoot. They were necessary since it was a while since she'd taken some and reviewing them in her camera she noticed Megaghy was featured, or was lurking in the background in a fair proportion of them. She didn't think her PhotoShop skills were quite up to exhuming people. She'd just crop him out and put it down to bad photography, that is, normal snaps.

Lourdes was once a small market town of no great significance unless you were a cow or a chicken; until 1858 that was, and some miraculous visions. Now six million people a year visit the place, and only Paris, in the whole of France, has more bedrooms. They were not going to use any of them, this was purely a trip to the shrine and out. Another 'done it' tick on the box of life.

It was a quarter to five and the sun was starting to find its way through the valleys when Ryder pulled back into the spot they'd stopped at seventeen days earlier and disturbed the lovers. Few if any lovers had been there since and with no rain, the bus's tracks were still evident.

Ryder pressed the buttons to start the speakers on the roof, slowly adjusting the volume. Ngoc was first out and immediately set about generating sounds from further afield.

The party came out in ones and twos and Sister Kris welcomed them explaining that they were in what she called 'a raw part' of the sacred area, one not normally accessible to the masses. It was not exactly where the vision appeared, that would be later, not the vision, but the spot, Virgin Mary was not one to milk a good appearance with an encore. That was something that could get the conservative Catholic Church back on track. Sister Kris explained that this area was special because it had retained the feeling that peasant girl Bernadette Soubirous perhaps experienced prior to her apparitions.

With no chance of bumping into any third parties, eleven tourists went about largely on their own. Eleven, because Jankowski and Nelson had remained in the bus to play another round of their virtual strip poker. It was a gesture that upset the misses Little and Temple, even though the Wailing Wall was more within the focus of the latter's faith.

The strains of 'Silent Night' came out of Ngoc's backpack and speakers. Ernie looked at Sister Kris in horror, they should never have left them to their own devices.

'They celebrate Christmas early here,' Arnold J offered.

'And in English,' Colino added.

Jankowski and Nelson, fascinated by the soundtrack, were out in the open. Ngoc had wandered to the back of the quarry quite unaware of his inappropriate contribution was echoing around the entire site and creating quite a stir. It sounded pretty spectacular, even if stunningly wrong.

Several of the party were drawn to the source, but the echoes disguised where Ngoc was and they cut left and right past discarded huge chunks of rock.

Sean Seamus, not the most agile of people even on a flat surface, found the terrain particularly challenging and uncertain of what lay ahead backed up. He went straight into Jankowski who hit Protz who stumbled and recovered only by hitting someone else. There was a scream and Rooster and Ernie looked up in horror to see Joyce Reid disappear over the edge of a cliff.

The scream was short. They rushed up cutting in between O'Reilly, Jankowski and Protz, who were frozen in uncertainty. 'Please somebody tell us what is going on?' shouted Janne. 'Say still, don't move,' shouted Rooster. What was next they couldn't say until they reached the edge and looked over. The rock-face was stepped and just six feet below them lay Joyce, face down in a pool of trapped water. Another two feet to her right and she'd fall a further thirty. She started to move and slowly got up to her feet. Rooster reached out the heavenly hands of Sister Kris to try and prevent her stepping out to certain death. 'Stop Joyce, don't move,' Sister Kris called out in Rooster's voice.

'Where am I, this isn't Lourdes,' she asked semi-dazed.

'Hallelujah I can see, I can see, I can see, I can see' she said in a slow and growing strength of voice.

'Hallelujah, I can see!' she screamed.

Joyce's joy was infectious and the other tourists dropped to the knees in prayer and personal hope that something bigger was about to happen to them all. Like chickens scattered by a fox, they jumped and leapt, stumbling into bushes and dipping their faces into rogue pools of water. Quicker than he'd ever moved Ernie shot off pulling back the most dangerous strays from the brink of an abyss.

Joyce took the hand of Sister Kris who had totally forgotten her role speaking only like the Rooster of old. She was hauled up and into the arms of the waiting nun.

'I don't know where I am, I don't know who you are, but Lord knows I'm so glad to see you. This is a miracle.'

It must have been, Ernie was on his knees, and crying 'Lord why me, why me, why always fucking me?'

44.
JUDGEMENT DAY

Eight months later – a courtroom in Phoenix, Arizona

Judge Heffner sat back in his chair as the clerk read out the charges. It was a very long list, each charge coming from the thirteen people in the front two rows, and the plea of not guilty would mean a very long trial. Elsewhere in the court sat a sizable proportion of the rest of St Anthony's inmates and staff. Dent sat beside Swallow, uncertain of how much fallout there would be on their lives. They hadn't contributed to the charge sheet, wanting to keep as much of themselves out of the headlines. Currently both suspended, the dismal degree of their fate would be decided in a boardroom once the outcome of this little show was concluded. With no timetable, other than a promised lifetime of hate, Angela was on the warpath and any ammunition brought out under oath would most certainly be turned against them. There was a new man beside Angela, her lawyer. It was a room full of losers.

Ernie had decided to defend the charges. He might not get a chance of a public performance for many years so grabbed this. In his heart he still believed that he could have made it as a legal eagle.

'Your honor, our defense rests on one small, but simple, fact. We offered the European Experience. At no point, and nowhere in print or on record, did we say we were going to go to Europe. It was all about the experience and we delivered, more than delivered.'

The courtroom fell silent and then into a growing swell of agreement. The thirteen started to nod in agreement and Protz shouted out 'that's right I don't recall them ever saying we were going anywhere and we had a great time, a great experience.' For over a minute the rest nodded or murmured agreement.

'Mr Zimmerman will you please take the stand,' Heffner instructed following a request from the prosecuting counsel. Ernie looked at the other two and lifted an eyebrow in a 'here we go' manner. He moved slowly and without panic to the stand, raised his hand and took the oath. He then launched into a solo performance that was not interrupted by the prosecuting lawyer who chose, for the moment, to let the little man hang himself.

'I will not deny that the original concept was to feed off an illusion, to make money through manipulation. When I first saw these people wandering around the paths of St Anthony's I was struck by how abandoned they seemed. Sure, they were all blind and they were, in a communal sense together, but they were alone. Stuck out in the Arizonian sun I wondered how often did they get visitors? They were sun-dried tomatoes, under watered, under visited, under loved. How often did someone come and take them into the world beyond the high walls? They were alive and well, but, well, they weren't having a life. The first European Experience trip was an experiment. Sure, the intention was to make money. This is America after all. There wouldn't have been any chance of a second one if we hadn't made money on the first. It sounds cruel, but we didn't pull the wool over these people's eyes, the wool was already there. What we did in 23 days was to give their other senses the holiday of a lifetime. It grieved us that we left with fifteen people and came back with fourteen. Jack Megaghy's death was from natural causes. It would have happened back in his room at St Anthony's, but on this occasion it just happened to be somewhere else and he had the best last eleven days of his life. Whether it was San Marino, LA or San Marino, Italy is of little consequence in the process of reuniting him with his family in Seattle. He died a happy man. Around the courtroom grew an ever-growing number of nods and smiles

'There were pluses aplenty, but none more so than the happy mishap that brought us here. Joyce Reid's freak incident went in a few seconds from horrific accident to a miraculous event. Perhaps it was because of her earlier generosity when she re-distributed the small fortune she came upon in,' he held back and looked at Joyce, 'Monaco or Carson City?' She smiled and gave a wave indicating it didn't really matter.

'Yes, it didn't really matter. It was remember, a fortune created on European Experience money. Those who accuse us are mostly $41,000 better off due to circumstances created by the Experience than they were before they left – so where's the fraud. By that change in fortunes we were so into the concept of giving these people what they needed and deserved, we never quibbled about who rightfully won it. It was my five dollars Joyce used. It kind of sums up the whole trip, if you can put a little in and get a lot more out, then do it. That is what we did with the European Experience. These people put a little in and after nineteen days I think they might agree, they have taken a lot more out. All that we owe them is the days they missed, through Joyce's second good fortune. They missed out on Paris, perhaps those who were contracted to care,' Ernie looked over to the wilting doctor and nurse, 'perhaps they could fill that gap.'

Harley stood up in the public gallery and ignored instructions to sit down. 'I too have had my life restored by this trip. Judge you are wearing a Tag Formula 1 watch.'

Heffner looked down at his Tag. The whole room looked at his Tag.

Joyce called their lawyer forwards and several of the party came together in an awkward huddle. She talked with them as Heffner called for silence and she talked with the lawyer. He shook his head and banged the rail several times. He then turned and came back towards Judge Heffner.

He lent forward and whispered to Heffner 'my clients wish to withdraw all charges.'

Heffner looked at the trio fondled the plastic tee in his pocket and for the first time in a morning, smiled, he might get some golf in after all.

Epilogue

Judge Heffner never suffered from hemorrhoid affliction again. He suffered heart attack after sinking a 35-foot putt on the 15th green to go one under. His golfing buddies, caring to the end and on similar life-defining rounds, put him in the golf cart, and played out their rounds. 'It is what he would have wanted.'

Harley settled out of court again for his out of court settlement and was allowed to keep twelve million for the discomfort and mental torment caused by the attempted cover-up by the local authority in an initial effort to throw the case out. He and Mrs 'Harley' Johnson opened a non-profit travel company for disabled people called Experience Europe, and they do. For real. They were expecting their first child at Christmas. If it were to be a girl they'd call her Joyce, if a boy, anything but Ernest.

Ngoc and Pang disappeared into the night, but there were reports of the mystery ownership of a highly successful online music and effects company called 'The Ricemen' operating out of the back of a mysteriously franchised Radio Shack.

Dent and Swallow were removed from their posts within minutes of the trial falling apart and moved to Chicago to start a new life. He was selling second-hand refurbished golf gear called 'Bunkered' and she kept the business out of the rough. As of last month, she was still waiting for a proposal.

Bradley Weston played the best round of golf of his life. He put it down to Dent's clubs.

Joyce Reid trained to became a pastor back home in Pensacola. Somewhat affected by the events, she changed her 'professional' name to ReJoice, with the capital J for Jesus. She preached about the vice of gambling and the virtue of giving without realizing that without the first she would never have experienced the second. She developed a rather passable singing voice and her theme was Leonard Cohen's Hallelujah. She sang it over the titles of the movie based on a book that somebody with a funny name wrote.

Arthur J also wrote the book about the experiences and went on lecture tours. When back at St Anthony's he'd drop in the fact that it was often a sell-out, failing to mention that most gigs were in tiny organic cafes.

The other tourists returned to St Anthony's to happily pass their time reminiscing. Those who had benefited from Joyce noticed an improvement in visitor frequency.

The remaining patients traveled with Experience Europe.

Ernie and Ryder bought the quarry and today entertain two thousand visitors a week in high season. Making $10 a-head just to get in, $5 a head on bandages and a further $20 on average on rock souvenirs.

They named it Hallelujah Canyon.

Printed in Great Britain
by Amazon